rule breakers fall hardest

USA TODAY BESTSELLING AUTHOR
MICALEA SMELTZER

© Copyright 2024 Micalea Smeltzer
All rights reserved. This book or any portion thereof may not be reproduced or used in any manner whatsoever without the express written permission of the publisher.
This is a work of fiction. Names, characters, businesses, places, events and incidents are either the products of the author's imagination or used in a fictitious manner. Any resemblance to actual persons, living or dead, or actual events is purely coincidental.
Cover Design: Emily Wittig Designs
Formatting: Micalea Smeltzer
Developmental Edits: Melanie Yu; Made Me Blush Books
Line Editing and Proofreading: VB Edits

rule breakers fall hardest
micalea smeltzer

For the girlies who like a man wearing a chain.
(TCB, I'm looking at you.)

prologue

DAIRE

THAT'S MY KID.

The thought is instinctual. One look at this tiny human, and I know in my gut he's my child.

The problem?

He's in my former professor's arms. A woman I should've never touched. A woman who wasn't mine to have.

The worst part of all?

Her husband is standing right beside her.

one

DAIRE

I'M IN HELL.

It's the only explanation for why I'm standing in front of Rosie Thomas, asking her for a favor. Although *favor* is too mild a word for what I'm proposing.

Literally proposing.

Marriage.

She gapes at me, blinking a pair of big round eyes that were my undoing when we were kids. Back then, all she had to do was look at me, and I was ready to do her bidding. She had me wrapped around her finger.

Until she didn't.

The look of shock slowly slips from her face, and then she starts laughing. Great big peals of maniacal laughter.

I look over one shoulder, then the other, to see whether students shuffling in and out of the dining hall are looking at us.

"I have to be dreaming, right?" She pinches her arm. "You can't be serious?"

I clench my fists at my sides. "As a heart attack."

I've been spiraling for weeks.

Longer.

Since the moment I saw my former professor holding a baby I know is mine. The kid looks just like me. I've been driving myself mad. Using my own money so my dad won't know, I've consulted a lawyer for help with figuring out the best way to go about this. According to her, if I were married and had my own place, it'd be much easier. I don't think she intended for me to immediately jump to the marriage portion of that equation, but I *will* have access to my child, no matter what. If that means getting married for the time being, then so be it.

That's why Rosie's perfect. We don't even like each other, so she'll be under no illusion that any of this is permanent.

She breaks into another fit of laughter. "Jesus, did you lose a bet with Cash?" She refers to one of my older brothers.

"*No.*" I grasp her hand and tug her into a quieter corner since we're drawing attention.

She yanks free of my hold the second we're tucked away and crosses her arms so I can't reach for her again. As if I *wanted* to touch her.

"Listen, I already explained the situation," I hiss. I have no reason to be annoyed with her—not when my proposition sounds absolutely insane. "It's temporary. Two years. Three tops, depending on how long court takes."

Her mouth drops open. "You want me to be fake married to you for *years*?" The bark of laugher that escapes her is humorless.

My gut tightens in a knot. I really wish she'd stop doing that. This isn't a laughing matter.

"All so you can get custody of a kid that may or may not be yours?"

"He's mine," I bite out. "I don't need a DNA test to know. But don't worry; we're working on that."

She sighs, pinching her brow. "This has to be a prank."

"It's not a prank."

She shakes her head. "Find someone else. You don't even like me."

That knot in my stomach does some kind of weird flip. *You don't even like me*. But she didn't say she doesn't like *me*. Interesting.

"I can't find someone else."

Huffing, she rolls her eyes. "Please, any girl would jump at the chance to marry you. Go ask one of them." She flutters her fingers at a congregation of girls outside the dining hall where I cornered Rosie as she was leaving.

"No."

She scrutinizes me for a heartbeat. Two. Three. "Why me?" Hands on her hips, she raises her chin defiantly.

"A multitude of reasons."

"Name one," she challenges, brows arched skeptically like she doesn't believe I can.

Teeth gritted, I rattle off the list. "You know me. We grew up together. We have history. It'll make the marriage more believable."

She wrinkles her nose and takes a step back. "You have me there, but my answer is still no."

She turns then, ready to walk away, but I clutch at her arm. She peers down at my hand wrapped around her bicep, eyes narrowed in annoyance. "Let go of me."

"I'll pay you. A million for every year we have to stay married."

"Mm, let me think about it." She twists her lips. "No."

"Do you want more?"

"I don't need your money, Hendricks. I have my own inheritance, thank you very much."

"Yes," I cock my head to the side, "but mine's bigger."

"Are you seriously trying to have a dick measuring contest with me? I assure you, I may be a girl, but mine's bigger."

"Your dick, sure, I'd believe it." I grin. "But we both know my family is richer."

She bristles at that, her posture going rigid.

"Your mother always wanted us to get married."

Her shoulders sink, and she takes a step closer. Fuck yes. I've found the magic words.

"My mother is an idiot."

Dammit. My stomach drops, along with my hopes. I guess not, then.

"You don't get to ignore me for years and glower at me every time you see me just to then beg me for a so-called favor." She wags a finger in front of my face. "A marriage isn't a favor, Daire."

She has a point, I know this, but I need her.

"Rosie—"

She holds up a hand. "I've heard enough. Fuck you."

With the flash of a middle finger, she hurries away, her glossy dark hair swishing over her shoulders. She leaves behind a cloud of fresh, sweet-smelling perfume. Something citrusy and—

Why the fuck am I thinking about what Rosie Thomas smells like?

I won't be deterred by her reluctance. She's the only one who can help me.

Despite how much I hate it.

She steps through the door and disappears. I don't go after her. No, while I need her to agree, I know her well enough to know she needs space.

Choking back my frustration, I turn for the dining hall. I don't really need to eat, but I'm here, so I might as well.

Some of the guys on my team gesture for me to join them at their table when they see me.

I shake my head and continue moving.

I've been distancing myself from everyone this year, even my roommates, not that it's been too difficult. Cree is always busy hanging out with his mystery girl now that he found her. Tutoring her? Please. He just wants to fuck her. And my *other* roommate, Jude, spends all his free time trying to get in our fourth roommate's pants. That's a whole other level of fuckery since she's Cree's sister.

Yeah, our off-campus townhouse is a whole fucking hot mess.

Under normal circumstances, I would've told them about the kid by now. A kid whose name I don't even know, since Danielle refuses to tell me. But while she's withholding that information, she's yet to deny that I'm his father.

Bitch.

Maybe it's wrong to think such a thing about my son's mother, but I can't help it. She probably assumed I wouldn't give a shit, that if I *did* find out he existed, I wouldn't care. Well, surprise, I do care. My kid is going to know me. End of discussion.

Our fling was short-lived. She claimed to be having marital problems because they couldn't get pregnant. Now I have to wonder, despite her assurance that she was on birth control and my strict use of condoms all except that one stupid fucking time, if she used me as a stud—an unwitting sperm donor.

After I've purchased a lunch, I find a spot in the corner and sit alone, ignoring the funny looks from my hockey teammates. It's shitty of me, but I don't want to talk to anyone these days. I have too much on my mind, and I'm too angry.

I'm not sure I'll ever get over the betrayal of not knowing about my own child.

Plenty of guys my age would be relieved that the mother didn't expect or even want them involved; not me. I was raised by a single dad. He was a workaholic, but he always made time for us. He made parenthood look *easy*, even as he ran a billion-dollar multimedia company. Sure, we had nannies, but he was *there* when a lot of parents in his position wouldn't have been. He made it to all our school events, and he was almost always home for dinner.

My mom was killed in a freak boating accident

when I was five. I have very few memories of her, all of which are hazy, and my dad only speaks of her on rare occasions. Even after all this time, it still hurts him. If it weren't for all of us boys, it's hard not to question whether he would've tried to join her.

Regardless, he stepped *up*, and I'll do the same. Not out of some sense of obligation, but because I *want* to. I don't want my kid to ever think that I didn't want to be there for him. I might not have planned on him, but he's here, and I want to know him.

If I told my dad what was going on, I have no doubt that he'd help. He'd be ready to throw money at the best lawyers. But I don't want that, even if it would be the easy way out. I want to fight for my son on my own … with Rosie's help. I'll gladly step up to the plate and prove that I can handle this on my own. I want my son to know that I'll do whatever it takes. That he matters that much to me.

If I eventually need help from my dad, then I'm not too proud to admit defeat. Not if it means having a relationship with my son.

Though my tray is full, I'm suddenly not hungry. I haven't been hungry much lately, which doesn't bode well. With the number of calories I burn between time spent in the gym and on ice, I need to eat.

But I can't make myself.

I stand and gather my tray, intending to throw it

away, but instead I shove it into an unsuspecting student's hands.

"Enjoy lunch on me," I mutter.

Head down, I stalk out of the building, already plotting ways to get Rosie to agree.

two

ROSIE

> Mother Dearest: Did you get that package I sent you?

I HUFF a humorless laugh at the text message and glare at the bottle she had delivered. Some new kind of diet pill she hunted down just for me, since my curves are apparently a disgrace. I'm a size twelve, for crying out loud. I'm *normal*. I've got a butt and boobs and hips and thighs and cellulite. It's not the end of the world. But tell that to my almond mother. I think she's on a diet involving cashews and raisins at the moment. Or maybe that was last month's craze. I can't keep up, and I don't *want* to. Truly, I feel sorry for her. She has an illness; it's consumed her life, and, unfortunately, mine by proxy.

> Me: Yep. Thanks for the box of condoms.

Don't parents usually send boxes of goodies from home to their kids? Fresh baked goods and cutesy things like notebooks and pens or even a stuffed animal?

> Mother Dearest: I didn't send you condoms! Who sent you condoms?

She's so dense sometimes. Sarcasm goes right over her head.

> Me: It was a joke.

> Mother Dearest: Did you get the package or not?

I sigh. She's not going to let it go, so I snap a picture and send it to her. This way she can see with her own two eyes that I received her lovely care package. The pills will be going into the trash as soon as this conversation is over. I should've thrown them away as soon as I opened the box, but I set them on the desk and stared at the label that promised I could lose fifteen pounds in one week, wondering if maybe I *did* need to lose weight.

Then I cursed myself for letting her issues get into my head.

At the end of the day, I pity her. It consumes her, the obsessive thoughts about every piece of food she puts in her mouth and its calorie content.

The most ironic part? While her BMI is probably in the normal range, mine would be in the overweight range. Yet *I'm* healthier. Her body has to be begging for proper nutrients.

> Mother Dearest: Oh, good. Muffy said she lost thirty pounds in less than a month using it. I got some for myself as well.

With a shake of my head, I use my foot to spin my desk chair in a circle. My dad forced her to check in to a facility that specializes in treatment for eating disorders. I told him it wouldn't work, not when she didn't want to go and refused to believe she had a problem, and shocker, I was right.

I want her to get better as much as he does, but she *won't*. At least not until she wakes up and realizes she has a problem with food, along with what could very well be OCD.

I don't want to talk about this anymore. It just makes me sad. For her. For me.

And, despite being happy with my body and being

comfortable in my own skin, my insecurities still claw their way out into the light of day from time to time.

Especially when my own mother makes it obvious that what I look like, the number on the scale, is more indicative of my value as a person than who I am as an individual.

> Me: I have homework.

I set my phone down, intending to focus on my textbook and push away thoughts of Daire's weird-ass proposal.

Literal proposal.

There's no way one of his brothers didn't dare him to do it. Or maybe it's some sort of hockey player prank.

When my phone buzzes on the desk, I know I shouldn't look, but I'm clearly a glutton for punishment.

> Mother Dearest: Let me know how it goes with the pills! Send a picture of the scale every morning. I'll track your progress! ☺

The stupid smiley face just adds insult to injury.

I will *not* be sending her any sort of pictures of a scale. I don't even have one in my dorm room. I *loathe* scales.

I take screenshots of her messages and send those, along with the photo of the pills, to my dad.

His only response is

I'M SORRY, SWEETIE.

He can't really do anything to help her, and it's not for lack of trying. When the rehab didn't work, he took her from therapist to therapist. There was acupuncture and even a hypnotist involved. Any time he's encountered a technique that has the potential to help her, he's tried.

I throw my phone onto my unmade bed.

Frustrated doesn't even begin to cover how I feel.

Is it too much to ask to be loved for who I am by my own mother?

God, what would she be like if I were bigger? Would she resort to pressuring me into even more drastic measures like surgery?

Sadly, it wouldn't surprise me.

You are not and will not become the product of her problems.

With a deep breath in, then back out, I focus on that phrase. In the past, moments like this would lead me to binge or even starve myself. Anymore, though, I can *mostly* let her words roll off my back.

I open my laptop, determined to focus on the essay I'm working on for my nutrition class. I have my mom to thank for my chosen career path. Not that I'll ever have to work. Not with the money I'll inherit from my dad, the heir to an entire hotel chain empire, as well as my mom, a successful nepo-baby model.

It's because of her that I'm pursuing this career path, a split between nutrition and therapy. I want to help people like her and maybe, in the process, save little girls from a life like I've led due to my mother's issues.

I've only written a few sentences, poor ones at that, when the door to the shared dorm space bangs open.

I stand up, my desk chair wheeling away.

"We're through! For real this time!" My roommate and best friend slams the door in the face of her on-again, off-again boyfriend. Storming through the open area between our rooms, she kicks her shoes off and lets out a small scream. "Oh," she says when she catches sight of me standing in the doorway of my room. "I didn't think you'd be back yet. Sorry about that."

"It's okay."

I never met Beatrice "Bertie" Carthwright before we were tossed together as roommates, but we clicked and became instant best friends. It's a wonder we never met before, with our families moving in similar social circles. Her family name is emblazoned on the packaging of one of the oldest candy bars in America. A person can't go into a grocery store or gas station without seeing a Carthwright Bar.

She runs her fingers through her hair in agitation. "He drives me nuts."

I struggle not to laugh from my perch in the doorway. "I'm aware."

Bertie and Tommy's relationship is volatile, to say the least. It's not abusive in any way, but they're both the jealous type and like to play games. See how far they can push the other's buttons. Tommy isn't a *bad* guy, but he's not *the* guy for her. She just hasn't seen that yet.

As her light blue eyes fill with tears, she wiggles her nose in an effort to keep them at bay.

"We're really done this time. I mean it." She throws her hands out in an X motion. "Done. I am *done*."

"What did he do?" I move away from the door and envelop my friend in a hug. She's one of very few people on this campus who actually likes me. I don't know what I'd do without her. While her ups and downs with Tommy can be exhausting, I want to be there for her like she has for me.

"He was flirting with Margo Thompson. Do you know her? Strawberry-blond hair?"

I shake my head. "Sorry, I don't."

Her lip quivers. "He said it was to make me jealous, but how did he know I'd be coming into the dorm at the exact moment? Huh? Answer: he didn't," she rambles, hiccupping through her cries. "I hate boys."

Forgetting about my essay for the time being, I hug her closer and give her a solid pat on the back. "Go shower and put on comfy clothes. I'll make brownies. We still have vanilla ice cream, right?"

"We should."

"Good. Now go." I shoo her out of the space and to the bathroom.

I'm not the best baker, but boxed brownies are pretty foolproof. I pull the box from the cabinet and dig around for our baking pan. The dorms at Aldridge are set up like apartments, with the bedrooms surrounding the living and kitchen area. The units in this building have either two or four bedrooms and share a single bathroom. We lucked out with a two-bedroom dorm, thank God. I'm not sure I'd survive living with three other girls.

I have the brownies in the oven and the sink full of dirty dishes when Bertie opens the bathroom door and a cloud of steam escapes.

"I already feel better." She inhales a lungful of air as she shuffles into her room.

I'm glad one of us does. My brain keeps seesawing between my conversation with Daire and my mother.

He wasn't lying when he said my mom always pictured the two of us getting married. Stupidly, I did too. For far too long. I shake my head to rid myself of the memories of a much younger Daire and me. He hung the moon and stars and all the planets in the sky when we were little. I thought he could do no wrong.

Until he did.

I check the timer on my phone. Twenty minutes until the brownies are done.

Bertie will be occupied for a while, doing her skin care routine, so I grab my computer and settle on the couch. Even if I only get a paragraph or two done before I'm interrupted, it's better than nothing.

As my shitty luck would have it, though, I've barely parked my ass on the couch when there's a knock on the door.

I groan. It's probably Tommy, tail tucked between his legs, coming to apologize.

The universe clearly doesn't want me to write this essay.

With an aggravated huff, I swing the door open. Only it's not Tommy on the other side.

Daire is so close that I could count each individual eyelash if I wanted, and he's got a lot of them. He towers over me, making me feel small, which, at five-ten, is rare for me. He's got to be six-four, maybe taller. I have to crane my neck back to peer up at him. It's been a long time since the two of us have been this close. Even earlier, as he *proposed marriage*, he kept his distance. Like he thought if he got too close, he'd catch cooties.

It takes everything in me to keep from stomping my foot. "What are you doing here?"

This is unfair on so many levels. Despite my best efforts, I've harbored a crush on this guy since I was eight and he was teaching me how to dive into his family's pool. Even after he broke my heart when we were sixteen, it lingered. And the damn thing persisted even when he accused *me* of following him here, even though we both know I'd always wanted to attend Aldridge University.

"I need you."

Without my permission, my heart does a somersault. Isn't that what I always wanted? For him to need me the way I needed him?

Remain strong.

"No."

"Rosie." My name rolls off his tongue in a growl. "I am begging you."

I turn to walk away, wishing I could slam the door in his face. But there's no point in trying to get rid of him. He won't walk away until he gets tired or hungry. Whichever comes first. I was lucky to escape him at lunchtime.

"Is that what you want?" he asks from behind me. "Do you want me to get down on my knees and beg? Because I will."

I turn around in time to see him do just that.

"Marry me, Rosie?"

A gasp sounds in the room. Not *my* gasp. Not even a ghost's gasp. Nope, it's Bertie, who's chosen this inopportune moment to finally come out of her room.

With a hand over her mouth, she squeals. "Yes," she

shouts, now clutching both hands to her chest. "You have to say yes!" She gives a giddy shimmy. "Oh my God, I can't believe this. It's so exciting."

My heart stops and my jaw falls open.

Blink. Blink. Blink.

The room remains in focus.

What the fuck is happening? I have to be dreaming.

"Come on, Rosie, say yes." Daire smirks up at me, far too smug for a guy who's literally on his knees begging me to marry him. He knows that I'm cornered.

I glower down at him. It's on the tip of my tongue to say no *again*, but in my periphery, Bertie is swooning at what she thinks is a romantic scene—apparently without a single concern for why I've never mentioned Daire to her before.

Panic crawls up my throat, and my heart starts again and instantly takes off at a breakneck speed.

"I ... isn't it too soon ... honey?"

He cocks his head to the side. "Darling, it's never too soon when true love is involved. Come on, say yes. Make me the happiest man alive."

Sweating through my clothes, I wring my hands, searching for a way to end this ridiculous moment. "I ... I ... are you sure? We should wait."

"Rosie," he grits out.

My knees wobble, and the room spins just a little. I feel like I'm going to pass out—from stress, certainly not from any sort of joy.

"We can make it work, baby," he goes on, ignoring my panic. "Whatever you're worried about, we'll get through it together. We're a team."

His eyes plead with me, begging me to give in.

They say *Rosie, I need you.*

And isn't that what I've wanted for years? For Daire Hendricks to need me?

But not like this.

"Will you marry me?"

"Yes," I bite out, not one bit happy about it. Jaw clenched, I narrow my eyes, silently telegraphing a clear *you owe me.*

I'm not doing it for *this* Daire. The one who's combative. The guy I've grown to loathe. I'm doing it for Daire, the boy who was once my best friend.

He gets up and pulls me into his arms, swinging me around. I roll my eyes as he spins me. This ridiculous display is solely for Bertie's benefit. Asshole.

He lowers me to the ground, and as I right myself, I take a step back, ready to put some distance between us.

Daire has other ideas. His warm hands swallow my face, and I barely have a second to comprehend what's happening before his mouth is on mine.

I used to fantasize about this moment. I was certain he'd be my first kiss, my last too, and every one in between. But that never happened. Now, I'm finally getting a kiss from my childhood Prince

Charming, but it's a kiss full of lies. A show for Bertie's benefit.

My body feels like ice, and yet it traitorously angles into him, responding to the way his mouth curves over mine. He slides one hand from my face, down my side, and settles it on my waist.

Twelve-year-old me is screaming with glee because I'm kissing Daire Hendricks.

Twenty-one-year-old-me hates that I like it.

My lips part beneath his of their own accord, and in response, he sweeps his tongue inside my mouth with gentle strokes.

Bertie makes a squeaking sound that has Daire letting me go and backing up to put a good foot of space between us. His eyes are hooded, and his normally light blue irises have darkened to a denim color. Chest rising and falling with labored breaths, he gives me a funny look, his gaze lingering on my mouth for a smidge too long.

"I didn't even know you two were dating!"

Bertie looks like the embodiment of the heart eyes emoji. Her cheeks are pink, and her eyes have tripled in size. She looks like she's going to swoon at any moment. All her anger and annoyance at Tommy has vanished. She's a sucker for love. The girl's room is lined with romance books, and we've just handed her what looks like an epic love story that I've been keeping a secret.

Frankly, I want to shake her for thinking I'd hide

something like this from her, but that's Bertie. She lives in her own little world most of the time.

"Six months, right, babe?" Daire recovers first, wrapping an arm around my waist and closing the space he created between us only a moment ago.

I plaster on a smile. It would be easy to tell her it was a joke. But instead, my mouth takes over and, with a mind of its own, says, "We reconnected over the summer."

"Why didn't you tell me?" Bertie skips toward the kitchen, practically floating on air. "Do we have wine? This calls for wine."

"That's on me. I wanted to keep it a secret."

My heart pangs at the lie and the confidence with which he spits it out. How is it so easy for him?

"A secret?" she repeats, searching for the wine we *don't* have because I drank the whole bottle by myself the other night when I was feeling particularly down. "Why?"

He shrugs and hits me with a smile that is anything but friendly. It's shocking, really, considering I'm not the one who needs a marriage. "She's dated most of my teammates. We figured it would be better to keep it quiet for a while."

And by dated, he means I've fucked them.

I don't *date*. Not for lack of trying, and not because I don't want to. But guys only seem to want me for one thing. I enjoy sex as much as the next person, so it's not like I'm going to deny myself. But it pisses me off that if I were a guy sleeping with half the cheerleading squad, I'd be applauded, yet because I'm a girl sleeping with athletes, I'm looked at as a slut even by the guys who use me for sex.

"I wish you would've told me. Did you think you couldn't trust me with your secret?" She sticks out her bottom lip, pouting. "I thought we were best friends."

I rack my brain for an excuse that will appease her. "I ... uh ... you've been, you know, having issues with Tommy. More so than usual. I didn't want you to feel bad that I was—*am*"—I shoot a panic-stricken look at Daire—"happy."

"Tommy," she says forlornly, tears returning. Sniffling, she turns away from us.

"Her boyfriend," I mouth at the man beside me. "They break up *a lot*."

He nods, lips twitching in an effort not to laugh.

Bertie snags a few tissues from the box on the counter and blows her nose. The sound that comes out of her is more fitting for a grown man than a petite college girl.

"That was sweet of you," she says, tossing the tissue into the trash, "but I still would've been happy for you."

"We can talk about this later," I assure her. If I don't shut this down now, we could be here having this conversation all night. "Right now, I need to speak to my fiancé," I say through gritted teeth.

Before either of them can protest, I grab ahold of Daire's arm and tug him into my room. Luckily, he doesn't put up a fight, because there's no way I'm strong enough to pull him by myself. I close the door and turn to face him, hands on my hips and ready to give him a piece of my mind. But he's not paying any attention to me. He's too busy looking around my room.

I wonder what it looks like through his eyes. The hints of red—my favorite color—the desk stacked with books and a worrying number of pens. My bed is made, the white comforter big and fluffy. I got it because it reminded me of marshmallows, and who doesn't think about diving into a big pile of those things from time to time?

He studies a picture on the shelf above my desk. In it, I'm flanked by his brothers. It's one of very few photos I have with them that doesn't include him.

"Why do you have this?" he asks, frowning at me.

"I still talk to them sometimes." I whisper the confession. Especially Roman, his younger brother. But that's none of his business. They were all my friends, but Daire was my *best* friend.

"Hmm," he hums, the sound full of what could be annoyance, though maybe it's only curiosity.

I cross my arms over my chest. It may come off as defensive, but I don't care. I learned a long time ago to guard myself against him in any way I can. Marrying him? Out of the question. "This isn't going to work," I tell him. "We hate each other."

He finally looks away from the picture. "That's exactly why it *will* work."

"Come again?"

"We hate each other," he reiterates. "Therefore, we don't have to worry about feelings getting involved."

I wrinkle my nose. "This is crazy. I ... you would owe me. Big time."

I'm not actually considering this, am I? Did I bump my head? Am I suffering from a concussion? Maybe all of this is a dream and I'm about to wake up and have a really big laugh about it.

"I know," he says. "Money, cars, whatever you decide you want, it's yours."

"All this because of a kid?"

I ignore the stabbing pain in my side at the thought. As a little girl and into my teenage years, I was convinced that *I* would be the mother of his kids one day. I even picked out names, for crying out loud.

"All because of *my* kid."

I wet my lips, stalling for time, turning his proposition over in my head. I hate that I'm even considering it, that even though I hate him, the little girl inside me is jumping up and down with excitement. Apparently, she didn't get the memo that this is fake.

"What are these?" he asks, picking up the diet pills and frowning at the label.

I close my eyes and pull in a breath through my nose. Dammit. Why didn't I throw them away the second I opened the package? I snatch the bottle from him and hold it behind my back. "Nothing."

"They're diet pills." His voice is higher than normal, and his eyes are wide. "Why would you need diet pills? Your body is perfect."

Those words send a bolt of elation through me. I try not to preen under that statement, but it's hard.

"My mother sent them."

He zeroes in on them as I drop them into the trash, then regards me, frowning. "She's still doing that shit to you?"

My heart speeds up, and a pit forms in my chest as a memory flashes through my mind. The day my mother took me dress shopping for the middle school dance. How she wouldn't let me buy the one I fell in love with because she said it didn't flatter my figure.

"Obviously," I bite out. The last thing I want to discuss with him is my mother. "Sit," I point at my bed.

He looks from the bed to me, arching a brow several shades darker than his natural blond hair. "Already inviting me into your bed? I'm not surprised."

I bite back a growl. I've never wanted to kick someone in the face more in my entire life.

"Don't act like you aren't familiar with falling into girls' beds." I cross my arms over my chest but quickly drop my arms to my sides. Something about him makes me incredibly defensive. "I need you to be straight with me. What all does this entail?"

My stomach rolls. Why am I even considering this?

He swallows, looking away like he knows there's a good chance I'll go running and screaming for the hills.

"We'll need to get a place together. I need to have a proper home." He glides his long fingers through his hair. "According to my lawyer, they'll do home checks." Rubbing his palms over his jeans, he cocks his head to the side. "They'll interview us too, to make sure we're competent."

Great, Daire getting custody of his kid is reliant on me proving I can handle a child.

My chest is so tight it's hard to breathe. "How old is this kid?"

"He's a few months."

I choke on my own saliva, hacking so hard that he actually gets up and hovers close, his hands held out in front of him like he's not sure what to do. Clearly, he has some work to do before he can be deemed competent enough to take care of a child.

Note to self—sign up for parenting classes.

Jesus, why am I taking this so seriously?

"Sorry," I say, breathless. "Swallowed wrong."

Instead of sitting on my bed again, he pulls out my desk chair. His big body makes it look like a child's chair.

He presses his hands together, almost in prayer. "I need you, Rosie." The words are soft, though his shoulders are rigid and his mouth is set in a firm line, like it hurt to make that admission. "Please don't back out on me."

I lower my attention to the floor between us. I can't look at him right now. "When would we have to get married?"

"As soon as possible," he answers without hesitation.

If my stomach sinks any lower, it'll be on the floor. "I want a wedding. A real one." I tilt my chin up defiantly. I've always dreamed of an elaborate wedding — thousands of flowers, an orchestra playing my favorite modern love songs, an elegant white gown.

The relationship may be fake, but that doesn't mean I don't deserve a wedding.

He groans. "No."

"Fine." I smile. "Then get out. No deal."

He clasps his hands and glowers at me. "I know you're not going to stop at a wedding."

"Obviously not."

He looks away. "We get married as soon as possible. A simple courthouse ceremony—"

"That—"

"But..." He holds up a hand, cutting off my protest. "Once we secure a custody agreement, *then* you can have your wedding."

We. Why the hell does that word make my heart squeeze in a giddy way?

"And you'll wear a tux?"

He blinks at me. "Yes."

"And dance with me?"

He sighs heavily, pinching his brow. "Yes—we do have to keep up appearances."

"What about…" Heat rises to my cheeks as I work up the nerve to get this next question out. I've never been a prude, but suddenly, I find myself embarrassed to put it into words. "What about relationships?"

Confusion ripples across his face. "I don't know what you mean."

Ducking my head, I survey the pale pink polish on my freshly pedicured feet. "Are you planning to stay celibate for this entire farce of a marriage?" I snap.

I have zero claim over Daire Hendricks, but that doesn't stop my stomach from turning over at the thought of him sleeping with other women while married to me. Even if it is *fake*.

You're so stupid. He was never yours and he's not yours now. Get over it. There's no quieting the voice in my head that's reminded me for years that he never cared about me the way I cared about him.

I inhale, waiting for his response, keeping my expression neutral despite the negative thoughts swamping me.

"I hadn't thought about it," he says carefully, like

he's wondering to himself *why* he didn't consider this fact. "I don't want either of us sleeping around until after custody is finalized. In case it could be used against me. Think you can handle that?"

"*Think you can handle that?*" I mimic in a sarcastic tone.

Sighing, he sits up straight. "It's a legitimate question, Rosie."

Annoyance crawls up my spine. "You know," I spit, "if I were one of your buddies or teammates, you'd give me a pat on the back and congratulate me for fucking my way around this school."

His eyes narrow on the word *fucking*, but I don't give him time to comment.

"Don't act so high and mighty."

"Fine." The word is hissed through clenched teeth. "Sounds like neither of us should have a problem with it then."

"Good." I lift my chin. "We're in agreement then."

We stare each other down for a long moment, neither of us breaking eye contact. It feels like a full minute, maybe even longer, before he looks away.

That's a point for me!

"I have one rule that you absolutely can't break." He wiggles his index finger at me.

I arch a brow. "What's that?"

His blue eyes narrow on me like he'd love nothing

more than to rip out my tongue right now. "You can't fall in love with me."

With a snort, I roll my eyes. "You don't have to worry about me ever breaking that rule." Not anymore, at least. "But the same applies to you. You can't fall in love with me either."

Silently, he holds out his hand, and we shake on it.

Daire gets up from my desk chair, leaving it spinning round and round in his absence, and heads for the door. With one hand on the knob, shoulders tense, he pauses.

One breath.

Two.

Three.

He glances back at me so quickly I almost miss it. "Thank you," he grits out.

Sure, I'm owed a thank-you—for even considering this, let alone agreeing—but I wasn't expecting one from him.

I'm frozen in place as he disappears. He mumbles something to Bertie on his way out, and then the main door shuts behind him with a loud click.

I can't believe I'm agreeing to this.

My bedroom door swings open, startling me and sending my heart racing.

With one hand encased in an oven mitt, Bertie holds the entire pan of brownies out. In her other hand, she holds up two forks.

"Spill everything." She plops onto my bed and offers one of the forks to me.

Quickly, I spin an elaborate story. A story that's far too easy to dream up, considering Daire and I have a shared past. It only serves to prove his point that I'm the only one who can do this for him.

three

DAIRE

"THIS IS BEAUTIFUL," Rosie says, taking in the open living space on the second floor of the townhouse. It's the third place we've looked at today. The tenth this week. "It's so open. Don't you think?" She turns to me, brows lifted and wearing a tentative smile.

I have to give her credit, she's trying.

"Mhm." I jerk my head in a nod.

"Don't forget to check out the deck," Lizzie, our realtor singsongs. "It's beautiful. Has a pergola too."

We take the stairs up to the top floor and check out the rooms.

"This one would be great for Junior, don't you think?" Rosie elbows me as she peeks into the large bedroom that looks out at the park behind the row of townhomes. Since I still don't even know my son's name, she's taken to calling him Junior.

"Yeah."

With a chest-heaving sigh, she cranes her neck, searching for Lizzie. When she confirms she's not within earshot, she pulls me into the room and shuts the door.

"Why do you act like *I'm* the one dragging you into this? Might I remind you, I'm the one helping *you* out? I actually enjoy living in the dorms with Bertie, but here I am, prepping to move out. Again, because I'm helping *you*."

I blow out a breath. My attitude is shit, and that's unfair to her. This isn't just a lot of change for me, but for her as well.

"I'm sorry."

Her jaw drops, but it only takes a heartbeat for that expression to turn into a sly grin. Then she slow claps. "Wow, mark this down in the history books. Daire Hendricks *can* apologize."

"Shut up," I grumble.

She sucks in a breath like she's ready to go on, but instead, she swallows down her next comment and squares her shoulders. "Do you like any of the places we've looked at?"

Rubbing at my jaw, I mutter, "They're okay, I guess."

With a frustrated groan, she drops her head back. When she straightens, several emotions flicker over her face—annoyance, exhaustion, resolve.

"All right, what are you looking for that these places are missing?"

I shrug, swallowing back my thoughts.

"Daire." She covers her face. "Use your big boy words. Give me something to work with."

There's a knock on the door then, and Lizzie cracks it open. "Is everything okay in here?"

"Oh, yeah." Rosie smiles at her. "Just give us a minute."

"Take your time." She backs away and eases the door shut, leaving us alone again.

"Think," Rosie says to me, hands on her hips. "What is it you want that none of these places have?"

I grit my teeth and duck my head. "It's stupid."

"I'm sure it's not. Tell me."

I look away, muttering, "A playground." But it comes out sounding more like a grunt than actual words.

"A what?" she asks, her voice pitched high. She's clearly trying not to laugh at me at this point. Can't say I blame her.

"A. Playground," I carefully enunciate. "I want to go down a slide with him and push him in a swing."

Fuck, it sounds so stupid coming out of my mouth, but I do.

She presses her lips together, fighting a smile, even as her eyes dance. "He's a little young, don't you think?"

"I mean when he's a little bigger. They have those baby swings and stuff." I scratch at the back of my head.

"We can have a playground installed at any of these places—does that make any of them more appealing to you?"

My chest tightens as I consider several we've looked at. "This one is nice, I guess. I like the kitchen."

"Okay," she says slowly. "Do you want to put in an offer?"

Do I?

How is it possible that proposing to Rosie was easier than committing to a house?

Probably because the marriage is entirely fake, while buying a house and being a father is all too real. I don't know how to be a dad. Why the fuck do they not have classes for this shit? I don't even know how to change a diaper.

"Why do you look like you're panicking all over again?"

I cover my face with my hands. "Because I don't even know how to change a diaper."

"Oh." She frowns, adjusting the strap of her purse. "I don't know how either." Quickly, she adds "We'll take classes?" with an ease that surprises me.

"Wait, there *are* classes?"

"Not at school, if that's what you mean, but there *are* classes at the hospital, or maybe a community center. I'll look into it for us."

My heart pounds out a quick rhythm in my chest. "Both of us?"

She lets out an exaggerated sigh. "I need to know how to do these things too."

"Right," I say, drawing out the word.

"What about a nanny? Are we going to need one of those? We still have to get through college."

I run my fingers through my hair, jittery with agitation. "I … I don't know. We'll have to figure that out based on what kind of custody I get."

"There's something else that's bothering you." I hate that after all this time, after all the distance between us, she still knows my tells so well. "Spill, Hendricks."

"It's stupid."

"*You're* stupid. Tell me something I don't know." She wipes beneath her eye with her middle finger.

This woman is infuriating. If I didn't need her so badly, I'd be more than happy to march her right out the front door and say *see you later*.

"I never planned on staying in this town."

She cocks her head to the side, but she remains silent, listening.

"I thought I'd leave after college. Move to Manhattan or Chicago or even London and work out of one of those offices for my dad. I didn't ... this isn't what I pictured, okay?"

But if I want to have any chance at a custody agreement and actually being in my son's life, I need to be here. The court almost always rules in favor of the mother, according to my attorney, so if having a relationship with my kid means I have to stay here in small-town Tennessee, then that's what I'll do.

Her shoulders soften, and sympathy floods her face. "That makes sense. I didn't even think about how much this changes your plans."

"Mhm," I hum, rubbing my jaw. "This is what I get for not using a condom *one time*." I grind out the last part. Fuck, I was such a fool.

"Well." She plants her hands on her hips. "All you can do now is make the best of it. So, what do you think of this place? Or should we keep looking?"

I sigh, taking in the details of the room we're sequestered in—the one she said would be perfect for ... *Junior*. I hate that her ridiculous nickname is sticking in my brain.

"I like this one fine."

"But you don't love it?"

I shake my head.

She nods once and heads for the door. "Then we keep looking."

HOURS LATER, I slide into the booth seat across from Rosie at the steakhouse she chose for dinner. It's a far cry from the usual place I hang with my friends closer to campus.

Exhaustion sits heavy in my bones, but I put in an offer on the final townhouse we looked at in the historic part of town. Rosie's eyes lit up the second we stepped inside. Even I had to agree it was nice. A sweeping staircase led to the second level, and the place was wider than the typical townhome. It felt like a home, which is what I'd been searching for but hadn't been able to voice. When we went out back and there was a playset in the small courtyard, one Lizzie confirmed would be staying, I knew we'd finally found the one.

"I'm *starving*." Rosie scans the menu, swaying slightly in her seat. She used to do the same thing when we were younger. "You're buying, right?" She arches her brow in question over the top of the menu. "Since you're going to be my husband and all, you have to take care of me." She tacks on a wink at the end.

"Yes." I slide the fancy-looking pepper grinder back and forth to busy my hands.

"In that case, we're getting appetizers."

I won't complain. I scarfed down a bowl of cereal for breakfast and haven't eaten since. She's probably in a similar situation, since we looked at homes straight through lunchtime.

Stifling a yawn, she sets the menu down. "Are you happy with your choice?"

"Our choice," I correct, picking up my glass of water. I gulp half of it down quickly, then wipe my mouth with the back of my hand. I might be an asshole, but I realize that Rosie is stuck with me through this for what could be a few years, so I want her to like the place too. "And yes, are you?"

"I think it's perfect."

"Hopefully my offer is accepted."

With a snort, she pulls a tube of expensive-looking lip balm from her purse. "You offered way more than they were asking. You'll get it."

I sit up straighter and swallow past the lump that's been lodged in my throat since the realtor submitted our offer. "I wanted to make sure we got it."

"We, huh?" Her lips twitch like she's trying not to laugh at me.

"It was a figure of speech," I grind out.

Just then, our perky waitress appears at the side of the table. She's probably a year or two younger than me, with glossy brown hair, big brown eyes, and pink lips. She's gorgeous and exactly my type, but alas, I'm celibate for the near future.

"What can I get you guys?" Her voice soft, almost shy.

"We'll take an order of the avocado egg rolls, and I'll

have a Caesar salad and fries." She passes over her menu.

"Uh ... the filet for me. Medium."

"Any other drinks?" she asks.

Elbows on the table, Rosie laces her fingers and rests her chin on the bridge they form. "Your most expensive bottle of wine."

"Oh?" The waitress smiles at her. "What are you celebrating?"

Rosie pastes on the biggest smile. "Our engagement." She holds up her left hand. "No ring yet. He was just *so* excited that he proposed without one. When you know, you know." She winks over at me.

I cover my face and huff out a long breath.

What the hell have I gotten myself into? Why didn't I listen more in sex ed?

"Wow." The waitress looks back and forth between the two of us. "That's so romantic."

"That's my little snuggle muffin." Rosie reaches across the table for my hand. "Such a romantic at heart. He learned to crochet this past Valentine's so he could make me a bear."

I'm pretty sure the girl waiting on us is about to swoon over these scenarios Rosie is fabricating.

"A bear?" she gushes. "That's so cute. Can I see your IDs first?"

Sitting up, I pull out my wallet and license, then slide it over. Rosie does the same.

"Great!" She hands our IDs back. "Let me go put this in and bring your wine."

"Thanks, Brittany." Rosie's voice is pure cheer.

"Her name's Brittany?" I ask, frowning at our server as she crosses the dining room.

Rosie rolls her eyes. "Yeah, she came up to the table and said *Hi, my name is Brittany. What can I get you guys?* Were you not listening?"

"I missed that first part," I mumble.

She takes a sip of her water and bites down on the straw as she mutters, "Of course you did."

I check my phone, hoping to find texts from my friends waiting, but there's nothing. Irritation has my teeth clenching. My world is imploding, and Cree is too busy running after a girl he thinks is the one who got away. Newsflash, she's just a girl. Nothing special. I shoot him a text, just a simple *Hey, what are you doing?* but I doubt I'll hear from him anytime soon.

"I don't think I've ever known of you to be this quiet." She takes another sip of water. "It's weird."

I look up and set my phone face down on the table. "I have a lot on my mind."

"Right." She cringes. "Makes sense."

Awkward silence settles around us. It's weird sitting across from someone I used to know everything about who is now a virtual stranger.

"What's your major?" I ask her.

She arches a manicured dark brow at me. "You're

seriously asking me about my major? That's like talking about the weather." With a shake of her head, she adds, "I'm studying to be a nutrition therapist."

"Because of your mom?"

She nods sadly, her eyes dropping to the table like the whorls in the wood are the most fascinating things she's ever seen. It pisses me off to know that her mom is still so obsessed over Rosie's weight. She's perfect the way she is. She always has been. "I'm sorry." I don't know what else to say. Sorry doesn't make it any better, and it certainly doesn't fix the problem.

"It is what it is, but yeah, she's why I wanted to go down this path. Not that I need to work, but…" She trails off, shrugging her shoulders.

She's right. Her dad is the sole heir to an entire chain of hotels, so she's set for life. I can't judge, not when I'm in the same situation with my own father. I have to applaud Rosie for going to college and working to get her degree when she could've spent the last few years partying and traveling. Her parents are far more lenient than my dad, who insisted that all of us boys attend college.

"Here's that bottle of wine for you guys." The waitress sets down two glasses, then she opens the bottle and fills each one halfway.

"Thank you so much." Rosie holds the stem, swirling the liquid around slowly.

I clear my throat. "Yeah, thanks."

"Your avocado egg rolls should be out shortly," she says cheerily, and with that, she bounds off to check on another table.

"Hmm, not bad." Rosie hums, bringing the glass to her lips for a second sip. "What do you think?"

"I don't really like wine in general."

She huffs in indignation. "Of course not."

Annoyance flashes through me. "What's that supposed to mean?"

She angles closer, elbows on the table, until she's close enough that she's able to whisper. "I know how you like your alcohol. Licked off the tits of whatever willing girl is throwing herself at you on any given night."

I bristle, hands clenching into fists on top of the table.

"But *I'm* the slut. Have you ever wondered why guys like you, ones who fuck anything that walks, think that *I'm* the one with a problem? You and me, we're the same."

"We're nothing alike."

She rolls her eyes, leaning back. "So you're telling me you don't like sex and haven't had a lot of it with lots of different women? You're the one who got your *professor* pregnant."

I grind my teeth but say nothing. I'm not interested in escalating this discussion into a full-blown argument.

"Yeah," she laughs humorlessly. Then she takes a gulp of wine. "That's what I thought."

We eat our meal mostly in silence, save for the sounds of our forks hitting the dishes. I feel like an asshole, because she's right. She's called me out on this before, and I keep falling into the same trap.

Will I ever learn from my mistakes?

Probably not.

four

ROSIE

> Daire: The offer was accepted.

I HAVE to read the text message three times before the meaning becomes clear. Once I realize he's talking about the townhouse, I want to smack myself in the face. My brain is officially fried from studying. It's time for bed.

> Me: That's good.

> Daire: Closing is in a month. We'll both need to be present.

> Me: Why me?

> Daire: So the deed can be in both of our names.

> Me: Why? You're paying for it. I don't need my name on it.

> Daire: <eye roll emoji>

> Daire: Because we're going to be married. I'm putting your name on it.

Now I'm the one rolling my eyes, but for real this time.

> Me: It's fine with me to leave my name off it. No hard feelings, I swear.

> Daire: Rosie?

> Me: Yup?

> Daire: Shut up and just accept it.

> Me: Okay.

It doesn't feel right that he's paying for the house, yet I'll officially be part owner. But arguing with Daire Hendricks is *exhausting*. I would know. I'm a pro at it.

As I scan my room, it hits me that I have a ton of crap to pack up. I'll have to notify the school that I'll be living off campus too and—

Let the anxiety spiral begin.

Deep breaths, Rosie. It'll be fine. Everything always works out.

I'm moving in with a man for the first time. Yet it isn't because we're madly in love and want to be together all the time. It breaks my heart a little, which is probably absolutely pathetic of me. It's like no matter how shitty I've been treated by the guys in my life, the small part of me that wants the fairy tale never gives up hope.

There's a soft knock on my door, and a second later, it creaks open a couple of inches.

"Hey, do you want to watch a movie?" Bertie asks. Her eyes are sunken and ringed in dark circles. She hasn't been sleeping much since the breakup, which seems to actually be permanent this time. Color me shocked.

"Sure? What did you have in mind?"

She grins, the gleeful expression at odds with her previous sullen demeanor. *"Barbie Princess and the Pauper."*

I lower my head. "I should've known."

Bertie is a sucker for the animated Barbie movies. I am too, not that I'll willingly admit that to her. I leave my phone in my room, not wanting to deal with Daire if he texts again.

"You seem like you have a lot on your mind." She stands on her tiptoes in the kitchenette, pulling out the big bowl we use for popcorn.

I open the pantry cabinet and shuffle our snack food around until I find the box of kettle corn stuffed in the back. There's nothing wrong with good ole butter popcorn, but I go feral for kettle corn.

Once I've got the plastic wrapping off, I put the popcorn in the microwave.

"I'm fine." I turn to her and pull my hair up into a bun.

She arches a brow, her face the picture of doubt. "Trouble in paradise?"

"No, we're great." I paste on a smile. "He just texted me to let me know our offer was accepted."

"Oh." Her face falls. "Really?"

I bite back a grimace. It hurts to know I'm disappointing her by leaving. But since it's so late in the semester, there's a good chance she won't be saddled with a new roommate. That knowledge goes a long way in easing my guilt.

"Yeah. Closing is in a month."

"Well," she says, pulling two cans of Sprite from the fridge, "congratulations."

I frown. Dammit. I'm such a fraud. I want to tell my best friend the truth. That none of this is real. That it's just a game of pretend to help Daire out. But I *can't*. I trust Bertie more than just about anyone, but even though Daire drives me absolutely insane, I would never do anything to compromise his chances of getting his son.

"Thanks." Just as I pop the top on the can, the microwave beeps, and Bertie yanks the door open and grabs the popcorn.

Once we've each got a bowl, we settle on the couch and cover ourselves with our favorite blankets, hers a pale blue color and mine red.

"I can't believe we're watching Barbie movies like we're eight," I say, adjusting the pillow behind me.

She laughs and pops a piece of popcorn into her mouth. "You never get too old for Barbie."

I point a finger at her. "Facts."

I IGNORE Daire as he tries to flag me down outside of my class. I'm not in the mood to deal with him. I'm blaming it on my period, but honestly, just looking at his face makes me angry on a good day.

I cut down the hall on my right, taking a shortcut with the hope of losing my husband-to-be in the process.

Unfortunately, there's one person in the world more stubborn than I am, and I'm marrying him.

I'm not the praying kind, but if I were, I'd be begging for all the strength and patience in the world right now. I'll need it to get through this impending marriage.

"Rosie!"

Ugh.

I come to a stop, and when he catches up, I cock my head to the side. "Yes? I have another class to get to."

"Did you not see me waiting for you?" He swings one arm around, gesturing behind us. "I need to talk to you."

"About what?" I stick my hands on my hips. "I really do have to get to class."

I have time, but not for him and his infuriatingly good-looking face.

He grips my wrist so I can't run away again. Smart man. His touch is firm but warm. "We need to get our marriage license," he whispers, looking around to make sure we're out of earshot of the students coming and going. "I want to go today."

"*Today?*" That simple sentence has my heart rate accelerating so violently I think I might pass out.

I knew this was coming, and soon, but now? Perhaps, subconsciously, I had an inkling, and that's why my natural reaction was to run when I noticed him.

"Yes, today. We need the license before we can have the ceremony."

I swallow past the lump in my throat, panic threatening to suffocate me.

Is this what a panic attack feels like?

"Rosie?" There's true concern in his voice.

I suck in a sharp, shallow breath. "Mhm?"

"Are you okay?"

"Just having a smidge of a panic attack." I take another breath, this one a little deeper. I no longer even remotely resemble the girl who wrote *Mrs. Rosie Hendricks* over and over again in my notebooks when I was a teenager, like I could somehow will it into existing.

I guess I did. *Huh*. Just not in the way I wanted.

His blue eyes widen. "You're not backing out on me, are you?"

"No, I ... this is a big deal, okay?" I push my hair out of my eyes and focus on taking another breath. "All of this ... the proposal, getting married at the courthouse, looks nothing like what I always wished for, you know?"

I've been doing my best to delude myself into thinking this whole thing isn't happening, but here he is, confronting me with solid evidence. We're doing this thing. This *thing* being marriage.

He rubs slow, soothing circles against the pulse point on the inside of my wrist with his thumb. "I can't keep apologizing to you."

"I know." I lower my head and study the shiny tiles beneath my boots.

He exhales heavily and squeezes a little tighter. "I need you, Rosie. But if you need to walk away from this, I'll..." He looks away, jaw pulsing. "I'll understand."

It's the first time since the fiasco in my dorm that he's voiced his reluctant agreement that I can say no.

It would be easy too.

I could walk away and forget all about this. *Him*. I've ignored him for years. I could certainly do it again. But if I do it again now, I'll always feel guilty, especially if it ends up costing him a relationship with his son.

Worst of all, I don't like the idea of him doing this whole fake marriage thing with someone else. Envy for a faceless, nameless girl rises inside me.

"No, no." I shake my head quickly. "I'm in."

I'm possibly the biggest idiot on the planet for not taking him up on his offer to bail out of this whole mess, but I can't back out now.

"Good." He lets out a breath and gives me a cautious smile. "When's your last class of the day?"

"I'm headed to it now."

With a nod, he releases his hold on me and steps back. "We'll get the marriage license after. I'll meet you outside the dining hall. Make sure you have your social security card, and license too."

Though panic once again washes through me, I dip my chin. "Okay."

"Okay," he echoes.

For a long moment, the two of us stand there, watching one another like idiots.

"I … uh … better go." I toss my thumb over my shoulder and take a step back.

"I'll see you soon." With that, he turns on his heel and strides away, towering above many of the other students shuffling their way to their next classes or just hanging around and catching up.

The whole way to class, I give myself a mental pep talk, but by the time I enter the classroom, I don't feel any better.

SURE ENOUGH, I find Daire outside the dining hall just as he promised, his hair damp from a shower. He probably went to the gym while I was in class. It wouldn't have made sense for him to go all the way to his off-campus housing just to turn around and come back to get me.

"I could've met you there," I grumble as I approach.

"And chance you not showing up?" He tugs on the strap of my backpack, pulling it easily off my shoulder despite the weight. "Not happening."

I roll my eyes. "I wouldn't have done that to you."

Because, apparently, I'm too honorable for my own good.

Outside, I follow him toward his sleek black Porsche 911, curious about whether he still trades cars as much as he used to. He went through at least five cars just while we were in high school. Last I remember, he had a motorcycle too.

"You know," I start as I reach for the door, only to

be gently moved aside so he can open it for me, "you're going to have to get a new car."

His lip curls as he looks from the sports car to me, then back. "Why?"

"It's a two-seater. Where are you going to put Junior? Strap him to the roof?"

"Fuck." The curse is a low sound.

I smile as I slide into the buttery smooth red leather seat, pleased with myself for thinking of something he obviously hasn't yet. It's a shame the Porsche needs to go. It's gorgeous. He could always keep it, I suppose, but what's the point?

Daire's phone automatically connects when he starts the car, and EDM music blares from the speakers.

He turns the volume down with the push of a button on his steering wheel, buckles up, and backs out of the parking spot. Despite the fancy cameras that show him a view all the way around the car, he puts one hand on the back of my headrest and cranes his neck so he can look out the back window. It's kind of hot, the way his bicep is flexed at my eye level.

Turning back around, he puts the car into gear. The engine *purrs*, the low vibration sending a shiver through me.

"When are we telling our parents about this?" I ask after several minutes of silence. "After the deed is done?"

He rubs his jaw with his left hand, then quickly

grasps the wheel so he can use his right to change gears as we navigate the small-town streets.

"I think that's best."

He's probably right. None of them would be against the union, but my mom would insist on having a wedding rather than waiting like we discussed.

"We'll make a trip home after it happens."

I hum in assent. "We're telling them together."

No way in hell am I facing the wrath of my mom on my own. I can already imagine the hysterics that are in my future.

"I figured," he says in that gruff way of his that has me wanting to smack him upside the head.

Some things never change.

Once we're parked outside the courthouse, Daire parks and hops out, waiting for me to join him. "Try to act like you like me." He slips his sunglasses off. "Think you can manage that?"

I roll my eyes. "I've faked a million orgasms. Pretending to like you is nothing."

"Faked. Right." He barks out a humorless laugh.

What would he think if I told him not a single guy has ever given me an orgasm? Not once. Not even with the ones who tried to get me there until I inevitably faked it just to get things over with. The only way I've ever gotten off is with the help of my trusty little toy. Maybe that's what has kept me chasing guys. The hope that, eventually, I find one who can. After so many, though, I'm thinking it's a me problem. I've tried and failed so many times that I get way too in my head about it, and that certainly doesn't help.

I trail behind him into the building. While he navigates the way and talks to the woman behind the counter, I paste on a smile and only say a word or two here and there.

I pass over every item they ask for, batting my eyes at Daire like I'm *so* in love with this man that I can't bear not being married to him for another minute. I put my hand on his arm and slide it down to entwine our fingers. His hand is stiff in mine, so I give it a squeeze, a silent reminder to play along. Who is he to tell me to act like I like him when he can't do the same? If one of us is going to give away our secret, it *won't* be me.

When we're done, we leave with the license in hand and another ten pounds of weight pressing down on our shoulders.

"Listen," I say once we're in the car, "I've agreed to help you out, but it's going to be a long ... who knows exactly, if we don't at least try to be friends. I'm here. I'll do what needs to be done. But I don't want to waste what could be years of my life tiptoeing around you."

With a sigh, he starts the engine. "I know."

"And don't tell me to fake it when you're the one who needs to work on his game face."

His mouth drops open. "Are you fucking kidding me? I was fine in there."

"Fine? *Fine?*" I drop my head back and cackle. "I'm pretty sure the clerk was concerned that I was holding you against your will."

He groans, rubbing a hand over his face. "Okay, perhaps I could've been warmer, but—"

"Perhaps," I scoff.

He backs out of the parking space, grumbling under his breath. "If I take you to get ice cream, will that make you feel better?"

A sudden lump rises in my throat. When we were younger, we'd always get ice cream when one of us had a bad day. I once told him that I was certain ice cream could solve any problem.

"If you're buying, then yes."

He scoffs. "As if you don't have a black AMEX in your purse right now."

I shrug, smiling. "Doesn't mean I'm going to turn down a treat on your dime."

Ten minutes later, I'm licking fresh strawberry ice cream from a cone and feeling like I won something, even if I'm not sure what.

five

DAIRE

A WEEK LATER, I'm dressed in a pair of dress pants and button-down shirt. I'm even wearing my good shoes. I had every intention of showing up at the courthouse in jeans and a sweatshirt, but Rosie reminded me that there's a chance we'll be asked for photos. How ironic that I have to jump through hoops in order to establish my parental rights. Samuel. *Sammy*. I finally know his name. It's not one I would have chosen, but somehow, it feels perfect.

Danielle put her husband's name on the birth certificate, which is complicating matters. He's certain *he's* the father, but I *know* I am.

> Me: Should I wear a tie?

I can't believe I'm even texting Rosie about this, but she's all I've got. I've yet to even mention the situation to my family. I don't want my brothers trying to talk me out of this or my dad intervening to fix my problems for me. Sure, my solution is unconventional, but it's going to work. It has to. I need to do this on my own, to prove to myself that I don't need my dad and his money. I'm a dad now. I have to come up with my own solutions.

> Rosie: I think so.

With a groan, I reach for the solid black one, then I get to work on knotting it. All my years of dressing up for hockey games are paying off.

Married.

I'm getting married today. It's certainly not how I thought it would go. There's nothing romantic about this, and even though I've never been in a serious relationship, I'm a bit of a romantic at heart. I've always thought about what it would be like to find that girl who's my best friend. A woman I share everything with, laugh with and—

Jesus. Things used *to be like that with Rosie.*

Our friendship ended messily, with way too much vitriol spewing from both our mouths. We're both passionate people, and that doesn't always bode well.

Over the past week, between getting the marriage license and dealing with house things, like a walk-through with the inspector, we've seen each other a lot. It's strange being around her again. Strange, not because it's bad, but because it's easy. Like it used to be. Sometimes it's all too easy for me to forget that we ever stopped being friends.

The house is eerily silent around me. A year ago, the place was always filled with people. We hosted parties every week. Now, Cree is too focused on wooing his mystery girl and Jude is too busy trying to get into Millie's pants.

None of my friends or my roommates know anything about what's going on with my life because none of them are even fucking around to talk to or answer my texts. Even though Cree and I are both on the hockey team, there's no time to talk because he's always disappearing.

In the bathroom, I fix my hair and spray on some cologne. I have no idea why I'm going through this much trouble. Rosie's request isn't a good enough reason. Cologne won't help, even if photos of our courthouse ceremony are brought up in court. But it's too late now.

I take the stairs slowly, each one creaking beneath

me on my way down, and swipe my keys up on my way out. Until Rosie brought it up, I hadn't even thought about my car situation. But she's right. I need something family friendly.

Me?

Family friendly?

It's laughable.

But I'll do whatever it takes, and that means my beloved car will have to go. I could purchase a more practical option and keep the Porsche, but I don't see the point. If I get the shared custody I want, there won't be much time to enjoy it anyway.

I'm still in the driveway when another text message from Rosie pops up.

> Rosie: I'm running late. I'll meet you there.
>
> Me: NO. I'm picking you up.
>
> Rosie: Don't be so stubborn. It makes more sense to meet there.
>
> Rosie: Stop frowning at me. I know you are.

Even though we haven't spoken in the past couple of years, she still knows me inside and out. It's maddening that she hasn't forgotten. Though I suppose I haven't either when it comes to her.

> Me: Fine. I'll be counting how many minutes you're late.

> Rosie: I'd expect nothing less.

I blast my music on the way to the courthouse. My tie is strangling me, but I don't dare loosen it. It's shitty of me, but I wish I were drunk right now. This is the last thing I want to deal with. I act like *I'm* the one being coerced into this, which is unfair to Rosie. I need to get my head on straight.

Parked near the front of the building, I sit and wait for her to arrive.

Sixteen minutes and twenty-three seconds later, her Mercedes-Maybach SUV careens into the lot. With the way she drives, I'm not sure how she still has a license. She's a menace to other drivers.

As she parks a few rows behind me, I climb out of my car, lock it, and lean against the passenger door to wait for her.

Fuck me.

My mouth goes dry and my heart just about leaps out of my chest.

Rosie's gorgeous. There's no denying that on any given today. But in this moment, she's fucking radiant. Her dark hair is pulled back into some sort of low bun thing, with a few shorter pieces framing her face. Her lips are lined in a vibrant red, and her white dress makes her tan skin almost golden.

I can barely breathe as I take in the thin cutouts along the fabric at her waist that reveal just a hint of bare skin on each side. Without my permission, my eyes continue their perusal. The dress has a high slit—but not too high to be inappropriate. It's not revealing—the top of the dress fully covers her breasts, and its sleeves probably help stave off the October chill—but god damn is it sexy.

With the way my cock strains against my pants, I send up a silent prayer to whatever god might be listening that Rosie doesn't notice.

"Sorry," she says, adjusting her dress. "I had to redo my eye makeup. I messed up my wing, and when I tried to clean it up, it just ... well." She waves a dismissive hand. "I had to start over."

I latch on to one word from that spiel. "Wing?"

"My eyeliner wing." She points to her face.

"Oh." I nod like I have the slightest clue what she's talking about.

"Ready?" she asks, smoothing a hand down her dress—her nails painted a bright red that matches her lips.

"As I'll ever be."

Laughing, she starts for the stairs. "You act like I'm the one dragging you here. Come on, Hendricks, let's get hitched." She crooks a finger for me to follow.

With my heart in my throat, I hurry to catch up

with her. If I don't, then I'm going to stare at her ass the whole way up the stairs to the main door.

Did I step into some fucked-up alternate universe this morning? It's the only explanation for why I'm checking Rosie out.

In the vestibule, I scan the directory posted on the wall, my hand automatically falling to her waist. She moves away instantly, so I let my hand drop. Shit. I'm already fucking things up. Sure, we need to make this look real, but it doesn't mean I get to touch her when no one is around.

"This way." My voice is gruff, annoyed, though I'm irritated more at myself than her.

If I had been smart rather than thinking with my dick, I wouldn't be in this situation in the first place.

Once we've found the correct office, we check in and hand over all our paperwork.

Rosie loops her arm through mine and leans into me. "Isn't he just so handsome?" she asks the bored receptionist, squeezing my cheek like my annoying aunt did when I was a boy.

"Mhm." The woman hums. "Here you go." She passes the papers back to me. "Go through those doors." She points to a large set of wooden double doors at the end of the long hall. "There are a few couples ahead of you, so just sit and wait."

"Thanks." Rosie lets me go as we head toward our fate.

"Wait!" The voice is high pitched and one I don't recognize.

Beside me, Rosie freezes, so I take her cue and stop too.

"Oh my God, no," she groans.

In unison, we turn around and come face to face with her friend ... *Belinda? Becca? Something with a B, right?*

"Bertie, what are you doing here?" she asks as the girl click-clacks down the hall to catch up.

"You need a witness!" She waves her hand wildly above her head as she reaches us. "And I volunteer as tribute!"

"Bertie." Rosie hangs her head. "There are already witnesses here."

"Yeah, but don't you want your friend here?" She frowns, her eyes growing round as saucers.

I swear if the girl starts crying, I'm going to lose my shit.

"And what about pictures? You need someone to take photos! I know you plan on having a real wedding, but this is still technically your wedding day. If you don't have pictures, you'll regret it."

Rosie sends me a look that's pure apology. "You're so right. Thank you."

Bertie beams at the praise. "I'm so happy I made it in time. When I got back to our room and you were already gone, I worried I'd miss it."

Rosie cringes, eyeing me in a way that makes it clear that she purposely left while her roommate was out.

I hold the door open for the ladies, and we find seats in the last row. There are two other couples ahead of us that haven't started yet, as well as one standing in front of the officiant.

While we wait, nerves and adrenaline course through me with such ferocity that I can't sit still.

Rosie puts her hand on my bouncing knee to settle it. "Babe," she says, clearly trying not to gag on the word, "it's cute that you're nervous."

"I'm not nervous," I grumble.

With her hand still on my knee, she leans over to Bertie and whispers something I can't hear.

As the couple rushes by us, it hits me that I'm so out of it I didn't even pay attention to their vows. I blow out a breath. With the next one, I will. The last thing I want to do is stumble over my words.

It doesn't take long for the two couples ahead of us to finish up, and when it's our turn, my heart beats so hard I can hear it in my ears. Why the hell am I freaking out so much? This isn't even real. It's temporary.

But it's still a marriage. It's still legal.

I hold Rosie's hands in each of mine and survey her. Her pulse visibly flutters in her throat. She swallows, forcing a smile. I paste on one of my own.

We're supposed to be happy and in love, I remind myself.

We each repeat the words when we're supposed to. Then it's time for rings.

"Oh, we don't—"

I clear my throat, interrupting her, and shove my hand into my pocket. Holding my breath, I pull out a ring for me and one for her as well. As she takes the thick silver band with a line of black through it that I got for myself, I don't miss the way her fingers tremble.

"I give you this ring as a sign of my love and devotion." I repeat the line I've been given, sliding the diamond eternity band onto her finger.

She swallows audibly, reaching for my hand. "I give you this ring as a sign of my love and devotion." The band is warm from her hand as it settles on my finger.

"You may now kiss your bride."

Kiss? Even as I watched the couples ahead of us, it never dawned on me that I would actually have to kiss her.

Rosie looks away.

It's just a kiss. You've kissed plenty of girls.

But girls who weren't Rosie—who weren't my *wife*.

I cup her cheek, brushing my thumb against her chin, right beneath her full bottom lip. Leaning in, I lower my head. Her eyes flutter closed in preparation, her breath stuttering.

I swear time stands still as I seek out her mouth. My intent is to press a quick kiss to her lips, but a wave of heat washes through me the second our lips touch.

More. I *need* more.

Not just more; I need everything.

I add pressure to the kiss and lick the seam of her lips. Her mouth opens slightly beneath mine, and a tiny sound escapes. I quickly swallow it down, relishing the warmth of her so close. The softness of her lips. She puts her hands flat on my chest, fingers flexing like she wants to clutch the fabric but is holding herself back. I kiss her harder still, with a desperation that shouldn't exist. Then she snaps, opening for me, letting me in. She kisses me back, nibbling on my bottom lip. Encouraging me to dive back in for more. I tangle my fingers in her hair so I can hold her where I want her, pulling it free from the bun. I don't stop. I can't stop, and I never want to.

A throat clears in the distance, but I pay it no mind.

"Excuse me?" The voice is male. Mostly unfamiliar.

I still don't stop.

Selfishly, I want to get my fill now, because I won't be kissing her again. I *can't*.

"Hey!" The command is louder this time, followed by a shake of my shoulder.

Finally, I pull my lips from hers. Her red lipstick is smeared, half of it no doubt on my face, and her eyes are hazy.

"We better get out of here." I wipe my mouth with the back of my hand. When I pull it away, it's streaked with red. I use my thumb to wipe at the lipstick smudged around her lips.

She lets me, still frozen from the kiss. If it weren't for the slow blink of her eyes and flutter of her pulse at the base of her throat, I'd worry I accidentally kissed her to death.

"Sir, you need to move. I have more couples to marry."

I glower at the guy. "I'm fixing her makeup. You can wait a minute."

The exchange snaps Rosie out of her trance. "It's okay," she breathes, stepping back. "I can fix it in the car."

"Are you sure?"

She nods.

With that, we rush from the room, Bertie struggling to keep up with us on the way to the parking lot.

"That was some kiss," she says from behind us, her shoes echoing off the stone floors. "I don't think Tommy has ever kissed me like that before. I'm definitely not taking him back after seeing that."

She rambles on as we burst outside. I don't know how Rosie feels, but I'm suffocating.

I kissed her and I *liked* it.

I *more* than liked it.

Worse yet, I want to do it again and I can't. It's *Rosie*.

"I'll leave you kids to it." Bertie adjusts her purse on

her shoulder. It's such a minute detail to notice, but I'm doing everything I can to keep my eyes off Rosie. "Have fun tonight!" She wiggles her fingers in a wave and heads toward her parked car. "I'll send you the photos later, Ro!"

"Thank you," Rosie calls after her, hands cupped around her mouth.

"What's tonight?" I ask her dumbly.

She rolls her eyes. "Our wedding night."

Fuck. I scrub a hand over my face. I hadn't even thought about that. I stomp toward my car, pretending I'm not leaving my *wife* standing on the sidewalk.

"Where are you going?" she calls after me, panic edging her tone.

I look back over my shoulder to where she's standing with her arms wrapped around her. "To get drunk."

"Are you serious?" She storms after me, her heels clicking on the concrete. "I can't go back to my dorm! You heard Bertie. It's technically our wedding night. She'll know something is up if I go back!"

I pull out my wallet and flick through my credit cards. I choose the one I want and shove it at her. "It has no limit. Get a hotel room. Buy a car. Go crazy. I don't fucking care."

"Daire!"

Without another glance her way, I get in my car and tear out of the lot like I have any chance of outrunning my demons. My brain is a whirlpool of spiraling thoughts about how I shouldn't have chased so many girls. How I shouldn't have gone after one of my professors. I've made poor decision after poor decision, and now I'm dragging someone else into my mess.

As I pull onto the road, I spare a brief look back at Rosie, at her stricken expression and her defeated posture, and guilt sinks like a stone in my stomach.

It's okay. I'll be drunk soon enough, and I'll forget all about that look on her face.

six

ROSIE

THAT BASTARD.

As the Porsche speeds out of the parking lot, all I can do is hope his sorry ass gets pulled over.

Staring down at the credit card he practically threw at me, I shake my head. Irritated doesn't begin to describe how I feel.

And what the hell was that kiss?

I've never been kissed like that before—with equal parts passion and desperation. It's like he wanted to sink inside me.

The worst part is that I would've let him.

Shame on me.

I cross the lot and climb into my SUV. For several minutes, I sit there, engine running, and soak in the warm air blowing from the vents. Today's harsh wind has caused a chill to settle in the air. Or maybe it's Daire's frigid behavior that's getting to me.

With my forehead pressed to the steering wheel, I swallow past the lump in my throat. I certainly didn't expect the traditional wedding night, nor would I let him touch me like that—even if I really, *really* liked the way he kissed me—but I can't say I envisioned him abandoning me in the courthouse parking lot either. I should've known better. If there's one thing Daire has been consistent about for the last few years, it's embarrassing me.

Meandering aimlessly down the streets of the small town outside our sprawling campus, I finally say *fuck it*, and drive the few hours into Nashville. I don't *need* to spend his money, but if he's offering, then why not put it to good use?

Asshole.

I don't even care if I'm behaving exactly like the kind of person he thinks I am. If he can't treat me with respect, then he doesn't deserve it either.

When I get downtown, I check into the Four Seasons. I didn't bring a bag with me, but I have no qualms about using Daire's card to pay for a change of clothes, pajamas, and toiletries.

Once I've got my keycard, I head back out and make my way to the mall. In the first store I come across, I change out of my dress and into a new pair of jeans and a light-weight sweater. From there, I continue to add to the bill. New boots at another store, a cute dress from a third, and a purse I've been eyeing for the last year but didn't want to pull the trigger on.

I don't care if our marriage isn't real. It's rude as hell that I've gone out of my way to help him, and in return, he's discarded me like a dirty tissue.

When I come across a furniture store, excitement flares inside me. We have a new home to decorate, after all. We need couches and tables and … well, *everything*. When I finish there, I charge a nauseatingly large sum, putting that "no limit" to the test. Sure enough, the purchase goes through.

If he gets text notifications for his card, he'll probably go into cardiac arrest.

"Thanks so much." I smile at the saleswoman, masking a pain so sharp I feel as if I've spent all afternoon wandering the mall with a knife buried in my chest.

Even so, I hold my head high, scoop up my bags, and continue on my merry way.

Retail therapy usually does the trick when my life goes to shit, but it's not making me feel better this time.

It doesn't stop me from purchasing another luxury purse, though, or a watch I certainly don't need.

The ring on my left hand feels like a weight threatening to drown me.

What have I done?

I never should've allowed myself to be suckered into a scheme like this. It was stupid. Downright foolish of me. There's a small part of me that remembers what it was like before, when he was my friend, and like an idiot, I let that small voice sway my decision. I just wanted to help. To make it all better for him.

It's late by the time I return to the hotel. Luckily for me, Daire's paying for the penthouse suite.

The bathtub is practically the size of a small swimming pool. I run hot water and add the bubbles and salt provided as exhaustion weighs heavily on me. I'm not even physically tired, just mentally strung out from the last few weeks. I better get used to it, I guess, because this whole thing is only beginning.

Slipping out of my clothes, I sink into the steaming water. An embarrassing sigh leaves me.

Alone.

It's my wedding night, and I'm all by myself.

Sure, it was never going to be a real wedding night, but I didn't realize I'd signed myself up to a lifetime of loneliness with this deal either. I thought … well, I guess I stupidly thought we could repair our friendship. Better friends than nothing, but apparently, he doesn't see it like that.

I snag my phone from the ledge around the tub,

desperately hoping to see a text or call for him, but there's nothing. The lack of notifications only leaves me feeling more pathetic.

When my fingers begin to prune, I wrap myself in a big, fluffy robe and scan the room service menu beside the bed. The last thing I feel like doing is eating, but my growling stomach disagrees with me.

By the time I've finished ordering, the hotel staff probably assumes I'm throwing a party. I ordered way more than one person can ever dream of eating. But now's a perfect time to sample a little bit of everything.

Remote in hand, I lie on my stomach and turn on the TV. The first menu I find lists a handful of early-access movies available for purchase, so I do what any sensible person in my position would do—I buy them all.

I desperately want to text him, check on him, but I hold myself back. I can't start down this path on night one. I'd rather not show him just how pathetic I can be so soon.

I click the icon for the first movie on the list and let it play in the background. There's a complimentary bottle of champagne chilling, so I pop the cork and pour myself a glass. I don't even like champagne, but I might as well drink it. It's not like I have anything better to do. I settle into the middle of the bed since I have it all to myself tonight and sip the bubbly.

The irony here isn't lost on me. All I wanted when I

was a little girl was to marry Daire and become Mrs. Hendricks. Now I've done it, but this scenario looks nothing like how I pictured it would.

You're helping him out. That's all. You knew what you were getting into.

I did, but that small part of me that hoped things would be different couldn't be quelled.

When room service knocks on the door, I hop up to let them inside. The guy scans the room, probably wondering where all my guests are, but he has the decency not to ask. I sign the slip for the food, and since he's keeping his comments to himself, I add a more than generous tip.

"Thank you," I tell him as he heads for the door. Just because I'm suffering in my feels doesn't mean I've forgotten my manners. Daire can think what he wants of me, but if there's one thing my parents and nannies instilled in me and my younger sister, it's to use our manners.

Being rich isn't an excuse to be a dick, my dad used to say.

To which my mom would berate him for saying the word *dick*, especially when my little sister, Grace, would repeat the word nonstop for the rest of the day. I miss my sister so much. It doesn't matter that I spent all summer with her in the Hamptons.

My sister was a welcome surprise for my parents and for me. I was ten when she was born. We knew from early on during my mom's pregnancy that she had Down Syndrome. My parents didn't once balk at the diagnosis, at least not that I saw. Instead, they embraced it with open arms. They've never treated Grace any differently than they do me. Okay, maybe that's not entirely true. They probably treat her a bit better, but only because she really is the best. It's impossible not to love her. She's a ray of sunshine, always smiling and giving hugs, but she can be brutally honest. Sometimes that's a great thing, other times, not so much —like the time she told our waitress she could see her boogers.

She's almost twelve now, so she's gotten a *smidge* better at filtering herself.

If she were here, she would read Daire to filth for his behavior. I smile, thinking about the way she'd call him a butthead.

She was only six when our friendship shattered, so she doesn't know him well, but she knows he broke my heart.

After I've inspected the spread of food, I grab the cheese board and take it to the bed with me. Cheese solves all problems. At least, that's what I'm hoping. It's nearly midnight, so the only lights outside come from the establishments nearby.

I haven't checked my social media in hours, and I always keep my notifications off, but I have nothing else better to do on my wedding night. So I wrap a small hunk of cheese in a piece of lavish bread and take a bite as I unlock my phone.

The second I open Snapchat, I nearly choke.

Video after video of Daire appears. It's a party at his house. Though I suppose the place isn't *his*, but it's where he lives. For now. Tears flood my eyes as I watch. The party isn't the issue. No, his meltdown is what steals my breath. It's like a dagger to the heart. He's trashed, his hair a mess and his eyes bloodshot. The guy is falling apart. Maybe I could feel a smidge of sympathy for him, but his words erase any softness I have toward him.

The phone shakes in my hand as I force myself to watch the video.

On screen, Daire stands in the middle of a living room, surrounded by people.

"Oh, and guess what? I'm fucking hitched now." He sneers the words, as if his marital status is a death sentence. As if he wasn't the one *begging* me.

He pulls out the ring I put on him only hours ago and slips it onto his right ring finger instead of the left.

"And no, not to the baby mama. She's a professor and a real bitch. She didn't tell me she was pregnant. She thought she could keep him from me, but I won't let her. No, sir." He smacks a hand roughly against his chest as tears slide down his cheeks.

Dammit, I hate myself for feeling sorry for him.

"So, now I'm married to Rosie—yeah, that girl I

can't fucking stand because—" He shakes his head. "That's not important."

That knife in my chest twists, the pain excruciating. I know he hates me, but I've never known *why*. At least I have a reason to dislike him. Even so, it hurts to hear those words out loud. God, I'm pathetic.

"Oh, but guess what, there's more." He tosses an arm over his friend Cree's shoulders, swinging the guy toward his other friend Jude.

Jude shakes his head and grasps Daire's shoulder. Even on this tiny screen, the pleading in his eyes is obvious. "Don't do this, man."

What's he so afraid Daire is going to do? Air all their dirty laundry?

Daire throws his head back and lets out an obnoxious bark of laughter. "But why not? It's so fun!" He squeezes his friend even tighter, smiling manically. He's clearly on the verge of a breakdown. "Are you listening, buddy?" Daire's mouth is almost on Cree's cheek in some sort of mockery of a kiss. "This is a big one. Are you ready?" Cree shoves him away, anger clouding his expression. Daire laughs, unbothered, as he stumbles and rights himself.

Instead of the normal sounds of a party—music, chatter—it's dead silent except for the conversation playing out on the screen. Every person in the room seems to be holding their breath, waiting for the other shoe to drop.

"What?" Cree asks Daire, the question so quiet I'm surprised it's audible. The grimace on his face makes me wonder if he really even wants to know. "Well, what is it?"

Daire looks off camera at someone. A war of emotions plays over his face. Anger, sadness, fear, maybe a little regret. He shakes his head, then and waves a hand wildly. "It's not important."

"It must be for you to be putting on this whole fucking debacle," Cree huffs.

A sneer forms on Daire's lips. "Don't be so quick to jump to conclusions, my dude. It's not like you're some holy saint. Nah, you like to think you're a good guy, but you're a liar just like the rest of us. And here's another little secret—*good guys don't lie*. Your sins might not be as shitty as the rest of ours, but a lie is a lie *is a lie*."

That's when the video cuts off. I'm sure if I scroll, I'll find one that shows what happens next, but I don't even want to know. I shake my head, a mix of emotions ranging from anger to downright pity rolling through me. It's like watching a train wreck and being helpless to stop it. The worst part is I'm stuck in the middle, right in harm's way if Daire crashes and burns.

I turn my phone off, fearing Bertie will come across one of the videos and call. What the hell would I even say to her if she did? I don't have a good explanation for Daire's rant or why he and I aren't together on our freaking wedding night.

I climb off the bed and set the cheese platter on the table with the other food. My appetite has officially vanished.

Breathing deep, I find a pair of pajamas purchased during my spree and slip them on. Then I turn the lights off and get back in bed, saying a prayer for sleep to come.

When it does, it's fitful, and I wake more exhausted than I was before.

I HEAD BACK to campus early since I have class, leaving most of my purchases in the car since it'll take multiple trips to get it all inside.

I take a few bags with me as I hurry into my dorm to get ready for class. All I've eaten since yesterday morning are a few pieces of cheese and bread. I can't stomach the thought of food right now, and the horrible part of my brain whispers *your mother would be happy*.

But I'm not intentionally starving myself.

After the scene in the parking lot yesterday and then the video of Daire, if I tried to eat, it would more than likely come right back up.

Once I've deposited the bags on my bed, I quickly apply my makeup. Today it feels like I'm painting on a mask for the world. The stares and whispers have already begun, and I've been on campus for five whole minutes. It's only going to get worse as the day goes on. I still haven't turned my phone back on. If I did, it would be to see whether Daire has tried to contact me. I hate myself for even caring. For even thinking he may have. It's unlikely I'll hear from him after the things he said last night.

When my makeup is done, I grab my backpack, making sure I have everything I need. And when I sling my bag over my shoulder and tuck my hair behind my ear, the ring on my finger glimmers in the light.

It sits like a heavy weight, a reminder that I'm stuck in this situation now. So I better put on my game face and make the most of it.

seven

DAIRE

IT'S BEEN eighteen hours since my drunken binge, and from what I've been told, the video of my meltdown is circulating everywhere. I didn't bother going to classes today; I'm too hungover to bother with it.

Every text I've sent to Rosie today has gone unanswered. I deserve to be ignored, but it still pisses me off anyway. So here I am, outside her dorm.

As I run my fingers through my hair, my wedding band catches. Shit. Why the fuck is it on my right hand? With a curse, I yank it off and shove it onto the correct finger. I send her another text, letting her know I'm here and on my way up.

Like all the others, it shows delivered but unread.

I hop off my motorcycle and secure my helmet. It's too cold to ride without bundling up, so I had already put it in storage for the winter, but I figured I'd take it out for one last ride before I sell it. With the way things have gone with Danielle so far, I could see her finding some way to sway a judge into thinking I'm not responsible enough because I have a motorcycle. So it, along with my Porsche, will be going soon.

Yeah, because your drunken rampage wasn't enough to completely sink your chances at receiving custody.

There's a group of girls outside the dorm. As a collective unit, they turn and look at me.

"Hey, Daire," one of them says.

I turn, vaguely recognizing her. "Hey," I answer as I close in on the door. "You mind letting me in?"

"I guess that depends on if you'll answer something for me or not." She flashes a flirty smile. "Is it true you're married? Some people are saying you were dared to say you were."

I wasn't expecting that, though I guess I should have been.

With my stomach in knots, I dip my chin. "It's true."

"That's too bad." She frowns, adjusting the strap of the bag on her shoulder. "We had some good fun."

Did we? I can't remember.

"Mhm," I hum. "Do you mind letting me in now?"

She puffs out her lips, which is entirely unnecessary given the amount of filler injected into them. "I don't think I will."

I bite back a grunt of annoyance. *It fucking figures.*

Normally I have zero problem getting anywhere I want to go. I'll need a little more patience today, but someone will come along eventually and let me up. So I step off to the side and take a seat around the corner on one of the many benches that dot the campus. Even though it's pointless, I send another text to Rosie, asking her to come down and let me in. She might not even be here, but I have to try.

Try for what?

To apologize?

An apology isn't anywhere close to enough in this situation, but it's all I have.

I spoke with Nina Voss, my lawyer, this morning and admitted to what a fucking idiot I am. Then I sent her the video. Understandably, she wasn't pleased. She can join the damn club, because I'm not happy with myself either. My life is an absolute clusterfuck right now. That's why I'm doing stupid shit. Nina wouldn't get it, because now definitely isn't the time for me to be pulling stunts like this.

So why did I?

Fear. As much as I hate to admit it, I'm terrified. And when I'm scared, self-destruction is my default.

I'm scared of graduating—of what I'll do with a future I'm still not certain about. I'm not like my older brothers, who've always had a clear path laid before them.

I'm terrified of being a dad, of fucking a kid up. I want to be a *good* dad. Like mine. Getting wasted and going on a drunken rant doesn't really align with the whole wanting to be a good dad thing, but I wasn't exactly thinking logically in the moment.

And now I'm scared of Rosie.

She's the only girl I can trust with this—and what does that mean? Does it mean deep down I never actually stopped caring about her? Do I have feelings for her after all this time?

To say I'm fucking confused is an understatement.

I've got my elbows on my knees and my head in my hands when I'm startled by a high-pitched voice. "Well, don't you look like a pathetic piece of shit?"

When I look up, I'm met with a scathing look from Bertie. She's clutching a textbook to her chest, her knuckles white like she's gripping it hard to keep from beating me over the head with it.

"I saw your childish meltdown."

I nod, eyes on the ground. "You and everyone else, apparently."

"How could you embarrass her like that?" She

snaps her fingers in front of my face, forcing me to look at her. "Rosie is one of the nicest people I've ever met. She's kind and caring and better than you could ever be. You two had me convinced you were madly in love, but you *both* lied." She clutches the book again. "Why did she really marry you?"

I look away, jaw clenching.

"Not as talkative as you were last night, huh?" Her glare burns a hole in the side of my face.

Rubbing at my jaw, I force myself to look up at her again. "Can you at least let me in so I can talk to her?"

Bertie tucks a piece of hair behind her ear and shrugs. "She's not answering me, so I'm not sure she's even here."

"Bertie, please—"

"You can come up with me," she snaps. "But only because you look so pathetic."

"Gee, thanks."

When she walks away, I haul myself up and jog after her, following close in case she changes her mind.

She doesn't speak to me again until we reach their dorm. She turns, standing with her back to the door, and says, "If you're not nice to her, I will drag you out of this room by your ear. You got me?"

I may be a foot taller than the girl and weigh a hell of a lot more, but I don't doubt her for a second.

"Got it."

She unlocks the door and lets me in first. I half

expect her to kick me in the back of the knee just so she can laugh as I flail.

The main room is dark and eerily quiet.

I shuffle to Rosie's bedroom door and knock. When she doesn't answer, I ease it open.

She's not here.

I flick on the overhead light and curse at the bags covering every surface of her bedroom area.

"What the hell?" I mutter, taking it all in.

I clear enough space on her bed to sit and wait.

Bertie appears in the doorway and scans the room. "I told you she might not be here. And apparently she went on a bit of a shopping spree. She tends to do that when she's feeling down."

I swallow thickly at that. Rosie was never like most of the girls we grew up with. So many of them were all too eager to spend Mommy and Daddy's money every chance they got. Rosie rarely asked for anything, but once in a while, she'd go on a shopping spree. That's when I'd know something had happened. Usually her mom had commented on her weight.

I fucking hate that I might have made her feel the same way that shit does.

"If it's okay, I'll wait here for her."

She shrugs. "Suit yourself."

I settle in, determined not to leave until we talk. It's probably foolish of me to stay, but if I went home, I'd be sitting around stewing too. At least this way I have a chance of seeing her.

I sit in that small patch of space for a long time, but eventually, I clear off her bed and make myself comfortable.

I swear I only close my eyes for a minute, but I'm startled by an ear-piercing scream. I jackknife up at the sound, my heart beating rapidly.

"What the hell?" Rosie is standing in the middle of her room with a hand pressed to her heart. She's damp with sweat and dressed in workout clothes, earbuds still in her ears.

I stifle a yawn. "I was waiting for you."

"Clearly." She pulls out her desk chair and sits to take off her tennis shoes. "What for?" she grits out, keeping her focus fixed on her shoes rather than looking at me.

I rub the back of my head and pat down my hair. "I'm sure you've seen the video by now."

She stiffens. "I already knew you hated me. I didn't need a video to tell me that."

My heart jerks in my chest at the hurt in her tone. Jaw clenched, I take a deep breath through my nose. "I wanted to apologize."

She sits up, one shoe still half-on. "What's the point, Daire? You'll still hate me, and I'll still hate you, and we'll still be married." Instead of flashing me her middle finger, she waves the one adorned with my ring. "The best we can do is be cordial."

I look away and bite back a curse. I'm livid, but not at her. I've been married for a matter of hours, and I've already fucked everything up.

She yanks the shoe off and drops it to the floor. "If that's all you came here for, I have a shower to take."

"I—"

She bolts out of her chair, ignoring me, and rummages through her dresser. Once she's found the clothes she's looking for, she walks out and closes the door behind her.

"Fuck," I mutter to myself.

I waited all this time to say I was sorry. For as shitty as my day has been, I can't imagine hers. And there's no one to blame but me and my big, fat, drunken mouth. Selfishly, it pisses me off that she doesn't want my apology. That she expected this kind of behavior from me.

And this video? It's exactly the kind of thing that can be used against me in court.

Fuck.

I cover my face and groan into my hands.

I could wait for her to come out of the shower, but what would be the point?

I get up and let myself out of her room. Bertie is sitting on the couch in her pajamas, legs curled under her and a rom-com playing on the TV. She shakes her head at me, tsking.

"You better fix this," she hisses. "She doesn't deserve to be treated like shit by you or anyone else."

I jerk my head in a nod.

I don't have the first clue how, but I have to try, because I need her.

eight

ROSIE

ALMOST ALL MY belongings are packed up and ready to be loaded onto the moving truck. Daire and I haven't spoken much in the past two weeks. The conversations we have had revolved around coordinating our schedules so we could sign the contracts for the townhouse and get our things moved.

Bertie watches me from my open bedroom door. She refused to help me pack. The day after the wedding, after my shower, after Daire left, I broke down and told her the truth. She'd already put a lot of it together, thanks to the video. Not to mention the girl is a hopeless romantic, so she thought it was weird that I'd never mentioned him before she witnessed the proposal.

She thinks I should have the marriage annulled and stay here. Thus, she refuses to help me move out.

She doesn't understand that even though he drives me insane now, I still hold so many good memories of him close to my heart. The Daire who used to be my best friend is the Daire I'm helping. Not this version of him.

"If you're not going to help me, you could at least go away." I stuff a sweater that fell behind my bed into a box with other miscellaneous things.

Getting down on the floor, I peer under the bed to make sure there aren't any other rogue articles of clothing hiding.

"Nah." She holds out her right hand, admiring her fresh pink manicure. "I like the view from here."

I turn to glare at her from my position on the floor.

"What?" She blinks innocently. "This is more entertaining than reality TV."

I dig my phone out of my pocket and turn the flashlight on to help my search. "I just need you to be supportive," I say with my head shove beneath my bed.

"I *am*," she defends. "I can support you and still think you're being dumb."

Finding nothing left beneath my bed, I rise from the floor and click the flashlight off. "I don't think those two things go hand in hand."

She shrugs. "For me they do."

I spin in a circle, surveying my progress. Daire is supposed to be here any minute with the moving truck, and I haven't even started on my bathroom stuff.

As if my thoughts have conjured him, there's a knock on our door.

"Shall I let Cujo in?" Bertie asks with a fake smile.

With a groan, I dump my cup of pens into the last open box in my room and reach for the tape. "I think you have to."

He knocks again, and this time, she disappears from my doorway.

When I'm alone, I inhale a deep breath, fortifying my strength so I can deal with Daire.

An instant later, he's standing in the doorway, his broad shoulders taking up the entire space and his eyes wide. "You're done already?"

"Yeah?" I reply, but it comes out as a question. "I haven't done my makeup and toiletries yet, though."

He scratches the back of his head, something he tends to do when he's uncomfortable. "I haven't packed yet."

I blink at him as annoyance builds in my veins. "You can't be serious."

He looks away, swallowing thickly. "It won't take me long. We'll go straight there after we get your stuff loaded."

Fists clenched at my sides, I spin and get back to work. I'm going to throttle him.

I've never wanted to wrap my hands around someone's throat and squeeze the way I do right now.

"By the way," he clears his throat, "I told Cree your dad bought us the house. So if he says something about it, just go along with it."

I spin and study him. His disheveled hair, the shadows under his eyes. "Why?"

"Fuck, I don't know," he snaps. Whether he's annoyed with me or himself is anyone's guess. "I guess I'm a compulsive liar." He holds his hands out and flexes his fingers. His attention lingers for a couple of heartbeats on the band around his left ring finger.

"Surely you must've put some thought into it."

Daire angles his head to the side, glowering at me. "I haven't put a single thought into anything for months. I've been living on rage and alcohol."

I press my lips together. "Noted."

I'm starting to think Bertie has a point—an annulment is sounding better and better.

Sighing, he steps into my room and sits on the stripped bed. "He kept asking if our parents knew yet, and I was already in the middle of telling him about moving out and the townhouse, and it just all kind of spiraled from there."

I tape up the last box in here, then pick up another to assemble for my bathroom things.

"You do realize you sound absolutely unhinged, don't you?"

He frowns, muttering, "I'm aware."

"As long as you know," I singsong, "then we'll be just fine."

I take the newly assembled box to the bathroom while my *husband* trails behind me. I'm not sure I'll ever get used to that word.

"Is all this yours?" he asks in an accusatory way, eyeing the makeup and hair tools scattered on the small counter around the sink.

"Some is Bertie's." I resist the urge to roll my eyes. I need to put my game face on if I'm going to make it through this day.

Forget this day—this whole marriage, however long it turns out to be.

At this point, I'm just tossing things into the box so I can get packing over with and get out of here. Not all of our new furniture has been delivered yet, but enough that we can move in and start getting settled.

So far, I've successfully avoided thinking about what it'll be like once it's just the two of us.

As I stick my acrylic organizer in the box, the makeup inside slides around, making an obnoxious sound.

"Why do you have so many of the same thing?" Lip curled, Daire points to the drawer with my liquid lip shades.

"Because they're all different colors," I answer, digging deep for patience.

"If it's okay with you, I'll head down to the truck with some of these boxes."

"That's fine."

When he's gone with the first load, Bertie appears again and watches me from the doorway. When she said she wasn't going to help, she meant it.

"I can feel your judgment from here," I mutter, head stuck inside the cabinet under the sink as I pull out my stash of shampoos and conditioners. What can I say? My hair is high maintenance and I have to swap out what I'm using often.

"Good. I'm glad."

I turn to glare at her, bumping my head in the process. I wince and rub at the now throbbing spot.

She presses a hand against her mouth, trying to hold in her laughter, but fails.

"I hate you."

Her laughter only grows. "No, you don't."

With a sigh, I drop several bottles of shampoo into the box. "You're right, I don't, but I should."

"And you should get an annulment." She shuffles closer, snags her lip balm from the counter, and swipes it onto her lips. "Helping him like this is beyond just being nice."

"I know." I double check that I have all my

toiletries, then carry the box back to my room where I left the tape.

"But you're not going to do anything about it?"

My shoulders droop. "Bertie, there's a child involved in this. I ... I can't back out now."

Her lips turn down in a frown. "You're a better person than me."

I laugh. "I don't think so. I'm just helping an old friend."

"But you're not friends now," she reminds me.

My heart lurches at the reminder. "I know." I pull my hair back into a ponytail and secure it with an elastic I always keep on my wrist. "I'm sure it makes no sense to you. It barely makes sense to me. But I know in my gut I have to do this."

Shaking her head, she opens her arms to me. "I'm going to miss having you as a roomie."

I step into her embrace and give her a squeeze. "You have no idea."

She picks up a box and balances it on her hip. "I'll carry this one box." Then she holds up her index finger and wiggles it. "But that's all I'm doing since I don't condone this."

I laugh, picking up a clear bin I filled with clothes. "Jesus." I grunt under the weight.

Bertie shakes her head. "Get a light one. Leave the heavy stuff for Daire."

"That's an excellent plan." I set the bin down, then

test the weight of a nearby box and find it manageable enough for me to carry.

Just as we're about to head out, Daire returns for more stuff. "Where did you get that?" I ask, pointing to the dolly he has now.

"Swiped it from the janitor's closet." He grins, clearly very proud of himself.

He wheels it into my room and loads a box onto it.

"Where's the truck? We'll head down with these."

"You'll have to wait for me." His biceps flex in a far too distracting way when he picks up a particularly heavy bin. "I locked it up before I came back in."

"Paranoid?" I question him with an arched brow.

"Absolutely." He stacks another bin on top of the first.

Bertie sets her box on the dresser while we wait for Daire to finish loading the dolly. He leads the way out the door and down the hall. While we're waiting for the elevator, he taps his fingers against the top box, drawing my attention to the band on his finger. He's not mine, but man does seeing that claim of possession fill me with a weird sort of satisfaction.

I look away before he can catch me staring.

Outside, Daire unlocks the back of the truck. Then he takes the boxes from Bertie and me, stacks them just inside the truck, and gets to work unloading the dolly and arranging my things near the front of the truck.

"You can wait down here if you want." He hops out

of the back. "There are only a couple left, so I can get them on my own. Unless there's something else you need."

"Can you grab my purse and backpack? They're still in the closet."

With a nod, he heads back to the entrance, leaving Bertie and me on the sidewalk. A gust of wind blows past us, making me wish I'd put a hoodie on. My short-sleeve shirt isn't doing much to protect against the cold that's beginning to leach into the air. It's my own fault for desperately trying to cling to the last dredges of summer.

"Well." Bertie turns to me, eyes downcast in an effort to hide her sad face. "This is it."

As I take her in, I'm hit with an overwhelming wave of sadness. Girls typically don't like me, but Bertie and I clicked from the instant we met.

"Stop making it sound like we're never going to see each other." I wipe away a lone tear. "You better come over for movie nights. I'll come here too. And don't forget our lunch dates."

We've always met at the dining hall for lunch on Wednesdays. Even when she was dating Tommy.

She rolls her eyes. "You can't get rid of me so easily."

I throw my arms around her and squeeze her tight. Being thrown together with Bertie at the beginning of our freshman year was such a blessing. I couldn't have made it these last three years without her. She's been my only true friend all this time.

"I love you, Bertie."

She laughs against me. "Stop getting sappy. You're going to make me cry, and then my mascara is going to run. But I love you too."

She waits with me on the sidewalk until Daire comes down with the last load of my stuff. He has my purse slung over his shoulder. I wish I could say he looks ridiculous, but with his confidence, he pulls off the look like it's the latest trend. His wide shoulders stretch the fabric of his school hockey hoodie taut. I hate that my mind immediately wanders to thoughts of what it would feel like to have him over me, caging me in with that big body of his.

My core clenches—the fucking traitor. I can't deny Daire is insanely good-looking, but my vagina is going to have to get on board with celibacy and quick, because I won't be having sex anytime soon, and definitely not with my husband.

Once Daire loads the last of my items—refusing the help we offer, of course—he heads in to return the dolly. While we wait, Bertie hugs me one last time. Then she hurries back inside, but not before I catch the tears in her eyes. I hate that I'm leaving her like this. Especially only a few weeks after she and Tommy have called it quits—for real this time, it seems.

Daire comes out, head ducked low like he's trying to

avoid eye contact with people milling around us. It's a strange sight. Usually, he's the big man on campus, commanding every space he enters and eating up his popularity. This new version of him is interesting, to say the least.

He climbs into the driver's seat of the U-Haul while I get settled in my SUV.

Then, we're pulling away from campus, my shoulders growing heavier with each passing mile.

nine

DAIRE

THE TOWNHOUSE IS PRETTY EMPTY, save for a few odd pieces here and there, like a couch and one random dining room chair that was delivered *without* the rest of the set or even the table.

Rosie, carrying a set of freshly washed sheets up the stairs, peers over her shoulder. "You don't think this place is haunted, do you?"

"No," I scoff.

As if to contradict me, the lights flicker.

Rosie lets out a squeak and drops the sheets on the

stairs. Hand over her heart, she asks, "Did you see that?"

There's no sense in lying. "Yeah."

"I think there are ghosts here. We come in peace. I promise." She holds her hands together like she's praying. "Or at least I do. I can't speak for him."

I roll my eyes from the bottom of the stairs. "They're ghosts, not aliens."

She screams again, pointing an accusing finger at me. "You said it wasn't haunted!"

I put my hands up and take a step back. "I just meant *if* there was something here, it wouldn't be aliens. You don't need to say you come in peace."

"Maybe we made a bad decision with this place." She scoops up the sheets and continues up the stairs, her head on a swivel.

I reluctantly follow. I need to get my bed ready too, and by bed, I mean a blow-up mattress. Our furniture is being delivered in phases over the coming weeks, thanks to Rosie and her ordering frenzy. She really did a number on my card, but I was an asshole, so I was asking for it.

"You loved it when we toured it."

She pauses in the hall that stretches in both directions—her room on one end, mine on the other.

"That was before it was dark and empty and creepy."

I sigh. "I can't help that. We're lacking on furniture at the moment."

"Speaking of furniture." She holds up a finger, but it gets stuck in the folds of the sheets she's holding. She flails until her hand is free and wags that finger at me. "I think we should paint before anything else arrives."

"What's wrong with the paint?"

She blinks at me, her mouth ajar. Clearly, she thinks my question is ridiculous. "It's very formal."

Sure, the colors are pretty dark and rich, but the paint looks fresh, and the colors aren't hideous. "So?"

"*Men*," she mutters with a shake of her head. "I'll call around and find someone who can do it in the next week or two."

"I didn't agree to this," I remind her.

Adjusting her hold on the sheets, she says, "The sooner you learn *happy wife, happy life*, the better."

With a grunt, I turn toward my room at the end of the hall on my right.

"Go for it, then," I mutter as I step across the threshold into my room.

I wrestle the sheets onto the blow-up mattress I bought when we stopped at Target on the way over. The furniture in the place I just moved out of belongs to Cree's parents. His mom did all the decorating, hence the feminine touch, despite it predominately being a bachelor pad.

I'm dropping my pillow onto the mattress when Rosie comes into the room.

"I was thinking pizza for dinner. Are you good with that?"

"Yeah."

She plants her hands on her hips. "You know, it is possible to reply with more than one word. What toppings do you like?"

"Supreme is fine with me."

"Perfect."

She stands in the doorway, watching me expectantly.

"What?" I ask when she makes no move to order the food.

With an evil little grin, she holds out her hand. "Card, please."

Right. I dig in my back pocket for my wallet and pull out my black credit card.

She takes it with a wink. "Thanks, *babe*."

"Don't call me that."

But she's already gone, out of earshot of my griping.

Running my fingers through my hair, I eye the boxes in the corner. I could get started on unpacking my clothes, but I've had enough packing for one day. Downstairs, I find Rosie sitting on the marble island in the kitchen, kicking her legs lazily back and forth while she scrolls on her phone.

"What are you doing?"

Without looking up from the device, she smiles. "Looking at paint colors online."

Of course.

I shuffle toward the refrigerator. The thing is giant. Inside one full-size door is the fridge, and inside the other is an enormous freezer. I'm sure it's a chef's dream—we have a similar setup at my dad's house—but it's a bit much for a townhouse outside of Nashville. Especially for two college-age kids.

"We need groceries," I mutter, eyeing the empty shelves before me.

"Mhm," she hums, legs still swinging. "I'm too tired to deal with it tonight. I'll go tomorrow."

"You won't know what I like."

She looks up from her phone, leveling me with a glare. "Then we'll both go, crybaby."

This woman. I can't win with her.

"We should go tonight."

She closes the app on her phone with a huff, crossing her arms over her chest.

Without my permission, my eyes drop to the swells of her breasts. Her position causes them to press against her sweater, emphasizing them. I shouldn't be staring at her boobs, but I can't seem to look away.

"Eyes up here," she commands, using two fingers to point from her eyes to mine. "Did you not listen to what I said? I'm tired, and the pizza is already on the way. It won't be the end of the world if we go in the morning."

"Fine," I say, because she's right, even if it feels weird not having a single item in the fridge. "We'll go tomorrow."

"Thank you for seeing sense." She hops off the counter and tucks her phone into the back pocket of her jeans.

Jeans that hug her ass like a second skin.

Stop staring!

Jaw clenched, I inhale through my nose, then hold the air in my lungs. It's going to be a long … what? Year? Couple of years? Regardless, our time together will be painful if I keep checking out my wife.

"Have you heard anything from your lawyer?"

"Nothing except her chewing me out over the video." Stomach twisting, I scrub a hand over my face. Dammit, I'm such a fuck-up. Getting drunk that night was the worst decision I've probably ever made, behind letting myself have such a public meltdown. Everything came to a head for me in that moment—the battle for my son, Rosie, my friends being nonexistent in my time of need—and I just lost it.

But I can't afford to *lose it* when I'm facing what looks to be a brutal court battle.

We haven't addressed the video much, Rosie and me, except for my apology. Since then, she hasn't brought it up. Regardless of our lack of conversation about it, I hurt her. Rosie might be a strong girl, but words can cut the deepest, and I know mine did just that when I said I hated her. The feeling is mutual, but that doesn't make my tirade okay. Especially when I'm the one who begged her to marry me.

I haven't talked to my lawyer about how she's going to play that whole thing off, but she'll figure something out. If I even consider an alternative, I'll spiral into an even more stressed-out and anxious version of myself, and that's saying a lot, because for the last couple of months, I've been nothing but a ball of nerves and anger. Every time I get a call lately, the urge to puke hits me. When my phone rings, my natural response is to freak out, sure that the video is finally coming back to haunt me even more than it already does. Nina has done her best to scrub it from the internet, but there's no way to erase every last trace of it.

Idiot that I am, I basically handed Danielle and her husband all the evidence they need to prove I'm not fit for any sort of custody on a silver platter.

That video paints a picture of a kid who isn't ready to be a parent. And if I were watching similar footage of someone else, I'd agree.

But that night, fear took over. I ran away and got drunk in order to avoid my feelings.

I can't do that anymore.

Silence stretches between us.

"The pizza should be here any minute," she says softly, passing by me on her way out of the kitchen.

Eyes closed, I focus on steadying my breathing. I

need to get my shit together. I asked Rosie for her help because even though our friendship fell apart, I've always known I can trust her. Now it's time to show her that. Regardless of how hard it might be. I've been fighting this battle on my own for months. I *wanted* to confess to Cree, but he's been too busy chasing after his girlfriend, Ophelia, to care. My meltdown nearly fucked up their relationship, but they've since made up. Doesn't make me feel any less guilty for being an asshole, though.

At the sound of the front door opening, I peek around the corner to see Rosie accepting the pizza and a bag with a smile. When she turns, I quickly duck my way back into the kitchen.

"Spying on me?" she quips, setting the food on the counter.

My stomach sinks. "No."

"Seemed like it to me." She takes out a liter of Coke from the bag. "We don't have plates, so you'll have to eat over here with me instead of sulking in the corner like a creeper." Flipping the lid of the pizza box back, she groans and inhales the smell of the peppers. "Get over here. I'm starving."

She hops up onto the counter again and picks up a slice. I close the distance between us and snag one of my own. Closing the box so the pizza stays warm, I lean against the wall across from her.

"What would your mom say if she could see us right now?"

Chewing, she holds a finger up. "Number one, this," she wags that same finger between us, "would probably have her spontaneously combusting with excitement, but you already know that. As for the pizza…" She shrugs, surveying the slice in her hand. "She'd probably go into cardiac arrest. She might be able to stomach a chef-prepared, fully fresh pizza. But Pizza Hut? No way in hell." She wipes the corner of her mouth with her finger. It comes away with a drop of sauce that she quickly licks away.

And now my dick is hard.

I send up a prayer that Rosie doesn't notice my current predicament. The last thing I need is her thinking I'm attracted to her.

"You know," she begins, lowering her focus to her lap, "Thanksgiving is next week. I'm expected at home, and I assume you are too. There's no way we can avoid telling them about this."

Them.

Our parents.

My brothers.

Her sister.

Keeping this from them has made it easy to ignore our reality. That's all about to change.

"I know."

"How should we go about telling them?"

I press my lips together and rack my brain but come up empty. "I don't know. But I don't think it matters *how* we tell them. They're not going to be happy that we didn't include them."

She huffs, probably annoyed I'm not offering a legitimate idea, and opens the lid, then drops a piece of crust into the box. "I'm going to shower, and then I'm crashing."

"All right." I reach for a second slice, leaving it at that. I'd rather avoid the conversation for as long as I can.

Maybe we should have called and broken the news. I'm suddenly regretting the idea of telling Rosie's father we're married while he's holding a carving knife. There's a good chance I'll be carved up right along with the turkey. But it's too late to change our plans now.

Within minutes of her departure, the room is *too* quiet, and I find myself missing her presence.

Not that I'd ever tell her that.

I finish up the pizza, stuff the box in the refrigerator, and wash my hands. Drying them on my T-shirt — since we don't have a single dish towel — I head upstairs for a shower.

I'm ready to crash. Once I get a few solid hours of sleep, this feeling for Rosie will go away.

It has to.

ten

ROSIE

AS I LIE on my back on my air mattress, my ears are hyper-tuned to every sound. I imagine mice skittering behind the walls, just waiting for me to fall asleep so they can devour me.

There's a creaking sound downstairs and then what sounds like a door shutting.

I sit up. "Daire?"

If he's moving around downstairs, there's no way he'd hear me call for him.

Be brave, I tell myself. *Go check.*

I ease the covers off my body and awkwardly climb

off the mattress. Outside my room, the hall is pitch dark. I make a mental note to pick up a few night lights.

"Daire?" I hiss, fingers skimming the side of the wall as I make my way toward the stairs. "Hey?" I start down them. "Are you here?"

At the bottom, I flick the light switch in the foyer and slam my eyes shut as the space is flooded with a blinding light.

A creak sounds to my right, and I jump. "Hey," I say louder this time. "You're scaring me. This isn't funny, asshole."

I move in the direction of the sound, silently urging myself to be brave.

But there's nothing.

No sign of Daire, like maybe I just missed him.

This place has mostly been brought up to date, but it's an older home, and old places like this have history. History means ghosts.

The door into the butler's pantry slowly closes in front of me.

The second I see it move, I'm gone, sprinting up the stairs. Halfway up, I fall, banging my knee harshly against the wood. Curses fly out of my mouth as I scramble to get my feet back under me.

I turn down the hall toward Daire's room, hoping like hell he's playing a prank on me and I'll find his bed empty.

No such luck. When I throw open his door, he's

asleep, one bare arm crooked over his eyes. I whimper, the sound doing nothing to stir him.

"Daire?"

Still nothing.

I move a little closer. "Daire?"

The guy is *out*. I bite my lip. Maybe I can move my bed in here without waking him up...

I don't particularly want to venture out of this room, but what choice do I have?

Easing out of his room, I tiptoe down the hall, keeping a careful eye out and praying we have a nice ghost that doesn't prey on twenty-one-year-old girls.

I get the mattress up on its side and push it out my bedroom door. By the time I make it down the long hall, I'm sweating. Clearly, my three-days-a-week workout routine is not enough.

I left Daire's door open a crack when I left, so I use the mattress to push it open.

Only I push a little too hard. The mattress turns into a battering ram, and the door flies back and slams into the opposite wall. As it bounces back, the mattress slips from my fingers. It falls into the room with a thud, taking me down with it. At least I have the mattress to cushion my fall.

Daire sputters awake at the commotion, arms flailing and dick ... dick swinging, because apparently, he sleeps naked.

Stop staring at this dick!

But I can't look away.

I'm dickmatized.

Dickstruck.

Dick—

"What the fuck, Rosie?" he bellows, breathing heavily with his hands fisted at his sides, ready to fight.

Words fail me. I'm too busy staring at him to even try to formulate a coherent thought.

Daire is a big guy. He's an athlete, so he kind of has to be. Hockey is a hard sport, and aggressive too. I'm relatively tall, so I'm not used to feeling small, but I'm absolutely dwarfed by his hulking form. Forget my early estimate. This guy has to be six-five or even six-six. He's a beast. His thighs are thick, his legs dusted with light blond hair that grows darker around his *very* big cock. The thing is nowhere near hard and looks like it could split me in half.

My mouth *waters*.

I take him in, perusing the perfectly sculpted planes of his chest. He's big *everywhere*. Built like a Viking.

"Rosie?" There's amusement in his tone now.

It hits me then—my blatant staring.

I zero in on the chain around his neck so my gaze won't drop south again. My cheeks are on fire. Dammit. He definitely caught me checking him out. But you know what? Sue me. It's his own fault for sleeping naked and looking like *that*.

"Um, h-hi," I stutter, struggling to stand up.

"What are you doing here?" he asks, planting his hands on his hips.

Do not look at his dick.

"Can you…" I swish my hand toward his nakedness, "cover up?"

"Why would I do that when you clearly want to look?" *Fuck me.* "Now, I'm going to ask you again, Rose. What are you doing here?"

I wrinkle my nose and huff. He knows how much I hate to be called Rose. Almost as much as I hate to be called Rosemary. I was named after my great-grandmother. Thank God my dad started calling me Rosie-Posie early on and Rosie stuck. Most people don't know my name is Rosemary, but Daire isn't most people.

"There was a ghost."

He gives a slow shake of his head, an incredulous laugh passing through his lips. "Sure."

"I'm serious. A door closed downstairs, and my first thought was ghost. But I told myself not to be ridiculous, that it was probably you. So, scared as I was, I investigated. As you can see, you were very much asleep. Ergo, ghost." I take a deep breath after my long-winded speech. "There's no way I can sleep by myself now, so I was bringing my mattress in here. I didn't mean to wake you."

His jaw is hard, his brow lowered. "Ghost aren't real."

"Says you. I disagree."

He pinches his brow, and my treacherous eyes use his momentary distraction to get another peek at his cock.

I've slept with a lot of guys, and I'm not ashamed of that, but I've never seen a dick like this in person before. I thought monsters like this only existed in porn. Daire could make some serious money if he wanted to venture down that path.

He clears his throat.

I've been caught ... *again*.

"You act like you've never seen a cock before."

Hearing that word, *cock*, coming out of his mouth, has my stomach performing somersaults.

"Not one like this," I admit. The second the words are out, I wince. The last thing I want to do is compliment the asshole. "Wait." I lean in, squinting. "What's that?" I point at its head. "Is that thing pierced?"

I've only heard of such things, never seen it in person.

"Uh, yeah." He rubs the back of his head, still not at all fazed by his nakedness.

"When did you do that?" I blurt.

He shrugs, keeping his gaze averted. "Drunken bet sophomore year. Hurt like a bitch. Couldn't have sex for months, but chicks love it."

I swallow thickly. I'll just bet they do.

"Anyway," I inhale a breath, "can I crash here?" I clasp my hands beneath my chin. "Please?"

I can't believe I'm pleading with Daire, of all people, to save me from the ghost, but I'll get no sleep otherwise.

Sighing, he surveys the mess I've made with my blankets and mattress. "Might as well. You're already here."

"Thank you! You won't even know I'm here."

He frowns, brow furrowed. "I already know you're here."

"It was a figure of speech." I straighten the sheet and scoop up my blankets. "This place really is haunted, though. You'll see."

"Mhm," he hums, watching me wiggle around in an attempt to get settled. "Impossible that it could be a draft or the house shifting."

"Are you going to put pants on now?" I ask, swiping a pillow off his bed because I'm not about to go back to my room and get one of mine. The one I had tucked under my arm is probably on the floor in the hallway.

"Nope." He settles on his bed, pulling the covers over his body.

It's quiet between us for so long I'm convinced he's fallen asleep.

But then, from the darkness, he says, "I'll take a picture for you."

I roll over so I'm facing him. "Huh?"

"A dick pic. That way you can look your fill any time you want."

With a squeak, I roll away again and bury my head under my blanket. "That won't be necessary."

He chuckles, amused by my obvious discomfort. "Good night, Rosie."

I don't respond, but I think it's a while before either of us goes back to sleep.

eleven

DAIRE

LAST YEAR, I missed Thanksgiving with my family since I had an away game that weekend. This time, I have no legitimate excuse to avoid going home, despite how badly I wish I didn't have to face this.

We board her family's private jet, since Cash called dibs on my dad's. Ironically, when my dad called to tell me Cash would be using the jet to fly home from Colorado, he'd already arranged for me to travel with Rosie, since we're literal neighbors. It would've been the perfect opportunity to say, "Cool, I was going to fly with her anyway, since she's my wife." But I kept my mouth shut.

It's been easy enough until now to ignore reality.

My family can't know the real reason I married Rosie. They have to believe this is real, just like everyone else.

The two of us don't speak until after the plane has taken off for New York. It's a short flight, so we settle in quickly. Rosie puts a corny rom-com on and slips a set of headphones onto her head. She's makeup free, which is a rare sight. It's been years since I've seen her when she wasn't completely made up. She looks softer without it. Younger.

She slides the headphones off and rests them on her shoulder. "I can feel you staring at me. What do you want?" She doesn't ask it with malice, but rather simple curiosity.

"Nothing." I reach for the bottle of water our flight attendant delivered earlier. I'd prefer something stronger, but I know better than to show up drunk to her family's home or mine.

"It must be something." She angles forward and pauses her movie.

"Nope."

She rolls her eyes. "Liar." Hands on her headphones, she moves to put them back on but stops. "You know, in order for this marriage to work, we need to communicate."

I snort. "This isn't a real marriage, *Rose*. Let's not get it twisted."

"You're impossible." She crinkles her nose in annoyance. "We don't know how long this is going to last. We need to at least try to get along. Think you can do that? Need I remind you, I'm doing you a favor, not the other way around? I also *really* miss sex."

The last part she tacks on has me snickering. "The eyeful you got of my dick didn't satiate you?"

"After I stopped gagging? Hardly."

"Please." I fight my smile. "You were drooling, but I could certainly make you gag on it if you'd like."

Rosie's cheeks turn a shade reminiscent of the bright red lipstick she usually wears.

"I'm done talking to you."

She slips her headphones on, but before she can settle them in place, I touch her arm, halting her. Lips pursed, she arches a brow in response, clearly annoyed that I'm interrupting her again.

"I don't want to tell anyone about Sammy yet."

She closes her eyes, inhaling a long breath. "No talking about Junior yet. Got it. Are we done here?"

I nod, and she puts her headphones back in place, then starts her movie once more.

Set on getting some much-needed sleep, I recline my chair and close my eyes. It's not a long flight, but hopefully with a nap, I'll be better prepared to handle whatever shit's about to go down.

"WHO ARE WE TELLING FIRST? Your dad or my parents?"

We probably should've discussed this before we boarded the plane this morning. At the very least, we should have worked through it before we got in the car that's taking us to our families' homes.

"My dad," I finally reply.

In front of us, the driver glances at us in the rearview mirror, brow arched. We've kept the conversation cryptic, since Tony has worked with Rosie's parents for years and will certainly tattle before we can confess.

"Good idea," she agrees, digging through her purse. She pulls out a mirror, then a small fabric bag. From there, she proceeds to apply a full face of makeup. I don't see why she needs it, but if it makes her feel better, then who am I to tell her not to? She wipes beneath her left eye where her mascara has smudged and then applies her red lipstick. Once she's capped the lipstick, she nods at her reflection, almost like she's giving herself a silent pep talk.

"How many of your brothers are going to be there?"

I look at my watch. "Cash should already be here, so all of them."

"Okay."

She's not at all unnerved by the idea of facing all

four of them. She actually *likes* them. I'm still wrapping my head around the idea that she stayed in touch with them after our friendship imploded. And not a single one of the fuckwit traitors mentioned it to me.

"Hey, Tony," she says, like he hasn't been eavesdropping on our conversation. "I'll get out at Daire's house. Let my parents know I'll be over later."

He arches his brows in the rearview mirror. "Do you want me to give them a reason why?"

"No," she says brightly, unfazed.

I shake my head. Tony probably suspects that we're dating. He assumes that's the news. We wisely removed our rings before getting off the plane since we weren't sure whether we'd be picked up by a driver or family.

The homes in the neighborhood we grew up in each sit on several acres. The wide-open space makes it feel like we're in the middle of nowhere, even though we're only an hour outside Manhattan. It's an exclusive area, though, and every homeowner here is making *billions*.

Tony stops in front of the massive gates at the entrance to the neighborhood. A hidden camera scans the car — the license plate and even the number of occupants — before they slowly swing open.

The road in is lined with trees for the first mile. As it opens up, we come upon the first house — or I should say property, since the house isn't visible from the road. I've never met the people who live there. Over the years, my brothers and I made up stories about who it might be. Asher, my eldest brother, is convinced it's owned by a European prince or something. While Roman, my baby brother, thinks it must be a spy, since we've never once seen any sign of life on the property — not even staff. I have a hard time believing a spy would have that kind of money, but who knows.

When we finally get to the driveway that leads up to my dad's house, Tony stops the car to wait for yet another gate. Not only is the entire neighborhood fully gated, but so is every individual house.

He follows the curve of the driveway and pulls up in front of the massive house. Growing up, this was all I knew. For the longest time, I had no idea that the vast majority of people don't live in houses this size. Even I don't understand why anyone needs a home so large. Now that I've been out on my own, I can't imagine ever living in a place the size of a shopping mall, no matter how much money I have.

"Thanks, Tony," Rosie says to him, getting out of the car.

He waits until I've climbed out too before he asks, "Should I unload your luggage here, Mr. Hendricks?"

The question stops me in my tracks. Stupidly, I didn't even think about what will be expected after we tell our families we're married. I've had too much other shit on my mind to worry about how strange it will look if we stay in separate houses.

Fuck.

"Yeah, you can leave it here." There's a good chance I'll have to throw it in my car when we head to Rosie's family's house, but I know better than to make this decision on my own.

Ice slithers down my spine.

We're *married*.

Not dating.

They're going to set us up in a bedroom together. Why wouldn't they?

The idea of sharing a whole bed with Rosie has me spiraling.

I'm borrowing trouble, though, so I shove those thoughts away.

Regardless, I stick to my decision. This way, I can prolong the inevitable. If I told him he didn't need to leave it here, then his suspicions would be confirmed, and I have no doubt he'd run right to Rosie's dad. At least this way, he can't be totally sure.

"All right," he says, mistrust gleaming in his eyes.

Rosie and I head for the front door, careful to keep almost two feet of space between us.

The door opens before we get to the top of the stairs, and Roman comes running out with a hoot of joy.

But it's not me he's happy to see.

He throws his arms around Rosie, almost tackling her to the ground.

Jealousy burns in my chest. Not because he's touching Rosie, and I'm hit with a wave of possessiveness over her. It definitely can't be that. No, I'm jealous because he's *my* brother, yet he's more excited to see her.

"What the hell are you doing here?" he asks, grasping her upper arms and steadying her before she falls.

I narrow my eyes on where he's holding her, even though she's got her feet firmly planted on the ground.

"This one dragged me along." She tosses a thumb at me.

My lip curls.

Roman chuckles, running his fingers through his shaggy blond hair. His is a shade darker than mine. Wavier too.

"You mean to tell me you two have kissed and made up after what…? Five years?"

Rosie side-eyes me. *Do we tell him?* That's what she's silently asking me.

I hold back a sigh. If we tell Roman, he'll save us the trouble of breaking the news to the rest of my family. But I can't imagine my father would appreciate that approach.

I give a subtle shake of my head.

"I guess you could say that," she replies with a genuine smile.

Her smile has nothing to do with me, and fuck if that doesn't make me all the more annoyed.

"Well, come on." He throws his arm around her

shoulders, tugging her up the last few stairs to the front door. "Get in here. Cash will be happy to see you."

I clench my jaw at the comment. My older brother had a thing for Rosie for years when we were growing up. For all I know, he *still* has a thing for her, since I had no idea they kept in touch.

Out of all my brothers, I'm the closest to Cash, who's only a year older than me, and Roman, who's two years younger.

I'll never understand how my parents handled having five boys practically back-to-back, regardless of how much help they had.

Inside the foyer, Roman hollers out, "Cash! Guess who's here?" To Rosie, he says, "I think he's in the kitchen. Are you hungry?"

"I could have a snack."

"Perfect."

I stand on the threshold, watching them head in the direction of the kitchen. Part of me is tempted to go off on my own, but a bigger part, the nosy part, wants to witness the way Rosie interacts with my brothers.

"Rosie!" Cash grins from ear to ear when he spots her. He's sitting on one of the barstools at the large kitchen island, mouth stuffed with a piece of the fudge Elsie, our family cook, makes every holiday season. "What are you doing here?"

He pulls her out of Roman's arms and envelops her

in a hug. I swear he even sniffs her hair. Cash holds her a little too long, at least in my opinion. Clearing my throat, I step closer and wait for him to let her go, but he doesn't.

Rosie doesn't encourage him to release her. In fact, she hugs him back just as tightly.

"You smell good," she tells him. "New cologne?"

"Maybe." He kisses her cheek.

Okay, now I'm pissed.

Rage courses through me, heating my blood, as I stride closer. "Hands off my wife, Cash."

Everyone in the room freezes, myself included, and every eye goes wide.

Fuck. Why the hell did I say that?

Rosie shoots a *what the fuck?* look my way. It's warranted, since I just told her not to spill the beans to Roman.

"Wife?" Cash laughs uproariously. "You're fucking joking, right?" He shakes his head. "I didn't know we were pranking each other this early, but this is a good one." With a wag of his finger, he spins, picks up a piece of fudge, and offers it to Rosie. "Fudge?"

She takes it from him with her left hand. Where, suddenly, her wedding band has appeared.

Hand trembling, I dig in my pocket for mine and wiggle it on.

Cash's jaw drops as he grabs her hand and gapes at

the ring. "You're going all out for this prank. Those look like real diamonds."

"It's not a prank," Rosie says softly, her cheeks pinkening. She glances over at me, lashes lowering so she doesn't fully meet my gaze. "We're married."

I lift my left hand as well, now that I've put my ring back on, and wiggle my fingers. The glower is still firmly fixed to my face, since my brother still hasn't removed his hands from my wife. I don't care if it's Rosie, if I still hate her. I'm legally bound to her now, and that should be enough of a reason for my brother to keep his distance.

"I'm not going to ask you again," I bite out through clenched teeth. "Take. Your. Hands. Off. My. *Wife.*"

Cash chuckles with a shake of his head, but he finally lets go of Rosie and holds both hands up. "How was I supposed to know? My invitation must've gotten lost in the mail."

Rosie's cosplaying as a tomato now. "It was pretty sudden." She darts a look at me, silently asking whether what she said is okay.

I eat up the distance between us and put a hand on her waist. I can't yell at my brother for manhandling her and then act like I don't want to touch her myself.

"Wait," Roman keels over laughing, "does Dad know?" When I shake my head, he sobers, his eyes going wide. "Do *your* parents know?" he asks Rosie.

"No." She bites her lip. "We're telling everyone today."

Cash reaches for another piece of fudge and pops it into his mouth. "I'm so glad I'm here to witness this."

I narrow my eyes on him. "Stop reveling in this."

He chuckles. "Nice try, but I'm going to enjoy every second of the show when Dad chews you out, and I thoroughly hope Chandler tears into you," he says, referring to Rosie's dad. "Oh, yeah." He rubs his hands together eagerly. "This is going to be great."

Brothers—we'd go to war for each other, but we also take immense pleasure in watching one another suffer the consequences of their actions when it comes to our dad.

"What's going on in here?" Elsie's voice echoes through the room. "Do I hear my favorite?"

"If by me, then yes, but you already saw me," Cash says as Elsie enters from the hallway on the other side of the kitchen.

As he goes in for yet another piece of fudge, she puts it into overdrive and reaches him in time to slap his hand away.

"You'll spoil your dinner," she scolds. With a big smile, she turns and stops in front of me. She has to stand on her tiptoes to take my face in her hands. "I've missed you. You don't come home enough."

My chest tightens. She's right. "Sorry."

"Sure you are," she harrumphs. An instant later,

though, her smile grows impossibly wide. "And you brought Ms. Rosie with you? I take it this means you two have finally made up. I've missed seeing you around, deary. Oh." She freezes when she notices my hand on Rosie's waist, and her eyes widen with excitement. "Are you two together?"

"Better," Roman replies, leaning against the counter with a smirk. "They're married."

"Married?" Elsie blurts, bringing both hands to her cheeks. "How come I didn't know? I would've made the cake!"

"It was a bit sudden," I answer, ignoring the guilt eating at me at the mix of excitement and hurt every person we've told thus far has displayed.

"Yes." Rosie beams, looking for all the world like she's truly in love with me. She wraps her arms around one of mine and gazes up at me adoringly. "Once we made up, we realized how much we actually love each other, and now, here we are."

Elsie puts a hand to her heart. "That's so sweet. But no wedding?"

"It's okay." Rosie flashes a smile. "My boo bear promised me the wedding of my dreams this summer." She pats my chest.

"Boo bear," Cash chortles, crossing his arms over his chest. He's not as built as I am, but he's plenty muscular. "You're never living this one down, baby brother."

I roll my eyes. He acts like I'm so much younger than him.

"Where's Dad?" I ask Roman, because Cash is currently dead to me.

"In his office," he replies, opening the fridge and sticking his head in. "What's for dinner, Elsie?"

"We better go talk to him," I whisper in Rosie's ear. Now that Cash and Roman know, it'll be no time before Asher and Hudson find out. The last thing I need is for my brothers to tell my dad before I can. I'm mostly certain he'll be cooler about this than Rosie's dad, but I worry he'll be upset if he hears the news from someone else.

"Okay." She gives my hand a reassuring squeeze.

"Good luck!" Cash calls, cackling like this is the funniest thing he's ever witnessed.

Ignoring him, I tug Rosie down the hall to the back set of stairs that will bring us close to my dad's office on the second floor.

"Did you have a thing with Cash?" My tone is harsher than I intend and laced with an anger I have no right to feel.

She startles at my question and pulls up short. "What?"

"You heard me." I squeeze her hand a little too hard as I try, unsuccessfully, to choke back my frustration.

"Ow." Frowning, she tugs her hand out of mine. "No, I never had a thing for Cash." She practically growls the words and heads up the stairs without looking back to make sure I'm following. "He wasn't the brother I was interested in," she whispers, like she hopes I can't hear her.

My heart pounds, and my feet freeze halfway up the steps. "Roman, then?"

She whips around and rolls her eyes. "What difference does it make who I had a crush on years ago? I was a teenager."

"It matters to me," I bite out, taking a step closer so we're eye to eye.

She scrutinizes me unblinkingly. "Are you really this big of an idiot?"

I open my mouth to reply, but she slaps her palm over it.

"Don't answer that. You'll just dig a bigger hole for yourself."

Lowering her hand, she spins and continues up the wide staircase.

I stay behind, but only because the view is annoyingly nice.

She waits for me at the top, then follows me to the office, even though she knows where it is. With a steadying breath, I wipe my sweaty palms on my pants, then knock on the door and wait.

"Roman," my dad hollers, "I told you already, I'm not building a skate park in the backyard for Christmas."

I chuckle. "It's me, Dad."

"Oh." He pauses. "Come in."

I shoot a look at Rosie. *Ready or not?* Then I open the door and usher Rosie in first, since it's the gentlemanly thing to do. Plus, it gives me a few more seconds to catch my breath before facing my father.

His mahogany desk is a monstrous thing. The wall behind him is lined with tome after tome of rare and collectible literature. My brothers and I used to poke fun at him for his love of old books. Regardless of where we traveled, he'd always cart us off to used bookstores.

With a smile, he slides his reading glasses off and sets them aside. The expression on his face has nothing to do with me, though, and everything to do with the woman at my side.

Despite our falling out, my dad and brothers still love Rosie.

"Rosie," he crows, getting up from his desk and coming around to pull her into a hug.

"It's good to see you, Mr. Hendricks."

He pulls away from the hug but keeps a hold of her shoulders. "How many times do I have to tell you? Call me Peter."

"Peter," she parrots with a tiny laugh.

I stand in the middle of the room, hands hanging limply at my sides now, eyes on the ceiling, doing my best not to be hurt that every person here is more excited to see an old friend than they are to see me, a member of the family.

"Daire," he says, finally turning to me. "I've missed you." He opens his arms for a hug.

The anger fades and is quickly replaced by a comfort I only feel when I'm with him, and I squeeze him back.

Despite his workaholic tendencies, he's been more present than most parents. When we were kids, he was always home by five. Even if he usually holed up in his home office after dinner.

Still, I can't complain. He lost the love of his life and runs a billion-dollar company, yet he still managed to be present in our lives.

"Does this mean you two have finally made up?" he asks me with an arched brow. "You guys were so close, practically attached at the hip, until you weren't."

"Uh … yeah, I guess you could say that."

I glance over at Rosie, who's worrying her bottom lip, silently urging me to get this over with.

I swallow back the trepidation rising inside me. I might be a full-blown adult, but that doesn't stop me from being mildly terrified of my father. As a teenager, I spent more than a few nights getting chewed out in this room. I earned each of those lectures, but that knowledge doesn't ease my feeling of dread.

"Dad." I clear my throat.

"Hmm?" He hums, cocking his head to the side.

Before I can answer, he blanches. "You didn't get her pregnant, did you?"

Rosie bursts into laughter. No doubt the little hellion is thinking to herself that no, she's not pregnant, but I did knock someone up. I'll give her credit, since she makes no move to rat me out.

"I'm not pregnant," she says through her laughter.

"Oh, good." His shoulders sag. "I'm too young to be a grandpa."

"Uh ... Dad? Asher's married. I'm pretty sure you'll be a grandpa in no time."

He waves a hand dismissively. "They've been fighting since they got here. I'm pretty sure a divorce is more imminent than a baby."

I frown. "Asher and Veda are having problems? I ... I didn't know." I actually *like* my brother's wife. She keeps him in line and is a pretty cool chick. They've been together for years. The idea that they could split has a pit forming in my stomach.

"You could pick up the phone and call your brothers now and then."

"We text," I say, though his comment hits with perfect accuracy. I've done a shitty job of staying in touch.

"In a group chat?" he asks, chin dipped and brows raised.

I run a hand down my face and swallow thickly. "Yes."

"And you think Asher is going to talk about it in a group text chat? Come on. You know him better than that."

I do. No one would describe my oldest brother as rowdy, like they would the rest of us. He's the kind of person who bottles up his emotions. So maybe it's possible that his marriage is struggling. If he can't communicate, then it's hard not to think he's destined to fail.

"I'll talk to him while I'm here," I mumble.

"Anyway," he leans back against his desk, "what was it you were going to tell me?"

With my heart in my throat, I loop an arm around Rosie's waist and tug her against my side. She's soft against me, her sweet-smelling perfume permeating the air.

My dad's eyes light up as he takes us in. "Are you two dating? I've been waiting for this day since—"

I clear my throat. "We're married, actually."

If I had to guess how my father would react to the news, I never would have even considered what happens next.

"What?" he asks, clutching his chest. "M-Married?"

"Dad?" I lunge forward, grasping his arm as he sways, unsteady on his feet. "Dad?" I say, louder this time.

His legs give out then, but before he can hit the floor, I catch him.

Behind me, Rosie screams.

Panic floods me, but I have the wherewithal to check his pulse. I find it, but it's weak.

"Call 911," I tell Rosie.

I think I just killed my dad.

twelve

ROSIE

I BURROW INTO MY SWEATER, seeking even a modicum of warmth. Though even if the waiting room was warm, it probably wouldn't matter. Ice has been coursing through my veins since the moment Daire's dad dropped to the floor.

Across from me, Daire paces from one side of the room to the other. Asher and Hudson, the two eldest Hendricks brothers, are speaking in hushed voices in the corner. Asher's wife, Veda, went to find coffee a while ago and hasn't returned. Cash sits beside me, drumming his fingers on the arms of the chair while Roman flirts with one of the nurses at the station to our left.

"This is all my fault," I whisper.

Cash stops drumming and cocks his head. "Your fault?"

Blinking back tears, I peer up at him. "Daire told him we got married, and then he just collapsed. So yeah, this is my fault."

He shakes his head. I don't think I've ever seen his usually golden skin so pale. As I frantically called 911, the boys appeared, one by one. The house is enormous, but apparently my panicked scream carried far.

Cash shakes his head. "This isn't your fault. Dad hasn't been taking the greatest care of himself. He's healthy enough, or so I thought, but he avoids going to the doctor like he thinks they're going to lock him away. God only knows what's going on inside his body."

With my lip caught between my teeth, I wrap my arms tighter around myself. "I can't help it. I feel guilty."

"Rosie." He says my name softly, pulling me into an awkward hug with the arms of the chairs between us.

There's a growl nearby, like an annoyed dog. "Stop touching my wife, Cash."

Huffing, I roll my eyes at my so-called husband. "Stop being a dick. How about that?"

Daire pinches the bridge of his nose. "Excuse me for not liking the way my brother is pawing all over you."

"Territorial much?" I fire back, sitting up straight. "It was a hug."

Every eye in the room is fixed on us. Shit. We're in a hospital waiting room while his dad is being seen for a possible heart attack. Arguing is the last thing we should be doing. But I can't seem to help it. He brings out the worst in me.

Veda returns then, wearing a cream-colored sweater. She's pushed the sleeves up to her elbows, revealing the floral sleeve tattoo on her right arm.

She scans the room, bracelets jangling on her wrists. "I feel like I missed something."

Asher doesn't stop talking to Hudson, despite the way she's focused on him.

"My little brother is feeling a bit ... challenged, which I find extremely interesting. What do you have to be insecure about?" Cash taunts Daire. "You're married."

Veda's eyes flash between me and the two brothers. Snickering, she raises the cup of coffee to her lips. "Oh, this is fun."

Before I can delve into what she means by *that*, my parents and my sister step through the sliding doors at the front of the building.

I stand up, leaving both annoying brothers behind me. "Mom!" I rush into my mother's arms. Though I called them soon after we arrived at the hospital to tell them what happened, I conveniently left out the part about being married.

She takes my face in her hands the way she used to when I was a child. "What happened?"

"He just collapsed," I explain. "It happened out of nowhere."

"Do you know anything yet?" my dad asks, scanning our surroundings like he's ready to take charge.

"No, nothing yet."

He disappears without another word, probably to go in search of hospital staff he can berate information out of.

"Hi, Rosie." Grace waves. The sound of her voice and her proximity alone bring my anxiety down to a manageable place.

"Gracie!" I all but tackle her in a hug, unable to keep from smiling. I've missed her so much. I force her to FaceTime me at least once a week, and it's still not enough.

"You're squeezing me too tight," she accuses.

I let her go, but not before planting a big, smacking kiss on her cheek.

"Ew." She wipes it away with the back of her hand. "You're gross."

"I'm going to check on the boys," my mom says, giving my hand a squeeze in passing.

She strides straight over to Daire and grasps his

face, like she did mine, and then gives his cheek a pat. While she speaks to him, Daire locks eyes with me, like he could sense me watching.

"He's staring at you," Grace points out from my side.

I turn away first and sling my arm around my baby sister's shoulders. "I've missed you, you know."

She rolls her eyes. "Duh. I'm amazing. I'd miss me too."

I laugh, feeling lighter than I have in weeks. Only Grace.

When I look back toward the waiting room, my mom's moved on to Cash, and Daire is standing with his arms crossed, surveying the space.

"I need to talk to him," I tell Grace.

She throws out an arm toward him. "Be my guest. I'm not holding you hostage."

Now's not the time to be laughing, but Grace has the most innate ability to lift my spirits. I can't help but giggle. She's so sarcastic, just like our dad.

As I approach Daire, I nod toward the hallway, silently asking him to follow me. I expect him to refuse, but he dips his chin in return. And with his hands shoved deep in his pockets, he shuffles out behind me.

I wait until we're a good distance away and tucked safely behind a vending machine before I speak. "We're going to have to tell my parents. Like *now*. Better for them to find out from us than your dad when he wakes up. Or your brothers."

Daire blinks at me, crossing those massive arms over his chest. The guy really is like a brick wall. Completely impenetrable.

"If he wakes up."

"Huh?" I voice, not catching up.

"*If* he wakes up," he grits out, wearing a glower that almost masks the fear in his eyes. "He had a heart attack, Rosie. That's not some minor thing—"

"They said it was a mild heart attack," I point out, but the assurance does nothing to ease the expression.

"I've already lost one parent," he reminds me, toeing his shoe against the stark white linoleum floor. "Excuse me for being realistic. Not everything is about you."

I lower my head and breathe through the ache in my chest. "I'm not trying to make this about me." It's like a knife to the heart that he'd even think that.

"Are you sure about that?" he retorts. "This is what your mother has always wanted for you, right? Marrying a Hendricks? I bet you can't wait to tell her that you succeeded."

His words hit me like bullets, one right after the other. I stagger back, shocked by the vitriol he's spewing.

Instantly, he grimaces, the look one of regret. But it's too late for that. The words, the accusation, it's all out there now.

"I know you're upset right now, but that doesn't give you the right to be an asshole."

He looks away, jaw pulsing. I'm not expecting an apology. Hell would surely have to freeze over for that.

Wrapping my arms around myself, I look up and down the hall and sigh. "I'll tell them myself."

I shimmy out of the corner, doing my best not to brush up against him as he stands as still as a statue. I'm halfway down the hall when he wraps a hand around my elbow and spins me around.

"What?" I ask softly. I don't have any fight left in me. Not with how today has gone.

"I…" He swallows, his throat working, and his eyes dart away for a moment before he forces them back to meet mine. "I'll tell them with you. You're not the one who got us into this."

I give a tiny nod, holding his gaze. Maybe there is hope for us. Maybe it's possible we can work as a team. "All right, come on, then."

My parents are both seated in the waiting room when we return.

"No updates yet," my dad says before either of us can speak. "I tried to get information, but…" He throws his hands up in annoyance. "Nothing."

"Mom? Dad? Can we talk to you for a second?"

My mom hops up, instantly alert. Her hair is styled perfectly, as always. It's the same dark, almost-black shade of hair as mine. Her eyes are identical to mine too. I get my height from her as well, though she comes in at a solid six-foot when she's not wearing heels. Even though she no longer models, she's still waifish. It hurts to see that she clings so firmly to the habits she created all those years ago. The modeling industry did a number on her.

My dad groans as he gets out of the chair, grumbling about his back.

With a deep breath in and a hand to my stomach, I start back down the hall, away from Daire's snickering brothers. Clearly, based on the looks and whispers, they know what's about to come.

"I'm coming too!" Gracie hollers, hurrying to catch up.

I stop in front of the vending machine we were just hiding behind and turn to face my parents. I'm still wearing my ring, and in the chaos of their arrival, they haven't noticed it yet. I find my thumb absentmindedly spinning it around and around as I collect my thoughts.

"I want to preface this by saying I'm sorry, and it wasn't planned."

Both my mom and my dad narrow their eyes on me, then on Daire, and in unison, they go ashen.

"Oh my God." My mother gasps and brings a shaky hand to her mouth. "You're pregnant."

My dad wags a finger in front of Daire's face. "Did you knock up my daughter?"

"Why does everyone think I'm pregnant today?

Jeesh," I blurt out, throwing my hands in the air. "Daire and I got married."

Boom.

Done.

It's there.

Out in the open.

In the aftermath of my confession, my family goes silent. As they gape at us, muffled conversations from the waiting room float on the air amid the incessant beeping of machines.

Grace is the first to break the silence.

"You can't be married." She stomps her foot. "You always said I could be your flower girl, and your maid of honor, and—"

"I know, Gracie." I reach for my sister. The tears in her eyes are like a knife to the stomach. Holding back my own tears, I squeeze her tight. "That's why we're going to have a real wedding. I want you to be all the things you want to be."

She sniffles, burying her face in my neck. "It won't be the same."

"I promise it'll be better than you think." I rub my hands up and down her arms, desperate to give her some sort of comfort.

"I don't believe you." Her bottom lip trembles as she steps back, cracking my heart right in two.

Beside me, Daire finally speaks. "It's my fault,

Grace. I..." He steps forward, putting his hand on the curve of my waist.

I shiver at his touch, hoping like hell he thinks it's from the cold air pumping through the hospital.

"I just love your sister so much." His eyes meet mine briefly before focusing back on my sister. "I couldn't wait to be married to her. I begged her to do it now. But she's right. We're going to have a big wedding eventually. I promise."

She sniffles. "You pinky promise like before?"

Like before? My stomach tumbles at those words.

He nods, holding out his pinky. "I pinky promise."

"No takebacks."

"None."

Finally, she wraps her little finger around his.

When they let go, I elbow Daire in the side. "What does she mean by before?"

"We used to pinky promise *all* the time when I was little," she informs me happily.

He shrugs. "Who wouldn't pinky promise Grace? She's the best."

He has me there.

"How did this happen?" My mom asks, running her fingers through her hair. "Don't get me wrong, I'm thrilled." She gives Daire a bright smile. "I always hoped you'd be a part of our family. But I thought you weren't on speaking terms anymore."

Daire and I exchange a look as my stomach sinks.

"We reconnected at the beginning of the year." The lie escapes me far too easily. "We started chatting and realized that maybe that hate was more like..." I clear my throat. "More like love." I almost gag over the word. "We knew right away that we never wanted to be apart. And like Daire said, he just loves me so much." I pinch his cheek a little harder than necessary. "I mean, who in their right mind could resist me?" I'm laying it on too thick, but I can't help myself. "So he proposed, and I said yes, and we got married the next day. The end."

My dad laughs, the sound far too loud for the quiet hospital, and there's not one ounce of humor in it. "You didn't think to ask her father for permission first? I'm an old-fashioned man."

"Chandler—"

My father holds up a hand. "That's Mr. Thomas to you."

I have to cover my face with my hand to hide my amusement, trying to appear hurt instead. Daire's always called my dad by his first name, so for him to suddenly demand the mister status, he must be pissed.

"You better not be snickering, Rosemary."

I cringe.

Not the whole first name.

Sobering, I say, "Definitely not, Dad."

"Liar," Daire whispers in my ear.

I pinch his side.

"Oh my God," my mom blanches, "is this why your dad had a heart attack?"

My face flames, and Daire lowers his head, kicking at the linoleum floor. "Unfortunately so, Mrs. Thomas."

"Oh, dear." She pats his cheek. "It's Lydia. It always has been."

My dad glowers at her for playing good cop.

"Remember, Dad," I say, because apparently I have a death wish, "we're adults. We made this decision together."

"The wedding is going to be beautiful," my mom says, clasping her hands in front of her chest and swooning. I have no doubt that she's already designing the whole thing in her mind.

Now that she doesn't think I'm pregnant, she's thrilled.

"Lydia," my dad snaps.

"I'm thinking white roses ... or maybe peonies."

She wanders away from us, tugging her phone out of her purse.

"She's going to be calling you for your tux measurements soon," I mutter to Daire.

One side of his mouth quirks up. "I'll be waiting for the call."

My dad shakes his head and crosses his arms over his chest. "I need you two to be serious for a moment."

"Can I go now?" Gracie interrupts.

With a sigh, Dad points to the waiting area. "Yes, go sit down. I'll be back in a minute, sweetie."

"Bye." She gives us a big smile and waves before all but skipping down the hall.

When she's out of earshot, my dad inhales, then lets it out in one big rush. "Did you two even think to have a prenup drawn up?"

My blood freezes in my veins. My whole life, my parents have drilled into me the importance of a prenup. With the inheritance I stand to gain, it's logical. Expected. The same is surely true of Daire with his father.

"Um ... I know you don't want to hear this," I say, cringing, "but no."

"Unbelievable." Hands on his hips, he lowers his head and paces a few steps away. "I'm calling my lawyer. Maybe we can get this annulled."

"Sir—" Daire's voice is strained, laced with panic.

"But Daddy, I love him!" I pull my best Ariel impression, hoping to add some levity to the situation, to turn this conversation around. I hate conflict more than almost anything. Daire's the only person who seems to bring out my combative side.

My dad blinks back at me.

Daire covers his mouth with his hand to hide a snicker.

"I'm not annulling the marriage," I say, lifting my chin and pulling my shoulders back. "Daire is my husband. We love each other." I look over at him, the lie thick on my tongue. "We're adults, and we made this decision together. Surely you can respect that."

Silently, I take a single step closer, begging him to understand. Hoping he sees that I'm just a girl in love and all the things he's worried about are silly. We both come from money; a prenup would hardly make a difference.

If I give in to what he's demanding and sign annulment papers—not that I think it could even be annulled—then all of this would have been for nothing, and despite myself, I want to help Daire with his custody situation. That probably makes me insanely stupid. I literally have the perfect out in front of me, and I'm turning it down.

"You're being ridiculous," my dad bites out. "The two of you clearly didn't think this through." He shakes his head. "I'm so disappointed in you, Rosie."

It's the worst thing he could've said to me. My whole life, I've gone out of my way to please my parents, and this feels like a sharp slap to the face.

Daire studies my face, his eyes wide with sympathy, like he can see just how much my dad's words hurt me.

"Hey." Daire jumps to my defense, putting his body in front of mine. "Don't talk to her like that."

My dad's face turns such a garish shade of red, I worry we might have another heart attack on our hands.

"You were almost like a son to me at one point, but you are *not* family, and you can't talk to me like that!" My dad's voice echoes down the quiet hallway.

Wincing, I peek over my shoulder, hoping we haven't garnered an audience. Unfortunately, all four of Daire's brothers are watching from the waiting room.

"You two are too young for this. Smarter than it too. Marriage isn't something you jump into on a whim."

Daire clears his throat. "Technically, sir, I am family. I'm your son-in-law." He speaks each word slowly, with inflection.

Fuck me, does the guy have a death wish?

I grip his arm. "Come on. Let's go for a walk."

My dad shakes his head, and with a huff, he walks away, not toward the waiting room but in the direction of the exit.

His silence is worse than his anger.

A lump lodges thickly in my throat.

"Rosie—" Daire steps in close, holding his arms out in an offer of comfort.

I shake my head, shrugging him off.

This isn't real.

He doesn't *actually* want to touch me, and I can't stomach the idea of accepting false affections from my fake-husband in a moment like this. I head back to the waiting room and park my butt in the seat beside Cash I claimed earlier.

"I'm sorry," Cash says softly, tilting closer.

I give a tiny nod of acknowledgment. He shouldn't have to worry about me. His dad is the one we should all be focused on.

While we wait for news about his dad, it's pretty damn clear that mine just might hate me.

thirteen

DAIRE

ROSIE'S BODY is stiff in the bed beside me. She's only just stopped crying, and she only gave in to the tears when she thought I'd fallen asleep.

We came home a few hours ago, after we found out my dad was doing fine. We haven't been allowed to see him yet, so we'll go back in the morning. This is certainly not the Thanksgiving weekend I imagined. The last thing I expected to happen when I broke the news of our marriage to my dad was that he'd have a heart attack.

For several minutes, I blink up at the ceiling,

arguing with myself over whether I should say something to Rosie, and when I finally decide to bite the bullet and do it, I'm at a complete loss for words.

But I do it anyway.

With a deep breath in, I lace my hands over my abdomen.

"Rosie?" I whisper.

She probably won't answer. If I had to bet, she'll continue to feign sleep. And if she does, then I won't have to come up with something else to say.

The sheets rustle, and the mattress dips. In my periphery, she rolls onto her side so she's on her back and cups her hands beneath her head.

"Yeah?"

I swallow and rack my brain for something that will ease her pain. "Your dad will forgive you."

She huffs a sigh. "Probably not before my mom's finished planning the wedding." A little laugh escapes her then, the sound slightly hysterical. "She already sent me a Pinterest board."

I cross my right arm behind my head. "Are you okay with that? With her taking over?"

She snorts. "Absolutely not. I've been dreaming of my wedding for years, but…"

"But this isn't real?" *Why* did that sound like a question?

"Right. But I still want it to feel like me. Not my

mom. Even if it's temporary. That's not really what's bothering me, though."

"Just your dad?"

She shakes her head. "Your dad's in the hospital, Daire. I feel so … guilty." Her voice wavers on that last word, like she's crying again.

My stomach sinks at the thought. I don't know how to handle a woman's tears.

"Don't cry," I practically beg. If she does, I'm worried my natural instinct will be to pet her on the head and say, "There, there."

"Sorry." She sniffles. "I can't help it. That was scary."

Her ghost-white face flashes through my mind. All the color drained from her the instant he collapsed. I'm sure I didn't look much better.

"It was," I agree.

She's quiet again for a long moment, the whirl of the fan suddenly the only sound between us. "Do you want to talk about it?"

I drop a hand over my face and shake my head. "No."

She huffs a sigh. "You never do."

Frowning, I roll over to face her. "What's that supposed to mean?"

Despite my glower and my tone, she doesn't cower. She shrugs, the sheets wrinkling beneath her. The bed is a king size, leaving plenty of space between us.

"You've never been good at talking about your feelings."

My chest tightens, but I breathe through it, forcing the ache to dissipate. "Why would I want to talk about them?"

"I don't know," she snaps. "Maybe so you're not holding on to every little thing that upsets you? You can share your burdens with people, you know. They'd be happy to listen. Especially about Junior."

"His name is Sammy," I grind out. I might not like the name, but it's *his* name.

Her teeth flash in the dark. "I prefer Junior." She tucks a loose strand of dark hair behind her ear. "Anyway, all I'm saying is you should talk to someone."

"I'm not going to a therapist, if that's what you're getting at."

I went a few times after my mother died and hated every second of it. I have no interest in being psychoanalyzed by a stranger.

"I didn't say anything about a therapist. Talk to your friends. Your dad. Your brothers. Talk to me. Just talk to someone."

"Is that not what we're doing?"

She closes her eyes and heaves out an exasperated breath. "That's not what I was getting at, and you know it. You're ridiculous."

She rolls away from me, taking the blankets with her.

Biting back a curse, I yank them back over to my side.

"Hey!" she snaps.

I pull them up to my chin and settle on my back again. "Don't hog the blankets."

"You're a child."

The glower she sends over her shoulder is enough to have most people shaking. Good thing I'm not most people.

I paste on a sarcastic smile in response.

"Fuck you," she snaps, climbing out of the bed.

I sit up so fast stars dance in my vision. "Where are you going?"

"To get a snack," she huffs as she walks out the door without looking back.

I flop back down, annoyed.

With her.

With myself.

I lie there for what feels like hours, fighting the urge to see what she's doing. Eventually, though, my curiosity gets the best of me, and I slip out of the bed and go in search of her.

Quietly, I take the main staircase to the first floor and trek to the kitchen. By the time I get there, I feel as though I've walked miles. Though I grew up in this house, it never fails that when I return, I've forgotten how large it is.

At the soft murmur of voices, I stop and listen.

"You and Daire, huh?"

Sounds like Cash.

A glass clinks, like maybe he's toasting our marriage, though his tone isn't overly congratulatory.

"Yep." She sounds bored by the conversation. I guess it's a good thing, but after the way he greeted her and drifted toward her at the hospital, I can't help but wonder if they planned to meet up like this.

"I'm not buying it."

She's quiet for a long moment, but finally, she says, "What exactly aren't you buying?"

"I don't know what went down with you and my brother, but he's a grudge holder. I can't imagine him forgiving you so easily for whatever you did."

She snorts, the sound pure annoyance. "I didn't do anything to him. He's the one who hurt *me*."

I rear back, and my lungs practically seize up. *What the fuck is she talking about?*

Cash chuckles, though there's no humor in the sound. "Whatever it is obviously still has you heated, petal. And you want me to think you're happily married?"

Petal?

My blood heats at the word. At the implication.

There's a crunching sound, like she's chewing. Then she clears her throat. "Don't call me that."

My brother has a pet name for *my* wife? I don't like that. Not one bit.

With a sharp breath in, I step into the kitchen, making my presence known. Instantly, my boiling blood turns to ice.

Cash has his hand on Rosie's cheek.

And I see fucking red.

Instinct takes over, and I rush up to them. I'm too irate to register Rosie's cry of "Daire, no!" as I cock my arm back and punch my brother in the face so hard he falls off the barstool.

He lies on the tile floor, his hand covering his face. A line of blood trickles out of his nose.

"I told you to keep your hands off my wife."

The bastard has the audacity to laugh at me. I've always gotten along with my brothers. There's never been any true animosity. Competition, yes? But never flat out hate. Right now, I think I hate him.

Cash chuckles, rubbing his jaw and ignoring the trickle of blood. "Maybe you really do care about her."

I have to fight the urge to take another swing at him. "What does that mean?"

He says nothing, just picks himself up from the floor and turns to Rosie. "It could've been us." And with that, he turns and exits the kitchen.

"What the fuck?" I turn my wrath on her.

Her shoulders are curled in on themselves, but as I step closer, she straightens and shoots figurative daggers my way. "Why are you pissed at me?" She grabs a half-eaten apple from the counter in front of her and takes a bite. "I haven't done anything."

"Why the fuck is Cash so into you? Did you hook up with him?"

She wrinkles her nose. "God, no."

I clench my hands into fists at my sides. "What's that supposed to mean?"

She arches a brow, cocking her head to the side. "Your brother is hot, but no, I've never slept with him. Is that clear enough for you?"

"He's into you." It's a statement, not a question.

"So?" she counters, kicking her feet up on the island and leaning back on the stool. "I'm married to *you*."

"He has a nickname for you." The rage that's taken over only grows at the memory of the way he called her *petal*.

"You weren't the only Hendricks I was friends with, Daire." Her tone has completely changed. These words are gentle, like I'm a bomb she's worried might go off.

"*Petal*," I spit, "doesn't seem to be the kind of nickname you give someone who's only a friend." My fists are clenched so tight the knuckles on my right hand are stiff. They'll no doubt bruise after the way I laid Cash out. The fucker didn't even attempt to fight back. That alone tells me he knows he's in the wrong.

"Just because you hate me doesn't mean the rest of your family does," she whispers, eyes dropping to the bowl in front of her. "He asked me out last year when we were home for Christmas."

This news is like a slap to the face. It's ridiculous, to feel this way, but it fucking stings. "Did you go?"

She hesitates, running her tongue over her bottom lip. "Yes. But while we were out, I told him I just wanted to remain friends."

"Why would you do that?"

She snorts. "Why do you sound so offended that I turned him down?"

"I ... I don't know." I rough a hand over my face. What the fuck is wrong with me? "He's a catch. You could do a lot worse than my brother."

She shakes her head, frowning. "You are so fucking hot and cold, Daire. I can't read you. I turned him down because *you're* the one I always had a big, dumb crush on. Not him, or Roman, or any of your brothers. Just ... you. You fucking idiot."

She shoves back the barstool and stands, never taking her eyes off me. I'm trapped in her stare, my heart in my throat.

"I know you hate me as much as I hate you. I thought the stupid crush would go away when you ... never mind." She drops her head and gives it a shake, letting out a self-deprecating laugh. "But it didn't. Don't think for a second I agreed to this hoping it would turn into something real. I know it won't. So don't worry about me and my feelings or your stupid rule. But no,

I'm not interested in your brother, even if he likes me. He wouldn't be you, and I'm not cruel enough to make him second best."

She hesitates for a second, focus fixed on the floor in front of her, like she's warring with herself about whether she should give me a chance to answer, but she ends up ducking around me, leaving me standing alone in the kitchen.

I drop my head back and mutter to the vaulted ceiling above me. *"Fuck."*

fourteen

ROSIE

AS WE SIT side by side at the ice rink, I find myself constantly peeking over at Peter to make sure he's okay. Out on the ice, the brothers and Veda are playing hockey three on three. Asher and Veda are on opposing teams, and although I can't hear what Veda is saying, it's clear she's taunting Asher.

Normally, the temperature doesn't get to me. Probably because I'm usually surrounded by fans. But Peter and I are alone, and it's borderline frigid. I tug a pair of blue mittens with pearl detailing from the pocket of my coat. They were a gift from my mom last Christmas.

Knowing her, there's a possibility that the pearls are real.

With a centering breath, I find my courage and ask, "How are you feeling?"

Have I been avoiding my father-in-law since his return home from the hospital? Most definitely. The last thing I need is for him to faint and fall down the stairs at the sight of me.

"Fine." His breath fogs the air, the tip of his nose pink. He fiddles with the scarf at his neck. "I wanted to ask you the same."

I laugh lightly. "I'm okay."

"Your dad called me."

The flinch is involuntary. The ache in my chest is one I've been ignoring since that day at the hospital. "He did?"

He pats my knee and gives me a look of pure apology. "He's not too happy with you, is he?"

"At least he didn't have a heart attack." Wincing, I give him a sheepish shrug. "Sorry. Bad joke."

Peter laughs anyway. "Fair enough. You two took me by surprise, and I guess that's all it took." He snaps his fingers.

I clutch my mittened hands, studying the pearl design. "I'm glad you're okay."

"Me too." He smiles at the boys out on the ice. "I love my boys, and I hope to have many more years with them. Now that they're starting to marry off, I hope to have some grandkids to love too someday."

I press my lips together and swallow back the sigh that tries to escape me. Daire needs to fess up, and soon.

"I'm sure you'll get some eventually."

Just not from me.

"Are you two going to move off campus?"

I wiggle my fingers inside my mittens. "We bought a house. It's beautiful. If you ever need to be near Nashville, you should come visit. Or just come for fun if you want."

Dammit. I'm rambling. Heat rushes to my cheeks as I bite my bottom lip to shut myself up.

"I'd like that." He shifts his legs slightly.

On the ice, Roman scores. He and Daire celebrate with Veda and taunt the others.

Shaking his head at their antics, Peter says, "These kids of mine never grow up."

"They're all pretty awesome."

My chest aches at the nostalgia of all of this. This family was an integral part of my life for years, but after Daire and I fell out, I missed all of this. These little things I loved so much. While I remained in touch with the others, mostly Cash and Roman, I no longer hung out with them. It would've been too awkward.

"Do you happen to know why Cash and Daire have been giving each other the silent treatment?"

On the ice, as if to demonstrate their father's point, they glower at each other but say nothing. Then Veda drops the puck, and they're off once more.

"I might," I admit, lowering my head.

Peter sighs, crossing his arms over his chest. "Growing up, Cash always had heart eyes for you. You were oblivious because—"

"Because I was always looking at Daire." More and more since I married Daire, that old heartache returns, but I swallow it down.

He flashes a smile. "Exactly. I thought things would change when Cash moved away, but apparently not."

I fiddle with my ring, spinning it on my finger. "He'll have to accept it eventually."

I might not have feelings for Cash, but that doesn't mean I don't sympathize with him. I know exactly what it's like to have feelings for someone and not have them reciprocated. Without my permission, my eyes find Daire. He streaks across the ice, working the puck back and forth with his stick.

Neither of us speaks for a few minutes.

"I really am sorry for ruining your break. I know it's a short one."

"Peter," I sigh, resting my head on his shoulder. "You did no such thing."

"It's hard to get all my boys together at the same time now that they're all grown. I finally made it work and…" He trails off, frowning sadly out at his kids.

"Things happen, but it's been nice to be together like this. Thanks for letting me stay with you."

Rubbing his jaw, he chuckles. "You're married to my son. You don't think I'd kick you out, do you?"

Right.

"Sorry." I shake my head, laughing softly. "I'm not used to it yet."

The smile on his face is nothing short of fond. "When I married Susie, it took a full year for it to sink in. Maybe two. I was so excited to call her my wife, but there were a few times I slipped up and said fiancée or even girlfriend. Believe me, she didn't let me forget it."

"You miss her."

"Every day." A sigh escapes him. "I wouldn't change a thing, though."

"Really?"

"Never." He looks over at me, tilting his head slightly. "A lot of people never have their great love. It might've been short, but I had it, and it was enough to last me a lifetime."

"That's…" Sadness floods me, and I have to choke back a wave of tears. "That's really beautiful."

"The game is over!" Daire bellows, his voice so loud it echoes through the empty rink. "We won. Get over it."

Cash isn't backing down. "By cheating."

Daire throws out his arms. "Where were we cheating? Tell me. Oh, you can't, because we did no such thing."

"Hey, hey, hey." Asher steps between his brothers and puts a hand on each of their chests in an effort to keep them apart. "Cash, they won fair and square. What are you going on about?"

"Daire is a lying, cheating—"

"No, I'm not."

"It's just a friendly game. Quit it," Asher scolds. He glowers at Cash, then Daire. I can't blame him for being annoyed. He's having to treat his grown brothers like children.

"Stop being such a douche," Roman adds unhelpfully.

"Me?" Cash seethes, pounding his chest with his glove. "What about him?"

"What the fuck did I do?" Daire volleys back, throwing one arm out. "I scored a point. We won. That's it. Why are we even arguing about this?"

Beside me, Peter shakes his head and mutters, "Boys."

Since I'm looking at Peter, I miss who throws the first punch, but suddenly, Daire and Cash are scuffling on the ice. Asher's trying to break it up. Roman is cheering them on. Hudson shakes his head and skates off toward the locker rooms.

"Guys!" I yell, standing up. "Quit it."

They're paying me no mind. I give Peter an apologetic look and hurry down to the ice. I'm not wearing skates, so I slip the second I step onto the slick surface. If not for Veda, who grabs me by the elbow, I'd already be on my ass.

"Thanks."

"No problem." She releases me with a warm smile.

"Guys, stop," I shout, shuffling closer.

It kills me to see them fighting. They've always been so close. It's especially painful knowing I'm probably the source of their frustration.

"Rosie, back off," Asher orders, putting a placating hand in my direction. "I don't want you to get hurt."

I ignore his pleas. "Daire, please stop. This is ridiculous."

I make the mistake of tilting forward and reaching for him. The instant I do, he's swinging his arm back to punch Cash, but he catches my face instead.

A bolt of pain works its way across my face as I drop to the ice.

Peter shouts from the stands, but I can't make out his words.

Shit. *Please don't let him have another heart attack.*

The pain is so intense that tears immediately fall from my eyes.

"Hey," a soft voice says.

Still stunned, I blink up at Roman.

"Let me help you up."

"Rosie!" Daire shouts. He shoves Cash away but

takes a graze of knuckles to his cheek in the process. Then he drops to his knees, sliding across the ice toward me.

The genuine worry on his face makes my treacherous heart skip a beat.

"Rosie, Rosie, Rosie." He chants my name, cupping my face gently with both hands—his gloves long gone from the tussle with his brother. He grazes a thumb around my eye, sending a zap of pain through me. "Shh," he soothes, ducking closer. "Fuck. I'm so sorry."

Behind him, a few feet away, Cash hangs his head and gives a sheepish look. "Sorry," he mouths.

"Was I the one who got you?" Daire asks, probing the back of my head in search of further injury.

I nod. "It was an accident."

"Doesn't matter," he mutters, shaking his head. "It shouldn't have happened." Without letting go, he twists at the waist and calls for Roman. "Go grab her some ice."

"Dude." Roman throws his arms out wide. "We're *on* ice."

Daire grunts at his little brother. "You want her to put her face on the slab of ice in the rink?" He turns back to me, continuing his examination of my head. "Idiot," he mumbles.

"Right. Ice. I'll get that now." Roman throws a thumbs-up before skating off.

"Come on." Daire takes my hands. "Let's get you up."

With far more grace than seems possible, he stands on his skates while hauling me up with him. And once I'm on my feet, he scoops me up bridal style.

Squeaking, I push against his shoulder. "I can walk."

In response, he just holds me closer. "This is quicker."

With a sigh, I hold on and let him do his thing. I can't argue with him there.

Off the ice, he eases me onto a bleacher. Peter has come down from where we were sitting a few rows up and slides in beside me.

"Are you okay, sweetie?" He angles forward and inspects my face with a frown.

"I'll be o—"

"She's going to have a black eye," Daire says, tugging at his hair. "This is your fault." He glares at Cash as he walks by on his way to the locker room.

Cash doesn't even bother replying, just shakes his head and continues on.

"The good news is, you took that like a champ," Veda says, settling in on the bleachers behind me.

"Really?" I ask, my tears beginning to subside.

"Totally."

"You're a bunch of infants," Asher mutters as he wanders by. "Grow up."

Hudson says nothing, just shoots me a concerned smile before going to change.

"Where the fuck is Roman with the ice?" Daire curses, straightening from his crouched position in front of me and scanning the rink. "I should've gotten it myself."

"I'll go check on him." Peter presses his hands to the cold surface beneath him, but before he can stand, Veda puts a hand on his shoulder.

"Stay put," she says. "I'll check on him."

"It's already bruising." Daire brushes his fingers ever so carefully over the sensitive skin around my eye. "I'm so sorry."

My first instinct is to tell him it's okay, that he doesn't need to fuss over me, but I keep my mouth shut because, selfishly, I *love* that he's doting on me right now. Even if it took an elbow to the face to receive the affection.

Roman returns, with Veda trailing behind him.

"This was the best I could do." He passes Daire a rag filled with ice cubes.

Daire says nothing as he takes the makeshift icepack and presses it to my face.

I wince from the icy chill of it, but it instantly dulls the throbbing.

Veda and Roman head off, leaving me with Daire and Peter.

"I've got this, Dad," Daire says, frowning at Peter. "You don't need to worry."

Peter gives a humorless laugh. "Don't tell me not to worry when you were just in a fistfight with your brother."

Daire sighs, his entire body deflating. "If he wasn't interested in fucking my wife, I wouldn't be fighting him."

Peter shakes his head. "Some fights aren't worth picking. Rosie is *your* wife. You already won." He gives Daire's shoulder a squeeze. "I'll be in the lobby."

It's strange, sitting here alone with Daire. So far, since we arrived, we've spent our days doing everything we can to not be alone together, and at night, we slip into bed without saying a word.

Daire's blue eyes swim with sympathy and remorse. "I really am sorry."

"You really need to stop fighting with your brother. Your dad's right."

With a sigh, he slides onto the cold surface beside me, careful to keep the ice gently pressed to my cheek.

"I don't know why I feel so territorial," he admits, lowering his head.

"I'm not sure either," I say, my heart beating a strange rhythm in response to his words. "You hate me, remember?"

I hate to admit it, but at least my reasons for hating him are starting to feel a bit juvenile.

"Right," he says softly, Adam's apple bobbing. "How does it feel?"

"Cold."

He laughs at my answer, the blue of his eyes lightening some. "I have to change, and then we'll go."

With a nod, I stand.

He rises too, his hands hovering around me like he's afraid I might fall over.

"I'm okay," I assure him. "I'll wait with your dad in the lobby."

He studies me, his lips turned down, like he wants to argue, but after a silent moment, he acquiesces.

I pull the ice away from my face and wander out of the rink. In the lobby, I find Peter sitting in one of the uncomfortable-looking chairs, so I join him, trying to ignore the pounding in my head.

He tilts forward and gently pats my knee. "I think I have ibuprofen in the car."

"That would be much appreciated." My smile is entirely grateful.

"I have some stuff for bruising we can apply to your face when we get back to the house too. With five roughhousing boys, I should've taken stock in arnica. It'll also help with the pain."

I press the ice to my face again. It's beginning to melt, leaving my fingers wet, but I keep it there anyway. The more I ice it now, the less swelling I'll have later.

"I always thought you'd be a part of this family."

My chest tightens at the sentiment, and I shift in my seat so I'm facing Peter. "Really?"

"I thought the two of you would go the more traditional route, but it was inevitable."

"Me and Daire?" Surely the hit to my head has given me a concussion. There's no way he means Daire.

He laughs quietly. "I questioned it there for a while, when you guys fell out of touch, but I had a gut feeling you'd eventually find your way back."

Daire and Roman appear, Roman knocking into his brother's shoulder. They're laughing, but when Daire spots me, he quickly sobers.

"How does it feel?" He crouches in front of me, gently pulling the ice away from my face. "It's not looking too bad."

"Is he lying?" I ask Roman.

Roman bends down too, peering at me. "It looks better than expected."

"Good." I stand, returning the ice to my face. "Let's get out of here."

fifteen

DAIRE

EVEN THOUGH I'M living with Rosie, along with a whole host of complicated thoughts and emotions, it's good to be home.

The trip to New York for Thanksgiving was nothing short of a shitshow I'd prefer to put behind me.

From the opposite end of the sectional couch in our living room, Rosie frowns at her phone.

I watch her, surveying her face. Guilt eats at me every time I see her black eye. I was so pissed at Cash that I had no idea she was even on the ice.

He'd been begging for a beating from the moment we

got to the rink. By the end of the game, I'd reached my breaking point, and when he tried to claim I'd cheated, I snapped. He was only trying to get a rise out of me. Even then I knew that, but I couldn't control my temper.

"Your face is going to freeze like that," I tell Rosie when her frown deepens.

She looks up from her phone. "Huh?"

I turn the volume down on the TV. Neither of us is paying it much attention anyway.

"You look annoyed."

"Oh." She sets her phone face down beside her. "Just my dad."

"Is he still not talking to you?"

She shakes her head. "He told me to stop texting him—that he doesn't have anything to say to me." Her shoulders sag. "Do you think now would be a good time to thank him for buying this house?" She jokes, her smile hollow.

"I really don't know why I told Cree that." I was panicked. In my brain, it made more sense to tell him that someone other than me had bought the house. My thoughts weren't exactly logical, but I can't recant the declaration now.

"It's whatever." She waves a dismissive hand. "I knew he'd be upset, but I didn't think he'd be so mad he'd stop speaking to me."

The sadness radiating from her is almost too much

for me to bear. I so badly want to make her feel better, but I don't have the first clue how.

I'm saved from possibly sticking my foot in my mouth in an attempt to cheer her up when the doorbell rings.

Arching a brow, I ask her, "Expecting someone?"

Brows pulled low, she shakes her head. "No. Did you order pizza?"

"No."

When the bell rings a second time, she rolls her eyes. "It's probably a delivery that needs a signature or something."

"It's after eight. Do they really deliver packages this late?"

She narrows her eyes at me and scowls. "I didn't invite someone over, if that's what you're getting at."

With a sigh, I stand. "I'll get the door."

"I'll get the door," she mimics in a sarcastic tone, following me.

As I approach, I make a mental note to have a peephole installed. If that's a thing. If not, I'll have a new door put in. Without a clue who's waiting on the other side, I swing it open.

"Bertie!" Rosie shrieks before the identity of the girl in front of me registers. Rosie practically shoves me out of the way so she can hug her best friend. "I missed you."

"You were going to see her tomorrow anyway," I grumble at the intrusion.

"Hey, just because you stole her from me doesn't mean you get to keep her all the time." Bertie pokes me in the shoulder. When she turns back to Rosie, she gasps. "What happened to you?" She makes fists at me, like she's ready to fight. "Did you hurt her?"

"What?" Rosie asks, closing the door. "Oh! My eye? It was an accident. I tried to break up a fight. I shouldn't have stepped in."

Bertie narrows her eyes on me. "I take it you were the one in the fight?"

Head tipped back, I plant my hands on my hips and sigh. "Perhaps."

"It's not a big deal." Rosie grabs her friend's wrist and tugs her over to the couch. "Look, we finally have furniture. I don't have a proper bed yet, but it's coming."

"How's this fake marriage of yours going?"

I stand awkwardly in the doorway of the living room, watching the two of them. I'm not exactly ready to go up to bed, but it feels weird interfering with their girl time.

Rosie settles on the couch, looking my way at Bertie's question. "It's going fine, I guess."

"Hey." Bertie snaps her fingers at me. "Make yourself useful and pop some popcorn."

Rosie laughs, her dark hair swishing around her

shoulders. I watch her for a moment too long before I shake myself out of my stupor.

With a grunt, I take a step back. "Any other requests?"

"Wine if you have it." Bertie snaps her fingers. "Ooh, or champagne."

"Why would we have champagne?" I mutter, turning for the kitchen. "I don't even know if we have popcorn."

I locate a bottle of wine in the fridge, but we don't have wineglasses. The girls will have to make do with plain ole drinking glasses. I fill each halfway, then search the pantry for popcorn. There's not much in there, so it doesn't take me long to deduce that there is none.

Taking their glasses of wine to the living room, I tell Bertie, "No popcorn."

"That's okay," she says with an unaffected shrug. "Order us pizza or something."

Rosie giggles, flicking a brief glance my way. "She's testing you," she mouths.

Testing me? Am I passing? And why do I care?

"What kind of pizza?"

"Veggie." Bertie tucks her legs under her and brings her glass to her lips.

"Anything else?" I arch a brow, waiting.

"Cheesy breadsticks would be great too."

I sigh. "You got it."

In the kitchen, I place the order. Then I pace. I'm full of restless energy without a good way to burn it off. A year ago, my life was vastly different. Now, I'm flailing around like a fish waiting for *something*. We're at a standstill in the custody petition while we wait for the DNA test to come back and confirm what I already know.

I text Cree to see if he's free but pocket my phone when he doesn't immediately respond. I doubt I'll hear from him. He's so far up Ophelia's butt it's not even funny. *All* my friends are settling down. It's fucking weird. Laughable, coming from me, since I'm the one who's actually married.

The worst part is, I'm starting to think I might be a little jealous of their situations.

I haven't had a girlfriend since high school. Sure, I've been out with several girls more than once, but I never stuck around long.

Rosie appears in the doorway, startling me from my wandering thoughts.

She shakes her head back and forth like I'm a mirage she can unsee. "Why are you sulking in the kitchen?" She grabs a glass from the cabinet and adds ice. When we came home after Thanksgiving, several large boxes full of dishes and glasses from Anthropologie were waiting on the porch. Rosie was like a kid on Christmas after I carried them in. She tore into each box, oohing and aahing over every piece. Literally every one. Even dishes identical to the previous one she'd opened.

"I'm not sulking."

As she fills her glass with water, she gives me side-eyed look. "Sure looks it."

I cross my arms over my chest. "Well, I'm not."

With a laugh, she sets the glass on the quartz counter. "Sure looks like it." She nods at my crossed my arms. "You can hang out with us. You don't have to hide away if Bertie is here."

"I don't want to intrude on your girl time or whatever."

"All right." She picks up the glass with a smile. "Suit yourself."

After the pizza arrives, I snag a plate for myself, then take the boxes to the girls. Look at me, being all domestic and shit.

Rosie's eyes follow me as I leave the room. I can practically feel her laughing at me.

Poor Daire. He doesn't know what to do with himself.

No. I shake my head and push away the thought. I can't imagine Rosie pitying me in any way.

Pizza in hand, I head to my room. I'm still sleeping on an air mattress and living out of a suitcase. Damn, it'll feel good to sleep in a real bed once the rest of the furniture is delivered.

I plop onto the mattress, making a note to add air to it before going to sleep, and turn on the TV I've got propped against the wall. As I scroll through the channels in search of something to entertain me, I take a bite of greasy pizza. None of the shows or movies I come across grab my attention, and I'm not in the mood to play video games. I'm still too damn restless. Now's the time I'd usually workout, but I no longer have access to an in-home gym like I did when I lived with my friends. I could use the one on campus, but I have no interest in driving all the way there.

"Maybe I should go for a run," I mutter to myself. If I do, though, I should stop eating. Otherwise, I'll get sick. I lower my head and inspect my slice of pizza. Nah. I'd rather eat.

A couple of hours later—after I've brushed my teeth and stripped down for sleep—my bedroom door eases open. Rosie pokes her head in.

"Bertie left. You can stop hiding now."

I stifle a yawn. "It's all good. I'm ready for bed, anyway."

Guilt prickles at me as I take her in. Her eye really does look bad. I didn't *mean* to hit her, but it doesn't change the fact that I did. Worry worms its way in along with the guilt the longer she stands there. Could her injury be used against me in the custody battle that's bound to ensue? I hate that my thoughts go there, that I'm so preoccupied with how her black eye could affect me, but I can't help it.

"What's going on in that brain of yours?"

I chuckle humorlessly, crossing my arms behind my head. I have to crane my neck to look up at her from the air mattress.

"You don't want to know."

She opens the door wider, crossing her arms over her chest. "Try me."

"It was selfish."

"You're a selfish person. I'm not surprised you'd have selfish thoughts."

The mouth on this girl.

I breathe through the guilt and the trepidation and the annoyance and force the words out. "I was thinking about how your black eye might be used against me."

"Used against—*oh*. Please." She rolls her eyes. "As if I wouldn't be honest about how it happened. Besides, there were witnesses. You don't think your dad would explain it? Or any of your brothers? You do realize you have to tell them about Junior eventually, right?"

"But they're my family—people will think they're lying to help me. Even if they do believe me, I still look shitty, since the truth is that it happened because I was fighting with my brother."

I ignore her question about telling my family. Obviously, I should have broken the news while we were there, but after the declaration of our marriage gave my dad a literal heart attack? No way was I going to risk killing him by telling him about my son.

Rosie throws her hands up. "You're borrowing trouble. Nothing has been said or done yet, so try not to worry until you have a reason to. Think you can manage that?"

"I'll try."

"Good." With a wink, she adds, "Lighten up, buttercup. Night."

"Buttercup?" I mutter to myself after she's gone.

Shuddering at the nickname, I replay her words in my head, considering her advice. She's right. Worrying about it now won't do me any good.

But I keep fucking up at every turn.

And it feels like my chance of getting any sort of custody is slipping from my fingers.

sixteen

ROSIE

BERTIE and I navigate the stands, searching for our seats near the box the guys will be in after they come out. As we get settled, my heart hammers with excitement. I've been called a puck bunny in the past, and sure, I have slept with several of the guys on the team, but I grew up around the sport thanks to Daire and his brothers. And I love it. I crave the thrill of the game.

I keep my jacket on for now because the arena is chilly, but once the game gets going, I'll warm right up. Sitting still at a game is virtually impossible for me. Through all three periods, I'm up and down. Cheering and yelling my annoyance when the ref makes a bad call.

Daire and I drove separately since he needed to be at the rink early and I was picking up Bertie.

Before I left, I expertly applied makeup to my bruised eye, following a tutorial I found online. Surprisingly, it worked well.

The attention of girls around us weighs on me, but I ignore their scrutiny. I've gotten good at it over the years. I've had to in order to stay sane. Girls are jealous, vapid creatures. It's why I've held on tight to Bertie. A truly good friend is a rarity; there's no way I'll let her go.

"These bleachers are so uncomfortable," she gripes, wiggling her butt. "You'd think Aldridge could invest in actual arena seats."

"They have plans to replace them, but they keep putting it off."

"How do you know that?"

I shrug, tugging the sleeves of my sweatshirt down to the tips of my fingers. It's less out of a need to warm my hands and more of a nervous habit—like a turtle burrowing into its shell.

"Slut." The word is a low hiss behind me.

It's directed at me, which is beyond laughable because these same girls have slept with multiple players too.

The difference?

I just married one — the one they all want but have never had.

Not that Daire doesn't sleep around. I've heard the stories, but it's a well-known fact on campus that he won't touch the puck bunnies. Maybe, in some weird, fucked-up way, that's why I became one. So I could convince myself that's why he didn't want me.

I brush my hair behind my ear with shaky fingers.

I've done my best over the years to act like losing Daire doesn't bother me, but in reality, it was, and still is, one of the biggest losses I've ever suffered.

I loved him.

As a friend.

As something more.

And then I lost him, and I was left floundering.

"You married Daire, right?" One girl snickers. I turn her way as the guys skate onto the ice. Cheers ring out, but the sound is dull thanks to the roar of blood in my ears. My face warms, and my heart rate picks up. I shouldn't have turned around. There's no way anything nice will come out of this girl's mouth.

I locate her behind me and over a few seats. She's smirking at me with one perfectly sculpted brow arched, like she thinks she's so much better than me. Her sleek blond hair is stick straight and her lips are glossy. She would be pretty if she wasn't giving me such a nasty look. With her upper lip curled like that, she looks like she ate something nasty.

"Yes," I reply, hoping my answer will be good enough.

I turn, desperately wanting to watch the game that's about to begin and to *not* engage with an army of mean girls.

"How does it feel to know you married a guy who hates you?"

This is the first game I've attended since we got married. The last few were away games. I knew going into this that I was bound to face some snide comments. Regardless, they still sting.

"Hey, watch your mouth," Bertie snaps, grasping my hand and squeezing gently.

I recognize the girl. We were in class together last year. It takes me a few seconds, but her name finally comes to mine. Hannah. A soft, pretty name. It doesn't fit the scowling ice princess behind me.

"It was an honest question," she says, her tone flippant. "He pity married you, you know."

I roll my eyes.

If anything, I pity married him, but go off, sis.

"You're nothing but a whore," another voice chimes in. "What would he want with you anyway?"

Despite how hard my heart is pounding, I keep my attention fixed on the rink and do my best to ignore them.

It's impossible to block out the words completely as

they pummel me from all sides, but I don't give them the satisfaction of speaking to any of them again.

It hurts that girls can be so vicious to one another when we should be on each other's sides.

Daire's on the bench, and every minute or so, he glances my way, wearing a worried frown. There's no way he can hear what the girls are saying, but it's obvious he can tell that something is off. I paste on a smile. The last thing I want to do is be a distraction for him.

"Hey." I turn to Bertie, being sure to keep my focus fixed on her and not the girls farther down the bench. "I'm going to get a Coke. You want anything?"

She shakes her head. "I don't think so."

I scoot my way to the stairs, then hurry up them. I'm winded by the time I reach the level where the concession and bathrooms are.

I bypass the food, ignoring the way the smell of buttery popcorn calls my name, and burst into the bathroom. Since the game is in full force, it's empty. I close myself in a stall and lean my back against the door.

The tears come in a torrent.

My makeup is going to be ruined, but I can't make them stop.

Normally I'm impervious to what people say about me. At the end of the day, they don't *know* me, and that fact alone usually keeps me from feeling bad about myself.

Today, their words cut me in a way nothing has before.

Wiping my nose with the back of my hand, I take one deep breath after another, willing the tears to stop.

The bathroom door opens with a bang, and I hold my breath.

"Rosie?"

Bertie.

"I had to pee."

I cringe. Shit. If my rushed response wasn't enough to make it obvious I'm upset, the thickness in my voice definitely is.

"Rosie," she says softly, her voice directly behind me. "I'm sorry."

I choke down a sob. The tenderness in her tone guts me. "Why are you apologizing?"

"Because you don't deserve to be talked about like that."

I suck my bottom lip between my teeth, biting down. "Can you just give me a minute?"

"Sure, but after you dust yourself off, come back down there and show those bitches that they can't touch you."

"Thanks, B."

"Anytime."

She retreats, her steps getting quieter, then the door squeaks shut behind her.

It takes me a few minutes to fully pull myself together, then another couple to clean up my makeup.

I grab a Coke and popcorn before returning to my seat.

Bertie flashes me a smile. In contrast, the girls around us glare daggers, clearly less than pleased by my return. They can kiss my ass.

I flip my hair over my shoulder, doing my best to appear unbothered. Whether they believe it or not, I stick with the act and pay them no more attention the rest of the game, even though they practically beg for it.

When the game is over and the players file off the ice, Bertie and I begin the slow exit out of the arena. The girls gossip ahead of us, talking about the guys and who they're dying to see.

Since I drove here, I plan to head straight to the dorms to drop off Bertie and then home. The rest of our furniture was delivered, and I've been enjoying every minute of my new mattress.

We're almost to the exit when my phone buzzes in my pocket. I pull it out and furrow my brows at the text from Daire.

"Daire wants me to wait for him outside the locker room."

"Oh." Bertie looks around. "Where's that?"

"This way."

I clasp her wrist, leading the way. I've waited in this hall an embarrassing number of times. But never have I waited for Daire—unless trying to catch a glimpse of him counts.

The group of girls who were being snotty during the game stand in a cluster. When they see me, they roll their eyes as a collective. It's like watching a flock of birds mimic each other.

Bertie scans the hallway, taking everything in. With the way she's worrying her bottom lip, it's obvious she's uncomfortable. She's never come to the locker area with me before. In the past, when she did attend games with me, she usually met Tommy after.

She's been doing well since the breakup. I'm hoping she'll get out there and start dating again soon, but I won't push her to move on if she's not ready.

I pull my phone out again, hoping for an explanation as to why Daire requested my presence, but the screen is blank. Blowing out a breath, I lean against the wall and settle in.

"Thanks for waiting with me."

"You are my ride," Bertie points out.

A little chuckle escapes me. "And I promise I'll get you home and tucked into bed soon."

She bumps my hip with hers. "I appreciate it."

"I'm sorry I haven't been able to hang out as much."

Smiling, she turns to face me and leans a shoulder against the wall. "It's okay."

It doesn't feel like it is. Not to me, anyway.

I want to say more. To promise I'll make time with

her more of a priority, but before I can, the locker room door opens, catching our attention. Justin, the team captain, heads over to his girlfriend. He wraps an arm around her waist and buries his face in her neck. She laughs and pushes him back gently with a hand on his chest. Love radiates off both of them.

A stupid pang of jealousy hits me.

Is it selfish that I want that? A guy who's obsessed with me? A love that's real?

A lump forms in my throat.

All I've ever wanted is to love and be loved in return.

A couple more guys head out, some ignoring the gathering as they stride by. A few guys hang back and approach the group of girls. Giggles ensue, and I can't help but roll my eyes. To think I was ever that ridiculous makes me want to throw up.

Finally, Daire emerges. At the sight of him, my breath catches. His blond hair is damp from the shower and a shade darker than normal. Denim blue eyes fix on me almost immediately. Face serious, jaw set, he stalks toward me.

I hold my breath, and my heart thumps against my sternum. What the hell is with the look?

"Whoa," Bertie whispers. Is she as taken aback by his intensity as I am?

He loops his arm around my neck and pulls me in with so much force I practically fall into his chest, fingers splaying over his shirt. Half a heartbeat later, his mouth descends on mine. Unprepared for the kiss, I freeze the second our lips touch.

He hasn't kissed me since we exchanged vows—why would he?—but now he kisses me like a man returning from war, desperate to reestablish a connection with the love of his life. It's the way I've always dreamed of being kissed. He runs his tongue along the seam of my lips, urging me to open up to him.

I shouldn't, dammit, but my body responds to him in a way it never has with anyone else. The heat of him seeps into me as he holds me close. I swear he's an actual, human furnace.

Every time he pulls back slightly, I expect him to sever our connection, but he just dives back in, practically devouring me.

Somewhere in the back of my mind, I know I should put an end to this.

Why is he kissing me? Obviously, it's not because he wants to. So what's his ulterior motive?

When he finally does release me, I'm embarrassingly out of breath.

He presses a tender kiss to the top of my head as I cling to him, steadying myself. The gesture is far too sweet to have come from the guy who doesn't like me.

"I missed you, babe." He nuzzles his nose against mine. "Longest game of my life."

What is he playing at?

"I missed you too."

"I have a few things to finish up here, and then I'll see you at home." He leans in, and in a hushed tone that's still loud enough to be overheard, he says, "Be wearing that black lacy set I love so much."

He kisses me again, so quick my head spins, and then he's gone.

What the fuck just happened?

Bertie blinks at me, her eyes wide. Her look says *you have some explaining to do*.

I'm hit with looks dripping with jealousy from every angle. Even from girls who've already secured a guy for the night.

A couple more guys exit the locker room, and one of them—Luke—takes an extra-long look our way. It's not me he's fixated on, but Bertie. I've never heard the guy speak more than five words at a time. He's a scholarship student, and from what I've heard, a bit of a bad boy. But he's a damn good hockey player.

In all the times I've stood in this very hall trying to score a hookup, I've never seen him pay attention to a single girl. If I hadn't heard rumors of his extracurricular activities, I'd think maybe the guy was a monk.

He faces forward, but before he turns the corner, he steals one more look at her.

Beside me, Bertie is checking her phone, oblivious.

Giddy, I grab her hand. "Luke Covey was totally

checking you out!" I sound way too excited. I blame it on the high I'm still experiencing from Daire's kiss.

"Who?" she asks as she loops her arm through mine and tugs me away from the other girls. Before I can answer, she leans in close and changes the subject. "What was that kiss about?"

"I have no idea." I slide my arm from hers so I can search through my purse for my keys as we walk.

"Did he tell you why he wanted you to wait?"

I shake my head. "No."

Her eyes narrow on me.

Keys in hand, I pull up short. "I'm serious."

With a sigh, she says, "Tommy never kissed me like that, and he supposedly loved me." She looks off into the distance, her mouth turned down at the corners. "I miss him. Is that terrible? I know I'm better off. True love shouldn't feel like an off- and on-again roller-coaster. Still, I'm sad."

"Aw, Bertie." I loop my arm around her shoulders and pull her in for a side hug. "It's okay to be sad. You were with him for a long time."

As we approach my car, I hit the unlock button on my key fob, and once we're settled with the heat blasting to ward off the chill, I turn to her and grasp her hand. "It might not feel like it now, but you'll find someone who treats you the way you deserve."

Maybe someone like Luke. If the way he was checking her out is anything to go by, there's definite interest there. "You're beautiful. Some guy is going to sweep you off your feet in no time."

She looks out the window, eyes swimming with pain. "I hope so."

I hate seeing her feeling down, especially over a kiss that was most certainly not real.

"Want to get ice cream before I drop you off?"

She perks up instantly. "I'll never say no to ice cream."

THE HOUSE IS dark when I step inside. Daire's car is still missing, so I assume he went out with the guys.

I let myself in and turn on the light in the tiny laundry room.

As the space brightens, a black eight-legged blur rushes past my foot.

The scream that comes out of me is shrill to say the least.

"Ew, ew, ew," I chant, shaking my hands and gagging. "Not a spider. Why me?"

I'm on the verge of tears, paralyzed by fear.

"Get into the house," I mutter to myself. "Don't be a weenie."

I scurry through the small space and open the door that leads into the kitchen, then I promptly slam it behind me.

Bile creeps up my throat and my entire body goes hot as I gag again. For a long moment, I stand with my back to the door, fanning my face and breathing through the nausea.

If Daire were home, I have no doubt he'd tell me how dramatic I am. I can't help it if the thought of a spider skittering through the house scares me.

The spider and I didn't come into contact with one another. Nonetheless, my skin crawls. Desperate for a shower, I sprint upstairs and say a prayer that there are no more little critters running around.

I close my door and strip my clothes off as I head into the bathroom. While the water heats, I pull a fresh towel from under the sink and drape it over the shower door.

When steam begins to fill the bathroom, I clip my hair up and step inside.

I scrub my body thoroughly, unable to fight the urge to decontaminate myself, and figure I might as well shave my legs while I'm in here.

I'm usually in and out of the shower quickly, but tonight, I spend a solid forty minutes under the scalding spray, letting it soothe my muscles and calm my mind.

Once my body is dry and I've slathered lotion over every inch of skin, I slip into a pair of black sweatpants and a purple cropped sweatshirt.

As I'm shaking out my hair, I hear movement downstairs—the squeak of a barstool—and an unbidden wave of comfort washes over me. Daire's home.

My stomach rumbles as I step out into the hall, reminding me I haven't eaten dinner. The popcorn I stuffed into my mouth and the ice cream with Bertie hardly counts.

I find Daire in the kitchen setting a hodgepodge of ingredients on the island.

"I'm starving. What are you making?"

He chuffs a laugh. "Not anything fun. Just chicken and veggies."

"Ugh. Boring." I flip my hair over my shoulder dramatically. "Can I have some anyway?"

He shakes his head, his upper lip curling in amusement. "Sure, as long as you don't tell me how much you don't like it."

I mime zipping my lips. "I won't say a word."

He washes his hands, then gets to work preparing everything.

As he works, I wait, thinking he'll bring up the kiss, but he remains focused on the task at hand.

Once the oven chimes, signaling that it's preheated, he slides the tray of chicken into the oven and washes his hands again.

"Daire?"

Holding a knife in one hand and a steadying a stalk of broccoli on a cutting board with the other, he flicks his head slightly to force an errant piece of blond hair out of his eyes. "Hmm?"

"Why … um … why did you kiss me?" I tap my nails on the counter softly while I wait for his answer, pretending my heart isn't racing a mile a minute.

He lowers the knife to the cutting board and narrows those denim blue eyes on me. "Why do you *think* I kissed you?"

A lump lodges in my throat, but I swallow past it and sit up straight. "If I knew, I wouldn't be asking."

With a sigh, he runs his fingers through his hair. Then he presses his hands flat on the counter, fingers splayed, and stares at me. Through me. Straight to my soul.

"I might not know exactly what those girls were saying to you, but I can guess. I wanted to show them you're mine."

My throat goes dry. I like the sound of him calling me his *way* too much for a fake relationship.

"Th-Thank you," I stammer.

"I saw how uncomfortable you were." He curls his hands into fists on the quartz countertop. "I didn't like that."

"It's just jealousy." I shrug, going for dismissive. "They want you."

"Doesn't matter." He picks up the knife and chops the stem off the broccoli. "I dragged you into this mess.

They might not know that, but it doesn't matter. They have no right to treat you the way they did."

I lower my head as tears spring to my eyes. I don't want him to see me emotional, but I can't help it. I have a thick skin, but sometimes, words cut deep. Those girls don't know me, but that doesn't stop it from hurting me.

The next thing I know, his hands are on my cheeks, tilting my face up so I'm forced to look at him.

"Listen," he says, his face a mask of pain. "I know I'm not the best person at times, but I won't stand for anyone being shitty to you like that. You and me? We're a team now. You hear me?" He holds tight, his eyes bouncing between mine.

With a sniffle, I nod.

"Good." With that single word, he releases me and steps back, returning his focus to preparing dinner.

I'm not quite sure what to make of this version of Daire — this Daire who's going out of his way to protect me like he did when we were kids.

I'm so used to the animosity between us that somehow it almost feels easier.

With a cleansing breath, I shuffle to the fridge. Wine bottle in hand, I pour myself a glass, then I take a seat at the island. I'd be crazy to turn down the opportunity to watch a hot guy cook.

He rubs his jaw and clears his throat. "I, uh — I need to get baby stuff. And I need your help."

I arch a skeptical brow, spinning my wineglass. "You're enlisting my help for baby stuff? Why?"

"Because you're a girl."

Huffing a laugh, I shake my head. "So because I have a vagina, I'm automatically supposed to know all things baby?"

He presses the heel of his hand into his eye and rubs. "I just figured you'd have a better idea than me. The DNA test is supposed to come back sometime this week, and I'm just ... trying to be prepared."

"I still can't believe you went through all of this," I flick my fingers lazily, gesturing to the house around us, then I wiggle my left hand, letting the light catch the diamonds, "before you had the DNA test done."

He narrows his eyes. "I know that's my kid. The DNA test is only a formality. The sooner I get things in order, the better, and there are so many things I need to take care of. A new car, the room, stroller, car seat ... fuck." He drops his head back. "My lawyer said I need to set up a trust in case anything happens to me and—"

"Whoa." I hold my hands up. "Let's take one thing at a time. What's something you can accomplish relatively easily within the next day or two?"

"Um..." He cocks his head to the side and presses his lips into a straight line, looking as though I've asked him a complicated math problem. "A new car shouldn't be a problem. I've only put it off because I really like the Porsche."

"You know you could afford to keep it and still get something else, right?" I mutter sarcastically, but before he can snap back, I wave a hand. "All right, the vehicle situation needs to be handled in the next three days—does that sound agreeable to you?"

He pulls the oven door open and bends to check on the chicken. "I suppose."

Men.

"You know what else is easy?"

He straightens, facing me. "What?"

I give him a blinding smile. "Shopping. Like you said, Junior is going to need a car seat, stroller, crib, bottles, clothes..." I heave a breath and cringe. "And whatever else babies need. Haul your happy ass to Target and get to shopping."

His eyes widen. "That sounds horrifying."

"Don't be dramatic. Shopping is fun."

"Maybe for you."

"Well." I place my palms down on the cool counter. "I'm not going shopping for Junior by myself, if that's what you're getting at. We can go this weekend. *Together.*"

Daire sighs and pulls the lid off the steamer basket to check the broccoli. "Fine."

"You should look online—find parenting blogs with recommendations."

He drops the lid and turns to me, wearing a scowl. "We can't just figure it out when we get there?"

"No," I drawl. "You need a list. I'm not the baby whisperer. I'm not going to magically know what your spawn needs just because I have ovaries. Figure it out."

I'm not trying to be *mean*, but I can't hold his hand through this thing. He's a dad now. He has to step up and learn how to parent.

"I can do this," he mutters more to himself than me. "I can handle it."

"I'll help some," I concede. He did help me out with the hockey bitches tonight, so I can certainly return the favor. "But I'm not handling all of it by myself."

He reaches out a hand to me. "Deal."

seventeen

DAIRE

A COUPLE OF MONTHS AGO, I never could have imagined I'd be perusing the baby care aisles of Target on a Saturday, much less with Rosie at my side.

Tucking a piece of dark hair behind one ear, she scans the lineup of pacifiers with a furrowed brow, her lips parted.

I stare at the choices as well, appalled. "Why are there so many choose to from? And why are they all shaped differently?"

She plucks one off the shelf and shakes the plastic package, like maybe it'll change form or something.

Lips pursed, she tilts her head, appraising them. "I don't have an answer for you."

With a sigh, she drops it into the cart, then she proceeds to add one of each kind.

I wince as each one hits the plastic cart, my eyes locked on Rosie.

"What?" she asks. "We don't know which one Junior will prefer, and you can afford it."

My chest goes so tight it's hard to breathe. "I can't do this," I say, clutching at the collar of my T-shirt.

She turns slowly and takes me in with a surprisingly gentle expression. "You can. You're his dad. You'll figure it out."

I haven't voiced this part out loud. I've barely even been able to *think* it. "I'm scared."

"Good."

My stomach drops. *I can't have heard her right.*

"Good?"

"Yeah." She turns back to the smorgasbord of baby stuff. "I'd be concerned if you weren't. This is a human being, not an old toaster you inherited."

My lips quirk. "An old toaster?"

She flicks her fingers lazily, moving down the aisle toward the bottles. "It was the first thing that popped into my head. Sue me."

She did that all the time when we were young. She'd come out with the most random explanations and scenarios. I think I missed that.

I think I missed *her*.

"Jesus. This is ridiculous." She huffs. "One of each," she declares, grabbing one bottle after another and tossing them into the cart. "Once we know what he likes, we can return what we didn't open or donate it and get him more of what he does like."

"All right," I agree. Down another aisle, she leaves me to pick a camera monitor for his bedroom while she picks out crib bedding.

Babies need a lot of crap. More than I ever realized.

I'm still looking at specs when Rosie waddles back to me with an armful of sheets and blankets and God only knows what else.

Hands on her hips she surveys the overflowing cart. "I better go get another."

Before I can protest, she's flouncing down the aisle, dark hair disappearing around the corner when she turns.

Pulling my phone from my pocket, I go over the list I made after I spent hours on the internet researching, then I cross off the things I know we've put in the cart. I was going to order a crib and stuff for his room, but Rosie gave me a look and said she'd handle it—then she started muttering about wallpaper and paint. I don't have the first clue what she'll turn the nursery into, but I'll let her have her fun.

I peruse the aisles, adding items to my overflowing cart and crossing them off on my phone as I go. I smile in satisfaction at all the checked bubbles. I'm finally starting to get somewhere.

Except I haven't gotten to meet my son yet.

What if he hates me?

That thought has plagued me since the moment I decided to pursue custody. I have no experience with babies. What if he senses that right off the bat?

Rosie steers an empty cart down the aisle. "What's put that look on your face?"

I almost don't answer her, but regardless of the distance we've maintained for years, regardless of our falling out, she's once again become the one person I feel like I can share my fears with. "What if he doesn't like me?"

"Who?"

I rub at my chest, hoping to dull the ache behind my ribs. "Sammy."

"Oh." She nods, appraising an aisle filled with diapers. "Junior. Got it. He's a baby, and babies can be weird … I think. I have no experience." With one hand still on the cart, she waves the other in circles in front of her. "It might take him a bit to warm up to you, but I'm pretty sure that's normal. You can't expect everything to be rainbows and sunshine from the get-go."

"I know," I grumble. "Jesus." I let out a low breath, overwhelmed by all the diaper choices. Every package is a different size, and they're all labeled with numbers that make no sense to me. "I don't know which one he needs."

With a sigh, she shrugs. "We'll just keep doing what we've been doing and get a few different kinds."

"All right."

By the time we check out, I've spent a ridiculous amount of money. I say a silent prayer of thanks that I have access to my own trust and that my dad can't monitor the money that goes in and out of it. If he could, he'd be calling before the end of the day with questions about why I dropped several grand at Target.

In the parking lot, I load up Rosie's Mercedes. Thank fuck we had the forethought to bring it. There's no way all this stuff would fit into my Porsche. I'm already mourning the loss of my motorcycle, and my beloved car is the next to go. I have a kid now. It's time to be responsible. Sports cars and motorcycles aren't safe, and I plan to be around a good long while.

My phone rings, and when I pull it from my pocket, my lawyer's name flashes on the screen. "I need to take this," I tell Rosie.

"I can finish this up."

I nod in thanks and slide into the passenger side of the SUV before I answer the call.

"Hello?"

"Hello, Mr. Hendricks," Nina croons over the line. Nina Voss is incredible at what she does. In the end, it'll be worth every penny I've given her. I have no doubt she'll do all she can to make sure I have rights to my son. "I have some good news."

My heart lurches. I've never heard that phrase—*I have some good news*—from her. "Really?" I straighten in the seat. "What about?"

"Now that the DNA is back and I've shown the court documentation that proves you've been working toward meeting your son for months, they've granted you a supervised visit."

Hand shaking, I press the phone closer to my ear. "Is that normal?"

"I might've pulled a few strings to make a visit happen this early."

I run my fingers through my hair. "When?"

"Tomorrow."

Despite how desperate I am to meet Sammy, my stomach drops out from under me. "Tomorrow?"

She laughs softly. "Yes. I'll text you the address. I'll be there. A social worker will be in attendance too."

"Okay, okay," I chant, on the verge of hysterical laughter. Fuck, my emotions are thrown all out of whack. I finally get to meet him. Hold him.

I don't want to fuck this up.

"Thank you."

"Sure thing." She clears her throat. "Bring your ... wife."

Nina was disgusted after she saw the video of my drunken tirade, but she expertly handled all damage control, and she has been working with me to figure out the best way to explain it if it comes up in court. So far, our best defense is that it was a massive lapse in judgment, mixed with too much alcohol, because I was coping with the unexpected news of finding out I had a son. It's mostly true. And the court doesn't need to know that I knew about it before that day.

As far as my comments about Rosie, we're blaming that on the alcohol as well. They won't likely view me in the best light. They'll probably see me as a dumb college kid, and they'd be right, but it's the best excuse I've got. Now I have to prove in other ways that I'm serious about this. I don't want to take Sammy away from Danielle out of spite. I simply want the right to know and help raise my son.

"I'll ask her."

"Bring her," she reiterates, and with that, she ends the call.

Rosie returns from putting the cart away and climbs in. When she turns the ignition, the dash lights up with a pink hue that amused me the first time I saw it.

"Is everything okay?" she asks, putting the SUV in reverse.

Woodenly, I turn to her. "I get to meet him tomorrow."

She stomps on the brake, forcing my head to hit the seat behind me. Behind us, a horn blares. "What?"

"I know." I rub at the back of my head. "I'm

surprised too. My lawyer …" I pull in a deep breath and let it out. "She wants you there."

With a nod, she murmurs, "Okay."

My stomach does a damn somersault in response. I was sure she'd argue. "Okay?"

Laughing, she navigates the oversized SUV into the Starbucks drive-thru. "Well, yeah. That's why we did this whole thing, right?" She flashes me her ring, the movement making it glitter in the sunlight. "The whole point is to help you get custody."

"Right."

So why do I keep forgetting that?

IF I'D EVEN HAD the forethought to imagine the moment I'd get to meet my son, my vision wouldn't have been anything like this. The room they put us in is fitted with dark paneling and dingy linoleum floors. It smells of antiseptic, and the chairs and table look to be relics from the eighties.

Rosie looks around, trying not to frown. The iced coffee she picked up on the way leaves a ring of condensation on the particle board table.

There's a scattering of toys in the corner, but they look like they're meant for toddlers or older kids.

My heart is racing. It has been all morning. There

are dark shadows under Rosie's eyes, and her face is pale, like she didn't sleep at all. I certainly didn't.

Nina paces on the other side of the room. Her fingers fly aggressively across the screen of her phone, making it look like she's chewing someone out.

"Take a breath."

At the sound of Rosie's voice, I turn to her and exhale loudly, only then realizing that my lungs are burning.

We've been here for twenty minutes already. I wanted to arrive early. But Sammy was supposed to be here five minutes ago.

Are they in the building? Or are they not coming at all?

Stupidly, that thought hasn't occurred to me until now.

When Nina's fingers slow and she holds her phone at her side, I clear my throat for her attention. "What happens if Danielle doesn't show up with him?"

Out of the corner of my eye, Rosie stiffens.

Nina slides her phone into her purse. "It would count against her."

At that moment, the door opens, and a social worker enters, holding a baby in her arms.

Big blue eyes the same color as my own study me. He's small, but he's already so much bigger than he was when I saw him at the start of the school year. He doesn't have much hair, and what he does have is blond.

Standing slowly, I approach the social worker carefully. "Can I..." I extend my arms. "Can I hold him?"

She smiles. "Yes. He's yours."

He's yours.

I swallow past the sudden lump in my throat. My hands shake and my heart races, but then Rosie's hand is at my back, instantly calming me.

I'll think about that detail later.

For now, I take my son from the social worker and hold him to my chest.

I wait with bated breath for him to cry or scream or try to get away from me. Instead, he settles against me, his tiny hands gripping the fabric of my shirt, and watches me with those eyes that already have the power to gut me to my core.

Rosie stands at my elbow, leaning in and running a gentle finger over his head. "He's so cute," she says, her tone full of reverence. "He looks just like you."

I'm racked with nerves, because holy shit, I'm holding my *son*. Even so, I grin at her. "You think I'm cute?"

Rolling her eyes, she huffs a laugh. "Sure." She turns to the social worker. "He's almost six months, right?"

The social worker studies her, then me, curious. "You don't know?"

"The information we've been given is limited." I look down at my son. I've been fighting hard for him, and he doesn't even know it. Months. It's taken me months and hours upon hours of work to even get to hold him.

Fuck Danielle.

"He was born July first."

"A little cancer baby," Rosie croons, gliding a gentle finger over his pink cheek.

He giggles in response.

"When did you first think he was yours?" The social worker asks me. I'm not sure whether it's out of curiosity or some sort of other motive. Regardless, I'm more than happy to answer honestly.

"I *knew* he was mine the moment I saw him. It was at the beginning of the school year. Classes had just started and I saw ... I saw his mom on campus with her husband. She was showing him off to some other professors. It was like gravity pulled me closer. I knew even before I looked at him that he was mine."

I feel Rosie's eyes on me, but I don't dare look at her.

Before Danielle could notice me, I turned a corner and threw up in a cluster of bushes. It earned me some dirty, questioning looks from other students who probably thought I was drunk in the middle of the day.

After getting sick, I locked myself in the nearest bathroom and hyperventilated for what felt like hours. I was terrified out of my mind. I wasn't ready to be a dad, but suddenly I knew I *was* a dad, and whether I was prepared for it or not didn't matter. Then I started to spiral. I sent Danielle God only knows how many texts. She never answered a single one.

I left that restroom with resolve, though, set on doing whatever it took to be in my son's life.

When Sammy fusses a bit, I adjust my hold on him, bringing him to the crook of my neck. Closing my eyes, I inhale his scent and let the calmness that comes with having him so close wash over me. He smells perfect.

"Look at you." Rosie smiles at us. "You're a natural."

"Do you want to hold him?" I ask her.

"Me? I ... no, that's okay." Her cheeks flush, and she takes half a step back. "This is your time."

"He's yours too," I remind her. "In a way."

She exhales a shaky breath. "Right."

She holds her arms out, and I gently transfer Sammy to her. Immediately, he tangles his small hand in one of her dark curls and tugs.

"Ow." She winces through a laugh. "You're strong, buddy."

I help her extract his hand from her hair and let out a low whistle. "Kid's strong."

With him in her arms, it allows me a chance to get a better look at him.

He's so beautiful, so perfect, that he takes my breath away.

"This isn't so bad." She rocks from side to side

gently and smiles down at him. "I thought he wouldn't like me. That I'd be terrible at this."

On instinct, I reach out and gently tuck her hair behind her ear. "You're a natural."

To the two ladies in the room, Rosie explains, "I've never been around babies before."

"What about Grace?" I ask, keeping my voice low so Nina and the social worker can't hear me.

"I was ten," she says by way of explanation. "I was excited to have a sister, but I wasn't into the whole baby thing. Besides, we had nannies."

"Ah, makes sense."

"Here, take him." She passes Sammy back to me with an encouraging smile. "Enjoy your time with him."

We only have another forty-five minutes with him, but it's better than nothing. I won't take a second of it for granted.

I look down at my son, doing my best to memorize every detail. I might not have been prepared for any of this, but already, I know that I was always meant to be a dad.

eighteen

ROSIE

I STEP OUTSIDE, groaning against the cold. Big, fat snowflakes slowly circle from the gray sky. I'm running late for class, having gotten lost in studying for too long. That's what happens when I have to play catch-up. I've been ignoring my schoolwork more than I should while I work to prepare the townhouse for Junior. Furniture for the nursery is ordered, as well as the cutest watercolor dinosaur wallpaper. As I head down the sidewalk, I make a mental note to hire someone to put it up. Already this morning, I spent an hour calling around in search of a person who could come babyproof the house.

Apparently, most people do that themselves.

I didn't know that, and frankly, I don't trust myself or Daire to get it right.

I unlock my car and toss my backpack in the passenger side. As I'm shutting the door, an unfamiliar vehicle pulls into the driveway. Immediately, my hackles raise and my heart rate kicks up a notch.

I'm not about to get kidnapped, am I?

Holding my breath, I take in the minivan, and as I squint at the driver, a laugh works its way out of me.

Why is Daire...? Oh my God.

I suck in one big, gulping breath after another, trying to rein in my hysterics. "Please tell me you didn't buy a minivan."

He opens the door and slips out. "Huh?"

With a hand pressed against my stomach, I grin at him. "Did you buy a minivan?"

He looks at the vehicle as if only now realizing what it is. With a shrug, he stuffs his hands into the pockets of his jeans. His breath fogs the air. His blond hair peeks out beneath a black beanie embroidered with the school's wolf mascot.

"I told the sales guy I needed a family vehicle."

"And he steered you toward a minivan? You could've gotten something like mine." I toss a thumb at my SUV.

"But look." Excitement lights his eyes. "The doors just slide open." He pushes a button on the fob, and both rear doors slide back. "And there are these anchor things in the seats back here that the guy said make the car seat more secure."

"I can't believe you got a minivan," I mutter, surveying the behemoth in the driveway. Truthfully, it's not the worst thing I've ever seen. It looks slightly more like an SUV than other minivans I've come across, but...

But it's still a minivan.

Daire Hendricks is driving a minivan.

Uncontrollable laughter bubbles out of me before I can stop it.

He crinkles his nose. "What's so funny?"

"What do you think your friends are going to say about this?"

Lips pursed, he examines the minivan, then focuses on me again. "I don't really care. I'm a dad now. This is safe and reliable." He pats the hood. "Besides, they're busy with their own lives."

The hint of hurt in his voice when he says that last part pierces my chest. "I'm sorry."

He shrugs like it doesn't bother him.

"It's senior year," he reasons, pushing a button to shut the door, "we were bound to grow apart."

He can rationalize it all he wants, but I think his friends are shitty. He needs them now more than ever.

But I don't have time to lecture him on that. Not that he'd want me to anyway.

"I'm running late. But this," I point at him where he stands beside the minivan and make a circle motion with my finger, "makes it worth it."

I turn to get in my car, but before I climb in, I pause and yank my phone out of where it's buried in my coat pocket. Whipping back around, I take a photo of Daire.

"What's what for?" he asks, face scrunched with annoyance.

"Photographic evidence—Bertie is never going to believe me otherwise."

He huffs something unintelligible as I get into my car.

With a wave, I'm off, and somehow, I make it to class on time.

"LET ME SEE IT AGAIN."

I hand Bertie my phone, and she cackles all over again at the picture of Daire standing beside the minivan.

"I can't believe he bought a minivan." She passes the device back. "Send that to me."

"For what?"

"For whenever I need a laugh." Her eyes dance as she takes a sip of her margarita.

I had no plans of going out tonight, but Bertie sent me a text inquiring about drinks, and I couldn't say no. I miss her, so I jump at just about any opportunity to hang out.

Harvey's is a staple for Aldridge University students. The building is huge, housing a massive bar in the center and a dance floor.

I've spent a lot of time here in my years at Aldridge, most of them pining over the athletes who hang out in the large U-shaped booth in one corner. I used to watch Daire with his friends, cursing myself and the longing that plagued me.

I can deny it to myself all I want, but I never stopped missing him after our friendship came to an end.

Back then, the booth was frequently occupied by some of the school's most popular guys. Mascen Wade—the son of a famous drummer—and his closest friends Cole and Teddy, along with Daire, his friends Cree and Jude, and others I couldn't name. Mascen, Cole, and Teddy have since graduated, and none of the other guys are here tonight. I recognize Luke there, though. He's got his fingers wrapped loosely around the neck of a beer and his eyes focused on the table. He doesn't seem involved in the conversation with the crowd around him.

Like he can feel my gaze, he looks over. His eyes glide over me and land on Bertie. Instantly, he sits up straighter and looks away. But a moment later, he covertly glances back and gives her a quick once-over.

"Luke Covey is looking at you again," I tell her.

"Who?"

I try to hide my smile. "The same hockey player who was checking you out by the locker room the other night."

"Which one is he?" She angles forward so she can peer at the group occupying the booth.

"Hold on, this will be easier."

I bring up my social media account and type in his name. Nothing comes up. I put in the handle for the Aldridge hockey team instead, then scroll until I find a picture of him.

"This guy." I pass my phone to her.

Her jaw drops. "Him?" A pink hue rushes to her cheeks. She sinks into the booth, shoving my phone back at me like it's a snake.

"Yeah. Why are you so freaked out?"

She leans forward, keeping her head low, and hisses, "I hooked up with him."

My jaw drops. "When?"

She exhales shakily. "Freshman year. It was before I met Tommy. Obviously." Her hand trembles as she tucks a strand of blond hair behind her ear.

"I need details. How come you never told me about this?"

She takes a sip of her margarita and holds it out in

front of her, surveying it. Wrinkling her nose, she goes in for another sip that turns into a gulp. "It was at the very beginning of the year. One of the first parties we went to. We weren't really friends yet, and after I met Tommy I just … didn't think about it anymore. It's not like we exchanged names."

"Was the sex bad?"

She snorts. "Far from it. It was…" The color in her cheeks darkens. "Phenomenal. Best I've ever had." She sinks down slowly in the booth.

"Wow." I lift my margarita glass and tip it toward her. "Good for you. It seems like he might be interested in revisiting it—fuck, he's getting up."

"What?" Bertie practically shrieks, her eyes going wide with horror.

"He's coming this way," I warn.

She looks one way, then the other, sinking lower, like she wants to melt into the booth behind her.

Luke stops beside our table and shoves his hands into his pockets. He tips his head at me in greeting before setting his eyes on Bertie. "Hi."

His voice is deep and sensual. As that one word settles over Bertie, her shoulders lower and her throat bobs with a swallow. "Hi."

"You wanna dance?"

I've been here at least a hundred times, and not once have I seen Luke pay any attention to a girl, let alone ask one to dance.

Bertie, bless her, points at herself. "Me?"

He chuckles, blue eyes sparkling. "Yeah. You."

"Go." I mouth the word at her.

"I ... okay."

I grin at her, my heart practically floating as she slides from the booth. Luke puts his hand on the small of her back, guiding her over to the dance floor. As much as I want to watch, I don't want to put that kind of pressure on my best friend, so I pull out my phone to distract myself.

There's a message from Daire waiting. It's a response to the one I sent telling him I was going out with Bertie.

> Daire: Text me when you're on your way home.

Home.

How strange is it that my home is with *Daire*, of all people?

> Me: I will. I'm probably going to head out in a bit.

He replies with a photo attachment right away.

> Daire: What's your opinion—do I need one of these?

The picture is of some sort of baby carrier that he could strap to his chest.

> Me: Absolutely.

> Daire: Adding it to my cart.

> Me: What else do you have in there for Junior?

He sends me a screenshot of the items, ranging from the carrier to a play mat to a set of hockey-themed onesies. I can't help but smile. This whole situation has to be mildly terrifying for him—how could it not be?—but he's stepping up to the plate and seems genuinely excited about it.

Baby Sammy is lucky to have him.

> Me: All excellent choices.

A reply doesn't come right away, so I set my phone to the side and spear a bite of the Caesar salad I ordered and have barely touched.

Luke and Bertie are still on the dance floor. For a moment, I can't help but watch them. Thankfully, she seems to have relaxed a little. Luke is holding her gently, careful to keep his hand in a respectable place above her hips.

Luke Covey is a gentleman—who knew? A little zap of envy hits me, because once again, I wish I could find a man who'd treat me with so much care. But mostly, I'm giddy for my best friend.

I polish off half of my salad and most of my side of fries before flagging down the waitress for a to-go box. My leftovers will make for a good lunch tomorrow.

My phone vibrates on the table.

> Daire: You think so?

> Me: Most definitely.

It's cute, the way he wants my opinion.

> Me: I was thinking—we should take a baby CPR class.

> Daire: Fuck. I never thought about that, but you're right.

> Me: I'll find the website again and look at dates.

> Daire: Thanks.

It's weird, how easily we've become a team. What's stranger is how much I *don't* hate him anymore. Not that I'm telling him that.

Bertie is still on the dance floor, but I'm ready to head home, so I catch her eye, finding it impossible not to smile at the way she's glowing. Bertie deserves to find some happiness—even if it's the temporary, sexy kind of happiness.

"I'm gonna head out. You good?" I mouth.

She nods, throwing me a thumbs-up.

After paying our bill, I gather up my to-go boxes and head out. It's strange, leaving alone. I can't remember the last time I didn't go home with a guy after a night at Harvey's. My, how things have changed.

Once I'm in the driver's seat with the doors locked, I shoot Daire a text that I'm on my way.

It's almost muscle memory to head back to campus and the dorms—so much so that I find myself ready to turn out of the lot in that direction before course correcting and turning toward downtown instead.

I have to stifle a giggle when I pull into the driveway beside the minivan. I'm not sure I'm ever going to get over Daire's dad-mobile.

With the back door open, I snag my backpack and slip it over my shoulder, then pick up the to-go boxes. Cursing when I reach the door, I set the boxes down at my feet to search through my backpack for the house key. Before I can get my hands on it, though, the door opens. I take in Daire from head to toe. Blond hair still slightly damp from a shower, curling at the ends. A gray Aldridge U sweatshirt hugging his muscular frame. Down my eyes go, taking in the loose gym shorts and stopping at his bare feet.

"I heard you pull in," he says by way of explanation.

I arch a brow, bending to retrieve the boxes, but he snatches them from the ground before I can.

"Sounds like you were waiting for me."

He shrugs, but he doesn't deny it, which brings a stupidly big smile to my face.

Once the door is locked behind us, I follow him to the kitchen, where he puts the boxes in the fridge.

Popping his head out, he holds up a bottle of wine. "Do you want a drink?"

"Just water, please." I set my backpack on the counter and pull out the books and materials I need. It's late, and the last thing I want to do is schoolwork, but I should get a jump-start on it.

Daire fills a glass with ice and water, then he sticks a straw in it like I always do. "How was your time with Bertie?"

"Good." I smile, feeling all warm inside at the memory of Luke asking her to dance. "I left her dancing with Luke."

"Luke...?"

"Covey. On your team."

Daire's lips part, and his eyes go wide. "Seriously?"

"Mhm," I hum, cracking the lid to my laptop to see how much life the battery has left. "He seems into her."

He scratches at his jaw and turns away. "That's shocking."

I close my laptop with a *snap*. "What's that supposed to mean?" There's more bite in my tone than is probably warranted, but I can't help but rush to Bertie's defense.

"I didn't mean it like that." He spins around and lifts both hands in defense. "Just that Luke doesn't really go out, and when he does, he tends to stick to himself. I know he hooks up some, but it's rare. He's a scholarship student. He's serious about all this. He wants to go pro."

He's certainly good enough to go that route.

"Good for him." I pull out my charging cord and plug in my laptop. "I'm going to shower. Are you going to be up for a while? I thought I'd come back down after and do some homework."

Nodding, he turns to rummage through the pantry.

Daire is *always* hungry. I guess it makes sense. He's an athlete, after all. But it's been an adjustment for me, as well as a stark reminder that while I might not live with my parents anymore, the way my mom used to monitor what foods I ate still haunts me. I have to remind myself often that Daire's snacking is not excessive. Logically, I understand that there's nothing wrong with having a snack, but being in his proximity like this has shown me that even though I've tried so hard to heal from it, some trauma lingers.

"I'll be down here." He shuts the pantry door.

I leave my stuff and head upstairs to my room. I've kept the space simple. That way, if we get caught with a social worker needing to do a home visit, it looks like a typical guestroom and not like my husband and I sleep in separate beds.

While the water warms, I reach for my speaker and turn it on so it can connect to my phone.

The EDM playlist I click on is probably not something most people would think I'd like, but the fast-paced music, usually accompanied by a booming bass, has always soothed me.

Under the spray, I work the sweet, floral-smelling shampoo through my long hair. As I rinse, watching the white soap suds swirl down the drain and disappear, my thoughts drift to Daire. How he greeted me at the door and chatted while I unpacked my things. Almost like he missed me. I gave up hope that our relationship could be repaired a long time ago, even as some little kernel inside me still stupidly yearned for him. But was it stupid? After tonight, I can't say for sure...

Shaking my head, I reach for conditioner. I squeeze a dollop into my palm and apply it to the ends of my hair. I take my time, stalling before I return downstairs and face him again. Things are changing between us, and while I hope it's for the better—while I *think* it's for the better—I can't help but want to protect my heart.

He already broke it once.

Who's to say he won't do it again?

nineteen

DAIRE

THE CHILD CPR class is filled with a mix of expecting parents, young women—probably nannies—and teenage girls that I assume are here because they're babysitters. Then there's Rosie and me.

"Like this." The instructor demonstrates CPR on the infant doll in front of the two of us. "You're being too rough. You don't want to crack ribs, do you?" She shoots me an accusing look.

"Sorry," I mutter at the chastisement, my face heating.

This is a lot harder than I expected. Especially since

I took a CPR class my freshman year. Coach requires it of all his players. He's never explained why, but rumor is that when he was younger, a friend collapsed in front of him, and no one knew how to do CPR properly. Whether it's true is anybody's guess. Most of my teammates are full of shit, so there's a good chance it's not.

"No, no, no." The short, older woman chastises me yet again. To Rosie she says, "Big men like this one here want to show off how strong they are. But death isn't cute."

The heat in my face has officially spread everywhere, and I've broken out into a sweat. I'm trying to do this right, but clearly, I'm failing at every turn.

"Fingers," she says, holding up her index and middle finger. "Like this."

She demonstrates again.

I shoot a pleading look in Rosie's direction, but from the twitch in her lips, she's far too amused to be any help.

"Now try."

I take a deep breath. At this point, the entire class is staring at me.

I try again.

She closes her eyes, pinching her brow. "Dead baby," she mutters.

Tossing my head back, I groan. "Please, help me. I need to learn this."

For the first time, she looks at me with a hint of

sympathy in her expression. Like maybe she gets how desperate I am. "Give me your arm."

I obey, extending my arm.

"You need to be firm." She presses her fingers into my skin. "But not *too* rough. Do you feel that pressure?"

I nod in answer.

"Good. Now try again."

Playing in front of an entire arena of hockey fans?

Not a problem.

Attempting to give this doll CPR while a dozen people watch me? I'm ready to run out the door and never come back.

This is for Sammy.

With a fortifying breath, I do my best to mimic the pressure she demonstrated and try again.

She nods in encouragement, so I continue. For a solid minute, no one moves or speaks while I practice, but eventually, she claps.

"And now you've got it, Mr. Hendricks. Good job."

The thumbs-up the instructor gives me feels as good as winning a game.

I switch with Rosie so she can practice while the instructor goes around to the rest of the group.

"The sight of you struggling brings me far too much joy," Rosie admits with a smile. Her dark hair is gathered in a ponytail, for an instant tempting me to wrap that hair around my fist and bring her mouth to mine.

I haven't kissed her since my last home game. I'm

fucking grateful she didn't seem to notice how hard the kiss made me.

"So, what you're telling me is you like to see me in a vulnerable position?"

She flicks her brown eyes my way, her lips tipping up again. "Can you blame me? It's so cute to watch you squirm."

I cross my arms over my chest and bite my cheek to keep from smiling.

Is she flirting with me?

My heart beats out an irregular rhythm, but I ignore it and jump in to tease her in return. "You think I'm cute?"

She puffs out her lips and narrows her eyes on me over the CPR doll. "That's not what I said, and you know it."

"Good, Rosie," the instructor says, passing by us again. "You've got the technique."

Rosie flashes me a triumphant smile.

"Yeah, yeah. Get your gloating over with now."

An hour later, we leave with CPR certificates in hand.

Rosie snickers as we near my minivan.

"Stop laughing at my car." I bump her with my elbow. "It's nicer than you thought it would be, and you know it."

"It is," she agrees, letting her hair down from the ponytail. She tips her head back and gives it a shake, causing the dark tendrils to cascade over her shoulders. "But even you have to admit the scenario is funny. Daire Hendricks, college hockey star, driving a grocery-getter."

"I guess," I mutter, rounding the hood.

I get in the driver's side, but when she tries to open the passenger door, it doesn't budge.

She glowers at me through the window. "Daire."

A zap of excitement courses through me. I get a sick satisfaction out of riling her up. "What's the password?"

She bats her eyes, a smile that's pure annoyance on her mouth. "You're an asshole?" she asks, her words muffled. "Is that it?"

"Close, but no," I say, hitting the ignition button.

She pulls on the handle again without success. "Let me in."

"Apologize for making fun of my dad car."

"This is a mom van."

I grin and pull my seat belt across my torso. "Have fun walking home."

"You dick!" She slaps the window. "Don't you dare!"

I wouldn't, but she doesn't have to know that. I put the van in reverse and tap the gas just enough to force her to jump away.

"Daire!" Her voice is so high pitched I expect dogs to start howling at any second.

"Apologize," I singsong.

She huffs, stomping her foot. "I'm so sorry for making fun of your mom-mobile."

"Mm," I reverse slightly again. "Not good enough."

"I'm sorry! Okay? Don't leave me here!"

The desperation in her voice hits me like a stab to the gut. I was just having a little fun. I would've never *actually* left her here. I'm not that much of an asshole.

I unlock the doors, and when she yanks the door open, I angle over the center console. "I wasn't going to abandon you."

She gets inside with a huff, her nose pink from the cold. "Sure, you weren't." She yanks the seat belt across her body, avoiding my gaze.

My heart pangs at the hurt and anger wafting off her after such a harmless joke. "I mean it, Rosie."

She crosses her arms over her chest. "You've done it before. Why would now be any different?"

With my heart in my throat, I pull back into the parking space. Once the van is in park again, I turn in my seat to face her, racking my brain for any memory of leaving her behind. But I come up empty.

"When?" I demand.

"The day our friendship ended." She wraps her arms around herself, looking away like she wishes the words hadn't tumbled out of her mouth. She bites down on her bottom lip, but not before I catch the way it trembles.

Fuck. I hate that she's on the verge of tears because of me.

"The day ... junior prom?"

She rolls her eyes and shakes her head, but she doesn't turn my way. "You have to remember."

I've never forgotten that fateful day, but I didn't leave her.

"You left with Brady Jackson."

Her lips part, and she whips around, eyes wide. "Brady? Are you serious? I hated him!"

I turn the music down and clear my throat. "That's not what I heard. Alyssa told me—"

"Alyssa?" She huffs. "I shouldn't be surprised that she's the one who spewed that bullshit at you. She hated me."

"What?" I rear back. "No, she didn't."

"Daire." She blinks at me like she's waiting for me to connect a series of dots I'm too dumb to see. "She was your girlfriend, and I was your best friend. She didn't like that."

My stomach twists itself into a knot. "Why would she—"

"Because I was in love with you!" Rosie screams, throwing her arms out. Her knuckles hit the window, and she winces, then cradles her right hand in her left. "Everyone knew." Her voice is softer, her arms wrapping protectively around her body again. "Everyone but you."

Everyone but you.

Clueless fucking idiot.

She turns back to the window and sniffles. "That night ... I don't know if she knew I was in the restroom, but I think she did. She was bragging about how ... about how you guys were going to finally have sex and..." Rosie drops her head. "I knew she was your girlfriend. I knew it was inevitable, but it still hurt. And then you were supposed to take me home, and you just ... left me."

I stare at her, my heart cracking wide open. Why the fuck was I so stupid back then? How the hell did we let this ruin our friendship?

"I was so fucking angry," I start, curling my fists like I did all those years ago, "when she told me you went home with Brady. I was jealous when I had no right to be. I liked you too, but I didn't want to ruin our friendship." I bark out a humorless laugh. "But after that night, it was ruined anyway."

She whips toward me so quickly I have to dodge the fan of her hair. "You liked me too?" she blurts, her eyes wide as they meet mine. "You ... I never had any idea that—"

I'm fucking helpless to stop myself.

I grab her by the back of the neck and pull her into me. Our mouths meet, and just like the times we've kissed before, it's an explosion of sparks. A kiss has always just been a kiss to me. With Rosie? It's an experience. One I want to savor.

A small sound leaves her, one I quickly swallow, and then her tongue meets mine.

More.

I want so much more of her, and that's fucking terrifying.

We're married.

But not for real.

Feelings would only complicate things, but I can't pull myself away from her.

I don't break the kiss, even though my subconscious is screaming that this is a terrible idea. The taste of her is incomparable. In this moment, I'm certain I could kiss her for the rest of my life and never get tired of it.

In the end, she's the one who breaks the kiss. I guess that's for the best.

She rests her forehead against mine. "What are we doing?"

"I don't know," I answer honestly, smoothing a hand down her neck and shoulder as I sit back. "I don't know."

We sit there for another minute, probably longer, watching each other, before she says, "I'm starving. Let's get burgers."

WITH A THANKS TO THE WAITRESS, Rosie squirts a ridiculous amount of ketchup onto her plate.

"Would you like some fries with that ketchup?" I quip, taking the bottle when she's done.

She laughs, unfolding the napkin from around the utensils. Knife in hand, she cuts her burger in half. "I like ketchup."

I add a much smaller amount to my plate. When she suggested burgers, I couldn't pull out of the parking lot fast enough, more than eager to put off talking about the kiss. Especially when I can't make sense of my own thoughts. It's like a maze with no way out.

She's had a few bites of her burger when she says, "I can't believe we've hated each other for years because your ex-girlfriend is a big, fat liar."

I nearly choke on my Coke. "I guess you're right," I say between coughs as I wipe my mouth with my napkin.

"Alyssa was always a bitch."

I chuckle, sorting through my fries for the crispier ones. "She was," I agree. It's why I broke up with her shortly after that. We didn't last through the summer before our senior year. By that time, though, Rosie was dating someone, and I was still angry enough that I didn't reach out.

Young and foolish.

That's what we were.

A wasted friendship for nothing.

If we'd just *talked*—used our words, like my nanny used to say—we could have easily mended our friendship rather than stewing in hatred.

Neither of us can go back and undo the past now. There's only forward.

There's an expiration date on our marriage, but that doesn't mean we can't remain friends.

"This burger," Rosie points at her plate, "might be the best thing I've ever eaten."

"Ever?" I laugh. "That's a pretty big declaration."

She picks up the second half of the burger and inspects it. "It's that good."

"Glad you like it."

"I haven't been here before." She surveys the restaurant, chin lifted high. "How'd you know about it?"

"Uh…" I scratch at my chest and consider a little white lie, but in the end, I go with the truth. "Covey mentioned it. His mom works here."

"Luke?"

I nod and pop a fry into my mouth. "Yeah, but he doesn't know that I know that. A couple of years ago, he mentioned that this place had the best burgers. I came by myself once, and his mom happened to be my waitress—I only know because she asked if I went to Aldridge, and when I said yes, we got to talking, and when she found out I played hockey, she said she was his mom. I don't see her today." I look around to be sure.

"He seems nice. For a hockey player," she adds with a wink.

I press a hand over my heart. "You wound me, Mrs. Hendricks."

I'm not sure exactly what made me call her that, but I'm rewarded with the pink flushing from her neck all the way up her cheeks.

"I can't believe I'm admitting this," the pink somehow gets brighter in color, "but in middle school, I wrote that all over my notebooks."

"What?" I grin, feeling lighter than I think I have in years. I know exactly what she's talking about, but I want to hear her say it.

She rolls her eyes. "Mrs. Hendricks," she says softly.

"Glad to know you always wanted me."

She tosses a fry at me. "Shut up."

It's surprising, how easy this is. The camaraderie. The connection.

It's almost like we've been friends all along.

twenty

ROSIE

ON MY WAY out of class, I dig my phone out of my pocket and groan at the name flashing on the screen. I normally don't mind talking to my mom, but I have a feeling I know why she's calling, and I'm not in the mood for this conversation.

I'm tempted to ignore the call, but she's persistent, so it'll only be a matter of time before she's ringing again.

I duck into an alcove and swipe to answer.

"Hey, Mom." I sound far more cheery than I feel.

She launches right in. "I made an appointment for

you at a bridal store in Nashville to try on dresses. It's—"

"Mom," I interrupt, "I really can't be thinking about dresses right now. Christmas is almost here and—" I bite my tongue. We still haven't told our families about Sammy.

We had a home inspection a few days ago—after we babyproofed the house and got started on the nursery, at least. The wallpaper finally came and is being put up this week. Now, if only the furniture would show up. Just about everything we picked out is on backorder, and they keep changing the dates on me. I'll have to cancel and order furniture elsewhere if it can't be delivered in the next couple of weeks. Sammy might not be my child, but I want his room to be special. Maybe that's silly. A room is a room.

"I know Christmas is almost here," she huffs. "I'm still upset that you're not coming to see us."

"Daire and I want to be here, just the two of us, for our first Christmas," I lie.

In reality, it has nothing to do with us wanting to be alone. We're supposed to get another supervised meeting with Sammy on Christmas Eve.

"I have an idea!"

I pinch my brow and close my eyes, guessing where she's going with this.

"Why don't we come there to see you guys?"

"Mom. No."

Setting boundaries with parents can be hard. She forgets that I'm an adult now, with my own life.

"Why not?"

I stifle the urge to groan. "Like I told you, Daire and I want to spend our first Christmas together."

"I think it's unreasonable that you don't even want to see us. It's *Christmas*." A sniffle echoes over the line. She's really laying the guilt on thick now. "Grace misses you."

"Just you and Grace, huh?" No mention of my dad. "We can FaceTime on Christmas morning."

She sniffles again for dramatic effect. "It's not the same."

The longer we talk, the heavier the weight pushing on my shoulders becomes. Not once has she mentioned my dad missing me too. I've stopped trying to reach out to him, deciding it's better to let him work through his anger.

I've always been a daddy's girl, so being on the outs with him *sucks*. We'll move past this eventually, but that doesn't keep me from wishing we could skip to that part now.

"Back to the dresses — I'll schedule a visit in January. Grace and I will be there. I'm *not* missing out on this. You already robbed me of the first wedding."

"It was in a courthouse," I remind her.

"I don't care. I would've been there."

No, she would've been dragging me out of there and demanding we have a real wedding.

"I don't know if I'll have time."

"Make time. And lose ten pounds. You'll fit in the samples ... more easily."

When she hangs up, all I can do is gape at my phone. I know she doesn't intend to hurt me with her words, but fuck, it feels like a stab to the heart every single time. Why does the size of my body matter so much to her? I'm the one living in this shell.

I tuck my phone into my pocket, inhaling a steadying breath. Even though I made Daire promise we could have a real wedding, I'm beginning to regret that part of the bargain. All because my treacherous feelings keep forgetting that this marriage isn't real.

And my stupid mother is telling me I need to lose weight to fit into a *dress*.

It's just a fucking dress.

Slipping out of the alcove, I start toward the dining hall. I've completely lost my appetite, but I could go for a hot chocolate. At this time of the year, they serve specialty hot chocolate, and I'm in desperate need of a peppermint cocoa with a snowman marshmallow.

"Rosie? Wait up!"

At the sound of my name, I look up and come to a stop. Daire—my *husband*—is jogging away from a group of guys, Cree and Jude among them, and he's headed my way.

"I—" The word dies on his tongue, and his face morphs into a mask of concern. "What's wrong?" He reaches for my wrist, warm fingers wrapping around the cold patch of skin. "Did someone hurt you?"

"Just my mother," I retort.

His eyes narrow. "Do I need to call her?"

Snorting, I pull my coat higher up around my face. I feel like a turtle poking its head out of its shell, but I can't bring myself to care.

"No. But don't be surprised if she shows up on our doorstep on Christmas, despite being told no multiple times. That word doesn't seem to exist her vocabulary."

"What did she say?" he demands, not letting it go.

"It really doesn't matter." I shake him loose, then turn and continue my trek to the dining hall.

He follows, matching my stride. "It does to me."

"Why?" I demand. I just want to get my hot chocolate and find an empty corner where I can let the tears fall.

"You're my wife."

Another snort rips out of me as my chest constricts. "In contract only."

A muscle in his jaw ticks. "That doesn't mean you can't talk to me."

"Daire?" I tug my beanie down lower over my ears. *Why didn't I pick a college somewhere warmer?* "Right now, I just want to get a hot chocolate and drown my sorrows in sugar. Is that too much to ask?"

He stuffs his hands into his pockets. "*Then* will you talk to me?"

I flash him a toothy smile. "Maybe."

When we reach the dining hall, he hustles past me so he can hold the door for me. Silently, he follows me over to the beverage station. I *never* get coffee here. It's nasty sludge, so I'd rather get it from the on-campus café, but the seasonal hot chocolate is a different story.

I step up to order, looking over my shoulder at Daire. "You want anything?"

He shakes his head. "No, I'm good."

With a quiet laugh, I say, "Two peppermint hot chocolates with the snowman marshmallow, please." I scan my dining hall card, and then we step aside to wait for the drinks.

"I told you I didn't need one."

"Who said the other one is for you? Maybe I'm choosing sweets instead of alcohol today."

I'm more than a little surprised that I can joke like this so soon after the conversation I just had. It won't be long before my mom's words are circling in my head once more.

"That bad, huh?"

I look away, lowering my focus to the tile floor that looks like hardwood. "You have no idea."

By now, I should be used to her saying things like what she did. My skin should be thicker.

Though I suppose it's not unfair to be upset when

my own mother makes negative comments about my body.

I don't for a minute think she hates me. She doesn't do it to be malicious. Honestly, that might be the worst part of it all. It would be easier for me to dismiss if she was a horrible mother in general, but she's not. She's wonderful in all areas but this one. I even have sympathy for her, because her critiques of my body have more to do with what she endured from her own mom and the modeling industry than with me.

When our drinks are ready, I swipe both off the counter and hand one to Daire. "Trust me, you'll like it."

He looks down at the large snowman marshmallow that nearly covers the entire top of the cup. "Cute."

His hand is a brand on my back—one I feel through multiple layers of clothes—as he guides me to a table in the corner. None of the other tables nearby are filled, so we've got plenty of privacy. I appreciate his effort, even if I'd rather run out the door than talk about my family problems with him.

He pulls out a chair for me, shocking me with the gentlemanly gesture, and I shrug my backpack off and set it on the floor before sliding into the seat.

For a moment, I'm silently focused on gently blowing on my hot chocolate before taking a tentative sip.

Perfection.

I hum at the taste and take another sip. "God, I love this stuff."

Daire smiles, raising his own cup to his mouth. His eyes widen at the first taste. Surprise coats his words when he says, "That's good."

"I told you."

He takes a few more sips before he sets his cup down and says, "Now, tell me what she said."

Daire isn't the kind of guy to give up. He's always been this way, so I set my cup down and smooth my hands down my thighs, then force myself to dive in.

"She called about wanting to schedule a time for me to look at dresses."

His brow creases. "Dresses?"

"Wedding dresses."

"Oh." He nods, picking up his drink. "Right. Go on."

"I told her I didn't have time." It's the truth. Between school and the house and Daire trying to get some sort of custody of Sammy, my days are jam-packed. "But you know how she is."

"Pushy." He chuckles, though he quickly sobers and rests one elbow on the table, shifting to face me. "But I don't see why that would've had you upset."

The snowman marshmallow in my cup swirls around, the edges curling in on themselves are a perfect representation of how I feel at the moment.

"It's what she said at the end of the conversation

that got to me." I tap my fingers against the side of the Styrofoam cup, stalling. The idea of saying it out loud is painful. Even more so than hearing it. "She told me to lose ten pounds before we go so that I fit in the samples easier."

With a thick swallow, I drop my eyes to the table, waiting for his reaction.

Daire goes eerily still at my side. He lets go of his cup, his left hand curling into a fist on top of the table.

I can't help but zero in on the ring on his finger, getting far too much satisfaction at the sight of it than someone in a fake marriage should.

"She said what?"

Cringing, I take a sip of my drink, wishing it were spiked. "Don't make me repeat it."

He fumbles in his pocket, then pulls out his phone. "I'm calling her."

"No!" I shriek, grappling to get ahold of his phone. "Don't do that."

He glowers, holding it in the air. "Tell me why the hell not."

"She's my mom. She didn't mean to hurt me."

He holds my stare. "It doesn't matter whether she meant to. She *did* hurt you."

I lift one shoulder and let it fall. "I'm used to it."

His gaze softens, and he sets the phone on the table. Slowly, he cups my cheek. With a soothing stroke of his thumb, he says, "You shouldn't be used to that. No one should."

"Well," I drop my eyes, "I am and I'm fine."

"No." Finger on my chin, he tips my chin up, forcing me to meet his eye. "You're not. It's okay to admit when someone hurts you. You've certainly given me hell all these years."

I let out a watery laugh at that. Tears burn my eyes, but I sniff them back. "It's all so stupid."

"There's nothing stupid about your feelings, and I'm sorry I hurt you too."

"Back at you." I nod and sit a little straighter. "We really made a mess of things, didn't we?"

Chuckling, he brings his hand back up to my cheek. His thumb moves in slow, careful circles. "I think we're starting to get it together."

With just a few simple words and a couple minutes of his time, he's managed to make me feel better.

Sometimes, all it takes is seeing that someone cares.

"By the way," he says carefully. "The guys are picking me up to go out tonight. They said that since I never got a proper bachelor party, they owe me one."

I eye him over the rim of my cup. "Why do I feel like I should be worried?"

"*I'm* worried. There's no telling what those fuckers have planned. Jude in particular."

"Should I wish you luck?"

He finishes the last dregs of his hot chocolate and sets his cup down. "Probably."

I pat his hand and grin. "Good luck."

This camaraderie we're building is all too reminiscent of our long-ago friendship. A part of me can't help but wonder how I'll survive it if I lose him a second time.

twenty-one

DAIRE

NOW THAT I'M not living with Cree and Jude, it's hard to see them. Cree and I practice together every day, though there's no time to really talk. And Jude's on the football team, and our schedules don't line up. When they cornered me earlier today and said they wanted to take me out for a bachelor party of sorts I was more than a little concerned about what they might have up their sleeves. Especially considering all the shit we've been known to get up to. I've been on my best behavior for weeks, avoiding anything that might make it seem like I'd be an unfit father. I haven't even gone to

Harvey's—the bar on campus that's been a staple for me and my friends for the last few years.

"Where are we going?" I gripe from the back seat of Cree's Bronco.

Jude's up front in the passenger seat—after the truth came out about Jude and Cree's sister, they've been surprisingly amicable. Cree can't be too mad when it's fucking obvious that Jude's obsessed with Millie. The guy worships the ground she walks on.

What was even more of a shock was finding Luke Covey in the back seat when I climbed in. He's always sort of floated on the outside edges of our friend group. Since he doesn't go out much, it makes it hard to get to know the guy.

"To get Mexican food and celebrate your nuptials. I still can't believe you're fucking married, dude."

"I feel like I'm being kidnapped."

At my grumbling Luke actually manages a laugh.

"Dude." Jude turns around, clutching the back of his seat. "You're too old to be kidnapped."

"We've been driving forever."

I might be a little cranky too. Practice was rough, and I'm pretty sure my ribs are bruised.

"Good food is worth the drive."

I look to my left at Covey. "How'd you get roped into this?"

He flicks his fingers lazily at the two guys in the front of the car. "I heard tacos, and I was sold."

"Fair enough." I watch the world pass by outside the window, wondering what Rosie is up to. We've gotten along well since we finally talked about what happened our junior year. We might be the two biggest idiots on the planet, but we were teenagers, and it became so much bigger than it needed to be.

After what feels like one hundred years, we finally pull into the restaurant parking lot.

"I gotta piss," I say, pushing my door open. Mostly, I just need to get out of the car.

For years, I've been hanging out with these guys, but suddenly, it feels weird. They've been caught up in their own lives for the past few months, and it's safe to say that I've gotten used to not going out. I hate to admit it, even to myself, but I'd rather be at home on the couch watching a game.

By the time I come out of the restroom and find the guys, they're already seated at a booth, but there's one new addition.

"Teddy?" I ask as I approach.

He graduated last year and moved to New York City. He popped up earlier this year when he stayed with his mom for a bit and I was still living with the guys, but I haven't seen him in months.

Teddy stands, a sombrero wobbling on his head. "You think I'd miss your bachelor party? Never." To Cree he says, "Who turns down an excuse to drink tequila? And don't worry, I got you a hat too."

He holds one out to me, and suddenly, the other guys are wearing them too. Luke is paler than he was before, his lips turned down in a frown. I bet he's regretting wanting tacos now.

"Great. Thanks for being sure to include me in all of this." I gesture to the table and take a seat.

As I do, Teddy plunks the sombrero down on my head.

I close my eyes and groan. "Are we going to get in trouble for wearing these?" I ask. "This feels wrong."

"No, the waitress gave them to me. They use them for parties."

Great. Now there is no getting out of this.

"Fantastic," I grumble, roughing a hand down my face.

The waitress stops by for our drink order and places two bowls of chips and salsa on the table.

Cree, Luke, and I dig in. I didn't have time to eat after practice, and it looks like they're just as ravenous. Jude and Teddy, on the other hand, look downright scared.

Teddy raises his hands. "I'll ... uh ... wait for her to bring some more. You guys have at it."

I still can't get over the fact that Teddy's even here. He's like a whack-a-mole that just pops up randomly and disappears again.

"Here you guys go," our waitress says with a smile, setting our drinks on the table.

I grab my Corona and squeeze the lime into the bottle. As I take that first pull, I survey my friends. Even though I was reluctant about coming out tonight—and still butt hurt that my friends weren't there for me when I needed them—I'm glad I did.

Every one of them had their own shit going on too, so I'm getting over it. After what I went through with Rosie, I've learned my lesson about holding a grudge.

Teddy gasps so loudly that beside me, Luke looks like he's ready to jump out of his skin.

"What the fuck, dude?" Jude shakes his head.

He shared a dorm room with Teddy until this year. He knows the guy too damn well.

"They have karaoke."

As a collective, we all groan.

Luke gives a chuckle. "Am I wrong, or did you sing karaoke at Harvey's dressed as Voldemort last year?"

Teddy's face splits in a grin. "Fuck yes. I'm glad my performance was rememorable."

"Rememorable?" Jude repeats, sneaking a chip while Cree isn't paying attention. "Dude, I think you mean memorable."

Teddy shrugs. "You knew what I meant."

With Teddy, you never know what'll come out of his mouth or what will happen next. It's best to be prepared for any scenario.

By the time I have a full beer in me I'm feeling mellow.

Maybe it's the beer, or maybe it's because I'm a fucking dad now, but I'm feeling nostalgic tonight. How many more nights will we have like this as a group? Graduation is only a few months away, and then we'll all be going our separate ways.

When my phone buzzes in my pocket, I dig it out, and I can't help but grin when I see Rosie's name.

> Rosie: How's it going? Do I need to call with a fake emergency to save you?
>
> Me: It's fine.
>
> Rosie: Okay. Have fun.

I put my phone away, and when I look up, every guy around the table is staring at me. "What?" I ask stupidly.

Cree is downright gleeful when he asks, "Was that Rosie?"

"Yes?" I'm not sure why it comes out as a question, but it does.

"He's got it bad," Jude says to Cree.

"What?" I look between the four guys, my brain clearly lagging after a single beer.

"You're falling for your wife," Cree chortles. "Oh, this is brilliant. You gave me such a fucking hard time over Ophelia, and now the universe is getting back at you."

"I ... no. I mean I *like* her—as a friend. We're patching things up."

"Dude." Teddy points a tortilla chip at me. "As someone who fell for my fake girlfriend, I feel like I'm more than qualified to speak on this subject. You've got the hots for your wife."

Do I?

Rosie's beautiful—she's always been—but getting feelings involved could make this arrangement messy. Right? It doesn't matter that when I kiss her, it's like ... like magic. As cheesy as that sounds.

I've tried my hardest not to think about those kisses, because I'll drive myself insane if I do.

When I made the rule about not falling for each other, there wasn't even a glimmer of a possibility in my mind that I would end up with all these complicated feelings for her.

Fuck, I think Teddy's right.

"Love is scary as fuck," Jude pipes in. "But it's worth it, man. With the right person, it's worth it."

Cree glowers. "You're dating my sister. I don't want to hear anything you have to say. *Bleh.*" He fake gags. "I can't believe I'm going to be stuck with you for the rest of my life."

Jude raises his hands and leans back in the chair. "What I said still stands."

"What about you, Covey?" Cree asks, lifting his chin. "You ever been in love?"

"No." He shakes his head. "I haven't."

Narrowing my eyes, I ask, "Have you been out with Bertie?"

A rush of protectiveness hits me. Rosie's best friend is a cool chick and doesn't deserve to get strung along.

Luke ducks his head, and I'd fucking swear the guy is blushing. "I asked her on a date. She said no."

"Oh. I'm sorry, man." I sit back, pushing against the edge of the table. "She just got out of a long-term relationship. From what Rosie's told me, it was messy at times."

"It's okay," he says, picking up his beer. "Sometimes timing is everything, and when it doesn't line up…" He shrugs in a *what-are-you-going-to-do-about-it* way.

"I didn't tell you this, but I'm pretty sure she likes you. Don't give up on her."

He sits up a little straighter at that, his expression brightening. "Really?"

I nod, bringing my beer to my lips.

"Cool. Okay. I'll text her or something."

Our waitress approaches with a tray full of food. "Here you go." She sets each of our plates in front of us, then tucks the tray under her arm. "Any more drinks?"

As a collective we say, "Yes."

"I'll be back with those in a minute."

I've already scarfed one whole taco down when she returns with our second round. I won't have more than this, but since we're celebrating, I might as well indulge.

Jude raises his bottle in the air, his sombrero tilting to the side. "To the death of Daire's bachelorhood."

I shake my head and bite back a laugh.

"To the death of Daire's bachelorhood," the rest echo the sentiment.

I tip my bottle at them and drink.

I'M MOSTLY sober by the time the guys drop me off, but it's late, so I fully expect to find Rosie in bed. Instead, I find her in the family room, burrowed beneath a mountain of blankets, haloed by the light of the TV.

I struggle to get my shoes off, having to lean against the wall and yank one off, then the other rather than toe them off like I normally would. Maybe I *am* feeling the effects of the alcohol more than I thought. "What are you doing?"

"Watching a movie." Her voice is muffled by the blankets.

My skin suddenly feels too hot, so I shrug out of my coat and drop it onto the floor. Then goes my sweatshirt and t-shirt.

Rosie's eyes widen comically. "Are you … am I getting a striptease right now?"

"I just wanna be comfortable."

When I reach for my belt, she yelps, covering her eyes with the blanket.

Once I'm down to my boxers, I grab a blanket and join her on the couch.

Slowly, she peeks out from behind her barricade, only revealing one brown eye to me. "Please tell me you're wearing *something* under there."

I smirk. "You've already seen my dick. What difference does it make?"

"Can you blame me for not wanting your bare ass on the new couch?"

I chuckle, my body lighting up with amusement. "I have my boxers on. You can relax."

She keeps her face mostly covered, but what I can see of her cheeks is stoplight red. She continues staring at me like she's in some sort of trance.

"Watch your movie." I point to the screen.

"This is so weird," she mutters, but eventually she turns her attention back to the TV.

The couch is big. I could've picked any spot. But I chose the one right beside her. It's weird, this feeling of wanting to be close to her, but I don't have the energy to fight it.

The movie is one I haven't seen before. One of those lovey-dovey kinds. But I get sucked in anyway. Eventually her toes find their way from her blanket to beneath mine.

"Jesus." I flinch. "Why are your feet like ice?"

"I don't know." She bats her eyes. "I'm cold. Care to warm them up for me?"

An embarrassingly high-pitched sound leaves me when she presses her entire ice-cold foot to my thigh instead of just her toes.

Grabbing her foot, I yank it into my lap and press my thumb into her arch.

A tiny moan escapes her full lips. "That feels so good," she admits, closing her eyes.

It takes concerted effort not to grin at her response. "Glad I could put my hands to use in some way."

She tugs her foot back at my comment, but I hold on tighter. "Nuh-uh. You're not getting away that easily."

I work my thumb around her whole foot, paying attention to the spots that are sore based on the sounds she makes.

Eyes closed, she rests her head back against the couch. "You're really good at that."

I bite the inside of my cheek to hide my amusement. "I'm good at lots of things."

She's quiet for a moment. Then she raises her head and levels me with a thoughtful look. "Why do I feel like you're flirting with me?"

My fingers still, along with my breathing. "Maybe I am."

Silence stretches between us.

"You shouldn't," she finally says, her chin lowering a fraction. "It's ... I don't want to get hurt."

Heart hammering, I blurt out, "Would it be so bad? You and me? For real?"

Her mouth pops open in an adorable look of shock. "I've admitted to having a crush on you for *years*, and you're asking me that? It's ... it's what I always wanted," she admits softly, her focus now fixed on the blanket she's snuggled under rather than me. "But Daire ... feelings would complicate things. We're doing this for Sammy."

I know what she's saying, and fuck, out of the two of us, she's being the smart one here, but I can't stop myself.

I lean into her, hesitating with my mouth millimeters from hers.

"Tell me not to kiss you, Rosie."

"I..." Her breath fans across my lips, warm and sweet. "I can't do that."

It's all the invitation I need.

I cup her cheek and angle her head back. Her fingers find their way around my neck, holding me to her as I deepen the kiss. She tastes of chocolate and something else I can't pinpoint.

Somehow, I get her on her back, our legs tangled in the blankets. I hold my weight above her with one elbow planted on the couch cushion, not wanting to break the kiss for anything.

There's a small voice in the back of my mind warning me that I shouldn't like kissing her so much. Because she's right—it could seriously complicate things. But instinct has taken over, and I make no move to stop. Stopping feels fucking impossible.

I want *more*.

I *crave* more.

I swallow the little sounds she makes, desperate to hear them again.

"God, Rosie," I groan, skimming my thumb over her bottom lip. She's flushed beneath me, eyes heavy. I brush my nose over the skin of her neck, smiling to myself when she shivers. "I want to make you come. Will you let me do that?"

Her eyes widen, and she goes rigid beneath me. "I ... I don't ... I've never..."

My heart lurches at her reaction. "What are you trying to say?"

She presses her lips together, turning her head to the side and breaking eye contact. "A guy has never made me come, okay?"

I stare down at her. Shock and anger on her behalf swirl inside me, mingling with a little awe. "Never?"

She presses her tongue against the inside of her cheek. "Nope. Not with his fingers. Or his mouth. Or his cock."

A primal need to rise to the challenge roars to life inside me, insisting that *I* can.

"Don't get me wrong," she goes on, "I've had orgasms, but only with my vibrator. I guess I'm broken." She gives a small, humorless laugh.

She makes a move like she's going to slip out from under me, but I tighten my hold, not willing to let her go. Not yet at least.

"You're not broken," I whisper, my lips close enough to brush hers. "Are you willing to let me try?"

Her lips part. "Try…?"

"To give you an orgasm."

"Daire," she scoffs. "I … this sounds like a bad idea."

I kiss just beneath her chin and inhale her scent. "I disagree. I think it's a very good idea. A great one even. Downright excellent."

She bites her lip, her eyes swimming with uncertainty. "And … when nothing happens, you'll be okay? You won't be mad?"

"First off, I would never be mad at you for something like that. Second, it *is* going to happen."

"How can you be so sure?" she argues, and I'd swear there are tears in her eyes.

"Because," I smile, slowly plucking the blankets away from her body, "you've never had sex with me."

Her pained expression lightens a fraction. "That cocky, are you?"

"If you want to call it cocky, then sure." I reach for the band on her sleep pants but stop there. I arch a brow, waiting for a signal from her. "I'd say self-assured."

"That good in bed, are you?" There's a little smirk on her lips—one I'm very much looking forward to turning into an O of pleasure.

"I've never heard any complaints."

Finally, as a pink flush creeps up her neck, she gives me a small nod, and I wiggle her pants down, panties with them.

It's kind of adorable, the way she presses her legs together in an effort to hide herself from me.

"Oh, come on, Rosie," I goad with a smile, "show me that pretty pussy."

She hesitates still, and I sit up, my stomach sinking.

"Are you okay? We don't have to do this if you don't want to. I wouldn't push you to do anything you're not comfortable with."

"I know." There's a quiver in her voice. "I know you wouldn't."

I swallow past the trepidation rising up inside me. "Then what's scaring you?"

Her stomach shakes with a laugh. "You. Me. *Us.*"

"I understand." I think I do, at least. "I'm terrified."

Of feeling something real.

Of fucking all this up.

Surprise lights her eyes. "You are?"

I nod, skimming my finger around her belly button. She shivers from the touch.

"Why don't we see where all this goes?" I hold her gaze, wanting her to know I'm serious about this. "We're already married. We might as well see what happens, don't you think?"

She stares back, a million thoughts swirling behind her eyes, and swallows audibly. "I ... okay."

"Okay," I echo. "Good. Can I *please* make you come now?"

She clutches my wrist. "You can't—"

I press a finger to her lips. "I *will*."

She scrutinizes me for a long, silent moment, then gives me a small nod.

This time when I put my hands on her thighs, she relaxes the muscles there, letting me spread them.

"Fuck." The word rips out of me. Her bare pussy is pink and glistening. She's fucking drenched. Like maybe she's been turned on from the moment I did my impromptu striptease.

Desperate to taste her, I lower my head and take my time licking her.

She whimpers beneath me.

"Does that feel good, baby?" I kiss the inside of her thigh. "You want more?"

Her breathless little "yes" has my cock aching.

I suck at her clit, and when she rocks her hips into me, I can't help but chuckle. Looping my arms around her legs, I hold her still. I've never understood why some guys don't like going down on girls. There are few things in this world more satisfying than working a woman up with my tongue and my fingers and watching her squirm beneath me, begging for more.

With one hand, Rosie rakes her fingers through my hair and grasps it roughly. I pull my mouth away from her core, looking up her body at her. Her lids are heavy and she's pulled her t-shirt up so she can palm her right breast.

Oh, fuck.

She's so fucking hot.

How the hell could I have so stupidly thrown our friendship away? Why didn't I try for something more with her?

When she loosens her hold on my hair, I shake my head. "Hold on to me, Rosie."

She whimpers at my words and obeys.

This time, I add my fingers along with my tongue, and instantly, she gets even wetter. Her legs begin to shake, her core quivering along with them, signaling that her orgasm is approaching.

It's sooner than I expected.

Much sooner, considering that a guy's never made her come.

Deep down, I hope it's because she was secretly always waiting for me.

I was always the man for her. I was just too fucking dumb to see it.

"Daire, I—*ohmygod, I'm coming.*"

I tease her through her climax, and once her shaking subsides, I move up her body until I find her lips. If she doesn't like the taste of herself on my mouth, she doesn't show it. She kisses me back, her arms wrapping around my torso.

My lips find the curve of her ear. "I'm not done with you yet."

She opens her mouth, but before she can speak, I grab her and roll onto my back, taking her with me.

"Wha—"

"Hold on to the back of the couch," I coax, fingers digging into her ass. "And ride my face."

"Oh." She looks down at me, her jaw unhinged.

I do my best not to laugh at her mildly horror-stricken expression. If I do, this will be coming to an end far too soon.

"I'm ... won't I be too heavy?"

"Rosie?" I squeeze her ass and look up at her, trying not to think about how her soaking wet pussy is pressing into the fabric of my boxes. "When a man tells you to ride his face, you ride his goddamn face, you hear me?"

She squeaks when I lift her up and put her right where I want her.

Too heavy? Her fucking mother.

There's no doubt in my mind that I'll be having a talk with that woman sooner rather than later. I hate that her mother, of all people, put those kinds of thoughts and feelings in her head.

Un-fucking-acceptable.

"You're hovering, Rosie," I singsong. "Give me more." I give her ass another squeeze and tug her down.

Her first instinct is to resist, but after about three seconds, she finally does.

At the first spear of my tongue into her pussy, she nearly falls off the couch. With one hand still on her ass, I slide the other up to her ribcage to steady her.

Her reaction might be funny if I didn't want to make her orgasm again so bad.

Maybe even a third time if she'll let me.

She holds on to the back of the couch like I told her. At first, she's stiff above me, but as I continue, she relaxes and begins to roll her hips against my face.

Fucking heaven.

I groan, deep in my throat, relishing in the absolute trust she's putting in me.

That little rumble is all it takes to have her crying out and falling over the edge.

She's certainly reactive with me. Obviously, she's wasted far too much time on boys who don't know what the fuck they're doing when it comes to women.

I barely give her time to come down from the high before I have her on the couch again. I sink to the floor between her legs and palm her inner thighs, spreading her wide.

I'm fucking desperate to stroke my cock, but I hold myself back.

This is about her.

It's *not* about my pleasure. Not tonight.

I want Rosie to enjoy herself without thinking she owes me anything.

"I can't come again," she whimpers, throwing an arm over her face.

I slide two fingers into her dripping pussy, and instantly, she quivers around me. "Your pussy disagrees with that statement." I crook my fingers.

In response, her back bows off the couch. "Holy fuck, Daire."

Fuck, I've never felt this satisfied in my entire life.

I work my fingers in and out. Slow. Fast. Hard. Gentle.

The second I add my tongue, she detonates like a bomb going off.

"Holy fucking shit."

Her skin glistens with sweat, her breasts heaving. I'm not sure when she ditched her shirt entirely, but I certainly appreciate the view of her full tits.

I lick my fingers clean, fighting a grin at her wide-eyed expression as she watches me.

"I didn't think that was possible," she admits, reaching for a blanket and pulling it over her torso.

With a tut, of disapproval, I swipe the blanket from her. I'm not done looking my fill yet.

"Glad to prove you wrong." I join her on the couch, ignoring the way my rock-hard dick is begging to be let free.

"That was ... wow."

I chuckle and drop a kiss the top of her head.

Her eyes drop to my lap. "Can I—"

I grab a pillow, covering up my erection. "No."

Her face flames. "Oh. I—wow. Okay."

Averting her gaze, she tries to scurry away on all fours to the other side of the couch. The sight alone almost has me coming in my underwear. She's killing me.

I grab her bare waist and pull her back down beside me.

"I didn't mean it like that. Believe me. But this was about you. Not me. I don't want you to feel like you owe me because I made you come."

"Three times." She holds up her fingers and wiggles them. "Three."

I snatch her hand and pull it to my mouth, nipping at them. "Next time I'll make it four. Maybe five if I'm feeling lucky." I wink.

Her mouth falls open. "Five?"

"Mhm. I'll make you count them."

Standing, I stretch my arms above my head. I revel in the way she watches me. It's not just blanket desire in her eyes. No, I swear that emotion is accompanied by something like admiration, maybe even—*nope, not going there*.

I hold out a hand to her. "We need to go to bed."

"I don't think I can move."

I shrug. "No problem." I haul her up and over my shoulder, eliciting a scream from her. Grinning at the response, I smack her ass, then I make my way for the stairs.

"Daire! Put me down!"

I do. On her bed.

I give myself a solid ten seconds to admire her lying on her bed naked, cheeks flushed from the orgasms that *I* gave her when no other guy could.

She scowls up at me. "Wipe that shit-eating grin off your face, Hendricks."

My smile only grows as my heart pounds harder in my chest. "You're welcome, *Mrs*. Hendricks."

Before she can retort, I walk out and close her door. A pillow hits it with a soft thud a second later.

It's late, but there's no way I'm going to sleep until I've had an extra-long shower.

Next time, I told Rosie.

Because there will be a next time. And a time after that.

And maybe, if we let ourselves, a forever.

twenty-two

ROSIE

AFTER THE WAY the last game went, I'm not exactly keen to attend another.

But when Daire pulled the puppy dog eyes on me and asked me to come, I was a goner. It's the team's last game before winter break. They've been playing well. Amazingly, really. They have a chance to make it all the way to the Frozen Four if they keep this up. It'd be an incredible way to end Daire's senior year as well as his hockey career, since he doesn't plan to continue beyond college.

Once I'm finished with my makeup, I fix my hair into a braid.

Bertie was apprehensive when I asked her—and she's been tight-lipped about whatever is going on with her and Luke—but I didn't give her an opportunity to say no. Besides, I don't think she'd let me face those catty girls alone.

My phone buzzes on the bathroom counter. I cringe, hoping Bertie isn't backing out after all, but the message is from Daire.

> Daire: You were still in your bathroom when I left. I put a gift for you on your bed. Wear it tonight.

I frown at the text message.

Wear it?

I crack my bathroom door open and venture into the bedroom. Sure enough, there's a hastily wrapped box on the mattress. I can't help but smile at the thought of Daire wrapping this up himself.

Quickly, I tear into the paper and lift the lid. Inside, I find a jersey.

It's blue and orange, our school's colors, with Aldridge Hockey on the front along with an angry-looking wolf.

A giddy sensation hits me when I turn it around and find Daire's jersey number, six, on it.

I expect the area above the number to be blank—or at the most, to say *Hendricks*.

But no, this is Daire. He doesn't do anything half-assed.

Mrs. Hendricks has been added to the top.

I trace my finger over the outline of *Mrs.*

Don't cry, don't cry, don't cry. You'll ruin your makeup!

It's hard not to break down at the thoughtfulness of the gift. It's custom, which means he had to have put the order in soon after that disastrous game, before we ever truly made up for the past. Before… Heat floods my body at the memory of what happened on the couch last week. Nothing remotely close has happened since. He hasn't even kissed me.

It hasn't been awkward, though.

I'm terrified to make a move, to show how much I actually want him. And by the way he watches me, so thoughtful and with what I swear is longing, I think he feels the same.

The changes are mind-boggling. Only a few months ago, I hated Daire with every part of my being. Now? I very well could be falling in love with him all over again.

I lay the shirt down on the bed, and as I pick up the box to throw it away, I find a note inside.

In case anyone ever doubts you're mine.

—Daire

Feeling like I'm floating along on a high, I stick the note in my nightstand drawer, then force myself to finish getting ready. The last thing I do is put the jersey on.

I don't bother texting Daire back. He's busy getting ready for the game. I'd rather thank him in person anyway. Preferably with my mouth in certain places he didn't allow me to explore last time.

I stuff my wallet with my ID into my pocket and shoot a text to Bertie to let her know I'm on my way.

Turning up the music in the car, I head toward campus, and by the time I pull up outside the dorm, I've already had a full dance party.

"Your bass is shaking. I thought it was an earthquake." Bertie has to yell to be heard over the music. She reaches over and turns it down. "Are you trying—what are you wearing?" She gapes at my jersey.

I grin, wiggling in my seat. "You haven't even seen the best part yet."

"Show me!"

I pull away from the curb and head toward the arena. "You'll see it when I get out."

"Fine." She crosses her arms over her chest. "Make me wait."

"So," I drawl, "what's up with you and Luke?"

Traffic is at a crawl as we approach the arena. We should've gotten here sooner. If the dorm wasn't five miles from the arena, I would've parked there and walked.

She picks at a loose thread on her jeans. "Nothing."

"Nothing?" I repeat, side-eyeing her.

"He's sweet."

"And hot," I point out. "A lethal combination."

"He's great in a lot of ways." She looks down at her lap. "But I dated Tommy for a long time. Don't get me wrong, I'm over him, but I'm not sure I'm ready to date. I would be okay with it just being a hookup sort of thing, but he said he's not interested in only doing the casual thing."

"Oh … wow."

"I know," she laughs. "A hot hockey guy who *wants* a relationship? A rarity. But I just … I don't think I can be what he wants."

The car in front of me moves a smidge, and I crawl along with it.

"From the way he looks at you, it's obvious you're already everything he wants. But I love and respect you, so if you're not ready to date, I won't pressure you about it."

"I just…" She studies the pale pink polish on her nails. "I don't know what I want. But he's a good guy, and I refuse to string him along."

I reach over and take her hand, giving it a gentle squeeze.

It hurts to see my best friend so lost. Even though she knows ending her relationship with Tommy was the right thing, she's still mourning the loss of a years' long relationship.

It doesn't help that I moved out right after everything went down.

"Why don't you come over tomorrow, and we'll order pizza and watch a movie or something?"

Bertie will be heading home for winter break soon, so I won't see her until January.

"Are you sure you're not too busy?"

"For you?" I scoff. "Never."

Traffic continues to move at a snail's pace. I have reserved seats, so we'll be fine, but I prefer to be settled in before the pregame activities start.

Eventually I'm directed to turn and end up parking what feels like a mile from the entrance. At least I wore sneakers.

Bertie and I hustle inside, and I head to the bathroom to pee while she gets snacks.

There's already a line for the bathroom, but since I started my period yesterday, I have no choice but to wait.

When I finally exit the restroom, Bertie is leaning against the wall nearby with an order of nachos and two soft drinks.

"Let me take those." I reach for the drinks.

She gladly hands them over, then we start for the stairs that lead down into the arena.

"Rosie!"

At the sound of Bertie's high-pitched shriek, I jump and spin around. "What?"

"Your jersey says *Mrs. Hendricks.*"

My stomach dips. "Oh. That."

"Yes, that!" She clutches my arm so violently I'm lucky I don't drop the drink I'm holding in that hand. "I didn't realize *this* was the best part."

My cheeks heat, and a smile splits my face unbidden. "He said he didn't want anyone to doubt I'm his."

I'm still swooning over that note.

"Wait," she leans in close and lowers her voice, "does this mean things are getting real?"

"I don't know." I shrug, biting my lip as my heart thumps hard against my breastbone. "But I think so."

The scream that flies out of her has the people nearby turning to look at us.

"We're fine." I wave. "She thought she saw a spider."

Most everyone returns to their own business, though several girls in a group nearby look around in pure panic at the thought of a spider.

"We need to get to our seats. I don't want to miss anything."

Ironic, since I didn't even plan to attend until Daire asked me to and provided me with the two tickets.

When we're finally in our seats, Bertie starts in again. I'd expect nothing less from her.

"He put his name on you. With *Mrs.*"

"We *are* married." I take a sip of my soda and survey the ice without really paying attention.

She swats at me. "You know what I mean."

I can feel the glares from the girls around us, but I do my best to ignore them and whatever venom they might spew.

Stealing a nacho from Bertie's order, I pop it into my mouth.

With a glower, she pulls the tray into her chest. "Mine."

I smile back. "You know you don't mind sharing with me."

"Only when I'm not hangry. I skipped lunch."

"Bertie," I scold lightly. "Why didn't you eat?"

She shrugs, pinching the cheesiest nacho chip she can find between her fingers. "I was busy and forgot."

Growing up with a mother who constantly skipped meals and claimed to forget means my first instinct is to question whether she's being honest.

But by the way Bertie goes to town on her nachos, I believe her when she says she forgot, so I keep my mouth shut.

I need to talk to her about coming with me to try on

dresses. There's no way I want to endure what my mother might say without some sort of backup. But this isn't the place to talk about it, not with potential eavesdroppers around us.

As the game begins, Bertie holds out a chip. "You can have one more."

I laugh, taking it from her. "Thanks."

As I'm chomping on the chip, Daire skates by and stops, ice spraying up around him. He taps the plexiglass with his stick, as if I don't see him already. He waves, and some of the girls around me giggle like he's waving at them. He frowns as he scans the bleachers around me, then points directly at me and makes a heart shape with his hands.

I try, and fail, not to smile. He taps the glass with his finger, waiting for…

I roll my eyes and make a heart hand back at him.

Cree skates up to him then, clapping him on the shoulder and pulling him away.

Bertie leans over, finding my ear. "Either he's got it bad for you, or he really doesn't want these bitches talking about you."

"He doesn't want them talking shit about me."

"Yeah, probably," she agrees, wiping her fingers on a wad of napkins, "but I still think he likes you."

Despite my best efforts, hope, the most dangerous feeling of all, springs up inside my chest.

twenty-three

DAIRE

"ADMIRING YOUR HANDIWORK?" Rosie asks from the doorway of the nursery.

All the furniture finally arrived, and while a good deal of it was already assembled, like the dresser beneath the window, a few things, like the crib, needed to be put together.

I turn to face her. "As a matter of fact, I am."

She's already dressed to go. If we don't leave in the next couple of minutes, we'll be late to our visit with Sammy.

My chest aches at the thought of holding him again.

This'll only be the second time I get to cradle him in my arms.

In his whole life, the amount of time I've gotten to spend with him can be counted in minutes.

She steps up beside me. "It looks nice, right? Cozy?"

I nod. She did an incredible job picking out the furniture and decor. It's ... honestly, it's perfect. But the thought that he'll never get to stay here with us is like a knife to the chest.

I understand and respect the court's caution with this.

But selfishly, I just want my son.

I step out of the room, and Rosie follows. She eases the door shut with a quiet click.

"Thank you for this. For all of this." My words come out thick with sincerity. Rosie didn't have to agree to marry me, to help me out the way she has. "I'm sure this isn't the way you hoped to spend Christmas Eve."

Her answering smile does something to my heart. "I'm right where I want to be."

Fuck. That means more to me than she can possibly know.

JUST LIKE LAST TIME, we're met by my lawyer and a social worker.

I cradle the present I got for Sammy in my hands, twirling the box around and around as nerves skitter through me. It's a silly little thing, but when I saw the tiny hockey jersey, I couldn't pass it up, so I had it customized with my last name. Maybe it's forward of me to want my son to share my last name, but it's hard not to dream about the prospect. Sammy might not like hockey as he gets older. He might prefer another sport or even no sport at all. But I can't help but envision us playing together when he's older.

"You're fidgeting," Rosie whispers, pulling out the chair at the table.

"I can't help it."

She points at the seat, silently directing me to sit.

I don't listen. Instead, I pace the room, filled with a nervous energy I can't expel.

Minutes pass, and my restlessness only gets worse.

Even my lawyer looks worried, eyeing her watch.

Eventually I stop in front of her, my heart lodged in my throat. "They're not coming, are they?"

She exhales a breath, exchanging a look with the social worker. Nothing is spoken, but information is conveyed, nonetheless. The social worker slips from the room.

"They should have been here an hour ago. That doesn't look good for them. We'll wait a little longer, but I can't force them to show up. The good news for you, however, is that going against a court ordered visit won't look good for them when it's time to make a decision about custody."

I nod, wiping my damp palms on my jeans. "All right. We'll keep waiting, then."

The thought of not seeing Sammy today makes me want to throw up. I've been counting down the days since we scheduled this visitation. But none of us can magically make Danielle show up with him.

Rosie's gentle hand lands on my back. "Hey," her soft voice coaxes, "are you okay?"

"I have to be," I reply, ducking my head.

"Is there anything I can do?"

Shaking my head, I reach for her hand and bring it to my mouth. "No," I say and press a kiss to her knuckles. "But thank you."

She gives me a reassuring smile. "Maybe they got stuck in traffic."

"Maybe."

DEFEATED DOESN'T EVEN BEGIN to describe how I feel when we get home. I drag myself into the house, and Rosie trails silently behind me. She hasn't said a word since we left the social services office. She understands that no words can ease the pain in my chest.

They never showed up.

I set the present down on the kitchen counter.

I've never wanted a drink more than I do right now, but I ignore the beers in the fridge and instead pull out ingredients for turkey burgers.

"I ... uh ... I'm going to shower," Rosie says from the archway.

I jerk my head in a nod. "Dinner will be ready in about an hour."

She hesitates, like she's hopeful I'll say more. When I lower my head and silently continue prepping the food, her footsteps echo on the stairs.

With her gone, I pause, giving myself a moment to break down.

I slam the side of my fist against the counter.

I'm sad. Hurt. Angry.

It's fucking Christmas Eve, and I didn't get to see my son.

The stupid fucking present I bought sits mockingly on the island.

I knew this wouldn't be easy, but I wasn't anywhere near prepared for all the emotions I've been hit with. Maybe this is my punishment for all the times I scoffed when my dad said we'd understand how he's always felt once we had kids of our own.

I prepare dinner on autopilot, and just as I'm finishing up, Rosie returns. It seems impossible, but she's beautiful in every state—even in an oversized hoodie and shorts, with her hair damp from the shower.

"You smell good," I blurt as she steps up beside me.

I squeeze my eyes shut. Fuck. I can't believe I said that out loud.

She tucks a piece of hair behind her ear, the move drawing my attention to her makeup-free face. "Thanks." She shuffles to the fridge and emerges with a can of ginger ale—something I've learned she likes to have nightly.

I grab a straw from the drawer and pass it to her.

"Am I that predictable?" She slips it into the can.

I set our plates on the table and take a seat. "I'm learning your quirks."

"I feel like that should worry me." She arches a brow as she slides out the chair beside me. "Cozy." Her arm brushes mine.

"I wanted you close."

No point in beating around the bush.

"Hmm," she hums, picking up a sweet potato fry. "You're starting to make me think you like me."

I bump her elbow with mine. "I *do* like you, Rosie."

Her eyes meet mine, and the room around us drifts away. I forget about dinner. About my disappointment. All I see, all I feel, is her.

Leaning in, I hesitate, giving her the chance to back away.

When she doesn't, I cup her cheek with my left hand. The second our lips touch, a fire ignites inside me.

Scooting my chair back, I pull her closer. At the

same time, she pivots and lifts her leg until she sinks down, straddling me.

Between kisses, she says, "This … is … crazy."

She's right, but I don't stop. I *can't*. Images of that night in the living room play on repeat in my head far more than they should. I've grown way too used to getting myself off in the shower to the memory of her taste and the way she writhed against me.

"Do you want me to stop?" I kiss down the column of her neck.

She pulls away, her eyes hazy. "Don't you fucking dare."

Dinner is forgotten in an instant. I wasn't hungry anyway. Without letting go of her, I stand and circle the table. I set her down on the surface, working the fabric of her hoodie up her body.

Fuck.

She's wearing nothing beneath it.

I press my forehead to hers. "You're killing me."

"You can touch me." She puts a gentle hand against my jaw. "I want you to."

Eyes closed, I inhale, relishing those words. Frankly, I don't fucking deserve them. Not after how I've treated her over the years. She doesn't have the first clue what her forgiveness means or what a privilege she's affording me by trusting me with her body.

I cup her breasts—so full and heavy in my hands. Bending down, I swirl my tongue around one nipple and then the other. I kiss my way down her stomach until I reach the elastic band of her sleep shorts. Without waiting for me, she hooks her thumbs under the fabric and shoves them down.

The chuckle that rumbles out of me is low and dark as I take in her naked body on the table before me. "Eager, are we?"

She cuffs the back of my neck and pulls me in until our lips touch. "You have no idea."

I wrap my arms around her and hold her tight. I can't get close enough to her. We're acting like horny teenagers, making out on the table like this. Like we're making up for lost time.

Giving her a gentle push back, I kiss down the column of her neck.

A shiver rolls through her, and she whispers a small "sorry."

"Don't be sorry." I take her right nipple into my mouth, sucking gently. Her little whimper has me smiling. I move to her other breast, giving it the same attention before I sink down to my knees, my face perfectly aligned with her pussy. I groan at the sight of her glistening, pink flesh.

But before I can taste her, my phone rings.

I let out a low curse and sit back on my heels. "I better get that."

It's not often someone calls me, and when they do, it's typically important. After what went on with

Sammy, there's no way I can ignore it.

Rosie nods in understanding and reaches for her sweatshirt. As she yanks it back on and hops down from the table, disappointment floods me.

With a sigh, I pull my phone from my pocket. When my lawyer's name flashes on the screen, my heart jumps. Even though I'm already missing the feel of Rosie's skin beneath my hands, I'm thankful I stopped.

"Hey, what's up?" The greeting is probably a bit too casual, but after working with her all these months, the formalities don't feel necessary.

"There's been an accident."

twenty-four

ROSIE

DAIRE SLAMS his palms on the counter, startling the nurse on the other side.

"Sammy—Samuel Jensen, where is he?"

The nurse taps her keyboard, her attention fixed on the computer screen. "And you are?"

"His father," Daire pants. "Please. I need to know if he's okay."

Sympathy fills the nurse's face. "He's been moved to pediatrics."

"Where's that?" I ask, gently grasping Daire's arm.

"Third floor. Take a left and then a right when you get off the elevators."

I give her a grateful smile. "Thank you."

When I turn around, Daire's already jogging for the elevators, so I have to run to catch up.

He holds the elevator doors open for me as I approach, his face a mask of panic. "Hurry."

I step on beside him and clutch his hand. He tugs it from my hold before I can get a firm grip. A violent wave of embarrassment floods me as he takes a step away.

"Sorry." He leans against the side of the elevator and hangs his head. "I just … I can't right now. Not until I know he's okay."

I nod in understanding, even if hurt still sits heavy in my chest.

When the elevator opens, he's running again. My fluffy boots make it impossible to keep up.

He pauses in front of the pediatric doors, panting.

I slide to a stop beside him and study his profile. "What are you waiting for?"

His Adam's apple bobs, and he turns worried eyes my way. "What if he's not okay? What if he's hurt? What if … what if—"

I shake my head and place a gentle hand on his arm. "Don't go there. Not yet."

He sniffles and takes a deep breath that quakes

through his whole body. "Okay, okay." He chants, rolling his shoulder back.

He shuffles forward and pushes the call button next to the double doors, then takes a step back.

A smooth voice echoes through the speaker on the wall. "How can I help you?"

"I ... uh ... I'm Samuel Jensen's father. I got a call that there'd been an accident and I needed to get here right away."

"Oh. Of course."

There's a buzzing sound, and then the doors glide open.

The desk is around the corner, lit brightly by the halogens above despite the late hour.

"I need to see your ID first," the nurse says, standing from her rolling chair.

Daire fumbles in his pocket for his wallet. When he finally gets it out, he hands her the whole thing, hands shaking.

She doesn't bat an eye, just opens it up and looks from his ID to her computer screen, then up at him.

Passing it back, she looks to me. "And you are?"

"My wife. She's my wife." Trembling, Daire runs his fingers through his hair. "Please, is my son okay?"

"Room six," she says, her tone gentle, and points. "It's that one."

Daire keeps his feet planted and turns to me, blinking. I nod, encouraging him.

Junior is in a room. In the pediatric unit. Not the ER. That has to be a good sign, right?

I put my hand on his back and whisper a gentle "go."

It's all the encouragement he needs. With a shuddering breath, he moves forward, his steps brisk, until he reaches the door to room six.

Inside, we both come to an abrupt stop. The social worker we met with this afternoon is standing on one side of the room, along with a police officer.

Daire assesses them and opens his mouth, but before he can speak, movement from the other side of the room catches his attention. Sammy is lying in a crib, wearing nothing but a diaper. He's hooked up to monitors, but he looks fine, at least on the outside.

"Hey, buddy," Daire croons, shuffling over and reaching his finger out to the baby.

Sammy stirs, closing his hand around Daire's finger, his eyes fluttering sleepily.

"Daddy's here." The gentleness in Daire's tone is so painfully sweet.

I take a step closer to the social worker and officer, arms crossed over my chest. "Can someone tell us what's going on?"

"We're waiting for your lawyer to arrive," the social worker tells me. He can't be more than a few years older than us, but he looks tired. Like he'd rather be anywhere else. "You might as well make yourselves comfortable." He motions to the chair on my left.

I don't feel much like sitting, so I step up to the crib beside Daire and run my fingers through Sammy's downy soft hair.

"It's weird that Danielle and her husband aren't here," I whisper. "Do you think they're talking to a doctor?"

Daire shakes his head. "I don't know."

Thankfully, Daire's lawyer strides in only a few minutes after we arrive. It's nearly one in the morning, yet her makeup is impeccable and there's not one wrinkle in her dress suit.

"Sorry I'm late," she says, setting her bag on a plastic chair. Clapping her hands, she turns to where Daire and I stand. "Have they given you any information?"

Daire shakes his head. "I got here as fast as I could after you called."

"We haven't been here long," I add, worry sitting heavy in my gut.

"All right." Nina tucks her hair behind her ear and clears her throat. "Then I guess it's up to me to inform you that Mr. and Mrs. Jensen have passed away."

My heart stops, and I blink, certain I've heard her wrong. "Passed away?" I look from her to Daire with a frown. "Like ... dead?"

It's perhaps the dumbest question I could possibly ask, but right now, my brain isn't firing on all cylinders.

Daire doesn't take his eyes off his son when he says, "You ... you said there was an accident. I thought you meant Sammy was hurt. I didn't..." He shakes his head. "I didn't think to ask about them."

Nina nods solemnly, hands gently folded together in front of her. "It's why they didn't arrive for the scheduled meeting. It ... um ... took a while to get them out of the car and for everything to get settled." She nods toward the social worker and officer.

Daire rubs the side of his face with his free hand. The other is still occupied with Sammy's fist wrapped around his index finger. "This is a lot to take in."

"I understand." Nina nods. "It's late. We'll discuss everything tomorrow. And by tomorrow, I do mean the twenty-sixth. I have to play Santa for my kids."

Shit. I didn't even realize it's already Christmas day.

"So, what happens next? Is Sammy okay?"

"A doctor will be in shortly to speak with you," the social worker pipes up. "I have some papers I need to go over with you—it's about temporary custody. We should do that while your lawyer is still here."

Daire nods, his complexion paler than normal. "Yeah. All right."

"There's a private room down the hall." This comes from the cop who hasn't spoken until now. I honestly forgot the guy was in the room.

"Okay." Daire nods woodenly. "Will you stay with him?" he asks me.

"Yeah." I give his arm a reassuring squeeze. "Of course."

When it's only Sammy and me, the room is eerily quiet. I stand beside his crib, watching him, at a loss for what else to do. After a few minutes, he flails and fusses.

"Shh," I croon, touching his cheek. I wish I knew more about kids and how to comfort him. The poor thing is hooked up to machines monitoring who knows what. I don't even want to think about how bad the accident must have been if his mom and … well, dad, for lack of a better way to describe the guy, didn't survive.

It hits me then—that Sammy has lost the only parents he knows.

And he's stuck with us.

His biological father and a … *me*.

Two people who've been doing all we can to prepare to have shared custody of him but who are sorely lacking in hands-on experience.

"Oh, Sammy." I smooth his soft blond hair back. "What are we going to do?"

His bottom lip juts out, wobbling.

"Please, don't cry," I beg. "I don't know what to do if you cry. I'm not even sure I'm allowed to pick you up."

What are we going to do?

The house is babyproofed, and we took the CPR class. We've even watched numerous videos, but all the information we've received feels useless when I consider having to actually care for a tiny human.

I find myself running through a mental checklist of what I remember and noting things we might still need to do.

It's all so overwhelming, but it pales in comparison to what this baby has been through in the past twelve hours.

I didn't know Danielle or her husband, but it doesn't matter. They lost their lives, and that's tragic.

I wipe a tear off my cheek. "We're going to take good care of you, Sammy," I say, stroking his head. "You're already so loved by us."

I pull the chair up beside his crib and sit. I don't have much of a voice, but I sing to him, nonetheless, hoping it'll comfort him since I'm not sure I can hold him.

Shockingly, it only takes a few moments for his eyes to grow heavy.

As he drifts off, I curl my legs beneath me and settle into the chair to wait for the others to return.

At some point, I doze off, but when my head lolls, I pop my eyes open and scan the room. Sammy is sleeping peacefully. I'm peering at him, studying his features and fighting a yawn when Daire enters the room. He smiles at the sleeping baby before crouching down in front of me.

Taking both my hands in his, he whispers, "I've been granted temporary custody. We'll have to attend a hearing to establish permanent custody, but Nina said it shouldn't be an issue. Danielle and her husband don't have any family that should give us any trouble."

I nod, wiping the sleep from my eyes. "When can we take him home?"

This cold, white place can't be good for a baby.

"The hospital wants to monitor him for another couple of hours to be sure they haven't missed anything." He plucks his keys from his pocket and hands them to me. "Are you okay to drive home? You could get a few hours of sleep and come back and get us when he's discharged. I didn't even think to grab his car seat or anything before we rushed out."

I take the keys from him, trying not to yawn again, wishing I could stay but knowing he's right. I'll need to prepare to bring him home. "Yeah, I can do that. Keep me updated, okay?"

He steps back, giving me room to stand. "I will." He drops a kiss to the corner of my mouth.

I close my eyes and breathe deeply, hating myself for wanting more. A *real* kiss.

"Be careful. Text me when you're home."

"I will." I look at Sammy sleeping peacefully in the crib, then I slip out of the room.

I get turned around approximately three times before I find the emergency entrance. When we arrived, I was so focused on helping Daire get to Sammy that I barely registered our surroundings and just how large the hospital is.

I'm dead on my feet by the time I enter the house and stomp snow off my boots in the entry. After hanging up my coat, I bend down to undo the laces, then pull my boots off.

Every cell in my body longs to be with Daire, but we need the car seat and supplies, and getting a few hours of sleep in my own bed before we bring Sammy home is probably a good idea.

My bed calls to me, but after being in the hospital, I want to shower first. I scrub my body practically raw and dive under the covers. I'm out within minutes, and when I wake up and check my phone, there's a text waiting for me from Daire telling me that the earliest they'll be discharged is ten.

"Holy shit," I mutter to myself, collapsing back on my pillows.

There's going to be a baby living here. Permanently.

The events of last night come rushing over me.

In a blink, everything has changed. Here we were, preparing for court and a fight to establish some sort of shared custody, and now ... now poor Sammy doesn't have his mom. It breaks my heart. I didn't know the woman, and I might've hated her for having Daire's child, but the fact that she's gone? Just like that? It's scary how quickly it can all come to an end.

I hastily make my bed and throw on a sweater and jeans. Then I hurry into the nursery I've worked so hard on creating. Thank God all the furniture has finally arrived.

Once I've tossed a couple of Sammy's new outfits, along with a few diapers and wipes, into the diaper bag I ordered, I spin in a circle. "Do I need anything else?" I ask aloud, filling the silence. "Blanket." I answer my own question.

I zip the bag, then carry it downstairs and set it, along with the car seat, by the door.

Munching on an energy bar, I pace the length of the kitchen. We have bottles, but we don't have formula, and I don't know what kind he needs.

"This is too much." I fan my face with my hands. "Get your shit together, Rosie."

With a calming breath, I pluck my phone out of my back pocket and text Daire;

> ASK A NURSE OR SOMETHING WHAT KIND OF FORMULA I NEED TO GET.

It doesn't take long before he sends me a screenshot of one.

> Me: I'll pick that up before I get you guys. Ten still seeming likely?

> Daire: Probably closer to 12. The doctor is running behind.

> Me: Anything you want me to bring you?

> Daire: Nah. I'll just shower and change when I get home. We can eat lunch then too.

> Me: All right. Keep me posted.

I set my phone down and resume my pacing. My brain is having an extra difficult time dealing with this rapid turn of events.

Why didn't we take more classes?

Read more parenting books?

Watching tutorials?

Wait, are parenting tutorials a thing? Probably not.

I'm a certifiable mess.

I didn't bother with makeup when I was getting ready, but since I have time to kill, I trudge back upstairs. When I'm finished, it's still a bit too early to leave, but I can't be in this house a second longer.

I shrug into my coat and swipe my keys and purse off the small table in the laundry room, then I'm out the door.

Walmart is on my way, and thankfully open, so I run in and get the formula, but once I'm back in the car, I freeze behind the wheel.

It hits me in intervals, what a big deal all of this is.

Daire's going to be Sammy's sole guardian. Sammy's mom is gone, just like that. It's easy to forget how fragile life really is. We take it for granted—believing we're destined to live until we're old and gray and die peacefully in our sleep, but that isn't always the case.

I take a deep breath.

Then another when that isn't enough.

Before I pull out of the parking lot, I send a text to Daire that I'm headed his way. He sends back a thumbs-up.

> Daire: We should be discharged by the time you get here.

We're bringing a baby home with us.

A real-life, screaming, eating, and pooping baby.

Daire's baby.

"You can do this, Rosie. It's a baby, not a snake. People keep them alive every day. You can do the same."

Right?

I put on a playlist and crank the music up to drown out my thoughts as I drive.

When I arrive at the hospital, I have to circle the lot a few times before I find a parking spot.

I take out the car seat, along with a stuffed dinosaur from the nursery that I thought Sammy might like and the diaper bag that I definitely overpacked.

My heart pounds the entire trek through the

hospital up to the room. By the time I step inside, I'm sweating. The doctor is just leaving, so I step to one side and give a polite smile as he passes.

"Hey, I'm here," I say, still breathless from the walk.

Daire turns around to face me, Sammy cradled against his bare chest.

And just like that, my poor ovaries implode.

"Where's your shirt?" I blurt.

He chuckles, kissing the top of Sammy's downy soft blond hair. "The nurse suggested that even though he's six months, skin to skin might help with bonding."

"Bonding." I swallow, taking in all six feet and four inches of a shirtless Daire holding a baby. "Bonding is fun."

I set the car seat on the floor while Daire puts Sammy into the crib and picks up the diaper bag. He shuffles through the clothes I stuffed in there and settles on a cute pair of footie pajamas covered in a caterpillar print.

Sammy wiggles around, giving Daire a hard time as he tries to wrangle him into the sleeper. Finally he manages, and then it's time to put him in the car seat. We're both silent as we stare at the contraption.

"You put him in." Daire holds the baby out to me.

"Me?" I practically shriek, holding my hands against my chest. "He's yours."

"I don't know how all those straps and things works. What if I put him in wrong?" He frowns, his eyes pleading. "The only reason he's still alive is because he was strapped into a good car seat properly."

I take a deep breath. "We're in a hospital. Surely a nurse could help us."

"A nurse," he practically shouts, his face lighting up. "Great idea."

He all but shoves the infant into my arms and runs out of the room.

Sammy blinks at me, his big blue eyes round with curiosity. "Hi." I put my hand behind his head. I'm not sure whether it still needs to be supported, but it makes me feel better to do it anyway. "How are you?"

God, Rosie, what a dumb question to ask a baby!

His little body stiffens, and he starts to fuss, so I gently rock from side to side while making a shushing sound. "It's okay, your daddy will be back any second."

Sure enough, Daire breezes back in a moment later with a nurse.

He's still shirtless, and the sight of his abs is enough to send my libido into overdrive. It's been way too long since I've had sex, and the craving is even worse after Daire proved how good an orgasm that isn't of my own making can feel.

"Can you put a shirt on?" I practically beg him.

He grins, eyes crinkling at the corners. "Like what you see, baby?"

Baby.

I think I just melted into a puddle.

I've *never* liked the endearment, but when Daire says it, I *love* it.

He scoops up his long-sleeve Henley and tugs it on.

The nurse clears her throat. My cheeks heat with embarrassment. I didn't mean to stare at his abs as they disappeared, but oops, guilty.

"You guys wanted some help strapping in the little one?"

"Yes, please." I smile gratefully.

"All right, go ahead and put him in, and I'll show you."

I crouch and gently set Sammy in the car seat.

The nurse lowers herself beside me, and then Daire joins us.

"First things first, put his arms through the straps. Then we're going to buckle it into the part down here. Now, this is the part that probably has you guys stressed." She taps the chest buckle. "Snap them together, and then we're going to tighten it. It should rest here at shoulder height. And you should have about this much room between the straps and his body." She demonstrates with her fingers by pinching the strap.

"What about a coat?" I ask. "It's cold out."

The nurse shakes her head. "We don't recommend putting coats on when kids are in a car seat. It can cause them to slip out of the straps if there's an accident because there's too much space here." She pinches it again. "It's overwhelming, but I promise it's easier than you think."

"Thank you for your help," Daire tells her, standing.

I stand too, my knee popping as I do.

The nurse leaves, giving us a small wave, and then it's just the three of us.

This weird pseudo-family.

And it's going to be the three of us from now on.

Until Daire and I divorce, that is.

Daire picks up the carrier and reaches for my hand. "Come on. Let's go home."

Home.

Yeah, that sounds good.

twenty-five

DAIRE

"WHO'S PARKED IN THE DRIVEWAY?" Confusion floods me at the sight of the unfamiliar vehicle parked in front of the garage. Is it child services? Did they change their minds? If they're here to take Sammy from me, we're going to have a problem.

"What?" Rosie clutches the passenger seat and leans forward, craning her neck. I asked her to sit in the back seat so Sammy wouldn't get scared or lonely. I have no idea if he recalls anything from the last time he was in a car. "I don't know. Looks like a rental car."

I pull into the driveway behind the black Tahoe and put the van in park.

The second I press the ignition button, the driver's door opens in front of me, and my dad steps out.

I nearly shit my pants as he turns to face me, his hands on his hips. When Roman climbs out of the passenger side, I slap a hand to my face. "What the fuck?"

I haven't told my dad about Sammy. Not because I'm trying to keep my kid a secret, but because I don't know how the hell to explain to him that I knocked up my professor.

With a deep inhale, I get out.

"What are you guys doing here?" The urge to drop an F-bomb is strong, but I bite my tongue since there are impressionable infant ears listening to everything I say now.

"I can't want to see my son on Christmas?"

Hands on my hips, I tip my head back and search the sky for answers. My dad had a heart attack when we told him we got married. I can't imagine what's going to happen this time.

"Sure, but Dad," I put my hands up in front of me, "there's something I need to tell you."

I look back at Rosie and give a nod.

She bites her lip but responds with a nod of her own and unlatches Sammy from the car seat.

When she steps out of the car, Roman bursts into

laughter. "Holy shit! You guys *do* have a kid!"

My dad staggers back, his face ghost white—but he better not even think about becoming an actual ghost any time soon.

"Dad!" I rush forward and put an arm around him. "It's not what you think ... I mean, it is, but it's not."

"That's a baby, Daire." He puts a hand over his heart. *Fuck*. I hope to God it's only because it's beating fast and not because he's experiencing chest pains.

There's been enough death in the past twenty-four hours.

"Let's head inside and talk about this." I step in front of him and urge him toward the house.

"Daire." Without budging, he says my name again slowly. "That's a baby." He points at my son in Rosie's arms.

"Yes, and we're going to talk about it inside. Where it's warm."

Roman cackles, shoving his hands into the pockets of his jeans. "You're so dead."

I glare at my little brother. "Go help Rosie," I snap at him. "I'll get Dad inside."

When I take my dad's arm, he tries to shoo me off like I'm a pesky fly. Not like I'm trying to help the man who had a mild heart attack a month ago. The man I'm concerned will have another any minute. "I don't need your help. I'm not old."

"But Dad—"

"No buts," he counters, making me feel like I'm eight years old again.

With a sigh, I throw my hands up in surrender and back away from him. When Rosie shuffles up beside me, I take Sammy from her so she can unlock the door.

"Get in everyone. It's cold." On the stoop, she stomps slushy snow off her boots. When everyone's inside, she goes into hostess mode. "Do either of you want coffee? Snacks? I can—"

My dad holds up a hand to silence her, the move making my shoulders tighten with anger.

"Don't hold your hand up to quiet my wife," I snap at him before he can speak. "This is her home, and she was asking a polite question."

Rosie presses her lips together, shooting me a soft, sad look.

Chagrined, he turns to Rosie. "I'm sorry. That was rude. No refreshments are necessary." He clears his throat and narrows his eyes on me. "Now, what the hell is this?"

Across the room, Roman flops onto the couch, scooping up the remote.

I hold Sammy tighter against me and garner all the courage I can before I speak. "Dad, I'd like you to meet Sammy. This is my son."

My dad looks up at the ceiling, then presses his fingers to his temples. "Unbelievable." He turns to Rosie. "As angry as your dad is now, it's nothing compared to how he'll feel when he finds out you've been keeping this a secret." He points back at the baby. "Now it makes sense why you two were so insistent on not coming home for Christmas."

"Leave Rosie out of this," I bite out through clenched teeth. "She hasn't done anything wrong."

"I beg to—"

"The baby isn't hers, Dad."

A vein in his forehead pulses. "What? Who's the mother?"

"I've got a lot to fill you in on." My chest aches at the thought of all the details I'll have to give him and how disappointed he'll be in me. "We should probably take this slow."

"I don't have time for slow," he grits out, sitting on the edge of the couch. "I might be dead by the time you finish."

"Don't joke about that," I beg, my stomach bottoming out. The whole Thanksgiving fiasco still weighs heavily on me.

"Stop stalling."

Rosie steps in close and holds her arms out to take Sammy. "You talk with your dad," she says as I carefully hand him over. "I'll take him upstairs. He probably needs a diaper change and a nap."

"Thanks." I pull her in close by her wrist and press a kiss to her temple.

Her breath catches, and she shoots a surprised look

my way. If she thinks I've forgotten about what we were doing when I got that call last night, then she's sorely mistaken.

I'm going to make Rosie Hendricks mine in every sense of the word.

"Start talking, kid," my dad says, once again making me feel like a child.

I lean against the wall and cross my arms over my chest. It's a classic defensive pose, but I can't bring myself to care.

"Sammy's mom was my professor last year."

Before my dad has a chance to voice his disappointment, Roman bursts into uncontrollable laughter. "You would hook up with a professor. You always like to break the rules, big bro." He cackles some more. "Was she at least a hot young professor?"

"Thirty-six," I mutter, looking down at my feet. "And yeah, she was hot."

Not nearly as beautiful as Rosie, though. As if anyone could top her.

"She never told me she was pregnant, though. She was on campus at the beginning of the year showing off her baby, and I just knew he was mine." I shrug. "She denied it, so I got a lawyer involved and—"

"Please tell me you reached out to Nina Voss," my dad interjects.

I chuckle. "Yeah. Nina's been incredible. We established paternity and have been working toward a custody agreement, but..." I take a deep breath. This part is hard, since I'm still processing it all myself and figuring out how this will affect Sammy as he grows up. "Danielle and her husband were killed last night. Sammy was in the car with them when it crashed, but somehow, he came out of it without a single injury. For now, I have temporary guardianship, and we're hopeful that they don't have family members who will fight me for permanent custody. Nina says I have a good case since I'm the biological father and we've already turned in the evidence to confirm it, and because I was already trying to get shared custody."

"The baby mama is dead?"

"Roman!" Dad scolds.

My baby brother rears back. "What? This whole thing is crazy."

"Believe me," I mutter, breathing through the tightness in my chest. "I know. I'm living it."

"How does Rosie play into all of this?"

This is my moment, my chance to fess up to the truth about our marriage. He'd probably even understand. But the words won't come. I don't want to admit to any part of our relationship being fake. Not when my feelings are turning very fucking real.

"Like we told you, we reconnected, and it felt right. We didn't want to waste any time."

He narrows his eyes as he scrutinizes me, like he doesn't believe me. Even Roman looks skeptical.

"This is a lot to take in."

"Believe me, Dad, I know."

He lets out a long breath, his expression softening a fraction. "You have a baby."

"Yep."

"A son."

My heart constricts at that word. *Son*. "Mhm."

"Dad," Roman says, "you're finally a grandad. You can lay off Veda and Asher. Pretty sure they're going to get divorced anyway."

"Roman," he snaps, shifting on the couch so he can glare at the idiot, "stop speculating about your brother's marriage."

"Hey." He raises his hands innocently. "Don't shoot the messenger. If you watch them, it's pretty obvious that they're struggling."

"Lots of couples have rough patches. It doesn't mean they're getting a divorce."

Clearing my throat, I step away from the wall. "If you two don't mind, I'm going to go check on Rosie and Sammy."

Before either can say a word, I make a mad dash for the stairs.

The second I step into the room, I'm hard. Fuck. What does it say about me that the sight of this woman holding my child is such a turn-on?

Rosie cradles Sammy in her arms, rocking him gently in the glider we purchased. Her voice is soft, melodic, as she sings a lullaby I've never heard. Not only does seeing her with my son turn me on, but it makes my heart tap out a strange rhythm. She's been scared about all this, and yet she's already handling it like a pro.

"You look good, Rosie."

She startles, and Sammy's eyes pop open. "Don't sneak up on me like that," she scolds in a whisper.

"Sorry." I grin, easing into the room. I shut the door quietly behind me. "He likes you."

She lets out a quiet, humorless chuckle. "He's just sleepy. He'd like anyone who'd rock him like this."

"You don't give yourself enough credit."

Sammy's eyes grow heavy once more.

"This is crazy, Daire." She looks up at me, her eyes full of both wonder and terror. "We're in charge of keeping this tiny human alive."

"I know."

"And your dad is downstairs."

I chuckle softly and rub at the back of my neck.

"How does it feel now that he knows?"

"My shoulder are lighter, that's for sure."

She wets her lips and regards me, wearing a nervous expression. "Did you ... did you tell him the truth about us?"

With a sigh, I close my eyes. I probably should have. She's got an easy out now, a reason to end this early. Here I was thinking I'd be the one eager to dissolve this as soon as possible, but instead, I'm holding on with both hands. I rub my thumb against the thick band on my ring finger. I *like* it there. I like the message it gives. That I'm taken. That I belong to her.

"I didn't tell him it was fake."

Fake.

The word tastes like acid on my tongue.

Standing, she nods. "Okay. I'm not sure how we should go about telling my mom about this one."

I arch a brow. "What about your dad?"

She gently transfers Sammy from her arms into the crib. When he stirs, she puts her hand on his belly and gently shakes him to mimic the rocking she was doing. The little boy immediately settles back down.

"My dad isn't talking to me, so he doesn't matter."

The hurt in her voice has me closing the distance between us and pulling her into my arms. Instantly, she melts into me. The reaction is surprising, but I'd be lying if I said I didn't like it. For a moment, it feels like we've gone back in time. To when we were teenagers, watching movies and falling asleep on the couch together.

"Baby," I say softly, holding her even tighter against me. "I'm sorry."

She clings to me, keeping her voice low so she doesn't wake Sammy. "It's okay." *It's not.* "I understand why he's upset, but it just sucks, you know?"

The warmth that spreads through me as I hold her

is spoiled by the pain in her voice. I wish I could magically make the situation with her dad better.

"You know," I tip my head in the direction of the crib, "you've got way more of a motherly instinct than you think."

She rolls her eyes up at me. "I don't think so, but thank you."

I cup her cheek and study her face, the urge to kiss her next to impossible to ignore.

She clears her throat, stepping out of my touch. "We should go back down. Your dad and Roman unoccupied for too long can't lead to anything good."

I can't do anything but agree. "Yeah, you're right."

Still, I'm disappointed she backed away.

I turn the monitor on and check my phone app to make sure it's connected before we leave Sammy in the darkened room.

Downstairs, my dad and brother are—thankfully—where we left them.

"Are you guys hungry?" I ask.

The fridge isn't exactly stocked, but considering it's Christmas day, it's not as if I can run out and pick up food. We've got chicken and veggies, salad fixings, and a horde of frozen pizzas, because I can never remember whether we have one, so every time I'm at the store, I grab another.

"Starved." Roman rubs his belly.

"I could eat," Dad says.

Frozen pizzas it is.

Rosie stands uncomfortably in the open archway into the family room.

My dad straightens on the couch and frowns down at his hands. "I'm sorry about earlier, Rosie. How are you?"

"Good," she replies quietly. "Let me go see what we have to eat."

With that, she darts away. I give my dad and brother a look that says *don't do anything stupid* and hurry after my wife.

She's already scouring the refrigerator when I step into the kitchen.

"Let's throw in a couple of pizzas," I say, sidling up next to her.

She nods, pulling two supremes out of the freezer. "We need to go for a grocery run soon."

I nod in agreement, searching through the fridge for drinks. We're low on those too, so I head to the cabinet and pull down glasses and fill them with water.

My dad and brother have no one to blame but themselves since they didn't give me a heads-up.

When I turn, Rosie's right there. On instinct, I hover close and press my lips to hers.

She startles, wide eyes big and bright when I pull away. "What was that for?"

"I haven't kissed you enough today."

Her cheeks are flushed when I step around her to

take the water glasses to the two idiots in the living room.

They seriously flew here unannounced, got the surprise of a lifetime, and are hanging out on my couch like nothing major has happened.

It's like I'm in the Twilight Zone or something.

When I return to the kitchen, Rosie is sitting on the island, chewing on the edge of her thumbnail.

"Nervous about something?" I ask, stepping between her legs.

If my family wasn't a room over, I would lay her back right here and now and devour her.

"Yeah." She swallows audibly. "I'm scared to tell my mom. She's not going to understand."

My stomach sinks. "What do you mean?"

She frowns, eyes dropping from mine. "She's not going to like that I'm playing house with you with someone else's baby."

"Oh." I rub the back of my head, shame washing over me.

She splays her hand against my chest, the warmth of it soaking through the fabric of my shirt. "You know how our world can be—she's going to see it as a failure on my part, since you already have an heir, so to speak."

I huff a laugh. "That's ridiculous."

"I know that. But it's the way she thinks."

Rosie's mom could be a hundred times worse, but between her antiquated ideas and the way she talks about Rosie's weight, it's enough for me to hate the woman.

"Your mom sucks, Rosie."

It's perhaps not the right thing to say, but I can't help it.

She lets out a heavy breath. "I know."

In an effort to distract her, I lean in, ghosting my lips over her right cheek to her ear. "I'm still thinking about last night. Your pretty little pussy was right there, and I didn't even get a taste."

"Daire." Her voice shakes, and she grips my shoulders. I'm not sure whether she's trying to steady herself or keep me at bay.

"Have you thought about it too? Do you want my head between these thighs?" I move my hands down her body and give said thighs a squeeze. "Do you want to come on my tongue?"

She whimpers and squirms against the quartz countertop.

"I fucking love knowing I've made you come when no other man could get the job done. It just proves it, baby."

"P-Proves what?" she stutters, peering at me through her lashes.

"That you're mine. You were always meant to be mine."

"Daire." My name is a small, throaty gasp.

The oven chooses that god-awful moment to chime,

signaling that it's preheated.

I curse, but it's not like I can do anything anyway. The universe is constantly interrupting us.

Once the pizzas are in the oven, I turn back to find Rosie watching me, wearing a panicked expression, her hands gripping the edge of the island so tight her knuckles are white. "What is it?"

Did I go too far?

"We have separate rooms," she hisses softly.

Fuck.

"I'll move your stuff to mine."

While she keeps an eye on the pizzas, I sneak upstairs and quickly and quietly move as much as I can from her room over to mine. If my dad and brother stay here, I wouldn't put it past either of them to snoop through the drawers. We Hendrickses are a nosy bunch.

When I finish up, I check the monitor app on my phone to make sure Sammy's still out. My whole body warms as I take in his peacefully sleeping form.

I wasn't planning on becoming a dad so young, but when I look at that little boy, all I feel is happiness. He's a piece of me, one I didn't know I wanted but absolutely need now that he exists.

Downstairs, Rosie's taking out the pizzas.

"I'll give them a minute to cool before I cut into them. You should go check on them. I'll let you know when this is ready."

I clear my throat, glancing across the way at my dad and brother.

She rolls her eyes, and a laugh bubbles out of her. "They're not going to bite."

"Right," I mutter, slapping on a brave face.

She shakes her head, the picture of amusement with the way her lips keep twitching.

Despite my apprehension about facing my family again, there's a lightness in my chest that I only feel when I'm around this woman. "Are you laughing at me, Rosie?"

She sobers, pressing her lips together. "Never."

I grab her by the waist and tug her against me. "I need a kiss to keep me going if I'm going to survive them."

She bites her lip and swats at my chest playfully. "You're such a dork."

"Rosie."

With a sigh, she gives me a peck.

I shake my head, smiling. "Not good enough, and you know it."

Cradling her head, I tangle my fingers in her hair and take her in. Fuck, she's gorgeous.

She lowers her gaze to my lips, and that's all the permission I need. Closing the space between us, I give her a longer, deeper kiss. It's a far cry from a make-out session, but I still find myself growing hard.

Fuck, I want her.

When I pull away, her eyes are dark and sparkling with desire.

With a groan, I release her and back away, forcing myself to join my family in the other room.

My dad looks over at me as I sit on the couch. His lips are set into an amused curl. "Are you done avoiding us?"

I lace my hands behind my head, focusing on the movie Roman has playing. "Yep. For now."

"You have a kid, Daire."

My heart clenches, but I keep my expression neutral. "Yep."

Roman pauses the movie and leans forward. "Holy shit, I'm an uncle."

I arch a brow. "Just now figuring that out, brother?"

"Hey." He waves wildly. "We weren't exactly expecting to see the two of you get out of the car with a whole-ass baby."

"Fair enough."

Rosie clears her throat from the archway between the living room and kitchen. "Food's ready."

As she turns and walks away, it hits me. I couldn't have done any of this without her. And I don't want to do any of this without her.

I'm so fucked.

twenty-six

ROSIE

THE SHOWER RUNS in the adjacent bathroom. As tired as I am, I should be fast asleep, not thinking about a very naked and wet Daire only a few feet away.

I take a deep breath and start counting backward from one hundred.

I'm only at eighty-seven when the shower cuts off.

An audible whimper leaves my lips.

The bathroom door opens, and a billow of steam wafts out.

I squeeze my eyes closed tight and hold my breath.

I will not look.
I will not look.
I will—
I look.

Abs for days—slick and wet. I want to run my grubby hands over every inch. I'm salivating for him. For *Daire* of all people. Only weeks ago, I still hated his guts, but here we are.

I roll over, forcing myself to resist the temptation to keep staring.

The towel rustles, then it lands with a soft thud on the floor.

God help me.

Pulling the covers up, I burrow down beneath them.

He pads around to the other side of the bed, and as he climbs in, I finally crack my eyes open.

"You're wearing boxers?" I blurt.

He rumbles with laughter. "I didn't know if you'd appreciate me sleeping naked."

"Good point," I squeak.

I'm acting like a nervous, scared virgin, when that's the furthest thing from the truth.

But thinking about having sex with Daire makes me feel like one.

"I want to touch you," he confesses, his warm hand landing on my hip. "But the things I want to do to you … they'll have to wait. Though…" He brushes over the band of my pajama shorts. "There are other things I could do to you. But only if you can be quiet. Do you want that?"

I nod, way too eagerly based on the laugh that leaves him. His breath is warm when he leans in and kisses my neck.

He slips his fingers beneath the fabric of my shorts and panties, skimming over my pussy.

I press my lips together, stifling a whimper.

"Fuck, Rosie." He presses another kiss to my neck. "You're so wet already. Were you laying here thinking about me while I was in the shower?"

I give a jerky nod in answer and suppress a moan.

"Mm," he hums. "Were you thinking about me naked?"

Another nod, my heart racing.

"Was I stroking myself?"

Heat pools in my core as I nod again.

"Words, Rosie. You're going to have to start talking to me."

"Y-Yes," I stutter, tipping my head back to give him better access to my neck.

"In this fantasy, did I shout your name when I came?"

"I-I didn't get that far."

He slips just the tips of two fingers past my entrance. Just a tease. I wiggle my hips for more, but it does no good. With my bottoms still on and his body against mine I have no room to move.

"The things I want to do to you," he murmurs, lips ghosting over mine.

I arch back, begging for more. "Do it."

He pushes his fingers in another inch. "In time, Rosie. In time."

Finally, he works his fingers in and out of me, pulling all logical thought from me. All I can do is feel. He presses his thumb against my clit, the sensation so acute it's too much.

Too much and he hasn't even properly fucked me.

My orgasm builds quickly but levels off before I can hurtle over that edge.

It's so reminiscent of many experiences. All the times I was left disappointed. Suddenly, fear takes hold of me.

What if the night in the living room was a fluke? What if he can never make me come again? Would he be okay with that? What about—

"Get outta that pretty little head, babe."

I exhale, releasing the anxiety trying to take hold. He's right. If I overthink this, I definitely won't orgasm. "Sorry."

"Don't be sorry. Focus on me. Focus on how you feel. Stop thinking."

I nod forcefully. "I'll try."

It's easier said than done, though, and moments

later, clearly sensing those worries taking hold again, he changes tactics.

He sits up, causing the comforter to slip off our bodies, and yanks my shorts down. Then he lowers to the bed, using his shoulders to wedge my legs open wider.

With the first swipe of his tongue I bow off the bed.

I clutch the sheets, fingers tangling in the fabric as he devours me.

Quickly, pleasure builds inside me again. His mouth on my core renders me thoughtless.

I've had plenty of guys go down on me before, but to no avail. None of them devoured me the way Daire is. It always seemed more like an exchange, not like they were getting any enjoyment out of it. But Daire clearly loves it. He doesn't hold back. Not with his mouth, tongue, or fingers.

I cover my mouth with my hand as a scream builds deep in my lungs.

He looks up from between my legs and fucking *grins*.

That little—

My thoughts die again when he sucks at my clit.

There's no stopping the orgasm as it barrels through me. I keep one hand securely over my mouth and reach down with the other to grip his hair.

I swear he says, "That's right, baby. Ride my face."

But I'm so far gone to the pleasure I might've imagined it.

As I slump against the mattress, drained, he climbs back up my body and gathers me into his arms. His hard length presses into my backside. I'm dying to taste him, but I'm too tired to even broach the subject of returning the favor, and within moments, I'm out.

IT'S STILL DARK when I wake. Even in sleep, my mind is fixed on Sammy and whether he's okay.

I reach out for Daire, but all I find are cool sheets.

My heart drops.

Did he move to the couch?

I slide out from under the covers, searching for my sleep shorts. When I finally find them stuffed under the sheet near the foot of the bed, I yank them on, then grab a pullover and slip it over my head.

Down the hall, I hold my breath and slowly turn the knob to Sammy's nursery. The last thing I want to do is wake the sleeping infant, but I can't rest until I check on him and Daire.

In the glow of the nightlight, I can just make out the form in the daybed we set up across from the crib. When I ordered furniture, it seemed logical to have a bed in here in case Sammy got fussy or sick and one of us needed to stay close.

Daire sits up as I enter the room.

"What are you doing?" he whispers, shifting over to make room for me.

"I was worried about Sammy."

The daybed isn't exactly big enough for two grown adults, but we make it work. He spoons me against his chest, wrapping his arm around me.

"Me too. But he seems fine."

I take in the baby's sleeping form through the slats in the crib. Peaceful. Unbothered. Too young to know about the cruelty of the world.

"Is this how all new parents feel? Scared out of their minds?" I ask him. "Not that I think I'm his mom or anything. I know I'm not, but I just—"

"Shh," he hushes. "I know what you mean. I can't say for certain, but I imagine, yeah this is what they feel like." He kisses the back of my shoulder through the fabric of my shirt. "Now go to sleep, Rosie."

I wiggle against him, trying to get comfortable in the small space.

He groans, his voice a low warning when says, "Rosie."

My heart lifts, even as he's reprimanding me. "Sorry."

My mind feels more at ease now that I'm close to Sammy. If he needs us, we're right here.

I drift off to sleep again, but this time, I sleep through the night.

AFTER AN EARLY-MORNING GROCERY run and a much-needed stop at Starbucks, I find all three guys in the kitchen playing with Sammy.

"Peek-a-boo." Roman open and closes his hands around his face. "Peek-a-boo."

Sammy giggles from his grandpa's arms while Daire watches with a grin I've never seen before. It's 100 percent a proud dad kind of smile.

I set down the bags and drink carrier. "I was going to make pancakes if that's okay with everyone."

Daire hits me with a different kind of smile, a much sexier smile, as he reaches over and snags the iced shaken espresso I got for him.

"I'll never complain about pancakes," Roman says, holding out his arms to Sammy.

Peter shakes his head and pulls the baby in closer, not wanting to give up his grandson.

After a few sips of my cold brew, I get to work unloading the groceries.

"Are there more in the car?" Daire asks.

"Yeah, I was going to unpack these and go back."

He presses a kiss to the corner of my mouth, and on instinct, I startle. I'm still getting used to this affectionate version of Daire. "I'll get them."

When he's gone, Roman gives me a smile that's pure

younger brother mischief. "Things are going well with you two, huh?"

"Well, we are married. I'd hope we like each other."

"Cash still says you guys are faking it." Roman swipes one of the grapes right off the vine as I pull them out of the bag.

"Ew, I haven't washed those yet."

He takes another. "Don't care."

"Cash is imagining things." I sort the groceries on the counter into categories, avoiding his gaze. I find it easier if I sort it all before I start putting it away. Otherwise I'm constantly running back and forth.

I always suspected Cash had a crush on me, but before he asked me on a date last year, he never pushed for more, even when we stayed in contact after my friendship with Daire imploded. Then, last Christmas, when I told him I'd like to remain just friends, he seemed perfectly content. After that, I figured he was over it.

"It's just funny." Roman goes on, crossing his arms over his chest and propping himself up against the counter. "He never mentioned you to any of us."

I narrow my eyes on him. The youngest Hendricks brother has always been the most laidback, but right now, I feel like I'm under interrogation. "He didn't tell you about Sammy either. Seems to me like he's keeping a lot from you guys. Maybe you should stop questioning my marriage and take a long look at yourself. Maybe you're the problem here."

Peter clears his throat. "Roman, leave Rosie alone."

A sharp pain lances my chest. God, I hope they never know that this whole thing was a farce.

Daire's family has always been almost like my own. I don't want to have to face the shame of disappointing them.

Daire returns while Roman and I are still eyeing each other and sets the rest of the bags on the counter, then looks between the three of us. It's like he could sniff out the tension before he even entered the kitchen.

"What's going on?" he asks warily. His eyes shoot to Sammy in his dad's arms. "Is the baby okay?"

"The baby's fine," Peter assures him. "Your brother here was giving Rosie a hard time."

Daire clenches his hands into fists and brings them to his hips. Whether he realizes it or not, he purposely positions himself in front of me in a protective stance.

"What's your problem with Rosie?"

"I don't have a problem." He leans around Daire to see me better. "You know I don't have a problem, right, Rosie? I'm just trying to figure you two out."

"Figure us out?" Daire fires the words back at his brother. "What does that mean?"

"Daire." I gently grasp his arm, ready to beg him to drop it. It's not a big deal, and it's not really surprising that they're suspicious.

Roman looks down at the ground, shuffling his feet. "I don't know, but Cash—"

Daire throws his arms up. "This is about Cash? I should've known. Why are you listening to anything he says? He's jealous because I got the girl. Is it not obvious to you how I feel about her?"

He looks at me over his shoulder, his blue eyes lit like twin flames, and I nearly collapse from the intensity reflected there.

I don't want to say I see love there, because I don't want to even give voice to that possibility—not even in my own thoughts—but the emotion is a strong one. Stronger than any I've ever seen focused solely on me.

Roman clears his throat, eyes dropping. "Yeah, it is."

Daire reaches for Sammy, and his dad quickly hands him over.

The second he's in his daddy's arms, Sammy laughs, and Daire practically melts. His rigid posture loosens, and his scowl disappears.

"How can you love someone so much when you don't even know them?" Daire asks his dad as Sammy wraps a tight fist around his index finger.

Peter chuckles, smoothing Sammy's downy soft blond hair. "That's what being a parent is like—instant love."

Rocking Sammy, Daire turns his attention back to his younger brother. "Just for being a jerk to my wife, you get to put the groceries away." He claps him on the shoulder, then he turns to me and holds out a hand.

I gladly give it to him and follow him out of the room. As he leads me to the living room, I can't wipe the stupid, goofy grin off my face.

I'm so screwed.

twenty-seven

DAIRE

THANK FUCK FOR WINTER BREAK. Getting used to taking care of the every need of an infant while attending classes and practices would've been a nightmare.

I unload the stroller from the trunk while Rosie takes Sammy out of his car seat.

I tested out the stroller when we bought it, to make sure I could get it to open up and fold down fairly quickly, but for some stupid reason, I'm struggling.

The whirl of the sliding door closing on the minivan signals Rosie's approach.

She's got a blanket wrapped around him to shield him from the cold on the quick journey from the car into the mall. My dad and brother left this morning, and we decided it would be good practice to get out with Sammy and practice parenting away from the comfort of home for a while.

"Did we bring the diaper bag?"

I blink at Rosie, my stomach sinking. "I didn't grab it."

She groans, biting her lip. "I didn't either. We're idiots."

"We're new at this," I argue. "We're going to f— mess up."

She rocks Sammy, watching me struggle to open the stroller. "Need some help?"

"No." Hands on my hips I glower at the folded-up monstrosity. "I can handle this."

I push the buttons on either side and lift, then shake it, but it doesn't release.

She cocks her head to the side, lips pursed. "I'm pretty sure you're doing it wrong."

"No. This is right." I shake it again, and the thing stays locked.

Sammy gives out a small, irritated cry.

"Shh," Rosie hushes sweetly. "I know you're cold. Your daddy is being stubborn."

"I'm not stubborn," I bite out between my teeth. "I just know I can do this."

"Mhm. Sammy and I will head on in and wait for you where it's warm."

"Good idea." I lean over, pressing a kiss to Sammy's beanie-covered head. "I won't be long."

She gives me a skeptical look, one brow raised, that I ignore.

It takes me fifteen minutes and the help of a guy walking by who says he has the same stroller to get it opened up. I try not to think about what kind of struggle I might have folding it up again. That's a problem for future Daire.

Inside the mall, I text Rosie to ask where she is.

Rosie: Food court.

Heading that way, I scan the people I pass, looking for anyone I recognize. I don't know why I care—after my recorded meltdown, practically the entire campus knows I have a kid.

My stomach roils at the memory of all the alcohol I drank that night.

Never again.

The mall is packed with people shopping and returning Christmas gifts, so it takes far longer than it should to navigate the empty stroller to the food court. I search the crowded tables for Rosie and find her waving her arm to get my attention.

Parking the stroller beside the table, I pull out a chair and plop down.

"Took you long enough," she snickers. There's a cup of Auntie Anne's pretzel nuggets in front of her.

I snag one and pop it into my mouth with a grin.

"Hey, those are mine. Get your own." She swats my hand when I reach for another.

"Nice try." I bite into my successfully stolen second piece. "I forgot how good these are."

Laughing, she puts Sammy in the stroller and straps him in. "I always get them when I'm at the mall. It's a tradition. Right, Sammy?" She taps the baby's nose.

He giggles and reaches for her finger. She smiles at him as he holds tight, but when he tries to bring it to his mouth, she gently pries his fingers loose.

I take a third pretzel bite, earning myself another glare. "I can get you more."

She perks up. "Before we leave?"

"Sure." I make a mental note to swing back by here and get another order to take with us.

"Will you FaceTime my mom with me?"

The idea of telling her mother about Sammy fills me with dread—not because of what she might say or think about me, but because there's a good chance she'll say something hurtful to Rosie. I won't be able to hold back if she does.

"Tonight?"

She puckers her lips and crosses her eyes at Sammy. He squeals with delight.

And me?

Fuck, I fall a little more.

Love.

That word echoes in my brain.

I'm falling in love with my fake wife.

It was the one rule I gave her—no falling in love.

I never expected to be the one to break it.

"Are you okay?"

The question snaps me back to reality, the sounds and smells of the food court coming back into focus.

"Sorry." I clear my throat. "I zoned out. What did you say?"

"I said tonight is probably as good as any."

"For what?"

She tosses a pretzel nugget at me, but I catch it and pop it into my mouth. "To talk to my mom, you idiot."

"Oh, right." I rub the back of my head. "Yeah, we'll call her tonight."

"Good." She stands and unlocks the wheels of the stroller. "Well, don't just sit there," she scolds when I stay seated. "We have to get Junior some more clothes. I didn't get enough. Who knew a baby could poop through so many outfits in one day?"

"Right, clothes."

That's why we're here, after all.

That and there was some designer purse Rosie wanted to look at.

I scoop up the trash and toss it. Then I fall into step beside her and peek over at my son.

Three of us.

A family.

My family.

I like the sound of that way too much.

twenty-eight

ROSIE

I'M SWEATING.

Like literally sweating through my shirt.

I rip my hoodie over my head, thankful I'm wearing a tank top underneath.

Sammy's already asleep upstairs, and I've checked the baby camera app no less than twenty times since he went down.

It's safe to say I'm even more of a worrier than Daire.

He pulls a beer out of the fridge and holds it out.

"What's this for?" I fan my pits frantically.

She smirks. "For you. I think you need it."

He's not wrong. With a sigh, I snag it and open the drawer where the bottle opener is.

When I tip it back and guzzle it, he snatches the bottle from my hand.

"Hey!" I wipe my mouth, glaring down at the wet spot on my white tank. "What was that for?"

"I wanted you to take the edge off, not chug it." He holds the bottle hostage against his chest, even though I haven't made a move to take it back.

"Can't I do both?"

He shakes his head. "Nope."

This video call is one I suggested, yet when my phone rings, I practically jump out of my skin, and when I pick it up off the counter with a shaky hand, I nearly drop it.

Daire gives me a look that I read as *get your shit together*.

I slide my thumb over the screen to answer and prop the phone up against the fruit bowl on the island so my mother can see both of us. "Hey, Mom!" I sound way cheerier than I feel.

Her eyes are narrowed, her nose crinkled. "What's on your shirt?"

"Oh." I look down, pretending like I'm just noticing it. "I must've spilled some soda on it. I'll change when we hang up."

Daire dips his head, his elbows resting on the island. "Hey, Mrs. Thomas."

"Honestly, dear," she tuts, "we're family now. Call me Mom."

"Um…" He shifts on his stool.

"Mom," I interrupt, pressing a hand to his bicep, "he's probably not comfortable with that."

Talk about insensitive. It probably didn't cross her mind that it might be an upsetting suggestion to someone who's lost their own mother, but it's still no excuse.

"Lydia works too. Rosie, darling, I've got the appointments finalized. The earliest I could get them scheduled is the first weekend in February. We're set to visit four boutiques and…" She claps, her eyes dancing. "I had my dress pulled from storage so you can try that on too."

"Oh." My heart sinks. At the same time, I see my face fall in the square in the corner of the phone screen that reflects my image. "That sounds … great."

I should've known she wouldn't listen to my pleas about not dress shopping. And her dress? I don't want anything to do with it.

It's actually beautiful—a timeless gown I admired every time I looked at my parents' wedding photos when I was a girl. I thought she looked like a princess.

But my parents were married during her peak modeling days, and my mother was scarily thin. There's no way in hell her dress would fit me, and the idea of what she might say when it doesn't makes me want to throw up.

Like he can sense the tension radiating from me, Daire puts a gentle hand over top of mine where I rest it on the countertop.

"Let's not talk about dresses right now, Lydia. We have something to tell you."

Before either of us can utter another word, she lets out a shrill squeal. "You're pregnant? Oh my God, I'm going to be a grandma. Do you know the gender? How far along you? I'll need to plan a—"

"Mom."

"—baby shower and you two should—"

"Mom."

"—make me a list of all the things you want. Oh my, this baby is going to be—"

"Mom! I'm not pregnant."

"—so pretty." She pauses, lips parted. "What?"

"I'm not pregnant," I repeat, tucking a piece of hair behind my ear with a trembling hand.

Naturally, Daire notices. He marks the subtle shake and when I lower it, he tucks it beneath his with my other hand. "But Daire has a child, and we've recently gotten custody and—"

"A ... a child with someone else?" Her whole face falls like I've delivered the worst news imaginable.

Daire steps in, filling her in on the situation. For

several minutes, I just breathe, so thankful I don't have to rehash the whole thing. When he finishes, there are tears in her eyes.

She presses a hand to her heart when she says, "That poor thing. What a wonderful thing you're doing for him. Taking him in like that."

"He's Daire's son. There was never a question about whether we'd take him."

"Yes, dear, of course," she says in a dismissive tone. "You'll have to call me again when I can see the little one. But I need to go."

"All right, love you."

She returns the sentiment and ends the call.

"I think that went well," Daire says with a smile, his hands finally leaving mine.

I snort, even as my stomach ties itself into a knot. "That's what you think. She's pissed."

"Why?"

"You'll see."

Less than thirty seconds later, the text comes through. I turn it around so he can read.

> Mother Dearest: His first-born son should've been yours, Rosemary.

"She only calls me Rosemary when she's feeling particularly pissed off."

"That's an archaic way of thinking."

"Yeah, well…" I shrug off my annoyance and turn

my phone off completely.

I'm in no mood to receive more texts like that.

"Your mom is a complicated creature." He passes me the beer from earlier, and this time he doesn't say anything when I chug it.

With a sigh, I set the empty bottle down and wipe my mouth with the back of my hand. "You're telling me."

I love my mom, I do, but she's a bit much.

"Are you okay?" he asks, genuine concern creasing his brow.

My responding smile is genuine. It feels good to know that he cares enough about me to ask. "Yeah. I'm used to it."

"What does she think is going to happen if you're not the one bearing my first-born son?" He laughs outright at that, grabbing a beer for himself and another for me.

I'm not a huge beer drinker, but tonight, it's just what I need.

"That he'll inherit the majority of whatever portion you get of the Hendricks fortune." I take a swig. "And that any kid I give you would get less."

He cocks his head to the side, frowning. "Doesn't she know that things can be split equally?"

"This is my mother we're talking about. She's a loony tune. God love her."

"I'm sorry she makes you feel bad about things."

"About myself, you mean?" I set my bottle down and laugh humorlessly. "The worst part is she doesn't even mean to be cruel. At least if it were purposeful, I could blame it on jealousy or pettiness. But she's not a shitty mother. No matter what she says, her goal isn't to make me feel bad. She's just ... Her way of thinking is twisted. I don't know whether it's from how she was raised or a consequence of being in the modeling industry for so long."

"Still, I wish she didn't talk to you like that."

Elbows on the island, I rest my chin in my hands. "I'm used to it."

He grunts and rounds the island until he's standing at my side. "That's what you always say."

"Because as sucky as it is, I am."

We're watching each other silently, both still processing the conversation, when Sammy wails from upstairs.

I tip my beer in Daire's direction. "Parenthood calls."

Without hesitation, he jogs out of the kitchen. He doesn't need my help. I could stay down here, sipping the rest of my beer, but I don't want to. Sammy might not be mine, but he's already got me wrapped around his chubby little finger.

I didn't know I liked kids this much.

Not until him.

As I hit the top step, Daire opens the door to the bedroom and disappears inside.

"Hey, little man," he croons, scooping the screaming baby into his arms. "What's wrong?"

Sammy continues to scream, not at all consoled by Daire's hold. It's pitiful seeing him like this, and we're two idiots who really don't know what we're doing.

"Want me to take him?" I step up to his side and hold my arms out for the baby.

Daire passes him to me, and he instantly nuzzles into me, his wails turning into sniffles.

"He likes you more than me." Daire doesn't sound disgruntled about it. If anything, he's amused.

I poke my boob. "I think it's because my chest is squishier than yours."

His laughter warms me as I sit down in the rocking chair. "Can't say I blame him."

Smoothing my finger over Sammy's cheek, I smile down at him. "Did you have a bad dream, little one?"

Teary blue eyes look up at me. My stomach is heavy—this little guy doesn't know how much his life has changed in the past few days.

"Do you think he misses his mom?" I whisper.

Daire sits on the floor in front of us, crossing his legs. "Probably."

"Poor little guy." Gently, I rub my finger over his eyebrows in an attempt to help him back to sleep.

"Could you find a pacifier for him?" The small table to my right, where we usually keep one or two, is empty.

He hops up and looks into the crib, then he tries the changing table and the dresser, opening drawer after drawer.

"How the f—" He catches himself with a shake of his head. "How did we manage to lose every single one in a matter of days?"

"I don't know." I rock Sammy carefully. "But obviously we have."

He gets down on his hands and knees, peering under the bed. "Ah, here are a few." He pulls out three. "I'll go clean these."

He hasn't been gone more than ten seconds when Sammy's stomach makes the worst rumbling noise I've ever heard.

And then he poops.

I gag at the smell. It's awful.

An instant later, a warm and wet sensation crawls up the arm I'm cradling him with. Bile rises in my throat as I realize he's had a major blowout that his diaper clearly can't contain.

Nope. No. I can't do this.

Gagging, I stand and hold him straight out from me. No wonder he woke up.

"Daire," I scream. "I need you."

After a heartbeat, I hear his feet pounding up the

stairs, and then he comes running back in from down the hall. "What is it? What's wrong?"

"He pooped."

He gives me a confused look, his nose wrinkling at the smell. "Okay?"

"Look at his back." I gag again, holding the baby out to him so he can see the massive poop stain. "It got on my arm," I whimper. "I have *poop* on my arm."

Daire takes Junior from me, probably worried I'll drop him.

I wave my arms as tears burn my eyes. I can't stop gagging.

"It's on me. It's on me. It's on me."

Jesus, I'm hyperventilating now. This is pathetic, even for me, but there's *poop* on me.

"Bathroom, now," Daire commands.

I don't even call him out on his bossy tone. Frankly it's the exact thing I need to kick my ass into gear.

"Breathe," he reminds me, flicking on the bathroom light.

He ushers me to the sink and turns on the water, then he grabs the bottle of hand soap. He squirts what feels like half the bottle into my palms and then puts a couple of pumps on my arm.

"I can't touch it." A whimper escapes me.

Daire sighs, holding a fussing Sammy to his chest. "My hands are a bit full, Rosie. You're going to have to do this one yourself."

I toss my head back and close my eyes. Chanting "ew" the entire time I wash up.

After I've scrubbed for a solid five minutes, I still don't feel clean. I'm definitely going to be taking another shower.

"Can you start a bath for him?" Daire asks when I turn the sink off. "I think it's the only way to get him clean."

"Him and me both," I grumble.

I turn on the faucet and wait for the water to heat, then make sure it isn't too hot.

Miraculously, we get Sammy out of the pajamas and diaper without making an even bigger mess. Both go in the trashcan, and I tie up the bag and set it outside the door.

"You made some kind of mess, little man," Daire croons, letting the warm water running out of the faucet clean Sammy's backside. "That was nasty."

When he's mostly clean, Daire finishes up by setting him in the bath support inside the tub and giving him a full bath. Sammy's eyes are heavy with exhaustion, and he's almost asleep by the time we get him out.

While Daire dries him off, I run into the bedroom and pull out a fresh diaper and footie pajamas.

Five minutes later, the little guy is back in the crib, dreaming away.

Easing the door shut behind us, Daire loops his arm

around my shoulders and tugs me into his chest. "We make a good team."

My stomach flips. "We do, don't we?"

"Yeah, baby," he presses a kiss to the top of my head, "we do."

twenty-nine

DAIRE

"HENDRICKS, what the fuck are you doing here with a baby?"

Shoulders tensing, I turn around to face Coach. Dammit. I was hoping he wouldn't notice me, but I should've known better.

The man can sniff this kind of stuff out.

Winter break is over, and a new semester has begun, but Rosie and I have had no luck finding a reputable daycare with openings for Sammy. After we exhausted all our options, we started searching for a nanny, but it'll take time to interview applicants and find the right one.

"A baby?"

"Yeah, the one you're carrying." He wags a finger at me. "You're supposed to be practicing, not babysitting."

The sounds of the guys changing into their gear in the locker room ahead echo down the hallway.

So close but so far away.

"I'm not babysitting," I correct, and Sammy giggles, making a noise I think might be his form of *hi*. "This is Sammy. My son."

Coach rubs the back of his head, sighing like the weight of the world is on his shoulders. "I was hoping those rumors weren't true." He straightens and hits me with a serious look. "Now, what are you planning to do with the little guy?"

"I had to bring him with me. Rosie's in class, and we haven't found a daycare, and I don't have—"

Coach holds up a hand. "That's a lot of *and*s, kid. Give him here. I'll watch him while you practice."

On instinct, I pull the car seat in closer, my chest tightening. "You … you're going to watch him?"

Coach rolls his eyes. "I had babies once too, you know. I can handle the little guy."

It's not that I don't trust him. It's just that the idea of handing him over to someone else terrifies me.

If the idea of trusting Coach to care for him scares me, then how the fuck did I think I could handle leaving him at a daycare?

It's obvious now that I wouldn't have been able to drive away.

"All right," I agree reluctantly. I really have no other choice.

I hold Sammy's car seat out to Coach and then slide the diaper bag off my shoulder and pass that over too. When Coach gives the baby a genuine smile, my stomach eases a bit.

"Hurry up and get ready for practice. If you're late—"

"Yeah, yeah. I know. Extra drills."

"You do listen when I talk? I'm impressed, Hendricks." He claps me on the shoulder, then gives me a little push toward the locker room.

I go, but not without turning around to get one last look at Sammy, who waves at me.

Fuck, he's cute.

NEVER IN A MILLION fucking years did I expect to find Coach with my son strapped to his chest. Clearly, he found the baby wrap in the diaper bag. It was a hysterical distraction for me and my teammates.

Off the ice, I hit the showers to wash away the

sweat, rushing through my routine so I can get back to Sammy quickly. I already miss the little guy.

The guys apparently have the same idea. As fast as I finish up, they're faster, and I come out of the locker room to find half my team playing with Sammy in the room we watch game tapes in from time to time.

My heart pangs as I watch the interaction. Fuck. I never expected my team to embrace my son as one of their own.

"Our new mascot is pretty cute, don't you think?" Cree holds Sammy out to me.

I carefully take him and pull him close, dropping a kiss to his head. "He got half his DNA from me. Obviously, he's going to be cute."

Sammy snuggles his little face into my neck. That little move makes my chest expand and my heart explode.

It's crazy to say, but I didn't know love, not true love, until he came along.

"Are you going to bring him to practice tomorrow?" Justin, our team captain, asks.

I shrug, scanning the room for his carrier. "Depends on whether I've found someone to watch him by then."

When I've located the seat, I crouch in front of it and strap him in.

"If you need to bring him to drylands, we can take turns watching him," Justin volunteers.

My throat tightens at the offer, and the backs of my eyes prick with emotion.

I didn't give my teammates enough credit, that's for fucking sure.

Clearing my throat, I give a gruff "thanks" in response. "I've gotta get going. Thanks for looking after him." I scoop up the diaper bag and position it over my shoulder.

The guys disperse, but Cree lingers. "Can we get coffee or something before you head home? I feel like…" He runs his fingers through his hair. "Fuck, I've been a shitty friend this year."

I grit my teeth and cover Sammy's ears. "Don't cuss in front of my kid."

He winces. "My bad. Sorry."

"We've both been bad friends this year," I admit. "We've had a lot going on."

He exhales, the breath heavy with tension. "It's been some kind of senior year, that's for sure."

"Coffee sounds good."

A light flurry of snow is falling outside, so I set the car seat down and dig a knitted hat out of the diaper bag.

Cree chuckles beside me as I adjust the hat on Sammy's head. "Look at you. You're a natural."

My heart pangs at the sentiment, but I breathe through the ache as I drape a blanket over the car seat. "Trust me, I'm not. But I'm all he has."

Cree turns to face me head-on and frowns. "What do you mean?"

Fuck.

I never filled my friends in on what happened to Danielle.

Picking up the carrier, I nod at the door, and we head out into the cold. "Danielle and her husband were in a nasty car accident."

"What?" He freezes, his eyes bulging.

"Yep." I don't stop, and Cree rushes to catch up. "They didn't make it, but Sammy wasn't injured, thank fu—thankfully." My stomach roils thinking about how easily I could've lost my son before I ever really had him. "I have temporary guardianship. With any luck, it won't take too long to make it permanent. I hope like hell none of her family gives me any trouble."

"F—"

I cut him off with a glare.

"Frick. That's crazy."

"You're telling me. It happened Christmas Eve night."

"I can't believe you didn't tell me." He doesn't sound angry, just surprised.

"I've had a lot going on. It wasn't on purpose, I promise you."

"Wow." He rubs his jaw. "I don't really know what to say."

I shrug. "We're just taking things a day at a time."

As we approach the coffee shop, the fatigue that's plagued me for days creeps in. The caffeine is going to be much appreciated. If I thought life was exhausting before—between classes, practice, gym time, and games—it has nothing on parenthood.

Especially parenting an infant while still in college. This isn't for the faint of heart.

The line for coffee isn't too long, but Cree shoos me toward a table with Sammy while he gets our order.

Sammy babbles, blowing spit bubbles, as happy as ever.

"Look at you." I pat his belly overtop the blanket. "You're learning something new every day. Can you say Dada? Da-da."

He blows more bubbles in reply.

"Dada." I point at myself. "I'm Dada."

He gives me a gummy smile that hits me straight in the solar plexus.

Rocking him gently in the car seat, I duck down and tickle his chin. "We'll keep working on it, all right?"

My phone vibrates from my coat pocket with an incoming text, and my heart lifts, knowing it's likely Rosie.

> Rosie: I'm exhausted. Do you mind if I pick up takeout for dinner?
>
> Me: Same. Takeout sounds great.

> Rosie: What are you in the mood for?

> Me: Whatever.

> Rosie: Ugh. Give me more information than that.

I grin at my phone screen.

> Me: I'm not falling into that trap. You probably already know what you really want.

> Rosie: Five Guys?

> Me: I'm not opposed to sharing, but Five Guys seems like a lot.

> Rosie: DAIRE

> Rosie: No food for you.

> Me: I take it back. Burgers sound great.

> Rosie: Too late. Sorry.

I chuckle, amused by her antics. God, she's cute.

It feels like it's been forever since I touched her, and I'm craving so much more. I want to feel her bare body beneath mine. On top of me. All around me.

"Black coffee with a *sprinkle* of sugar. Seriously, what the fuck does a sprinkle of sugar mean?"

I take the offered coffee from Cree. "Language, my

friend. We have impressionable ears listening now. Isn't that right, Sammy?" I say, smiling down at my son. "Say Dada."

Cree slides into the chair across from me and sets his cup on the table. "I'm going to teach him to say Cree first just to spite you. Or maybe something silly like scooter."

"Yeah," I say, biting back a smirk, "because if Dada's too complicated, then surely he can say scooter."

Cree tips his coffee cup back, and instantly, his eyes go wide and he sputters. "Sh—shoot, that's hot."

Amusement curls my lips. "Did you think it would be cold?"

He tosses a napkin at my head, but I dodge it easily, and it lands on the floor beside me.

Sammy giggles, the sound enough to have me grinning in a way I don't think I ever did before him.

"You think that's funny?" I ask the baby, gently poking his belly. "Hmm? You thought it was funny that Uncle Cree threw something at Daddy."

"Whoa." Cree nearly chokes—I'm guessing on his saliva because he's shoved his coffee away from him like it's the coffee's fault that he's an idiot. "That's so weird."

"What is? Talking to a baby?"

"No. You calling me Uncle Cree and yourself Daddy."

I laugh. "I am Daddy."

He turns his head and gags. "I don't want to hear about your weird kink things in public."

"God, you're so easy to rile. For the record, I'm not into being called Daddy in the bedroom."

Though I have recently developed a kink for making my wife come. Watching her face flush and the way her body shakes all over. I'm going to lose my shit when I finally get to sink my cock inside her and watch her come on my dick.

Cree pops the lid off his cup, and steam billows in front of his face. "No wonder I burned my tongue," he mutters.

Sammy gives another giggle, pulling my attention back to him. I rock him gently in his carrier. It's wild how I don't want to take my eyes off him—not because I'm scared something will happen to him if I look away, but because I'm so captivated by him. By his big blue eyes and his gummy smile. Everything he does is cute, from the way he scrunches his nose when he sneezes to the curl of his tongue when he yawns.

I've only ever heard women talk about baby fever, but I think I'm experiencing it right now.

I could have a million more of these.

Well, if I didn't have to deal with waking up in the night. That part isn't fun. But everything else? I'm surprisingly okay with it. Even the diaper changes don't bother me.

Cree and I catch up, but it isn't long before Sammy

is yawning and rubbing at his eyes, signaling that it's time to get home so I can get him fed, then bathed and ready for bed.

For such a small human, he's incredibly time-consuming.

When I pull into the driveway, Rosie's Mercedes is already there.

I unbuckle Sammy and scoop him into my arms. Then snag my backpack and the diaper bag with my free arm. I'm halfway up the walk when Rosie opens the front door and steps back to let me in.

"Thanks." I give her a grateful smile, dropping the bags to the floor in the foyer.

She shuts the door quietly, turns the lock with a *snick*, and snatches the baby from me, burying her face in his neck.

"I missed you." She smacks a loud kiss on his cheek. "Were you good for your daddy?"

My stomach flops around like a fish out of water at the sight in front of me.

Then I'm hit with a vision of Sammy in a few years, with more kids running around. Ones with dark hair and Rosie's attitude, and fuck, *I want it*.

But does she want it too?

Does she want *me*?

I rub at my sternum, easing the ache there. I've been too scared to talk to her about the future or my growing feelings. I'm too damn terrified of the possibility of her not wanting the same.

But we let a miscommunication tear us apart once, and it took years to find our way back to one another. There's no way I'll let that happen again, so that means I have to be honest about my feelings.

And soon.

"Is he hungry?" she asks, already heading for the kitchen.

I follow behind, taking a moment to appreciate how well her jeans hug her ass.

"He's probably getting there."

Sammy's just starting to eat solids, but he's not completely sold on them yet. I wouldn't be either if I had to eat mushed up peas and sweet potatoes. He devours the fruity ones, though, especially bananas.

Rosie straps him into the highchair. The second highchair we've purchased since bringing him home on Christmas day. He hated the first one, flailed and kicked and cried every time we put him in it, and I'm learning that I'll do just about anything to make sure my little guy is happy.

"I just got home, so burgers and fries are still in the bag." She gestures to the greasy takeout bag on the counter. "Can you plate everything up?"

"No problem."

She wheels the highchair over to the table, and

Sammy chills there while she gathers the half-eaten jars of baby food from the fridge.

I grab two plates from the cabinet, and as I open the brown bag, the smell of cheese and salty fries hits me. The temptation to grab a fry and pop it into my mouth is impossible to resist.

I groan as the flavor explodes on my tongue. Delicious.

Beside me, Rosie searches through the drawer for the baby spoons.

"Dishwasher," I say. "I ran them through this morning."

"You're a saint." She opens up the dishwasher and plucks one out.

Sammy, suddenly impatient, lets out a wail and bangs his chubby fists against the tray.

Hands full, Rosie shuffles over to the table. I can't help but watch her, amazed by how natural this feels. As she's taking lids off jars, I realize she's forgotten the bib. They're one of several necessities we failed to purchase before Sammy came to live with us, but it only took a matter of days to discover just how much we needed them.

Swiping one from the drawer, I take it over and fit it around Sammy's neck.

"Oh, thank you." Rosie peers up at me, her eyes bright. "I forgot."

"I got you. We're a team." As if it's the most natural

thing in the world, I kiss the top of her head.

The scent of her shampoo sends a comforting warmth through me. I'm a fucking goner.

In response, she gives me a confused smile. I don't blame her. I never knew I had it in me to be this affectionate. But here I am, and I wouldn't change it.

After plating up our dinner, I set them both on the table and join my two favorite people.

"We've established that you missed Sammy, but what about me?"

Rosie looks me up and down slyly. "What about you is it that you think is so miss-able?"

With a lighthearted scoff, I put a hand over my heart and rear back. "A wound straight to the heart."

She uses the spoon to clean sweet potato puree off Sammy's face. "You're the one that asked."

"So you didn't miss me at all? Not even a little bit?"

She spares me a glance, lips twitching with a desire to smile. "Maybe a smidge. Like the size of my pinky nail. If that."

"Well, baby," I lower my voice as I lean into her, brushing my lips over her cheek, "I missed you a whole lot."

Her breath stutters, and I sit back with a smirk, more than a little satisfied.

Rosie can pretend all she wants that she's not affected by me, but it's all for show.

She wants me as badly as I want her.

thirty

ROSIE

CROSS-LEGGED on the floor of my bedroom, I sort through a box of papers I should've cleared out a long time ago but held on to for stupid sentimental reasons.

God, if Daire ever saw this stuff, he'd realize how obsessed I was with him as a girl.

Mrs. Rosie Hendricks is scribbled on page after page of notebook paper. I take those out and set them aside. It's ridiculous that I lugged all this stuff with me to college, but stupidly, I wasn't ready to throw any of it away—not even when I hated his guts.

I pull a yearbook out and flip through it until I find my photo. I couldn't have been more than seven or eight, and I was sporting two missing front teeth and pigtails. Daire is easy to find. I'd recognize that blond hair and those blue eyes anywhere. Even as a little boy, he was beyond cute. Young Rosie had great taste. Older Rosie? She still has great taste.

But damn if our relationship isn't complicated.

This was a short-term arrangement, and we vowed not to get feelings involved. But day by day, it's getting harder to remember that.

With a huff, I close the yearbook and go back to sorting through the box.

I lift a small stack of journals out of the way, then flip through random pictures.

A drawing at the bottom catches my eye. I had to have been about fourteen when I drew it. I'm not an artist, and I don't pretend to be, but I went through a phase where I thought I might become a fashion designer.

My favorite item of clothing to draw?

Wedding dresses.

Particularly dresses I envisioned myself wearing on the day I married Daire.

God, I was delusional. Like most teen girls, I suppose.

My bedroom door swings open, and Daire bursts in

unannounced, scaring the shit out of me. I let out a scream and scramble to collect the papers scattered around me. Hastily, and with my heart beating out of my chest, I stuff as many as I can into the box. As I'm grasping at them, one of the drawings goes flying through the air and lands at his feet.

I slam the lid back on the box, panting.

The drawing is the least of my worries. I definitely don't want him to discover my journals or the pages upon pages of *Mrs. Daire Hendricks* written in a dozen different ways. In print, in cursive, with hearts over the i's, you name it.

Bending, he scoops the piece of paper up, studying it with a wrinkled brow. "What's this?"

"Do you always barge into people's rooms without knocking?"

He lowers the page and arches a brow at me. "When I'm lonely and want to snuggle my wife, yes."

My breath catches.

We haven't shared a bed since his dad and brother left. He tried that first night they were gone, but I told him it wasn't a good idea. Not because I didn't want him to sleep with me, but because I wanted it *too* much. It sounds stupid now that I think about it.

"And clearly," he continues when I say nothing, "you couldn't sleep either. Now, what is this?" He holds the paper out for me to see.

I slide the box under my bed and stand.

"A wedding dress," I mutter, tugging on the hem of my t-shirt nervously, as if he hasn't seen every inch of me already.

"A wedding dress," he parrots. "Why?"

I shrug. "I had this insane idea when I was a teenager that I'd design my own wedding dress one day. That was one I liked, so I kept it."

For a long, silent moment, all he does is study the photo. Finally, he holds it out to me.

"You could still do that, you know."

I slide the drawing into my bedside table drawer. Right next to my vibrator. Very appropriate.

"Do what?" I turn back around to face him.

"Design your own wedding dress."

With a sigh, I yank the covers back and slide into bed. "Maybe one day."

"Correct me if I'm wrong, but we're having a wedding this summer. It was one of your requests, remember?"

I stare up at the ceiling, my heart sinking. I don't even balk when he gets in bed beside me. "We don't actually have to do that. I know this isn't real." I close my eyes and breathe through the prickle behind my eyes. God, it's crushing to say that out loud. "Knowing my mom, she probably has everything booked already and is just waiting to spring a date on us. But designing a dress takes time and … it's not worth it, okay?"

He huffs a harsh breath. "You mean I'm not worth it," he says, his voice low and strained.

I turn my head to face him. "You're the one who told me not to fall in love with you. I'm just following your rule, Daire."

He rolls to his side, propping his head in his hand so he can look down at me. "Fuck that stupid rule."

My heart pounds out a rhythm in my chest, but I maintain my cool, rolling my eyes. "You're just saying that because you've been celibate for months and you're horny. I get it. You'd probably fuck a cactus at this point if it wouldn't hurt. I know this has an expiration date and—"

He puts his hand over my mouth. "Fuck what I said before. You and me?" His Adam's apple bobs, eyes skating over my face with an intensity that sends a shiver down my spine. "We're the real deal. We always were."

My eyes burn, and my heart threatens to burst right out of my chest.

What he's saying feels too good to be true.

I grasp his wrist and slide his hand away from my face. "Daire—"

He slants his mouth over mine, silencing me.

I close my eyes and melt into the mattress as he comes to rest over top of me.

So good, so good, so good. They're the only two words my brain can conjure.

He fits his leg between mine, his knee pressed right up against my aching pussy.

"You know I'm right," he murmurs between kisses. "I'm sorry it took me so long to see. If you want me to stop, I will, but fuck, Rosie, I don't want to. I want you so bad." With a hum, he brushes his nose against the column of my neck, sending a shiver down my spine despite how hot I feel all over.

It's what I've always wanted.

Him.

But along with desire, I'm filled with a sense of terror.

I finally have him back in my life, and as much as I want more, I'm scared of taking that step and losing him.

Losing him once was heartbreaking.

Losing him twice?

Devastating.

I exhale, my breath shaky.

He hovers above me, those denim blue eyes regarding me so sincerely, like he can read my mind.

"Baby," he murmurs.

I close my eyes at the tone of his voice—the understanding.

"I'm not going anywhere." The assurance is genuine, pleading. "Not again. Do you feel this?" He grabs my hand and presses it against his rapidly beating heart.

"It's yours. No one else's." He cups my cheek, inhaling the breath I exhale. "I love you."

The world around me goes silent.

I no longer hear my fan whirring in the corner of the room or the sound of our mingled breathing. Not even the rustle of the sheets reaches my ears.

Daire Hendricks loves me.

My *husband* loves me.

Love. Love. Love.

Those words echo like a pinball through my skull. My heart bursts at the notion, my lungs burning with the need to respond.

"Say it again," I beg on a whisper.

He lowers over me, hands braced on the mattress on either side of my shoulders like he's doing a pushup.

"I love you." He enunciates each word, focus fixed intently on my face, making sure I don't miss it.

I and *love* and *you*.

Three of the simplest words in the English language, but when they're put together like that, an entire universe exists in them.

"You love me?"

"That's what I said, Rosie girl."

"Have you ever told another girl you love her?"

My stomach twists while I wait for him to respond. I don't know what makes me ask it. Maybe a sprinkle of jealousy, but mostly curiosity.

"Never." His eyes, shining with honesty, never stray

from mine. "It was always meant to be you. I'm sorry I was such an idiot."

I giggle, the bed jostling with my laughter, but Daire never wavers above me. The chain around his neck dangles close to my face. I grab it and gently pull him closer.

"We were both idiots." Arching up, I close the distance between our mouths and kiss him.

When I pull away, he groans, the sound rumbling through us both and sending sparks skittering down my spine.

"By the way," I whisper, biting my lip, "I love you too."

Always have and always will.

He brushes his nose along the curve of my cheek. "Are we doing this?"

I don't hesitate. "Yes."

With that single word, whatever leash he had on himself snaps.

He kisses me with unrestrained passion. Pushing my t-shirt up and over my head until I'm bare to him, he peppers kisses all along my chest and stomach. Then he settles between my thighs.

"D-Daire, no." It's a breathless plea. I give him a gentle shove and he rolls over, taking me with him so I'm on top.

"Don't want me between those gorgeous thighs

tonight, baby?" He grins up at me, crossing his arms behind his head.

"Maybe later." I grin back. "But I want to do something I've been thinking about for a long time."

"What's that?" His tone is curious, but by the sparkle in his eye, it's obvious he already has a pretty good idea.

I rub my hands over his warm, muscular chest. He's hard everywhere. "I could bounce a quarter off these things if I wanted to." I flick one of his prominent abdominal muscles.

He laughs, the whole bed jostling with the movement. The motion slides me farther down his body. My thin cotton sleep shorts do next to nothing to protect me from the giant bulge in his pants.

It takes my breath away.

Nerves bubble violently inside me.

I'm certainly not inexperienced when it comes to sex, but this is Daire. The man I've loved all my life. That little factor changes it all.

He grips my ass with both of his big hands, rolling me against him. I hiss out a breath, suddenly certain I could come just like this.

"Daire." His name is a whimper. "You're distracting me."

Sitting up, he takes my lips in a breathless kiss. "Good," he murmurs, cupping the back of my neck.

His eyes are heavy-lidded, his lashes enviously long.

I scoot farther down his body, yanking his pants and boxer briefs down as I go.

His hard cock springs free. I whimper at the sight. It's been too long, and I'd be lying if I said I haven't been imagining what this thing would feel like since I burst into his room that first night.

He's long and thick, and the piercing on the head glimmers in the low light.

I bite my lip, both in anticipation and trepidation, and wrap my hand around the base, stroking once. Twice.

Daire groans, crooking his elbow over his eyes. "For the love of God, Rosie, if you keep looking at my dick like it's an ice cream sundae on the hottest day of July, I'm going to explode."

I huff a laugh, my breath fanning across the head of his cock.

"Rosie," he groans. "That isn't helping."

I swipe my tongue out, licking around the piercing, and in response, his hips buck off the mattress and a low curse flies from his lips.

"Is that helping?"

He lifts his arm and stares down at me with hooded eyes. "You're going to be the death of me, woman."

"Mm," I hum. "We can't have that. I'd like to keep you around."

I lower my mouth over him and continue until he hits the back of my throat and I gag.

"Fuck, Rosie." He fists my hair with both hands, gently guiding me up and down. As he sets the pace, I moan around him, making sure he knows I approve.

As I suck. I dig my fingers into his thighs, more than likely leaving half-moon indentions from my nails, but if it hurts, he doesn't complain.

I take him as far as I can once again, his piercing hitting the back of my throat. My core clenches in anticipation. It's impossible not to fantasize about what that thing will feel like inside me.

Daire brushes his fingers along my neck, gathering my hair away from my face.

When he murmurs "pretty girl," I think I might come on the spot.

This man turns me on and fills me with comfort in a way that no other guy has ever been able to.

Because he was always meant to be yours.

As that little voice in my head encourages me, I look up at him, finding his eyes hooded as he watches me. The muscles in his abdominals flex. He's holding himself back.

I smile around his length, then release him, a string of saliva clinging to my mouth. He groans at the sight, his eyes somehow getting heavier.

I wipe it away, tilting my head to the side. "Why are you holding back?"

His eyes widen with surprise, like he didn't expect me to pick up on it. "I'm not."

I grin. "Liar. Fuck my mouth like you want to."

He closes his eyes, breathing out slowly. "Are you sure?"

I nod, clenching my abdominal muscles to stave off the desire that courses through me at the idea of it. "Give it to me. I can take it."

He sits up, forcing me to crawl backward.

"Stay like that," he orders.

"On all fours?"

"Yeah, baby." He strokes my jaw and rises up on his knees. "Fuck, your lips are all puffy already." He rubs his thumb over my bottom lip. "So beautiful. Now open up."

I do as he says, keeping eye contact with him. Gripping the base of his cock, he guides it into my waiting mouth.

Then, with a hand in my hair, he guides my speed and picks up the pace. When I choke, he pulls back.

Peering up at him, I shake my head.

I can take it, I say with my eyes.

And he gives it to me, not holding anything back this time.

I revel in it—in making him lose control like this.

When he pulls back a second time, I whimper, but the sound dies off as he gently pulls me up and covers my mouth with his.

"If we don't stop, then I'm going to come in your mouth."

Breathless, I say, "I wouldn't mind."

"Next time." With a quick peck to my lips, he grasps me and lays me down flat on the bed. Holding himself above me with one hand, he yanks my shorts down and off my legs, then tosses them aside. "Are you wet, Rosie?"

I nod, biting my lip as my pussy clenches with anticipation. I've been waiting so long for this.

With one finger, he finds my core, letting out a low hiss. "Fuck, you're soaked."

Arching my back, I cup his cheek. "Please."

Please, fuck me.

Please, love me.

Please, never leave me.

"Are you on birth control?"

With my heart in my throat, I nod in answer.

"Do you want me to wear a condom?"

His thoughtfulness floods me with warmth. Finding my voice, I say, "I trust you."

In response, he lets out a shuddering breath and kisses me.

Giving him my trust might be even more powerful than giving him my love.

Gripping his cock at the base, he guides it to my entrance and pushes in only an inch or so. In unison, we moan. I might have been embarrassed of the sound if it wasn't so obvious that his feelings are just as intense.

"Jesus, Rosie." He pulls back out, then slowly pushes in again. This time a bit farther.

The piercing on the head of his cock feels foreign but strangely good.

"Daire," I practically beg, clutching at his arms. "Stop teasing me."

With a chuckle, he pushes in all the way. I gasp at the fullness and tighten my hold, my nails biting into his forearms.

He rocks his hips in and out, tortuously slow. "Look at the way you take me. Your pussy was made for me."

Dizzy with desire, I follow his line of sight. The vision of us connected this way is enough to cause fireworks to erupt in my chest.

"I love you." He kisses me.

Pressing his forehead to mine, he rocks gently in and out of me. The rhythm is at odds with the way he fucked my mouth, but it's not any less erotic. This is what we need for our first time. Soft and slow.

"You feel so good, baby."

I bite my lip, at a loss for words, let alone thoughts. I'm simply a big ball of emotions. This moment is too intense, but in the best way.

With his thumb, he finds my clit, pressing in slow, steady circles that quickly send me hurtling toward climax.

Curse this man for knowing exactly how to play my body. Why him when no one else could?

But as quickly as the impending orgasm barrels down on me, it fades.

Though I hide my disappointment, he knows me too damn well. "Let go, Rosie," he murmurs. "Get outta your head. Eyes on me."

I do as he says, pushing all thoughts but him from my mind. As I focus on the need in his eyes and the way he moves over me, that sensation quickly builds again. And then I'm careening over the edge before I can get too in my head about it again.

"Beautiful. So beautiful," he croons, lazily tracing my body with both hands.

I feel like Jell-O in his arms.

Without a word, he pulls out and turns me around so I'm on my stomach. Grabbing my hips, he props me up and enters me from behind.

"Oh, God," I cry out, clawing at the sheets when he fills me in the most delicious way.

I can feel him everywhere, and that piercing hits a pleasure button inside me I didn't even know existed.

He picks up the pace, pulling curses from my lips. It's not frantic by any means, but it is harder than before.

Impossibly, another orgasm builds.

I close my eyes, not thinking, just feeling.

When it hits me, I cry out and fall flat to the mattress. As I come down, his hand is warm on my back, steady, a reassurance that he's got me.

"I'm right here," he whispers, like he knows I need to hear the words.

His big body covers me from behind, the motion pressing him impossibly deep inside me. With a kiss on my shoulder, he gently pulls me up until my back is to his front.

Hand on my throat, he holds me flush against his body.

His thrusts are gentle once more. My whole body feels like it's shaking, though it could be that he's completely rattled my brain with pleasure.

When he pulls out, I whimper at the loss.

But before I can complain, he guides me to turn around and lie on my back once more. Then he's pushing back in. My body welcomes him eagerly, used to the size now. Gripping my legs, he pushes them up toward my head.

"Oh, fuck," I gasp.

Good. It's so good.

He clenches his teeth, his necklace dangling above my face. "I'm close," he groans. "Do you think you can come again?"

I whip my head from side to side. There's no way.

His response is a grin. Dipping low, he kisses me. "Challenge accepted."

I should've known better.

He reaches over to the drawer where I stuffed my drawing earlier and rummages around blindly.

"I figured you'd have one of these," he says, straightening and holding my vibrator up triumphantly.

Turning it on, he presses it against my clit.

I nearly fly off the bed like he's exorcising demons from my body.

The sensation is ... too much. Too good. Too intense.

"Oh, yeah." He smiles, pleased with himself, and thrusts deeper. "You'll come again."

In a matter of seconds, he works me into a frenzy.

Somehow, when the orgasm shatters through me, it's even more intense than the other two.

I'm exhausted.

Completely spent.

Turning the vibrator off, he tosses it aside, and then he's gripping my hips and pounding into me.

The sounds he makes as he comes ... I want to remember them forever. I've never witnessed anything hotter than the sound of his moans as he tumbles over the edge.

He pulls out of me slowly, watching me as I watch him, both of us catching our breath.

I'm simultaneously the most exhausted and the most energized I've ever been.

With a long exhale, Daire lies beside me, pulling me against his body. His lips press against my neck in a gentle kiss.

He doesn't say anything and neither do I.

We don't need words.

There isn't a single one that could encapsulate what exactly that was.

I close my eyes and drift off to sleep to the sound of his steady breathing.

I awake only a few hours later to the sound of Sammy's cries, and truthfully, I still couldn't be happier.

thirty-one

DAIRE

"YEAH, I UNDERSTAND. MHM. THANK YOU."

I end the call and turn to Rosie. She's never looked more beautiful than she does right now, sitting on the floor with Sammy, playing peek-a-boo.

I asked her to marry me because I was desperate to know my son. I never considered that she might treat him as her own. But it's so clear in this moment that I couldn't have picked a better person to do this life with.

"What was that about?" she asks, setting a dancing cactus toy in front of him.

"It was Nina." I let out a long breath. "The funeral is this weekend, and we need to go."

Rosie flinches. "Is it bad that I forgot there would be a funeral?" She bites down on her lip and surveys Sammy. "That makes me feel awful. I've been so caught up in settling into this new routine, and ... wow, I feel like a selfish asshole. They died, and the thought has barely crossed my mind."

I run my fingers through my hair. "Me too," I admit with a flinch. Fuck, I'm an asshole. Adjusting to parenthood isn't a good excuse, but it's the only one I've got. "It's been three weeks already. It seems like a long time to wait, but according to Nina, the family needed the time to prepare arrangements and travel."

"Makes sense." Rosie wrinkles her nose. "Um ... does this mean they've been, like, refrigerated all this time?" She flinches as soon as the question is out of her mouth. "I just can't imagine being frozen for that long."

"I'm not sure," I answer, sitting on the floor with her and Sammy.

He's only beginning to sit unassisted.

Danielle might've thrown me for a loop, and I've been angry at her for a long time, but now all I can think about is that, while I missed out on his early milestones, she'll never see the rest. And the realization makes me feel mildly ill.

I hope like hell I can do a good job raising this kid.

Rosie's hand is warm against my cheek as she turns my face so I'm forced to look at her. "What are you thinking about? You look sad."

I could lie, but what's the point in that?

"I was thinking about how I missed out on things like his first smile and first laugh. Rolling over. But Danielle? She's not getting any more of those firsts. Ever. And despite what she did to me, she is—was—his mom."

Rosie slips her hand to the back of my neck, pulling my head down so she can rest her forehead against mine.

"You're a good man, Daire. And an amazing father. I hope you know that."

I take her free hand and kiss her palm, then I lace my fingers with hers.

Sammy giggles. Every time he does something cute, the smile I wear is instantaneous.

"God, he's cute." I ruffle his downy soft hair.

"I have to admit, I think most babies are ugly, but he's perfect."

I throw my head back and guffaw. "Only you would admit to thinking babies are ugly."

"What?" She blinks innocently, moving to sit with her back against the couch. "Most of them are. Parents are just biologically programmed to think they're adorable or some shit."

Sammy teeters, and I dart a hand out to steady him before he falls. He babbles nonsense that I'd like to think is his way of saying thank you.

"Rosie?"

"Mhm?" She hums, her head lolling in my direction.

"Just so you know, there's no one else I'd rather do this with than you."

"Not even Miley Cyrus?"

I drop my head back and groan. "How dare you bring up my Miley Cyrus obsession."

"Remember that summer you insisted we watch *Hannah Montana* at my house because you didn't want your brothers to know you loved the show?"

I cover my face with my hands. "Well, you were obsessed with the Jonas Brothers," I counter.

"What girl my age wasn't?" She tucks her legs under her, smiling at me.

The warmth in her eyes matches the heat radiating from my chest at the memories.

Sammy slaps his hand against the rug, catching our attention.

Rosie scoops him up, peppering kisses all over his cheeks. As his responding giggles fill the air, I decide it's one of my favorite sounds.

This right here?

My little family?

It's all I never knew I needed.

SAMMY IS STRAPPED to my chest because I'm too fucking paranoid to carry him in my arms where someone might take him from me. It's ridiculous; these people are his family, but to me they're strangers.

As if sensing my tension, Rosie stays by my side, her arm looped through mine as we move around the room.

The funeral was an awkward affair that left me feeling ill.

Lots of crying. Lots of hugging—which I wasn't prepared for. And lots of questions.

There were some scathing looks from Danielle's husband's family. I can't totally blame them, I guess. It was a joint funeral, and I'm proof, along with Sammy, of Danielle's infidelity. It's not my fault she cheated on her husband. For all I know, they cooked up the plan together. It would've saved thousands of dollars if they were considering the IVF route. Not that I'll ever know whether that was their goal.

As uncomfortable as the service was, the awkwardness of the luncheon is so much worse.

"I'm Julie, Danielle's aunt," a woman with brown hair and a hint of gray at her roots says. "That makes me this little one's great-aunt—I think that's right." She moves in close and tries to pet Sammy's head, but with my height, she ends up getting nowhere close.

It doesn't help that I'm trying to sidestep her in an awkward mockery of a dance.

"Cool. I'm Daire. Sammy's father." I've said this at least five million times today. "And this is my wife, Rosie."

Rosie waves with her free hand. "Hello."

"Hi, dear." The aunt, Julie, doesn't even make eye contact with her, which instantly grates on me. "Can I hold him?"

She already has her hands outstretched for him.

"No."

Her mouth parts and her eyes go wide with shock, just like everyone else I've encountered today.

Sue me for protecting my kid. I don't know any of these people, and in a crowd this size, there are germs galore. I don't want him getting sick. And frankly, I'm paranoid enough to think that if I hand him off, I might not get him back.

"Why?" She's bold enough to ask, unlike the others I've turned away.

"Because I said so."

I don't owe anyone an explanation.

Rosie snickers at my side and tries to hide the sound with a cough.

Julie, clearly flabbergasted, stammers, struggling to find words.

Before she can formulate a response, I simply move

to another corner of the room and start the whole process over again.

"Do you want me to grab a plate of food for you?" Rosie asks, eyeing the buffet set up in the corner. Her nose wrinkles with displeasure.

"Fuck no. We're getting Chipotle after this."

She presses a hand over her mouth to hide her laughter. "You've already thought about this."

"Baby, I've already got the order ready to submit."

She sticks her lip out in a pout. "You didn't ask me if I wanted anything."

"I already know what you want."

Her brows furrow. "We've never had Chipotle together before."

"Rosie." I cock my head to the side, staring her down. "I know you." I pull my phone out and bring up the app, then I pass it to her.

Slack-jawed she reads the details of bowl I have saved for her. "You really do, huh?" She slides my phone back into my pocket for me, her hand lingering on my thigh a few seconds longer than necessary. "How much longer do you think we need to stay?"

I twist my head from side to side, considering the people mingling around the room. It's already been an hour.

"Another twenty?" I suggest.

She nods. "Sounds like a plan. I've gotta go pee, though."

My heart lurches at the notion. "Don't leave me," I practically beg.

The idea of facing these people without Rosie by my side for even a second makes me want to throw up.

She dances back and forth on her tiptoes. "But I really have to go."

"Then I'm coming with you."

"To watch me pee?" she asks a little too loudly, causing more than one person in our vicinity to turn in her direction.

"I meant I'd stand outside the door. Jeesh. I don't have some weird pee kink, if that's what you're thinking."

"Fine," she agrees, releasing my arm. "Let's go before my bladder explodes."

I follow her down a long hallway and park myself against the wall while she steps inside the ladies' room.

It's pathetic of me to hide like this, I know. Nina told me that none of the family has stepped forward in any way to try to claim rights to Sammy, but I still find myself scared to death that someone is going to take him from me.

I have no problem with Danielle's family wanting to know him and be involved in his life. They are his family, after all. But until he's 100 percent mine by law, it makes me uncomfortable.

I'm probably overthinking things, but I can't help it.

And being here makes me uncomfortable in other ways too.

Like a semi at full speed, it hit me, in the middle of the funeral. Where would Sammy go if something happened to me? He's not Rosie's, not by blood, but I still think she'd take care of him. Maybe one of my brothers would help her.

Immediately I picture Cash moving in to help her and how, from there, they'd fall in love.

Get married.

Have a kid of their own.

And now I want to throw up.

I haven't spoken to my brother in months. If he knows about Sammy, then it's because my dad or one of my brothers told him. While my dad and Roman were visiting, they forced me to tell Asher and Hudson, but I refused when it came to Cash.

It probably makes me territorial as fuck, but I don't like that he wants Rosie.

She's mine.

The bathroom door opens, effectively cutting off my train of thought, and Rosie appears, head tilted to the side, appraising me.

"Why does it look like you're freaking out?"

I clear my throat and cup the back of Sammy's head. "Because I am."

No sense in denying it when it's blatantly obvious.

"About what?"

We head back into the large room, where mourners stand in circles talking to each other. This looks like it's as good a time as any to sneak away.

I came. I've done my part.

So I steer Rosie toward the exit, and she doesn't protest.

"You didn't answer the question," she accuses when we reach the car.

I push the button on my key fob, and while the door slides open, I work Sammy out of the carrier so I can strap him into his car seat.

Side-eyeing her, I mumble, "I was stressing about what would happen to Sammy if I were to die."

"Oh." She presses her lips together. "For starters, let's not think negatively like that. Second, I hope you know I'd never let anything bad happen to him."

I jerk my head in a nod and cover him with a blanket now that he's all strapped in.

As I push the button to close the door and step back, Rosie places a gentle hand on my arm.

"Hey." Her tone is soft, comforting. "Don't freak out. If this is something you're really worried about, then let's call Nina. She can help you set up whatever you need to in order to make sure he's taken care of."

Leave it to Rosie to talk sense into me.

Feeling a modicum lighter, I press a hand to her cheek and bring my mouth to hers.

Before Rosie, kissing was just kissing.

With Rosie, it's an experience. One I'll never get sick of.

I press my forehead to hers.

"Why do you always do that?" she asks, her breath fogging the chilled air.

"Do what?"

"Put your forehead against mine." She pressed warm palms to my cheeks.

"I don't know. I guess it makes me feel centered. All the worries and negative thoughts fade away."

Her eyes shine, making my heart sink. Shit. Did my confession upset her?

"What?" I ask dumbly.

"Nothing." She shakes her head, stepping away.

Gently I grasp her wrist and take a step toward her. "Did I say something wrong?"

She wraps her free arm around her torso and shakes her head. "No, I just … I think that's the nicest thing anyone has ever said to me."

I tug on a piece of dark, curled hair and wrap it around my finger. Its softness distracts me momentarily. Does she do something special to make it that way, or is her hair naturally that soft?

"What I'm hearing is that I need to give you compliments more often."

She lets out a watery laugh, but her eyes still swim with sadness. "What can I say? I guess my love language is words of affirmation."

I take her in my arms and hold her for several heartbeats.

I'm going to tell this girl every day for the rest of our lives how much she means to me.

With a kiss to her forehead, I release her and reach for her door. "Let's go, baby."

thirty-two

ROSIE

DESPITE USING my best methods of persuasion, I was never able to convince my mother to cancel the appointments she made at several bridal boutiques. I'm not surprised she wouldn't give in, but man, did I hope she would.

I leave Daire and Sammy at home and head for the hotel to pick up my mom and sister.

My mom didn't want to stay with us because, in her words, she needs her sleep and can't have a baby waking her up.

I park in front of the hotel and send her a text that I've arrived.

The day hasn't even fully begun, and I'm already exhausted. I asked Bertie to come, but she gave me a vague excuse about having a prior obligation. Something's going on with her, I can sense it, and I'm going to have to get to the bottom of it.

But I can't dwell on that today. I have to focus on surviving a shopping trip with my mother.

Under other circumstances, I would've loved seeing her and Grace.

While I wait, I take a long gulp of my iced espresso—then another for good measure—and let out a sigh.

"You can do this," I mutter to myself.

Five minutes later, my mom and Grace stroll out of the hotel. Once they're settled, my mom in front and Grace in back, I turn in my seat and give my little sister a wide smile. "Gracie! I missed you!"

"I missed you too." She clicks her buckle in place. "Do I get to wear a pretty dress too?"

I bring a hand to my chest, smiling at her honest question. "Absolutely. You're going to be my maid of honor—if you want to be, that is."

"I get to wear a pretty dress?"

Amusement bubbles up inside me. Clearly, the dress is what she cares about most. "Of course."

She nods succinctly. "Then count me in."

My mom clears her throat, garnering my attention.

She's buckled, purse sitting primly in her lap. "Your father sends his love."

I flinch and face the windshield. "I'm sure he does."

For months, I've been doing my best to avoid thoughts of what a mess my relationship with my dad is. I've always been a daddy's girl, and not talking to him has been hard. But we're both annoyingly stubborn, and I refuse to apologize when I did nothing wrong.

My mom reaches over, tucking a piece of hair behind my ear. "I'm sorry, sweetie."

There's no point in rehashing this, so I unlock my phone and click on the map icon. "What's the address for the first place?"

She gives me a concerned frown, but she goes easy on me and simply rattles off the address so I can put it in my phone.

Twenty minutes later, I pull into a parking spot at a small boutique.

Show time.

I take my coffee with me, knowing I'll need the caffeine to get me through the day.

The boutique is small but cute, with walls lined with dress after dress in varying styles.

My mom goes straight for the sleek, fitted dresses, while Grace is drawn to the big princess ballgowns.

Me?

I park my butt on a chair and simply wait for my mother to pick dresses she wants to see me in.

I know her well enough to understand that this is purely about her living out her own fantasy. What I like won't matter, so why get my hopes up?

If Daire and I are going to have a real wedding, I'll have to find a dress on my own another time. Maybe I can convince Bertie to come too.

I cross my legs, smiling when I get a text from Daire. It's a photo of Sammy's mostly gummy smile. His bottom two teeth are fully in, and he has one coming out on the top that's been giving him a fit. Drool clings to his chin, but he's still the cutest thing I've ever seen.

"What are you smiling at?"

I turn my phone around so my mom can see. She wrinkles her nose. "Your kids will be cuter."

"Mom!" I scold, tucking my phone away. That one simple sentence sends fissures spreading through my heart.

She sniffs, lifting her chin. "It's true."

I shake my head and stand so I can get away from her. "Sammy is a beautiful baby," I mutter as I walk away.

Can this day be over yet?

Stopping in front of a rack of dresses, I browse through them mindlessly, distracted by anger and disappointment.

A throat clears nearby, catching my attention. A woman dressed in head-to-toe black approaches, wearing a friendly smile. "I'm Amy. I'll be helping you today. Has anything caught your eye?"

I open my mouth to tell her I haven't even really looked yet. That this is for my mom's benefit not my own. But, of course, my mother beats me to it.

"I have a few over here I want you to pull for her to try."

So it begins.

"I DIDN'T CHOOSE THIS PLACE." My mom sounds rather proud of this odd statement as I park in front of the final bridal shop. From the outside, at least, it's a tiny hole-in-the-wall place.

"What does that mean? You gave me the address." I turn in my seat and assess her, confused.

"Daire made this appointment for you."

"Huh?" My heart pounds out a strange rhythm in my chest. "Why would he do that?"

"I don't know, but he's so in love with you, Rosie," she gushes, clasping her hands in front of her. "I see now why you rushed into marrying him. If I found a man that obsessed with me, I wouldn't want to wait either."

I rub my face and force myself to breathe, trying to grasp what she's saying. "He made this appointment?"

"Honestly, Rosie," she sighs heavily, "you can be so dense sometimes. That's what I said."

From the back seat, Gracie groans. "Can we hurry up? I want dinner."

Honestly, same.

My mom's been on a rampage, determined to find the perfect dress, and forced us to skip right over lunch. I haven't scored any points with her yet. I'm definitely on her shit list after finding fault in every ballgown she's trapped me in. I wouldn't put it past her to buy one anyway, just to spite me.

She looks out the window now at the tiny shop, nose wrinkling in distaste. "I wonder how he found this place. It looks ... quaint."

By *quaint*, she means not good enough.

"I don't know, but we might as well go in."

The bell above the door chimes pleasantly, signaling our arrival, along with Grace's loud "something stinks."

"Oh my God." The girl behind the tiny desk up front slowly pulls her Tupperware container of food closer to her. "I'm sorry. I lost track of time. I was starving, and I know it smells like garlic, but I was so hung—"

I hold up a hand and bite back a laugh. "It's fine. Please eat. We'll look around while you finish up."

"Are you sure?" She grimaces, her face etched with what I swear is fear. "I can put this away."

"No, go ahead."

Beside me, Grace pinches her nose and huffs.

I quickly swat at her arm. "Stop that," I whisper. To the girl working in the store, I say, "Ignore her. Grace has an incredible talent for being dramatic."

The concern on the girl's face is quickly replaced by amusement. With a laugh, she agrees, and we head off to browse the selection.

I drag Gracie over to a row of dresses that look like what she's been fixated on all day, hoping to distract her.

I think she's as obsessed with turning me into her own living doll as our mom.

After the girl finishes up her lunch or dinner or whatever meal it's supposed to be, she comes over and introduces herself as Taylor.

"Your fiancé made the appointment for you and sent over a picture for inspiration. Do you have anything else in mind? Fabrics? We'll talk about the sketch too and make any tweaks you want."

I blink at her, confused by the words coming out of her mouth. It all sounded like gibberish to me.

"Huh?" I blurt.

My mom steps up, a hand on my shoulder. "What are you talking about? A sketch?"

Taylor looks between the three of us. "Uh ... her fiancé emailed over a sketch of a wedding dress. He said it was something you drew when you were younger and that he wanted you to have your custom dream wedding dress. It's all paid for. Whatever you want, it's yours."

As I gape at her, all the blood rushes to my head. I feel heavy. Like I might fall over.

Daire set this up?

Reached out to the store? Set up this appointment? And showed them my silly little sketch?

I don't know whether to laugh or cry.

It might be the sweetest thing anyone has ever done for me.

"A sketch?" my mom asks me. "What is she talking about?"

"I … uh … I was going through a box of old things, and he saw a sketch of a dress I created when I was a teenager."

My mom puts a hand to her heart, looking as touched as I feel. "It's so sweet that he set all this stuff up."

Taylor clears her throat and points behind her. "If you're ready, we can head back and discuss what you want."

I swallow past the lump in my throat. "That would be great."

I ENTER the house and follow the sound of the TV to the family room, where I find Daire and Sammy on the floor playing. Daire is on his back, holding Sammy in the air. The sound of Sammy's giggles warms me from the inside out and make it impossible not to smile from ear to ear. God, I missed them. It's only been hours, but all day, I found myself wanting to be with them.

For a long moment, I stand in the doorway, just soaking it in. Happy. For the first time, I truly know what it means to feel that way.

All in all, I've led a great life, but I've never felt this content. Things have never been this right. This complete.

Clearing my throat, I step into the room and shuffle closer. When I plop down on the floor beside them, I smooth a hand over Sammy's head. "How are my boys?"

Daire turns his head and gives me a panty-melting smile. "Having a little play time before this little guy's bath."

He sits up, hugging Sammy to his chest. The baby holds his arms out to me, and I gladly take him from his dad. With a deep inhale, I relish his sweet scent and snuggle him closer. Who would have thought that I would have a motherly bone in my body? I'd never put much thought into having kids before, but suddenly, all of me belongs to this little baby. He tugs on my hair, and I gently extract it from his hand. I kiss his pudgy fingers and then his cheeks. He's perfect.

"How did it go?" Daire asks me.

"The last store was certainly a surprise."

He grins, eyes crinkling. "A good surprise, I hope."

I nod, fighting tears yet again. "It was the best surprise. I can't believe that you thought to do something like that for me."

Impossibly, his smile grows bigger. "I love you, Rosie, and I want you to have the dress of your dreams when you finally walk down the aisle to me."

"Are we really doing this?" I whisper. "Are we really going to make this real?"

He cups my cheek and leans in until his lips gently brush mine. "It was always real. We just didn't realize it yet."

"My mom picked a venue and chose a date in September," I warn him. "She told me over dinner. She's already put a deposit down. Are you okay with that?"

He chuckles and sits straighter again, amusement sparkling in his blue eyes. "The better question is, are you okay with that? Do you like the location? Is it what you want? I only care about you being happy, not your mom."

"It's my dream location," I admit. "A long time ago, I mentioned that I'd love to get married there. Apparently she never forgot. The day after we told her that we were married, she booked a date."

"Your mom." He shakes his head, laughing. "She's something."

"Tenacious, that's for sure."

"So what's the location?"

With a smile so big it makes my cheeks ache, I launch into a lengthy explanation of the elegant gardens I visited before for a party my father attended. Daire would probably rather I shut up instead of talking about flowers and the best spots for photos, but he never once looks bored.

I'm still wrapping my head around the idea that this thing between us is real.

He's my best friend again, the person I'm most excited to see, the person I want to spill my secrets to. He's the love of my life.

Being with him is effortless, and to think, if it weren't for Sammy, we probably would have continued to be too stubborn to forgive each other for our teenage stupidity.

Standing carefully with Sammy in my arms, I say, "Let's get this little guy his bath and go to bed."

"Bed?" Daire asks, hopping to his feet. "Or *bed*?"

I swat him, my cheeks flaming. "Just sleep. I'm tired."

Stepping in close, he grips my hips and places a gentle kiss to the crook of my neck. "I know you weren't gone that long, but I missed you."

I sigh, melting into his touch. "I missed you too."

It's strange, to miss him so acutely after only a few

hours. But I suppose that's a sign that this connection is real.

"Come on, we need to get this little guy in the bath."

"And then bed?" He winks.

I pat his chest, my stomach dipping. "We'll see."

He grins back, his expression making it clear he knows he's going to get what he wants, because I want it too.

I've never been able to resist Daire. I certainly don't expect things to change now.

Starting up the stairs, I hold my hand out behind me. An instant later, his fingers entwine with mine.

This is the life I always wanted—always hoped for.

It doesn't feel real that I finally have it.

thirty-three

DAIRE

ROSIE and I haven't found a nanny for Sammy yet, but we're making it work. With graduation on the horizon, I'm beginning to think we shouldn't even bother. The real world awaits us, sure, but we have time. We have money. So why not spend time with Sammy, at least for a little while? Maybe that's selfish, but I don't like being away from my son. He and Rosie have become my two favorite things in the entire world.

We're still jumping through ridiculous hoops to get permanent legal custody of him. Since I wasn't listed as his biological father on his birth certificate, the process is a complicated one. Regardless of DNA, things have to be handled in a certain way. Nina says I have nothing to worry about and to be patient. That's hard, though.

After practice, I shower and change, then head out of the locker room to find Sammy. It's become an after-practice tradition to hang out with him in the game tape room with the team.

When I step into the room, Sammy is babbling nonsense to Luke.

The big guy grins and mimics him.

"Hey." Cree elbows my arm. "I'm mad at you."

I arch a brow. "What for?" I rack my brain for a reason but come up empty. I've been on the straight and narrow for months. I'm a *dad* now. I have to set a good example for my kid.

"You asked Jude and Millie to babysit. What's wrong with Ophelia and me?"

I wince, because yeah, I asked them. Rosie and I spent Valentine's Day at home with Sammy, but I planned a little surprise for her for this weekend, which meant needing a sitter. Honestly, I considered asking Luke. The guy and I might not be best friends, but he's a cool guy and really great with Sammy. In the end, though. I decided Jude and Millie were my best bet. Now that Jude's with Millie, he's about as mellow as they come—and fully obsessed with that girl—and Millie has experience babysitting, so it was a no-brainer to me.

I didn't even entertain the idea of Cree and Ophelia, and that's probably even worse.

"Millie has babysitting experience." It's a plausible enough excuse, right?

He arches a brow. "Did you ask me if I have any experience?"

"Well ... no. Do you?"

"No," he sighs. "Did you ask Ophelia?"

I scratch the side of my nose. "No."

"You still don't like her." It's a statement, not a question.

I shrug. "It's not that I don't like her, but I..." I press my lips together and weigh my reasoning. In the past, I wouldn't have even stopped to consider if my words would hurt my friend, but I've matured enough recently to hesitate.

"Just say it," he mutters.

"You weren't there for me when I needed you, so I guess I'm not used to thinking of you first when something comes up. I'm sorry."

Cree nods, solemn. "Fair enough. I really am sorry. Don't get me wrong, I wouldn't take back anything with Ophelia, but if I could do it over again, I would've done whatever I could to help you out."

"I know."

I've forgiven him, I really have, but apparently my brain hasn't moved on from the hurt his abandonment caused.

Coach pokes his head into the room, then. "Hendricks, just the guy I was looking for."

My stomach sinks. I'm in for it after the way I stumbled during practice and had a nasty fall. It was a total rookie move, but he didn't comment on it other than to yell about what a little bitch I am when it happened. He covered Sammy's ears for the bitch part, otherwise I would've been pissed.

The sight of our burly, gruff coach wearing Sammy strapped to his chest at practice is one I'm not sure I'll ever get used to.

"I got something for you," he says, stepping into the room and holding out a box. "Well, for the little guy."

Sammy lets out a giggle like he knows Coach is talking about him. He claps his hands, flashing his toothy smile.

I take the box from Coach as the guys near me lean in to see what it is.

With a quick look at Sammy, I lift the lid and set it on the floor. Inside is a baby-sized pair of skates.

Fuck.

I actually choke up.

I swallow past the lump in my throat and grit out, "Wow, thanks, Coach."

He nods once. "You're welcome, kid."

"We have to try them on him," Justin says.

Luke holds Sammy out to me, so I take him and fit the skates onto his socked feet. They're a perfect fit.

"That's pretty cute," Cree chuckles.

"Thanks again, Coach," I say to the older man standing in the doorway watching us.

"Don't mention it." With a wave, he backs out of the room.

Sammy yawns and rubs at his eyes, so I quickly take the skates off and carefully put them back in the box.

"We better head out before this kid goes from cute and cuddly to angry and screaming."

Cree laces his fingers behind his head. "I still can't believe you're a dad."

I arch a brow at my best friend. "Dude, are you going to say that every time I see you?"

He grins back at me. "Yeah, at least until it sinks in."

I shake my head. "Come over when he's crying because he's tired but won't go to sleep, and then maybe it'll be real for you."

"Mm." He tilts his head back, pretending to consider the idea. "I'll pass."

As I get Sammy buckled into his car seat, the guys disperse in a flurry of back slaps and hollers.

Once the little guy is secure, I pull out my phone and send a text to Rosie.

> Me: Are you still on campus?

> Rosie: Yeah, are you done with practice?

> Me: Finished up and heading out. Do you want to get dinner out?

> Rosie: Like pick it up and take it home?

> Me: No, I mean actually go out to eat. As a family. We haven't tried it out with Sammy yet.

She doesn't respond right away, and I worry she doesn't like the idea.

I'm almost to my car when she responds.

> Rosie: Sorry, I ran into Bertie. She's acting funny. But yes, sounds great. Where do you want to go?

> Me: The Italian place in town?

> Rosie: Yum. I'm in.

Fifteen minutes later, I pull into the lot of the restaurant. Sammy has babbled the entire way, playing with his feet and flailing his arms.

Rosie isn't here yet, so I hop out and grab the diaper bag and quickly make Sammy a bottle. I packed a couple of jars of baby food as well that I can feed him in the restaurant if he gets fussy. Sitting in the back seat, I hunt for the socks he took off on the way—the kid seriously pulls them off each and every time he's in the car—and take him out of his seat. Once he's settled in my arms, he greedily takes the bottle, his chubby hands holding on.

I smile down at him, heart full, and soak in the quiet moment.

I thought my life was good before, but fuck, I didn't know what—no, who—I was missing.

A knock on the window startles both of us. Sammy quickly smiles around his bottle, formula dribbling out of the side of his mouth, as Rosie presses the button to slide the door open. She climbs in, and my chest instantly goes tight. She's so damn beautiful. Her cheeks are tinged pink from the wind and her eyes are bright.

"Good idea," she says, nodding at the bottle.

"I figured it might save us some crying and screaming."

Sammy's about as easy as they come, but when he's hungry, he's not to be messed with—throw in the fact that he's teething, and his meltdowns have the ability to escalate into disaster-level proportions.

When Sammy's done, I pass him to Rosie and pack his bag up again. My stomach rumbles, reminding me that I stupidly skipped lunch.

A fifteen-minute wait later, we're seated at a table.

"Hi, I'm Rory. I'll be your waitress this evening."

I look up at that, smiling. "Hey, Rory."

Aurora, better known as Rory, is dating Mascen, a buddy of mine who graduated last year. I haven't seen her around much, but frankly, I haven't been hanging around in my usual haunts. A lot has changed for me this year.

"Oh, hi, Daire." She smiles. "Rosie. And look at this cutie."

"This is Sammy," I say proudly, smiling at my son in the highchair.

"Do you guys know what you want to drink?"

We both opt for water, and Rory goes off to get those and a basket of breadsticks.

"I don't know what I want," Rosie whines over the menu. "Everything sounds good." Sammy giggles at that, and she smiles over at him. "Did you think that was funny?"

He laughs again, smacking his hands against the table.

"How is it that everything he does is cute?" Rosie asks me.

I shrug nonchalantly. "That's my half of the DNA hard at work."

She rolls her eyes playfully. "I should've expected that."

When Rory returns with our waters and a basket of breadsticks, she pulls out her order pad. "Have you guys decided what you want?" She lifts both brows as she digs in her apron and pulls out a pen. "And please, for the love of God, don't order the steak. Mascen always gets it just to mess with me. It's an Italian restaurant. I highly recommend sticking with the pasta."

My lips twitch at her sass. She's literally exactly what Mascen Wade needs to keep him in line.

Rosie laughs, closing the menu. "No worries. We're definitely not here for steak."

"Have you decided yet?" She clicks her pen.

Rosie's lips twist back and forth. "I think I'll go with the carbonara."

"Excellent choice. And for you?" Rory sizes me up like she expects mischief.

"The lasagna."

"Mid-choice, but I accept it." She winks.

I shake my head at her antics.

When she walks away, I text Mascen.

> Me: Your girlfriend is giving me a hard time. I see why you're perfect for each other.

It's comical how fast Mascen replies.

> Mascen: Why are you with my girlfriend?

> Me: Calm down, jackass. I'm getting dinner with my wife.

> Mascen: Dude. I heard you got married, but I didn't quite believe it. Also heard you've got a pet?

> Me: A pet?

> Mascen: Your spawn.

> Me: Yep, and he's just as cute as I am.

I snap a picture of Sammy's drooly smile and send it to Mascen.

> Mascen: Don't stay there too long or Rory will start asking me when we're having one.

> Mascen: Make sure to tip her well, or else.

I chuckle to myself and tuck my phone away.

"What was that about?" Rosie asks, dipping a breadstick in marinara.

"Just texting Mascen."

"Ah." She nods, taking a bite. After she chews and swallows, she says, "I guess he told you to get away from his girlfriend?"

"Yep. How'd you know?" I ask jokingly.

Her eyes dance as she wipes her mouth with a napkin. "It's Mascen."

Sammy lets out an excited scream just then, causing a few heads to turn our direction. Enthused by the interest, he does his new favorite thing and blows a raspberry.

This kid.

He's already the biggest flirt. I'm going to have my hands full as he gets older.

"I'm really worried about Bertie," Rosie says, bringing my attention back to her.

Resting my elbows on the table, I lean forward, frowning. They haven't really been hanging out lately, but I figured it was because they're both so busy. Graduation is fast approaching, and just about every free minute of Rosie's life has been consumed by Sammy and me.

"Do you think she's upset about something?"

I'm not quite sure what kind of wisdom I could impose on this situation, but I'll try my best if that's what she wants.

She shakes her head, tearing a chunk of breadstick off. "No, I don't think it's that. But she's avoiding me. I'm worried about her."

I reach out and cup my hand over one of hers. "I'm sure everything is fine."

She hums in response, but she doesn't look convinced.

"She could be stressed about finals and all that has to be done before graduation."

"Maybe, but I feel like it's something more. I'm going to have ambush her."

"Ambush her?" I repeat with a laugh.

"Yeah, show up at the dorm with snacks and movies so she's forced to let me in. Her favorite wine too."

"Do you think she'll go for it?"

Rosie waves a dismissive hand. "If she really doesn't want to see me, then she's going to have to give me a plausible excuse."

I just shrug, because frankly, I'm at a loss. I don't know Bertie well enough to understand her motivation for avoiding Rosie. The whole thing does feel a bit weird, but I'm not about to delve into Rosie's business with her friend.

When our food comes out, my stomach rumbles with approval.

"Let me know if you guys need anything else."

"We're good for now," I tell Rory.

Rosie points her fork at her carbonara. "I'm convinced pasta could save the world if it wanted to."

I suppress an amused smile. "You think so, huh?"

She twirls her noodles around the fork and holds it up in front of her. "I know so." Sammy darts a hand out and snags a noodle from her plate. "See? He agrees."

I extract the noodle from his closed fist. "Mhm, I'm sure that's exactly what he was doing. It has nothing to do with him being a baby and grabbing anything he can get his hands on."

Rosie juts her bottom lip out in a pout. "Don't mock me."

"I'd never dream of it."

After dinner, we head home in our separate cars. It

comes as no surprise that Sammy drifted off on the way, but it doesn't bode well for our bedtime routine.

"Aw, look at him," Rosie says, coming up beside me in the driveway. "God, what I would give to sleep like a baby."

I laugh at that. Rosie is a wild sleeper, constantly rolling from side to side and taking the covers with her when she does. I've learned to sleep under my own blanket.

As I unlatch the car seat, Sammy stirs a bit but doesn't wake up.

"I think I'm going to skip bath time," I tell her, heading for the door.

She unlocks it and steps inside, then holds it for me. "Are you sure?"

We give Sammy a bath every night. I read somewhere that establishing routine helps a child feel secure, and since Sammy's whole life was upended overnight, it seemed important.

It still makes me sick thinking about him being in that car—how easily I could've lost my son for good before I ever got to know him.

"I guess it depends on him," I hedge.

Rosie nods, dropping her purse to the counter. "If you're okay on your own, I'm going to shower."

"I've got it handled," I assure her.

She leans in, giving me a quick kiss. "I love you. You know that, right?"

Hand on her waist, I pull her in again for a deeper kiss.

It still blows my mind that I get to kiss this woman any time I want. "I love you too."

I head up with Sammy while she puts our leftovers in the fridge and set the car seat carefully on the floor beside the changing table.

Once I've got him unbuckled, I ease him out of the straps, but as I lift him out, he gives an annoyed grunt, and his eyes fly open. From there, the screaming sets in.

I internally cringe. I tried so hard not to wake him, but it was futile. "Sorry, bud."

He continues to cry, bottom lip shaking.

Holding him close with one arm, I sway from side to side and snag a set of pajamas so they're ready for afterward. Then I carry him into the bathroom.

Bath it is.

The kid loves bath time, so with any luck, this will calm him down.

I turn on the water, checking to make sure it's the right temperature, and wait for the tub to fill before I undress him. While the kid loves baths, he doesn't like the whole getting naked part.

His screaming intensifies once his clothes are off, but the second I get him settled onto the bath support, he calms down. As he hiccups, looking pitiful, I wet a washcloth and lay it over his chest to keep him warm.

Using the sleepy time soap, I wash him up with

another cloth, making sure to clean beneath his chin and the rolls of his skin.

Finally, he smiles and kicks at the water, splashing me.

"Did you get Daddy wet?"

He giggles in response.

"Ooh, sounds dirty."

I turn at the sound of Rosie's voice. "Oh? I thought you were showering."

She shrugs, one hand on the doorframe. "I decided to wait for you."

I try—and fail—to hide my smile.

If I could spend every second of the day buried inside Rosie, it still wouldn't be enough, but between Sammy and finishing up our degrees, we're tired … a lot. Which means sex isn't happening as often as either of us would like.

"Don't look so smug." She steps into the room and pokes the side of my neck where she knows I'm ticklish.

I lift a shoulder, shrugging her off with a laugh. "I can't be excited about getting my girl alone in the shower?"

"Well, when you put it like that." She sticks her tongue out at me.

When Sammy's clean and calm, I wrap him in a towel and pass him to Rosie so she can dry him and lotion him while I clean up the bathroom. Since I let Sammy splash around so much—he's a baby; he's allowed to have some fun even if it makes a mess — I typically have to dry the edge of the tub and the floor around it when we're finished.

Back in Sammy's room, Rosie is already zipping up his jammies. She's talking to him in a soft, soothing voice, but I can't make out the words from the doorway. She's in her own little world and hasn't noticed that I'm done yet. Holding him to her chest, she settles in the rocking chair and sings, her voice soft and raspy. Sammy looks up at her with an adoring expression.

I never in a million years believed it was possible for my heart to feel so full — near bursting at times.

By the time she finishes the song, Sammy's out like a light. She looks up, smiling when she sees me in the doorway.

Somehow, in the blink of an eye, I got everything I didn't know I needed.

Sammy and Rosie changed my life in the best possible way.

With a steadying breath in, I cross the room and dip low to kiss her forehead.

Silently, she gets up and deposits him in the crib.

Together, we tiptoe out of the room and ease the door shut behind us.

We wait, counting to ten before we shuffle to our room.

What was once solely hers has now become our

space. Admittedly, I kind of forced my way in. I was tired of not sleeping with my wife.

Rosie turns the shower on in our bathroom while I lean against the counter and turn on the baby monitor.

"Would you ever want to do that?"

She looks over her shoulder at me. "What do you mean?"

"Have another kid?"

"Um…" She turns away to pull her towel from the bar. "I guess I haven't really thought about it much, but yeah, maybe in a few years." She turns back to me, her lip caught between her teeth. "Another could be nice, but let's make sure we can keep this one alive first. Deal?"

I laugh, holding my hand out to shake on it. "Deal."

With her hand still clasped in mine, I pull her into me, covering her mouth with mine.

I've been waiting all day to kiss her.

She melts into me as I slide my hands under her shirt. We stay like that, slowly exploring one another's mouths, for a long moment. Then she pulls back and raises her arms so I can pull the fabric over her head.

Groaning, I kiss the skin of her neck.

I don't know what kind of perfume she wears, but it's intoxicating — soft and sweet and slightly floral.

Hands on my cheeks, she pulls me back to her lips.

Fuck, I can't get enough of her.

We take our time getting undressed. There's something special about being unhurried, appreciating every second.

The spray is perfectly warm when we finally make it into the shower.

Water sluices down Rosie's body, tempting me to follow a drop between her breasts with my tongue. Once I reach her belly button, I work my way back up and circle her nipple.

Moaning, she bows into my body. "Daire." My name is a whimper on her lips.

"Hmm?" I hum, gripping her hips. My cock hardens, pressing into her stomach.

"Please."

"Please, what?" I grab her chin, holding her still as I kiss her.

She pulls back and licks water from her lips. "Please fuck me."

I don't have to be told twice.

With a hand behind one thigh, then the other, I guide them around my waist and lift her, making sure to keep her back pressed against the tile.

Guiding my cock to her entrance, I push in about an inch and pause, knowing how wild it'll make her.

"Daire, so help me God, don't tease me right now."

Amusement laces my voice when I say, "My needy girl."

I slide in all the way, swallowing her moan with my mouth, relishing how incredible it is to be buried in her wet heat. Her pussy clenches around me, and since it's been days since I've been inside her, I find myself dangerously close to the edge already.

"Fuck, Rosie. You feel so good."

She grabs my cheeks between her hands and kisses me. "Shut up and fuck me."

I don't have to be told twice.

By the time we leave the shower, the water has turned cold. I drag her into bed without letting her get into her pajamas, despite her protests.

I've barely got her tucked into my body when sleep takes me.

thirty-four

ROSIE

"WHEN CAN I TAKE THIS OFF?" I whine, tugging at the blindfold Daire tied around my head. "Not being able to see is making me car sick."

"We're almost there."

Since we weren't able to celebrate Valentine's Day on the actual day, Daire insisted on taking me somewhere this weekend. We dropped Sammy off with Jude and Millie before hitting the road. The idea of leaving Sammy in the care of someone else still sends a wave of anxiety through me. I'm attached to the little guy and don't like to be without him.

"Where is there?"

Daire sighs, his jeans rasping against the leather. My hearing seems to have magnified now that I've lost my sense of sight.

"Have some patience."

I purse my lips and let out an annoyed huff. My patience evaporated the second he made me wear a blindfold.

His warm hand settles on my knee, giving it a squeeze before he slides it up and settles it on my thigh.

What feels like an hour later, but in reality is probably about ten minutes, the car stops.

I reach to take the blindfold off, but he grabs my hands and stops me.

"Not yet."

"Daire," I groan, dropping my head back against the seat.

"Not much longer," he assures.

I jolt when his lips press against mine.

He hops out of the vehicle, and the back hatch beeps and lifts.

What is he doing?

He's back there for at least five minutes. Then, finally, the passenger door opens and he reaches over me to undo my seat belt.

He takes both of my hands, probably to keep me from ripping the blindfold off, and guides me out of the car.

When we come to a stop, he says, "All right, now you can take it off."

Quickly, so he doesn't have a chance to change his mind, I whip the blindfold off and drop it to the ground.

My jaw drops, and my heart rate kicks up in speed. The outdoor screen is large, spanning a wide-open space. There are no other cars around, only us. I turn to Daire, astonishment making it hard to form words.

Finally, I ask, "How did you do this? How did you even remember?"

He shrugs like it's not a big deal, when, to me, it means everything. When I was little, I talked about wanting to go to a drive-in all the time. It was a dream of mine. I thought it looked so cool, but my parents never would've dreamed of sitting in the car to watch a movie.

"I found the location and set it all up."

"But aren't these places usually closed in the winter?"

"Yeah." He puts his hands into the pouch of his hoodie. "But if you offer enough money, you can get people to do things they wouldn't normally."

I shake my head. God, I don't even want to know how much he spent to make this happen for me.

The thoughtfulness, though?

You can't put a price on that.

He cuffs my upper arms and slowly turns me. As the van comes into view, I gasp, and I swear my heart floats right out of my body. The cargo area of the minivan is set up like a bed, complete with fluffy blankets and pillows. There's a basket sitting in the middle too, like he packed a picnic dinner.

I will not cry. I will not cry. I will not cry.

It's single-handedly the kindest thing someone has ever done for me.

I throw my arms around Daire's neck with so much force he stumbles. Quickly, though, he rights himself and squeezes me tight.

"Thank you," I murmur into the skin of his neck.

"You're welcome."

I step away and crawl into the back of the car, excitement bubbling inside me.

"What did you bring?" I point to the basket.

He opens it up, revealing sandwiches from one of my favorite little shops back home. I stare in wonder. "How did you pull off *this*?"

"They put it on ice and overnighted it."

"You ... I ... I don't have words."

He leans in, brushing his thumb over my cheek. "Isn't it clear by now that I'd do anything for you?"

Tears burn my eyes, threatening to fall. I'm overwhelmed by the thoughtfulness.

With a sniff, I rein in my composure and sit straighter. "What movie are we watching?"

"What movie did you always want to watch at a drive-in?"

I slap a hand to his forearm. *"Angus, Thongs and Perfect Snogging?"*

He nods, trying not to laugh at my excitement, if the twitch in his lips is any indication.

When I was a tween, I was certain it was the best movie in history. A young Aaron Taylor-Johnson had a lot to do with why I was such a big fan.

I swallow past the lump in my throat and regard Daire.

I love him. I've known that for a while, and he loves me. There's no doubt. But seeing it like this? In the things he does for me? It's monumental. The way he went all out for our first Valentine's Day means the world to me. I would've been fine eating pizza on the floor while hanging out with Sammy. But he wanted to give me something I will never forget.

"Are you ... fuck, baby, I didn't mean to make you cry." He pulls me into his arms, knocking the basket over in the process. The opening credits of the movie start, but I bury my face in his hoodie and sniffle.

"Thank you."

Those two words aren't anywhere near enough to encompass the gratitude I feel.

This man listened to my ramblings for years and somehow remembered so many small details all these years later.

Finally, I compose myself and settle on my side of the cargo area. As I shift and get comfortable, he eyes me like he's waiting for me to break down again. When I smile at him, he blows out a relieved breath and hands me a sandwich.

"I have popcorn and drinks too."

The smile that splits my face is so big my cheeks hurt. "You've thought of everything."

"I tried to." He picks up his own sandwich and a can of Coke from the basket.

I peer inside and have to suppress a laugh at all the options he brought. There's even an assortment of movie theater candy. He truly has all the bases covered.

I'm not normally a Coke girly, but suddenly, I crave the sweetness. He fights a grin when he sees what I've chosen but doesn't comment.

Once I've got the can in the cupholder beside me, I settle into the pillows and cover up with the blankets. It's cold out, but thanks to the heat lamps set up outside the car—another impressive detail Daire considered—it's surprisingly nice.

Daire turns to me and opens his mouth, but I shush him, solely focused on the movie now. The car shakes with his silent laughter. I'm glad my enthusiasm for this great piece of movie history amuses him.

When the movie is over, my eyes are heavy and I'm dangerously close to falling asleep.

Daire, thankfully, doesn't call me out on it as he opens the passenger door for me.

I grasp his arm and turn to face him full-on.

"Tonight…" I start, clearing my throat. "Tonight meant more to me than you'll ever know."

He caresses my cheek, and I sink into his touch. "Good. I wanted it to be special."

He glides his lips over mine in a featherlight touch, leaving me wanting more.

"I don't know how you're going to top this."

He laughs as he steps back and guides me into my seat. "I don't think I can. But I'll thoroughly enjoy trying." He winks, and my stomach somersaults in response.

We drive back toward town, heading to Jude and Millie's, holding hands the whole way.

I don't tell him, but teenage Rosie is currently giggling and kicking her feet giddily.

How is this my life?

AFTER CLASS, I'm headed to my car when I spot Bertie ahead of me.

I can't say she's flat-out ignoring me, but she's certainly shifty.

I hurry after her before she can get too far away.

"Hey! Bertie!" I call out as she approaches the entrance to my old dorm.

She turns around, eyes widening like a deer in headlights.

What the hell is going on with her?

Luckily, she doesn't run away from me.

"Hey," she replies, voice soft. She clutches a book to her chest and drops her attention to the ground between us. "What's up?"

"What's up?" I repeat with a laugh. "Bertie, something's going on with you, and I'm worried. I'm your best friend. I can sense these things."

She frowns, biting her lip, and her eyes go glassy like she might cry.

My heart aches at the expression. What the hell could have her so upset?

Exhaling a heavy breath, she grabs my hand and tugs me into the building with her. She won't meet my eyes on the way up to the room, but I keep my mouth shut, resigned to be patient. When we get inside, she throws her bag down on the table and walks into her room.

I stand in the middle of the living space, scanning each detail.

This was once my home too, but it feels like a stranger's place now. Like it belongs to a Rosie from an alternate universe.

For a moment, I consider following Bertie, but I don't want to push too hard, so I wait here.

She comes out a moment later and drops a plastic object onto the coffee table.

It clatters, startling me, and when it stops, my heart drops.

"Look at it," she gasps, wrapping her arms around herself.

"Bertie." Her name is a quiet exhale.

"Look at it," she says again, bottom lip wobbling.

I don't need to look. I already know what it's going to say. "You're pregnant."

At my words, she bursts into tears.

"Aw, Bertie." I wrap my arms around my best friend, absorbing her sobs with my shoulder. I guide her to the couch, and she clings to me the whole way, clearly needing to be held. There's no way I'll let go until she's ready.

Eventually her sobs turn into hiccups, and she pulls away to dry her eyes.

"I'm sorry for snotting all over you." She gives a watery laugh, wiping her face with the cuff of her sleeve.

"Eh." I wave a dismissive hand. "I'm used to all kinds of things, thanks to Sammy. Snot, pee, poop. I've seen it all."

She inhales a shaky breath and lets it out slowly. "I'm going to have a baby." For a moment, she's silent, then she drops her head back and laughs hysterically. "Wow, that's crazy to say out loud."

"You're going to have a baby," I repeat.

She nods, rubbing her lips back and forth. "I'm going to be a mom."

"How long have you known?"

She tucks a piece of hair behind her ear with shaky fingers. "About two weeks. I ... I didn't tell you because, at first, I didn't know what I wanted to do, and then after that, I was scared to say it out loud. The timing ... it sucks." She rubs a hand over her face. "I didn't plan to become a mom until I was thirty. *At least*. I hardly feel mature enough to live on my own, let alone be someone's *mom*."

"Who's the dad? Please tell me you didn't hook up with Tommy again."

Bertie laughs, her cheeks pinkening. "It's Luke." She clears her throat, wiping her palms on her jeans. "Luke Covey."

I suck in a sharp breath. Though I can't say I'm surprised. The chemistry between them has been palpable every time they're together.

"Does he know?"

With a shake of her head, she stands and heads for the kitchenette. Pulling a ginger ale from the fridge, she unscrews the top and takes a sip. "No, you're the first to know. I feel like throwing up every time I think about telling him. Frankly, I feel like throwing up without even thinking about it."

"You've been nauseous?"

"You have no idea. I'm living off this," she holds up

the ginger ale, "and saltines. I've been living a glamorous life over here."

"I'm sorry if I pressured you into telling me before you wanted to. I've just been worried about you."

"It's okay." She takes another long sip of the soda. "I think I was mostly embarrassed. I swear we used protection, and I'm religious about my birth control, but…" She trails off, shrugging. "This one got through." She presses a hand to her flat stomach, turning a bit green. "Fuck." She sets the can down on the counter, nearly knocking it over in her haste, and takes off for the bathroom.

I follow and pull her hair back as she retches. "Oh, Bertie." I rub her neck.

Once she's finished, she slowly stands and shuffles to the sink to wash her hands and brush her teeth.

"Do you want to watch a movie or something?"

She shakes her head. "I appreciate it, but I'm exhausted all the time. All I want to do is shower and crawl into bed. Okay?"

I nod, my chest aching for her. "Okay."

I pull my best friend in for a hug. "Are you sure you don't want me to stay?" I ask one last time.

"I'm positive, but … I have an appointment tomorrow for an ultrasound." She wrings her fingers together, nervously biting her lip. "Do you think you could come with me? If you have class, it's okay — I can go on my own. But —"

"Text me the information. I'll be there."

She lowers her head and sniffles. "Thank you."

I hate to leave her, especially when she looks like she's on the verge of tears again, but I want to respect her wishes. And frankly, if I was in her spot, I'd want alone time to process.

"If you need anything before then, call me."

She squeezes me in a hug. "I will."

She leads me to the door, and with one more hug, I head out. I don't have any more classes, so I head home. Daire should already be there with Sammy. We should've hired a nanny, but neither of us is ready to trust a stranger with him yet. At least school will be over soon.

I stop at the coffee shop on campus before heading home to my boys. The caffeine is a must if I'm going to finish up my essay for my public health nutrition class.

When I step through the front door, Daire's in the family room with Sammy asleep on his chest.

He gives me a shy smile like he's been caught doing something he shouldn't. "He fell asleep, and I didn't want to move him."

My chest expands at the sight of them. "I don't blame you. I wouldn't either."

Sammy is snoring lightly, his little mouth open. Beneath his little cheek, there's a wet spot on Daire's shirt from the baby's drool.

I drop my bag onto the floor and take a sip of my

coffee. I tell myself I can sit on the couch for five minutes with my boys before I have to get to work on my paper. It's my last big essay for this class, and I want it to be good.

I tuck my legs under me, getting comfortable. "I ran into Bertie on campus."

"Oh?" He arches a brow. "Did you get to talk to her?"

I nod, debating about whether I should tell him. "I did."

"And?"

I bite my lip. I might as well fill him in. It's not like he's going to tell anyone. "She's pregnant."

His lips parts in surprise. "What?"

"I know. I'm going to go with her to her appointment tomorrow."

"Is she okay?"

My heart softens at the thoughtfulness behind the simple question. "I think so. Scared, obviously, and she said she's been really sick, but I think she's wrapping her head around it."

"How far along is she?"

"I didn't ask, but she hasn't been to the doctor yet, so I don't think she's too far."

"Wow." He rubs the baby's back. "I guess Sammy will have a friend to play with."

That comment takes a modicum of weight off my

shoulders. I hadn't even thought about that. Sammy and Bertie's baby will be close in age.

I take a couple of sips of my coffee and stand. "I have to go write this paper."

He brushes his lips over Sammy's head. "All right. We'll be right here."

Upstairs, I settle cross-logged on the bed and log on to my computer. My brain is frazzled, and I'm still processing Bertie's shocking news, so it takes about a solid ten minutes—and playing classical music—to get in the zone.

Two hours later—because I keep second guessing everything I write and deleting and rewriting it again—my rough draft is finished.

I am nothing if not an overthinker.

And when I check my phone, I find a text from Bertie. Her appointment is scheduled in the middle of one of my classes, but I don't care in this instance.

My best friend needs me.

IT'S POURING rain as I pull up outside the dorm to wait for Bertie. The plan was to meet at the doctor's office, but there was no way I was letting her take the bus in this weather.

I've just put the car in park when she dashes

outside, holding the hood of her raincoat firmly to her head so it doesn't go flying off in the wind.

"This is some kind of weather, huh?" She closes the door behind her. "Not going to lie; I'm glad you're the one driving."

I pull away from the dorm, turning down the music.

"How are you feeling?"

"I only threw up twice this morning, so I'm counting it as progress."

I shoot her a concerned look as I turn onto the main road around the campus. "Is there anything the doctor can give you for it?"

"I don't think so. It's just one of those pregnancy things." She drops her head back against the headrest with a *thump*. "I'm pregnant." Her voice shakes around the two words. "There's a baby inside me." In my periphery, she puts a hand on her stomach. "God, this is so weird. I'm not going to lie, the idea of feeling it move really freaks me out."

It freaks me out too, but I keep that to myself. Instead, I say, "I think by that point, you'll be excited to feel it."

"I hope so," she sighs.

I hate seeing my bubbly, vivacious best friend like this. Stressed. Sick. Worried.

With a painted-on smile, I glance her way. "I'm going to spoil this baby silly, just so you know."

She laughs at that, and I swear some of the weight

visibly lifts from her shoulders. She's not alone in this, and I want her to know it.

"You'll be the best Auntie, Rosie. At least you'll be able to give me advice. I'm terrified, and I don't have the first clue about how to take care of a baby."

The defeat in her voice breaks my heart. Our situations are different, but many of the feelings are the same. I think she'll be surprised by how quickly she'll adapt. Parenting is challenging, for sure, but I find that a lot of the little stuff I was worried about feels insignificant now.

"Yep, and we'll have playdates with the baby and Sammy. It's going to be great. And you know I'll be there for any advice you need." My priority today is to cheer her up, but I might be laying it on too thick, so I snap my mouth shut.

"Yeah, that'll be fun," she says in a detached tone, turning to the window. "How are things with you and Daire?"

As much as I want to help her work through this, I give in and let her change the subject. "Good, really good ... they're ..." I rack my brain for the right words. "Real. It's real."

She shifts in her seat and gives my wrist a squeeze. "I'm so happy for you." She's quiet for a few minutes, watching the scenery passing by.

I remain silent too, unsure of what to talk about if not this situation she's found herself in.

Eventually she asks, "Do you think you and Daire will have kids?"

I laugh at that, which probably isn't the best reaction when she's in the predicament she's in. "One day. But not now. We have our hands full with Sammy. I can't imagine another one any time soon."

"Sammy's lucky to have you both."

Emotion clogs my throat. "Thank you."

It's hard most days, not only parenting a child, but digesting all he's lost already. I never knew Danielle, and Daire didn't know her *well* either, so at some point, after everything is settled, we'll have to meet up with her family and learn what we can so that Sammy always knows about his mom.

The whole situation might've been fucked, but she doesn't deserve to be erased from his life. Neither of us would ever dream of doing that.

As we pull into the parking lot of the OBGYN's office attached to the hospital, a shaky breath flutters out of Bertie's lips. "I think I'm going to throw up."

Quickly, I reach for the grocery tote I keep in the back seat and shove it at her.

She opens it, taking a few deep breaths, while I watch her, unsure of how to help.

After a solid minute passes and nothing happens, she nods. "I think it passed."

"Maybe take the bag with you. Just in case."

"Yeah." She folds it up in her lap. "Good idea."

The office is on the first floor to our left. Bertie signs in while I find a chair in the corner.

"I'll just wait out here for you, okay?"

She shakes her head vigorously, her eyes going glassy. "I want you to come back with me."

Trepidation rolls through me, but I want her to be as comfortable as possible. "Are you sure?"

"Yes." She rubs at the side of her nose, breathing a rapidly. "Fuck," she says in a low whisper, knocking the back of her head against the wall behind us lightly. "I'm going to have to tell Luke."

I clasp my hands in my lap and shift to face her. "When do you think you'll do it?"

She holds her hands out in front of her, stretching her fingers. "I don't know, but I can't put it off forever. He's ... he's such a good guy. I've been avoiding him because I'm so fucking scared. But I can't be one of those girls who waits until there's no hiding it before breaking the news or, God forbid, never tells him at all."

I reach for her hand where she's begun tapping her fingers against the faux wood armrest.

"Sorry." She gives me a sheepish smile. "I'm nervous."

I give her hand a squeeze. "Everything is going to be okay."

She inhales a long breath, then lets it out slowly. "I hope so."

My stomach is twisted into knots over it all, so I

can't even begin to imagine how hers feels. But I'm so glad that she's allowed me to be here. With any luck, she feels at least a modicum of relief having my support.

Like most doctors' offices, the wait is long, but I follow Bertie back when her name is called.

She has her weight and blood pressure checked before she's put into a room, and once she's situated, the nurse asks her a list of questions like the date of her last period.

After she runs through the gambit of questions, the nurse hands Bertie a gown and pee cup, telling her to change in the attached bathroom and to put the cup in the collection basket when she's finished.

The door closes with a soft click behind the nurse.

Wiggling the cup between her fingers, Bertie says, "Wish me luck. I always struggle with these."

I give her an awkward thumbs-up and a smile. "You can do it."

While I wait for her, I check my phone, finding a string of texts from my mom about the wedding.

What kind of cake flavor do I want? Almond? Lemon? Chocolate?

Am I okay inviting Great-Aunt Linda?

What kind of food do I want served? She suggests surf and turf.

I roll my eyes at the questions. What's the point of asking when she's probably already ordered the cake and food and invited Great-Aunt Linda, who smells like cheese and mothballs?

I answer anyway, saying I'll talk to Daire about it. It's his wedding too.

I'm still trying to wrap my head around a *real* wedding. Sure, it was one of my stipulations, but now it's because, somewhere along the way, we fell in love. Playing house is seriously dangerous.

Bertie waddles out of the bathroom, awkwardly holding the back of her gown closed.

"Ugh," she groans. "The smell in here is killing me."

"The antiseptic?"

"Yes." She huffs as she plops herself on the table, the paper rustling as she wiggles and gets herself settled. "It burns my nose and makes me gag."

I sniff the air, but the room just smells clean to me.

She looks at me, wearing a pleading expression. "Distract me so I don't get sick."

"Uh … my mom is driving me nuts with wedding stuff, but I knew that would happen."

Bertie pales. "Oh my God, I'm going to be ready to pop at your wedding. What if I go into labor *at* your wedding? What if I've already had the baby and my boobs leak and I ruin my dress?"

I hop out of my seat and grab her flailing hands. She's damn close to hyperventilating.

"Whoa, whoa," I say, affecting a soothing tone.

"Let's not dwell on that right now. One thing at a time, okay?"

She covers her face with her hands and takes in a shuddering breath. "Easier said than done, Rosie."

"We'll figure it out when the time comes."

She nods distractedly, biting her lip. After a long moment of silence, she says, "My parents are going to disown me. My inheritance is down the drain." She puts a protective hand over her flat stomach. "But I can't ... this is my baby."

My heart squeezes in sympathy for her. "Aw, Bertie. No they're not."

"Yeah." She wets her lips, her eyes pooling with tears. "They are. Something like this—a baby out of wedlock and with a man they'll hardly see as proper? They'll be furious. It doesn't matter that he's been drafted to the NHL. He won't be good enough in their eyes. You've met them. You know how they are."

I have met them a few times. They're your typical stuck-up, rich upper-class people. The kind who look down on everyone else. But surely they wouldn't be so nasty as to disown their daughter.

My thoughts are interrupted by a light knock on the door.

Bertie sends me a panicked look as the door opens and her doctor steps inside.

"Good morning, Beatrice, how have you been?"

"Pregnant," she blurts.

I slap a hand over my mouth to stifle my laugh at her deadpan answer and shuffle back to the plastic chair against the wall.

Her doctor's lips twitch, as if she's holding back a smile. "Yes, that was in the notes. But more specifically, I want to know how you've been feeling."

"Sick," she says, her tone bland. "All morning. Sometimes all night. Random smells make me vomit. Sometimes just thinking about what I might possibly be able to eat sends me running to the bathroom."

"Okay." Her doctor takes notes, nodding along. "Anything else?"

She shrugs. "Other than the throwing up, I've felt fine. I'm a little more tired than normal, but it's also crunch time at school, so that could be contributing to it."

More nods. More notes.

The doctor asks a few more questions before she says, "All right, Beatrice, lay back and let's take a look at your baby."

Bertie's eyes widen comically, and a gasp escapes her. "Wait, I'm going to get to see the baby today?"

The doctor gives an amused laugh and stands from her stool. "Since you're not that far along yet, we have to use the internal ultrasound, but yes, you'll be able to see the baby today."

Bertie's eyes dart toward me. They're swimming with panic, but the smile that creeps up her face is pure excitement, as if she can't decide how she should feel.

"Do you want me to go?" I ask, straightening in my seat. I don't want to make her uncomfortable.

"I want you to stay. Please." She reaches out a hand to me, and I go to her, clutching her hand tightly.

"It might be too early to hear a heartbeat," the doctor says. "I don't want you to be worried."

"Why wouldn't there be a heartbeat?" Bertie's eyes shoot from me to the doctor and back again.

"Before ten weeks, it's not detectable, but..." She pauses and looks at Bertie's chart again. "Was your last period December twenty-seventh, or is that the conception date?"

"Conception."

"Okay, then you're about thirteen weeks."

"Thirteen weeks!" She blurts. "But that wasn't thirteen weeks ago."

The doctor gives a soft laugh. "I know it sounds weird, but we count the weeks from your last period, so basically, we add two weeks."

"Oh." Bertie's cheeks turn a bright shade of red. "I didn't know that."

The doctor smiles kindly. "Lots of women don't. Don't feel bad. If you're ready, go on and lie back. Feet in the stirrups."

Bertie lies back, positioning her feet. Her eyes widen in panic at the sight of the internal wand as the doctor holds it up and explains how it works. Even I'm surprised by the size of the thing.

"A little pressure," the doctor warns, lifting the sheet covering Bertie up to her knees.

Bertie scrunches her nose, squeezing her eyes shut, as the doctor lowers the wand.

A moment later, a black and white image appears on the screen. Bertie slaps her hand over her mouth, stifling a sob. "That's a baby. There's a baby inside me. I didn't think it would look like one yet."

It's small, but she's right. It's distinctively baby-shaped already.

The doctor pushes a button, and a moment later, the sound of a heartbeat fills the room.

Tears stream down Bertie's face. "That's my baby," she says to me, clutching my hand. "Do you hear it? It sounds strong."

After the doctor takes measurements, pointing body parts out as she goes, she gives Bertie a string of photos. Once Bertie is sitting up again, the doctor goes over a list of things with her, like foods that are off limits and prenatal vitamins she'll need to take.

By the end of it, Bertie's shoulders are slumped with exhaustion, but her eyes are brighter than before. She keeps looking down at the ultrasounds and smiling.

When we finally get back to the car, I ask her, "Are you hungry at all?"

"Not really." She bites her lip. "But I actually think a milkshake would be good."

"Hey, whatever you want, you get."

"Man, I would have gotten pregnant a long time ago if I had known I could get princess treatment."

I laugh at her joke, navigating out onto the winding road that leads from the hospital parking lot to the main intersection.

"How are you feeling now?"

She cracks the window a bit, letting in fresh air. "Shockingly, I feel better, but I'm still scared. Being a mom? That's a huge deal. I'm going to have a child to take care of—to try to raise into a good, decent human being. What if I suck at it?"

My chest gets tight at the concern in her voice. "You're not going to suck at it."

"How do you know?" she counters, folding up the ultrasound photos to put in her purse. She hesitates with her hand on the zipper, then chooses to keep holding them instead.

"Because I know *you*. You're one of the best people I've ever met. This kid is going to be lucky to have you as a mom."

She's quiet for a solid twenty seconds before she utters a quiet "thank you."

I pull up outside the shake place, half-expecting her to have changed her mind, but as soon as I parallel park, she's hopping out of the car with much more zest than she had before.

The rain stopped while we were in the doctors' office, but the sidewalk is still covered with puddles that we dodge on our way to the entrance.

The Shake Palace has been a favorite of ours since freshman year. With everything that's happened since the school year began, we haven't been even once. My stomach sinks at the realization. Who knows where we'll end up from here and whether we'll have any more opportunities to do all the things we've always loved before graduation. Daire and I haven't talked about it, but now with Danielle gone, there's no reason we can't leave Tennessee. And Bertie? She has a lot to work out now. Eventually, she'll have to break the news to Luke, and he's already been drafted by the NHL.

Bertie steps up to the counter and orders her usual butterscotch milkshake.

I used to make fun of her for the old lady flavor, but that stopped when she forced me to try it.

It was phenomenal—enough so that after that day, I stopped ordering cookies 'n' cream and copied her instead.

"Butterscotch for me too," I tell the girl behind the counter.

I tap my card to pay, practically shoving Bertie out of the way to beat her to it.

"Bitch."

I bump her hip lightly with mine. "I wanted it to be my treat."

"Yeah, but you missed class to drive me."

With a shrug, I stick my wallet back into my purse. "This is your day."

She gives me a playful shove. "Next time, it's on me. No arguing."

"Sure thing."

When our shakes are up, we sit at our usual booth in the corner.

I almost don't want to ask her, but I'm curious, so I go for it. "Are you feeling any better?"

She stirs her shake with her straw, mixing in the whipped cream. "Yeah, I am, actually. I feel ... still scared. But seeing it? That's my baby, Rosie. My little boy or girl. So yeah, I'm terrified, but I'm excited now too."

A weight drops off my shoulders at that admission. I hate that she's been dealing with this alone for the last couple of weeks.

Reaching across the table, I give her hand a small squeeze. "I'm going to be there for you. Whatever you need."

"Thank you." The smile she gives me is small, but there's a bit of happiness in it that's been missing all day.

It's going to be hard not to spoil her kid. I already go overboard with Sammy.

"I think..." She pauses, stirring her shake again, her focus set on the movement. "If you don't mind, before you drop me off, could we go to Target or somewhere and look at baby clothes?"

"Yes!" I blurt way too enthusiastically.

Shopping for baby clothes has become an addiction. I absolutely wouldn't mind picking up a few things for Sammy while we're there. And it seems like we always need diapers and formula, so it'll save us a trip later this week.

"I'm glad I have you," Bertie says, pulling me from my thoughts of all things baby.

"Don't you dare make me cry," I warn her, sniffing to alleviate the tingling in my nose.

She smiles, taking a sip of her shake. "I wouldn't dream of it."

Both our lives have changed drastically this year, but the one thing that hasn't is the way we have each other's back.

thirty-five

DAIRE

TIME IS MOVING at a speed I can't comprehend. Graduation is around the corner, and hopefully custody of Sammy will be finalized soon. Nina keeps telling me these things take time, and I understand that, but fuck, I hate all the waiting.

The front door closes, and Rosie's high-heeled shoes make a sharp clacking sound against the wood floors.

"My boys," she chimes, bending to scoop up Sammy from the floor and smacking a kiss on his head.

"Where's my kiss?"

She rolls her eyes, sticking her tongue out. "Don't be jealous."

"Me? Jealous?" I scoff. "Never."

"You're a bigger baby than Sammy."

She leans in, gently cradling Sammy's head, and presses her lips to mine, her kiss soft and tender. I cup her cheek, deepening it. I can't get enough of her. For someone who was hellbent on this never being real, I don't know what I'd do without the connection we have. I have a feeling when she walks down the aisle in September, I'm going to cry.

"How'd it go at the dress place?"

She had to go in for more measurements and to discuss any adjustments she wanted to make.

"Great." Her eyes light up with excitement. Sammy's balanced on her hip, smacking his hand against her collarbone for attention.

I pinch his cheek lightly. He's so fucking cute.

I figured this new parent glow would've faded by now, but it's just as strong as the day we brought him home, if not stronger. I'm not saying it's easy. In fact, it's probably the hardest thing I've ever done. But it's also the most rewarding, and damn, do I love being a dad. I'll do this ten times over if Rosie will let me. Well, maybe not *ten*, but four wouldn't be so bad.

"What are you thinking about?" she asks, no doubt having noticed I zoned out.

Heat burns my cheeks, giving me away. "Nothing."

She bounces Sammy, making him giggle. "Liar. You wouldn't be blushing if you were thinking about something innocent."

I tickle Sammy, and in response, he grasps my finger with a surprising amount of strength.

"I don't think you want to know."

"If it involves you and me naked, then I'm game."

I laugh, ruffling my little guy's hair when he lets go. "Shockingly, that wasn't it."

She cocks her head to the side, nose scrunched in curiosity. "What then?"

I blow out a breath, knowing she isn't going to let this go. "More kids."

It's her turn to laugh. "I thought we talked about this."

"I'm not saying it has to happen anytime soon. I know you're not ready, and honestly, I'm not either. But this little guy makes me think about things I never did before. I *like* this life. I like being at home, just us, our little family. I love playing with him and taking care of him. I just love being a dad."

Her face softens. The warmth of her hand on my cheek is like a soothing balm.

"There's nothing wrong with loving a more domestic life. We were raised to feed into the hustle and bustle. We grew up thinking being raised by nannies was normal, but in reality, very few people live that way. Choosing a different path for yourself isn't wrong."

I can't help but smile. She's voicing things I've been avoiding thinking about.

"You're not going to judge me if I want to be a stay-at-home-dad?"

Her laughter is warm and kind. "No, never. It's the twenty-first century. It shouldn't be frowned upon if you're a stay-at-home-dad and I'm the money-maker."

Heart hammering against my sternum, I pull her in for a kiss.

Neither of us takes for granted the privilege we've been born into—the extensive trust funds that allow us the freedoms to essentially do what we want.

"I love you."

She smiles, setting Sammy on the floor. Immediately, he crawls away. This is a new development that already has me dreading when he learns to walk.

"I know. I'm pretty easy to love."

I grab her hip, pulling her into me. "That mouth of yours."

Her eyes sparkle with challenge, a silent dare. "What are you going to do about it?"

"Oh. Don't worry." I look her up and down. "I'll take care of you later."

A FEW DAYS LATER, I pull into the driveway beside an unfamiliar car. Immediately, my heart begins to race, and I break out in a cold sweat.

Someone's here to take Sammy.

I'm half tempted to put the car reverse and flee, but the instant the driver steps out of the vehicle, my fears over Sammy halt in their tracks, and brand new fears rear their ugly heads.

Oh, shit.

Rosie's father closes his car door and eyes me as I idle at the end of the driveway.

Has he finally come to kill me?

Since he's already seen me, I've lost my opportunity to flee.

I pull all the way into the driveway and park beside the silver car.

Sammy babbles in the back seat, the sound easing my trepidation a fraction. He says a few words here and there, but we're unfortunately still working on Dada. I swear the kid refuses to say it just to spite me.

The instant I step out of the car, her dad is *right fucking there*.

Papa Mode Activated.

Hand on his chest, I give him a light shove. "Move back. I have to get my baby out of the car."

Silently, he concedes, taking a step back and shoving his hands into the pockets of his slacks.

With a wary look at him, I turn and slide the back

door open, then unlatch Sammy's car seat so I can carry him inside. I don't say a word to Chandler as I pass.

This unexpected appearance has me fuming.

How dare he say the things he did to Rosie, then just show up here out of the blue?

He follows me to the door, not saying a word.

I unlock it, but instead of pushing it open, I swing back around to face him, nearly taking him out at the knees with the car seat carrier.

"I didn't invite you in, Chandler."

He arches a brow. "Are you seriously not going to let me in?"

I stare him down, puffing out my chest. Maybe the move is an overreaction, but I can't help but feel protective of Rosie and Sammy. "I'm thinking about it. You hurt my wife. I don't take that lightly."

The muscle in his jaw ticks. "That's why I'm here. To apologize."

I snort. "Took your sweet time, didn't you?"

He blows out a breath, looking up at the sky like he's hoping he can gather strength from the heavens. "Yeah, I did. Are you going to let me in or not?"

"Might as well. You *are* my father-in-law."

He flinches at that, which only serves to make me grin with amusement.

"Is Rosie home?"

Hand on the knob, I turn my head dramatically. "Well, her car isn't here, so it's safe to say she's not."

Rather than admonishing me for my sarcasm—he is my elder, after all, and in our parents' social circles; that kind of behavior is highly frowned upon—Chandler silently follows me inside where I set the carrier down on the floor and unstrap Sammy.

There's a disgusted curl to Chandler's lip, which only makes my hackles rise.

Sammy might've been an unexpected surprise, but that doesn't make him any less loved or special to me or to Rosie.

I get my little guy settled in his highchair, then head for the fridge. He smacks his palms against the plastic tray, chanting *blana*, which I've deduced means banana, one of his favorite foods.

"Feel free to sit and wait for her," I offer with a wave at the couch.

The last thing I want is for Chandler to make himself at home in our house, in our safe space, but even though Rosie is hurt, I don't think she'd take too kindly to me kicking her dad out on the street.

That means I get to sit and awkwardly wait with him for who knows how long. Rosie and Bertie were headed to the wedding store after class to work on the design for the bridesmaid dresses.

I gather up the little glass jars of food and a spoon, then I pull out a chair and sit in front of Sammy. Almost immediately, I jump up, muttering "bib" to myself. Somehow, I always forget the damn thing.

Chandler watches my every move, wearing a shrewd expression. It causes tension to build in my shoulders, and I have to bite down on my tongue to keep from getting defensive.

"Do you need something?" I ask, giving Sammy his first bite of the mashed bananas.

Chandler shakes his head, pulling out a stool at the island. He's still too close for comfort, but it's better than him hovering.

Ignoring his presence, I continue feeding Sammy, talking to him about our day like I always do. When he's finished, I set him on the floor with his toys. He's due for a nap soon, but I like to give him a little time to crawl around when we get home.

"He looks like you."

I turn at the sound of Chandler's voice. "That's what Rosie says."

He looks away at the comment. "Do you really care for her? You're not just using her?"

I wouldn't dare tell him about the origins of our romance. If I have my way, we'll take that truth to our graves.

"I love Rosie more than you can imagine."

He dips his head in acknowledgment.

I always liked Chandler, but I'm afraid that even if Rosie forgives him for his bullish behavior, I never will. Anyone who hurts Rosie hurts me tenfold. Her pain is my pain, and it's one of the worst things I've ever experienced.

I sit on the floor with Sammy, stacking colored blocks that he knocks over, until his eyes are heavy.

"I'm going to get this one down for a nap. You can stay here."

In other words, *Don't even fucking think of trying to snoop around my house.*

He nods. "Have you heard from Rosie?"

With a shake of my head, I stride to the kitchen so I can make a bottle to take up with me. "No, she's busy, and I'm secure enough to let her do her thing without expecting her to check in with me every five minutes."

His lips flatten. "You don't like me very much, do you?"

Hands on the counter, I stare him down. "I used to like you. I even respected you. But you made my wife cry. You *hurt* her when she didn't deserve it. So, no, I don't like you, and I'm not sure I ever will again."

Picking up Sammy, I leave him behind to chew on that.

Sammy struggles to stay awake while I change his diaper and put him in clean pajamas for his nap. Once I've laid him in the crib, I rub his tummy until his eyes close and stay that way.

With a flick of the knob on the sound machine, I ease out of the room and shut the door.

Escaping into my room, I send a text to Rosie to

warn her that her dad is here. Maybe it's shitty of me to rat him out, but it would be even crappier to not give her a heads-up before she gets home.

My phone rings an instant later, and a picture of Rosie with Sammy illuminates the screen.

"Hello?" I answer, pacing the bedroom.

"My *dad* is there?"

"Yep. He's downstairs. I just put Sammy down for a nap."

She's quiet for a moment. "I can't believe he just showed up."

My stomach churns with nerves. "If you don't want to see him, I can send him away."

She gets quiet again and stays that way for so long I pull my phone away from my ear to make sure the call hasn't been disconnected. "No, I … I'll hear him out when I get there. We're almost done."

"Take your time."

I might not want to be stuck here with her dad, but I won't beg her to come home early. With her mother taking over the wedding details—which, shockingly, Rosie doesn't mind, at least for the most part—I want her to enjoy the few things she does have control over.

"I'll let you know when we leave here."

"All right. Love you."

"Love you too. Bye."

As I end the call and slip my phone into my pocket,

I inhale a steadying breath. I have no choice but to go downstairs and entertain her dad now.

This ought to be fun.

IT'S the most awkward hour and a half of my life.

When Rosie pulls into the driveway, I'm up and moving before Chandler can blink.

She strolls up the walkway, as beautiful as ever, with her dark hair cascading over her shoulders. Arching a brow when she sees me, she says, "Why are you standing at the door like a dog ready to greet its owner? Are you that desperate to get away from my dad?"

"It's awkward," I defend, locking the door behind her.

"Where is he?" She looks around like he might jump out from behind me and scare her.

"Family room."

She inhales a deep breath, then lets it out shakily. Her eyes dart in the direction of the family room, and she wrings her hands together in front of her.

I grasp her upper arms gently, hoping my touch soothes her at least a little. "If you want me to ask him to leave, I will."

She shakes her head. "No. Thank you. I know I need to talk to him."

"Do you want me to be with you or give you space?"

Before she can answer, Sammy cries, and we both turn toward the stairs.

"I want you by my side," she says, stepping in closer. "Let's get Sammy. My dad can wait."

Chances are he can hear our entire conversation, but I don't care.

Upstairs, we find Sammy attempting to stand up in the crib. We're both frozen just inside the doorway, staring at him. I can't speak for Rosie, but the sight fills me with not only awe but apprehension. While we're frozen in place, he straightens his legs so he's fully upright, clinging to the crib railing, and grins around his pacifier. The little guy is clearly pleased with himself.

I turn to Rosie with a laugh. "He can stand up in the crib, but he can't say Dada? I'm offended."

She pushes my shoulder, lightly shoving me aside. "He just doesn't want to give you the satisfaction because he's going to say Rosie first. Isn't that right?" she asks him, scooping him up. She plants a kiss on each cheek, earning a giggle from him.

There's no doubt in my mind that she loves Sammy as much as I do.

She lays him down on the changing table, peels his pajamas off, and changes his diaper, all the while cooing and talking to him. I stand off to the side, soaking in their interaction.

I don't know how I got so lucky.

"Did you miss me?" she asks him in a high-pitched voice.

He kicks his legs in an excited response.

"I'll take that as a yes." She blows a raspberry on his stomach.

His answering giggles make my heart hurt in the best kind of way.

"What do you want to wear?" she asks. "What about this little overall set? It's cute." She holds it up for his inspection.

He claps his hands, his arms flailing.

"I'll take that as a yes too."

She changes him easily, not having to wrestle him into the clothes like I normally have to. It's safe to say that Sammy has already chosen Rosie as his favorite person. I can't even be mad about it. She's my favorite person too.

When he's all clean and changed, she holds him against her chest and faces me.

"I guess I can't stall any longer."

"No," I agree, a lump lodged in my throat. "We can't leave him waiting forever."

She straightens her spine and nods, preparing herself to face what's to come. Fuck, he better be here to apologize and make amends. He should have done it months ago. Hell, the whole thing should've never happened in the first place. I couldn't ever imagine myself saying the things he did to my own daughter.

I follow her down the stairs, and then we face Chandler together, as a family.

He stands the moment he sees Rosie and rubs his hand awkwardly over his shirt. I don't think I've ever seen this man nervous, but it's clear that he is right now.

He clears his throat. "It's good to see you, Rosie."

She looks him up and down. "Hi, Dad. You could have called. You didn't need to waste your time coming all the way here."

It's not what I was expecting her to say. And from the way Chandler flinches, he wasn't expecting it either. Her tone matches the words — chilly, distant. The meaning behind that comment, that a call would have sufficed, shows how deeply he hurt her.

By the anguish in his eyes, it looks like, in this moment, he realizes that he's going to have to put a lot more work into repairing this relationship than he thought.

Rosie hasn't talked to me much about her feelings when it comes to her dad, and I haven't pushed her. Maybe I should have.

"I know," he nods, swallowing thickly. "I felt like it was better to talk in person."

She presses her lips together, looking away, clearly

struggling to keep it together. Fuck, it kills me that she feels this way.

I put a hand on her waist, offering her as much comfort as I can.

"Better for you or me?"

Chandler flinches again. "For both of us, I hope."

Rosie sets Sammy down, his little legs working quickly as he crawls over to the corner where we keep his toys.

"A little warning would've been nice."

He hangs his head and lets out a defeated sigh. "I know, but I didn't want to wait."

"Dad." The pain in that single word feels like a stab to the gut. "You've had *months*." I think that's what bothers her the most about him being here. He's had a long time to get his head out of his ass. Why is now different? "Did Mom make you do this?"

He shakes his head, scrubbing a hand over his jaw. "No. I mean, she's told me I'm being ridiculous, but no, she's not why I'm here."

Rosie's hands shake at her sides. I reach for one and squeeze, silently willing her to take strength from me.

"Let's ... uh ... sit down and talk," I say. I hate seeing her like this, the pain she's trying to hold back to keep him from having the power to hurt her any more.

From the toy corner, Sammy tosses his soft blocks, babbling away. He gives us a toothy grin, happy and completely oblivious to the tension swirling the air between the three of us.

Chandler sits on the ottoman directly in front of Rosie. By the way her grip on my hand tightens, it's clear she doesn't care for this proximity. Even so, she doesn't tell him to move.

"Rosie, the way I reacted…" He lowers his head in shame. "It was reprehensible. I was hurt. You're my little girl, and this wasn't how any of this was supposed to go. But my pain didn't give me the right to hurt you in turn."

His speech sounds rehearsed to me, but I'm not going to call him out on it.

"We've always been close," he goes on when it becomes obvious Rosie isn't going to respond, "and it's been awful not talking to you."

Not awful enough to apologize until now.

Again, Rosie says nothing. Chandler tugs at his collar, the corners of his mouth turned down in unease.

Sammy crawls over, using my leg to get into a standing position.

"Rosie, I—"

"Dada."

My heart stops, and I dart a look at Rosie. "Did he say—"

Her smile is so bright it hurts to look at. "He did."

Ignoring the man in front of us, I scoop my son into my arms. "Say it again," I beg.

I'm aware that begging a baby to say a word again is futile, but I can't help it.

Sammy smacks his open hand against my cheek. "Da." Another smack. "Da."

Fuck. I'm going to cry.

"Dada," he says again.

My heart lurches, and my chest aches in the most perfect way. "That's right. I'm Dada. And who's this?" I point at Rosie. We've been working on getting him to say Ro-Ro.

Sammy claps and lunges for her. "Mama."

I freeze, and at the same time, the color drains from Rosie's face. Her eyes are comically large when she asks, "Did he call me Mama?"

I let out an uneasy breath, not sure how she's going to feel about it. "He did."

"Mama," he says again, opening and closing his hands. His bottom lip begins to tremble when she doesn't take him.

Shit, Maybe she's upset. We've been careful not to refer to her as that—not wanting to be disrespectful to Danielle's memory—but so many of the books we read to him reference mother figures. Apparently he's picked up on it and decided she's supposed to be Mama.

Tears pool in Rosie's eyes, and she finally snaps into action. With shaky hands, she takes him from me and holds him close, kissing his cheeks. "Sweet boy," she says.

Rubbing the back of her neck, I ask, "Are you okay? Is it okay?"

She nods, the motion causing a few tears to slip down her cheeks. "It's okay. I don't ... we'll always make sure he knows about his mom, but I'm okay with whatever he wants to call me now and whatever he decides to call me in the future."

I lean in, kissing her. God damn, how did I get so fucking lucky?

Chandler watches the entire exchange, not saying a word. In fact I kind of forgot he was there until he clears his throat.

"You two ... you're really in love."

I chuckle and press a kiss to the side of Rosie's head. "I tried to tell you, sir. It's why we couldn't wait to get married."

A laugh bursts out of Rosie, because that's *not* the reason, but what her dad doesn't know won't hurt him.

Chandler rubs his hands against his pants. "I just wanted to come here in person and apologize. I know it doesn't erase how I behaved, but I felt like it was better to come here and see you than to call. So..." He stands slowly, like his joints hurt. "I'll head out and leave you to it."

He's halfway across the room when Rosie says, "Dad, don't go. At least stay for dinner."

My sweet Rosie. She's too kind even when people don't deserve it. I should've known how good her heart was when she agreed to marry me. This woman is one-of-a-kind, and she's all mine.

"Are you sure?"

"Yeah, and if you want to stay, we have a spare room."

The last thing I want is Chandler staying here after how he's treated her, but if she's okay with it, then I'll keep my opinion to myself.

He shakes his head. "Dinner would be nice, but the flight crew is on standby, so I have to head home tonight."

"All right, dinner it is." She shoots me a look that asks if I'm okay with this.

With a dip of my chin, I give her an encouraging smile and stand. "I'll order dinner."

Phone in hand, I position myself in the kitchen, giving them some privacy while keeping an eye on the interaction.

I order a spread of food from a local restaurant that offers delivery. No chance in hell am I leaving him alone in the house with Rosie while I pick up dinner. Then I busy myself wiping down the counters. I rinse the washcloth, and when I turn the water off, the house is strangely quiet. I spin, ready to step in if necessary, but Rosie is already off the couch and coming into the kitchen with Sammy still in her arms. I know I'm biased, but I'm pretty sure he's the snuggliest baby to ever exist.

"This is awkward," she mouths.

"It's not like he'll be here much longer," I whisper back.

She exhales heavily, looking back toward her father. The look in her eyes breaks my heart—the longing for everything to be okay, but the fear that it never will be. I might be angry at Chandler for hurting her, but at the end of the day, I want whatever Rosie does. If she wants to repair this rift, then I'll support her 100 percent.

Her bottom lip wobbles. "How did things get so messed up?"

Fuck, I don't want to see her cry. Wrapping an arm around her shoulders, I pull her into me. My lips find her forehead, offering her silent comfort.

This situation with her dad can't be rectified tonight, or tomorrow, or even next week.

Regardless of how badly they want to heal their relationship, it's going to take time.

thirty-six

ROSIE

I CRAWL into bed beside Daire, emotionally exhausted after my father's unexpected visit and our awkward dinner. It's wild how quickly a person I love so much became a stranger. The part that hurts the most is that even if we can repair our relationship, it will never be the same. What he said to me all those months ago was extremely hurtful, but the radio silence was worse.

Despite his claims, I can't help but think my mom convinced him to come apologize. She's probably been driving him insane about walking me down the aisle. I didn't mention anything about the wedding over dinner.

Frankly, I'm not sure I want him to walk me down the aisle. It's what I always envisioned, but right now, it doesn't feel right.

"Hey, baby," Daire says, pulling me in close.

His voice is gruff. Like maybe he dozed off while I was in the bathroom.

I throw my arm across him and lay my cheek against his bare chest. His heart thunders beneath my ear. I close my eyes, just listening to the sound of it.

He twines his fingers in my hair, and soon, he's massaging my scalp.

"Ugh," I groan. "If you keep doing that, I'm going to fall asleep."

He laughs, the sound a low rumble against my ear. "Isn't that the point? Aren't we going to bed?"

I sit up and regard him. My hair brushes against his chest as I do, and he shivers.

I arch a brow. "Are we?"

He grins, his eyes more alert than they were only a moment ago.

My body is aching for his touch more acutely than I've ever experienced before.

Sure, I've always enjoyed sex, but until Daire, I didn't know what it was like to want one person so desperately.

He sits up, cupping my cheek. His warm lips mold to mine, sending warmth and desire through me. Will the craving I have for him ever go away? Or will it only get stronger?

His tongue pushes past the seam of my lips, and I open for him.

Hands on my thighs, he pulls me onto his lap. I moan at the feel of him already half-hard beneath me. He still sleeps naked, and it's pure torture. Especially on the nights where I want him so badly but I'm too tired to do anything about it.

I'm exhausted tonight too, but I need to feel him.

The warm press of his body.

The comfort of his arms.

The tenderness in the way he makes love to me.

He kisses a path down the column of my neck, and I drop my head back to give him more access.

"These fucking gigantic shirts you wear shouldn't be such a turn-on, but fuck, they do something to me."

He pulls the fabric up and over my head, leaving me bare except for my panties, then kisses over my collarbone and down between my breasts. I grab ahold of the chain around his neck and tug, bringing his mouth back up to mine.

His eyes flash, and a grin splits his face. "Does my girl want me to kiss her?"

"Yes," I breathe, wrapping my arms around his neck.

My hips rock against him with a mind of their own. I'm cursing myself now for putting on panties before getting into bed. I'm desperate to have that thin barrier gone from between us.

"What else do you want?" he asks between kisses. "You want my mouth anywhere else?"

I moan at his words, and visions of exactly where I want his mouth swarm me.

"Use your words, Rosie. Tell me what you want."

He rolls us so I'm beneath him, the move so swift that it knocks the breath out of me.

Kissing his way down my body, he groans like he can't get enough of me. Licking and nipping at my flesh, he works his way lower until, finally, he stops with his mouth hovering just beneath my belly button.

"Rosie," he taunts. "You haven't given me instructions."

I inhale an unsteady breath. "You know what I want."

He shakes his head, teasing me with a stupid grin. "Not good enough."

I grip the sheets and arch my back. "Daire."

"Rosie."

I take a deep breath. "I want … your mouth … on … my pussy."

"See?" His grin broadens. "Was that so hard?"

He pulls my panties down and takes his sweet time to drive me crazy. I wiggle in annoyance, which only makes him chuckle against my flesh.

Once he's removed them, he balls them up in one

hand. Then he moves his way up my body and holds them against my lips.

"Open up."

Heart stuttering, I gape at him. "Wha—"

He shoves them in my mouth. "You don't want to risk waking up Sammy, do you?" With a kiss to my neck, he groans. "I don't think you realize how loud you get when I'm inside you."

It's not like my hands are tied. I could easily pull my panties out of my mouth. But it's so unexpected, I find myself frozen as he slips back down my body.

With the first swipe of his tongue, all logical thought leaves me.

Daire has single-handedly made me a huge fan of oral sex. I always thought it wasn't for me. He proved that all I need is an enthusiastic partner. Though I can't help but think that, even then, I would have been destined to only enjoy this with him.

I rock my hips against his face, and in response, he moans. Fuck. The sounds he makes while going down on me should be illegal. I'm pretty sure that if I recorded his moans and played them back, I could orgasm without ever touching myself.

He slips his right hand down and strokes his erection without losing focus on the task at hand—or mouth. The sight of him getting off on this is so unexpectedly *hot*, it nearly sends me over the edge.

I rake my fingers through his hair and tug, and he

moans, digging his fingers into my thighs as he spreads me open wider.

I'm so close it won't take much to get me off.

An inferno ignites in my core, burning me from the inside out.

He reaches up, yanking the panties from my mouth. "I want to hear the sounds you make when you come," he says, his breath warm against my aching pussy. "I want to hear what I do to you."

Dropping his mouth back to my core, he adds two fingers and hooks them slightly. That simple move is all it takes to send me hurtling toward release. I scream his name, begging for him to have mercy on me in one breath and begging for more in the next.

As I come back down, my chest heaving and my body trembling, he moves up my body, hair mussed, and grins, clearly pleased with himself.

He kisses me, long and slow, making sure I can taste myself on his mouth.

With a whimper, I reach between us, wrapping a hand around his cock, desperate for more of him.

He bucks against my hand. "Rosie," he groans, lowering his head so his hair brushes my forehead.

I guide him to my pussy, and he sinks in an inch, closing his eyes.

"Daire?"

"Mhm?" He nods, eyes still firmly shut.

"Are you going to fuck me or not?"

"In a minute," he croaks. "I want this to last."

Hand on his jaw, I coax him to open his eyes. He does so, slowly, his pupils blown so wide the blue of his irises is almost entirely gone.

I trace the shape of his lips with my thumb. "I love you."

I loved him as a girl.

Hated him as a teen.

And now I get to love him again as a woman.

He rocks against me, sliding in all the way and pulling a gasp from my lungs.

Wrapping my legs around his hips, I pull him close. Being fused to him like this, skin to skin, heart to heart, is the most intimate experience I've ever had.

He brushes the hair back from my eyes. "I love you too, Rosie. More than a lifetime will ever allow me to show you."

But he tries, at least, to show me, and man, do I feel it.

SPRING HAS FLOWN BY, and we're only a week from graduation when the call comes from Nina.

"Everything is settled," she says over speakerphone. "I called in a favor, and we have a court date two weeks from now. This will make it official."

"I'll have full parental rights?" he asks, his leg jostling beneath the table.

I reach over, putting a hand on his knee, hoping to imbue him with at least a little comfort.

"Yes. You have nothing to worry about."

"I know you keep saying that, but I can't help it. I don't want anything to go wrong."

"Everything is set, Mr. Hendricks. The law is on your side. I'll email over some more details and what to expect the day of. Take a breath. This is almost over."

"Okay." Daire scrubs a hand over his jaw. "Okay," he says again. "Thank you."

"If I have any more information for you, I will call," she assures him. "But everything should be set. Congratulations."

He clears his throat and says, "Thank you," his voice thick with emotion.

In the grand scheme of things, Daire's journey to getting custody of Sammy has been relatively short, but it feels like it's taken forever to get to this point. Soon, Sammy will officially be ours. No more questioning the possibility of him being taken away. For as much as it eases my fears, I can only imagine how relieved Daire is at the news.

He hangs up the phone and turns to me, his eyes filling with tears.

Angling closer, I take his cheeks in my hands. "It's almost over."

He sniffs back his tears. "Almost," he agrees, his voice cracking.

"You're going to be all mine soon," Daire says to his son. It means the world to him that Sammy will be officially his.

Have you heard from your dad lately?" he asks me, roughing a hand down his face.

"Every day."

His eyes widen at my response, but he presses his lips together, quietly waiting for an explanation.

I lean my back against the couch. "I know. I'm surprised too. It's usually nothing important, just asking how my day is." With a shrug, I swallow past the lump in my throat. "I appreciate him coming to apologize, and I want to forgive him and move on from this, but I'm more hurt than I thought I would be. I've always been a daddy's girl, and I've always done everything in my power to make him proud. I understand why he was upset with us. With me. But his words cut me like a knife." I play with a loose thread on my shorts in a poor effort to distract myself from the emotion rising up inside me. "The worst part of it all is how that one moment forever changed our relationship. Words have power, you know?"

"I know," he says carefully, squeezing my thigh. "My words hurt you once too. But you forgave me. So maybe, one day, you can forgive him too."

It's a valid point. I bite my lip, thinking over what he said.

"Maybe. It's just going to take time." I tuck a piece of hair behind my ear. "I think it's hard because he's my dad. I never expected him to hurt me like this."

With an arm around me, Daire pulls me in close and kisses the top of my head. "I know, baby."

thirty-seven

DAIRE

GRADUATION IS A BLUR. My dad takes Sammy to the stands while Rosie and I find our spot. Since she changed her last name, we get to walk across the stage one after the other. Our degree programs held separate graduations—mine yesterday evening and hers this morning—but now it's time for the biggie. Rosie wanted to skip this one, but I wouldn't hear of it.

Getting to this point means something to me. It feels like I'm putting the past behind me and stepping into the next stage of my life. Technically I've already done that, but the ceremony makes it feel final.

With the large class size, it's going to take forever to get through all of us.

While we sit and listen to the keynote speaker, I reach for Rosie's hand, twisting her wedding band around and around on her finger.

It's wild that our time at college is coming to a close. I came to Aldridge absolutely despising Rosie, yet here I am, married to her and happier than I've ever been. Not only have I repaired the most important relationship I'll ever have, but I've grown as a person. I've let go of my immaturity. I feel like an adult now—well, maybe not a full-blown adult, but at least a few steps closer to it.

And in just a few short months, Rosie will walk down the aisle to me.

When it's our turn to get up, I don't let go of her hand. Our line slowly snakes toward the podium. When my name is called, I reluctantly let go. Rosie's name is next, and as she exits the stage, I hold out my hand to help her down the steps.

"What are you thinking about?" I ask when we return to our seats. We stay standing, waiting for the rest of our row to fill in. "Don't tell me," I say, before she can answer. "You're thinking about getting me naked later."

She squeezes my hand, her nails digging into my palm. "*Daire*," she hisses.

I laugh and lean in to kiss her cheek. "Oh. So it's

just me?"

"You're thinking about getting yourself naked? Weird."

Biting back a chuckle, I pinch her side. "No, *you*. We have babysitters for once."

A laugh bubbles out of her. "You know there's no way we're going to be able to leave Sammy with your dad or my parents. We're way too overprotective for that."

"Yeah," I groan. "We are, aren't we?"

When our row is full, we sit and wait for the rest of the names to be called. By the end of the ceremony, I'm so close to dozing off that Rosie has to nudge me to keep me from closing my eyes.

"Sorry," I mumble.

Reaching over, she rubs my neck. "Don't worry about it. I'm bored out of my mind too."

When it's finally, blessedly over, Rosie drags me with her in search of Bertie.

Wading through hundreds of students is a nightmare—especially when I'm stopped by people I know every three feet.

"This is insane," she mutters, pulling me along. "Do you know *everyone* at this school?"

I give her hand a playful squeeze. "Pretty much. Here, hang on."

I let go of her hand and move in front of her, crouching down slightly.

"Uh." She stands behind me, her body going rigid. "What do you want me to do?"

"Hop on."

"You're giving me a piggyback ride?"

"It'll be faster. Promise."

With a huff, she climbs on and loops her arms around my shoulders.

I grasp her thighs and hold her easily, plowing through the crowd. "Beep, beep," I tell people as I pass. "Coming through." To her, I ask, "Do you see her?"

She cranes her neck and scans the crowd. "To your left," she directs.

Hiking her up higher on my back, I turn and head that way. "Now to your right a bit. Perfect. Straight ahead."

When her best friend is only a few feet from us, she hops down from my back. Luke hovers near Bertie like a protective bodyguard. They're not together, but it's obvious from the way he looks at her that he wants more.

"We did it!" Rosie throws her arms around her.

"Yeah, we did," Bertie says, her tone and expression more subdued.

"Are you coming over tonight?" Rosie asks, not letting Bertie's melancholy deter her from her own joy,

Her mom wanted to throw a huge party for us, but we managed to talk her down to a family dinner.

Bertie peers up at Luke, and I try not to smile. The

look on her face reminds me of the way I so adamantly denied my feelings for my wife during those first couple of months. "We might stop by."

"We?" Rosie can't hide her grin.

Bertie playfully elbows Luke in the ribs. "Only because he won't leave my side."

His fingers graze her hip over her gown.

"Okay, I'll see you later, then." Rosie gives her another hug. "We need to go save Sammy from our families."

I crouch down and wait for her to hop on again, then we're off. We made plans to meet them at the campus coffee shop, hoping it would be easier to find one another away from the crowd. Keeping a firm grip on Rosie once we're off the field, I stride quickly down the winding sidewalk.

"You can put me down," she says. "I'm heavy."

I snort. "Rosie, you're the furthest thing from heavy."

Up ahead, our family members are clustered in a small group. Roman is the only one of my brothers to have come. The longer I go without talking to Cash, the more it hurts, especially because it's caused strife between me and my other brothers. But I'm not ready to get into our issues just yet, and he hasn't reached out, so it's safe to say he feels the same.

As we get close, I set Rosie down, and when Sammy sees us, his face lights up and he reaches out for Rosie.

"Figures my favorite person would also be my kid's favorite person." I ruffle Sammy's blond hair. It's starting to thicken up.

"Dada." Sammy claps, and my heart leaps. I'll never get tired of hearing that word.

I hold my hands out to take him from Rosie if he wants, but he lays his head on her shoulder and smiles, patting her collarbone with his little fist. "No. Mama."

Her mom clutches her heart. "I can't believe he calls you Mama."

Her mom hasn't been thrilled about the fact that I have a child, but it's impossible not to love Sammy. It feels good to see that she's coming around.

"Are we heading back to the house now?" Rosie asks leaning into me when I put my arm around her waist.

Knowing her mom, it's entirely possible she's concocted an alternate plan we don't know about.

"Yeah, can we go to Rosie's house?" Gracie begs. "This was *so* boring."

"Gracie," her mom admonishes in a hushed tone. "Your sister only graduates from college once."

Gracie blows out a breath that has her bangs fluffing. "Twice, Mom. This morning and now. That's two times. *Two*." She drives home her point by wiggling her fingers in front of her mom's face.

"All right." She grabs Gracie's hand and tugs it down. "I get your point. We're headed back now."

Due to the size of the graduating class, we have to catch golf carts that take us to our cars. Her mom, dad, and Grace pile into their rented SUV, while my father and Roman are with us in the minivan. And Rosie thought it was a ridiculous choice. But look at us now.

thirty-eight

ROSIE

WE PULL in only moments before my parents and are still piling out when my mom hops out of their vehicle, vibrating with excited energy.

Her behavior instantly has me worrying about what we might find inside. I say a silent prayer that it's not a party and just the dinner she promised us.

"Mom," I warn in a stern tone. "What did you do?"

"Nothing," she says in a voice that very much means *something*.

I turn a worried look in Daire's direction as he's

getting Sammy out of the car. He gives me a confused frown in response.

He's known my mom his entire life, yet I swear he forgets how she is.

Shoulders slumped, I pull my keys from my purse and head for the door. I might as well get it over with. Whatever waits inside isn't gonna go away.

Once I've gotten the door unlocked, I step inside and pull it open farther to let Daire in after me. Rather than being hit with a loud *Surprise!* the only thing that assaults me is the smell of a home-cooked meal. Instantly the delicious scent makes my stomach rumble, reminding me that I haven't eaten since this morning, and all I had then was a little bowl of fruit.

I figured my mom would have this meal catered, but I assumed we'd eat later. I have to say that I'm glad that it's now. My stomach rumbles again in agreement.

In the dining room, I find a lavish setup. Plates that certainly aren't ours adorn the table. They look expensive and possibly antique. Every place setting is affixed with a small bouquet, the fragrances of which can just barely be detected over the herbs and spices permeating the air.

My mom steps up beside me, eyeing me cautiously. What do you think?" she asks, her expression uncertain, like she's worried I might hate this. But it's perfect, and I'm glad she listened to my request. A dinner party is more intimate.

"This looks amazing. Thank you, Mom." I wrap her in a hug. "Thanks, Dad," I add, though I don't reach out to him. Our relationship is going to take a lot of work.

"You're welcome." There's a sadness in his eyes, a longing for what we used to have. In the past, my reaction toward him would've been more enthusiastic, but he doesn't comment or force an interaction.

"This looks great, guys," Daire says, putting a hand on my shoulder. "Thank you for doing all this."

"Should I let Bertie know we're having dinner earlier than we thought?"

My mom shakes her head. "No, I let her know. Go wash up. The meal will be served when we're ready."

Relief washes through me. I could use a moment to freshen up. I'm pretty sure there's an inch of sweat dried onto my skin from sitting in the sun for hours in the heavy gown.

Grace pops up behind me, poking her head around my arm. "Those plates are so ugly. Did you pick those out, Mom?"

My mom sighs, throwing her arms out. "I swear, God sent me you to keep me humble."

Grace giggles in my ear. "You're welcome."

Chuckling, Daire bounces Sammy lightly in his arms. "I'm going to go change this one."

"I'm going to go change myself." I motion to my dress, thankful I chose black so the dried sweat isn't visible. I fully plan on hopping in the shower, even if it's only for five minutes.

Upstairs, we part ways when he turns into the nursery. In our bathroom, I turn the shower on and then scour my closet for a change of clothes. I settle on a simple green sundress. It probably won't be dressy enough for my mom's tastes, but I'm in my own home, I'm tired, and I want to be comfy more than anything else.

I hop in the shower and scrub my body quickly. I don't have time to linger like I want to, so I hop out and dry off quickly, then try to tame my hair into something that looks intentional.

Daire steps into the bathroom and sets Sammy on the floor. "You showered?"

"I had to. I thought I was going to sweat to death out there."

With a chuckle, he reaches in to turn the shower back on. "Same. It was hot as…" He looks at Sammy. "Heck."

After he's showered and changed as well, we venture back downstairs. Bertie has arrived, with Luke in tow, and my mom is fawning all over her. I'm happy to see it. Her parents didn't take the news of her pregnancy well, and it put a damper on the day for her.

Once we're all settled at the table, the catering team my mom hired serves us.

"This is incredible, Mom. Thank you for organizing all this."

She beams at the praise. "I'm glad you like it."

While we're eating, the topic of conversation turns from the ceremony to Sammy and custody.

"Everything will be settled in a few days," Daire says. He reaches for my hand beneath the table. "We'll go to the courthouse, and it'll be taken care of."

"That soon?" my mom asks, turning to me with a frown. "Why didn't you tell us?"

I shrug. "I'm sorry. I didn't think it was that important to you."

She presses a hand to her heart. "Of course it's important. Sammy is your boy."

Those words instantly have a lump forming in my throat. I'm not his mom, and I never want to replace her, but I feel like his and he feels like mine in all the ways that matter.

This morning, she cooed over what a sweet boy he is and refused to give him up. The relief I felt as I watched the interaction was instant and acute. I don't *need* my parents to accept everything I do with my life, but it doesn't stop me from wanting them to understand and love the people I care about, and that includes Sammy.

She turns to my father. "We're staying."

He looks from her to me and gives a simple "okay."

Daire's father pipes in. "I'll stay too."

Roman throws his hands up. "What am I, chopped liver? I'm staying."

Daire and I exchange a look. He looks as surprised as I feel. Neither of us expected this to matter to our families so much.

"All right," he says, squeezing my hand. "We appreciate it."

"Do you wanna go?" Luke asks Bertie.

"Only if you two are okay with us being there," she says, giving me a small smile.

"We'd be happy to have you guys there."

It warms my heart to know that our family and friends care so much about us and Sammy that they want to be there when he officially becomes ours. I suppose we should have expected that, but it never crossed our minds that they'd be interested in witnessing the moment.

With the chaos of the past eight months or so, it's been easy to forget how much our families do care about us.

We don't have to do everything alone.

We're surrounded by love.

I smile at Daire, and in response, he leans in and presses a quick kiss to the corner of my mouth.

The look on his face echoes my thoughts. Life isn't perfect, and it never will be, but we've been pretty lucky.

I'VE CHANGED my dress three times.

I shouldn't be so nervous. This day isn't about me. This moment will be between Daire and the court. I can formally adopt Sammy in the future, but I'll only do that when he's older and if he requests it. I don't want to take the choice away from him.

"Rosie." Daire's voice is tight with stress. "We have to go."

I turn to find him at the doorway of the closet. He looks good enough to lick in his dress shirt and dress pants. His tie is askew, thanks to Sammy, who keeps tugging on it.

"I'm sorry." I smooth down the dress. It's a simple black number, nothing flashy. I'm worried I look too much like a politician's wife in it, but it's too late now to try a fourth dress.

"Everyone is waiting on us."

"Crap. I'm sorry," I apologize again, scouring the floor for a pair of heels.

"Rosie," he warns.

"I need shoes." I clutch his arm as I slip one shoe on, then the other. When they're on, I smooth my hair down and nod. "All right, I'm ready."

"Mama." Sammy reaches for me, and I take him, settling him on my hip.

I follow Daire downstairs and out to the car. As we approach the van, he takes Sammy to strap him into his seat. It's just us, since his dad and Roman are riding with my family. They decided that the three of us should have this time alone in the car before and after.

It's been good, having them all here, especially as they've all had more time to come to terms with our decision to get married. It's also given them time to bond with Sammy.

Daire is silent on the drive to the courthouse. His body taut with nerves. It hurts that I can't take the stress away, but I'm resigned to the understanding that he won't feel better until all this is over.

He turns the radio off, his fingers tapping against the steering wheel while he waits for the light to change so he can turn into the parking garage.

With a steadying breath, I put my hand on his knee, offering my silent support.

After we get into the garage and park, he puts Sammy in the stroller, and I grab the diaper bag.

The wait for the elevator is achingly long, which leads to Daire pushing the button in rapid succession like somehow that will make it appear faster.

As he's reaching to jab it again, I grab his hand.

"You poking it like that isn't going to make it appear."

"Maybe not, but it makes me feel better."

With a small smile and a shake of my head, I pull

out my phone. I send a text to my mom, letting her know that we're in the garage waiting for the elevator. She replies quickly, informing us that they're all waiting in the lobby of the courthouse.

Finally, the doors open, and we get on. As we ride, Sammy giggles at his reflection in the shiny silver doors. "Hi." He waves.

Daire grins, looking more relaxed than I've seen him all day. "He's so smart."

I can't help but smile. Daire is the definition of a proud papa bear.

When the doors open onto the ground level, we walk out into the sunshine and stop at the curb, waiting to cross the street.

I reach for Daire's hand, finding it clammy with sweat.

"Sorry," he mumbles, cheeks flushing. "My nerves are getting to me."

"It's okay." I give his hand a squeeze.

We cross the street and enter the courthouse lobby, where we find our friends and family waiting for us, including Daire's best friend, Cree, and his girlfriend, Ophelia. Beside me, Daire sucks in a surprised breath at the sight of them but quickly recovers.

Nina Voss waves us over and pulls Daire aside, no doubt running through what he should expect.

I've been okay so far, but suddenly, I find my pulse racing.

And in the next instant, I swear my heart falls out of my chest. Because an older couple I recognize from the funeral step inside the courthouse doors. Danielle's parents.

Daire must see them the same moment I do because he blurts at Nina, "What are they doing here?"

For an instant, worry flashes across her normally composed face, but she quickly schools her expression. "I'm not sure," she admits.

Daire lifts a shaky hand and runs his fingers through his hair, clearly agitated. "If they try anything—"

"There's nothing they can do at this point," she assures him. "This hearing is a formality. Take a breath. It's almost our time." With that, she turns and heads toward a man I don't recognize.

"Rosie," Daire whispers, his eyes swimming with terror. "If they—"

I grab his wrist and give it a gentle squeeze. "You heard Nina. They can't do anything. Breathe."

He rubs a hand over his jaw. "Should I go talk to them?"

"No," I insist, tugging him back when he takes a step in their direction. "I don't think that would be a good idea. They seemed kind enough at the funeral." At least in our brief interaction. "Just focus on getting through this, and don't worry about them. Okay?"

"Okay," he agrees reluctantly.

Ten minutes later, Nina comes to get us, and our family and friends follow behind us. I assume Danielle's parents are back there somewhere as well.

The courtroom is identical to the one we got married in, which brings me some level of comfort. I'm not sure Daire feels the same.

As we settle, Nina guides me to the bench where our family is sitting. It kills me to do it, but I have to sit back here while Daire and Sammy stand before the judge.

My mom grips my hand on my lap, her touch warm and reassuring.

I don't hear a fucking word the judge says as it starts. It's like I'm here, but not, a total out-of-body experience.

My heart is racing so fast it pounds in my ears and my vision blurs.

"Breathe," my mom whispers. "You're going to pass out if you don't."

She's right. With a thick swallow, I let out my breath slowly and focus on getting a handle on myself.

The judge speaks, and Daire replies, but the roaring my ears is still too loud for me to make out their words. Despite my confidence until this point that everything would be fine, I find myself panicking in these final moments.

But in a matter of a few blinks, it's over and Daire is

making his way to me, wearing a gigantic smile, with Sammy held firmly in his arms.

"He's mine," he says when he reaches me. "He's ours. Finally."

I take his face in my hands and kiss him with every ounce of relief I feel. "We did it."

thirty-nine

DAIRE

THIS PROCESS HASN'T BEEN easy, especially with the unexpected curveball of the car accident, but we've made it out on the other side.

A throat clears behind us, garnering our attention, and in unison, Rosie and I turn, finding Danielle's parents approaching. Her dad extends a hand to me.

"We wanted to be here today. To show our support."

My heart lurches, and I reel back in surprise. That was the last thing I expected to hear. "Thank you, sir." I take his hand. "I appreciate it."

"We want to be a part of his life," his wife says, her

eyes welling with tears. *Sammy's grandma.* "I really hope you'll let us."

"It's been hard," he says, his voice thick with emotion. "Losing a child is ... indescribable. I know it sounds awful, but before now, we weren't ready for all of this. We still aren't, I suppose. But we're getting there."

"I understand." I adjust my hold on Sammy. "I'm okay with it." I press my forehead to the Sammy's, smiling when he grabs my cheeks. "Let me give you my number," I tell them.

After they take my number, they say their goodbyes, smiling at Sammy and promising to reach out to set something up in the next few weeks.

"How are you feeling?" Rosie asks when they've left.

I let out a long breath, my shoulders lowering. "Relieved."

Looping her arm through mine, she guides me toward the door. Our family trails after us, her mom pushing the empty stroller.

Outside, it's raining, but the sun shines brightly above us. Rosie lets go of my arm, spinning in a circle while wearing a blinding smile. With a gasp, she points to the sky above the courthouse.

I turn and tip my head back, finding a full rainbow arching above us. How fitting.

I chuckle, shaking my head. "Would you look at that?"

Sammy laughs, holding his chubby hands out to catch the rain.

"Do you like the rain?" Rosie pinches his cheek lightly, making him giggle. She turns to me, rain dripping down her face. "I can't believe we finally did it."

When we stepped inside the same courthouse all those months ago, this moment was our end goal. It's felt like an endless process, but we've made it.

"Yeah." I grab her by the waist, pulling her into me. "We did. But there's one last thing we have to do."

She blinks rain from her lashes. "What?"

"Get married—for real, this time."

"For real," she echoes.

epilogue

September

DAIRE

BEAUTIFUL DOESN'T EVEN BEGIN to cover the way Rosie looks as she glides toward me down the aisle. For a while, she wasn't sure she wanted her dad to walk her, but in the end, she asked him, knowing she'd regret it if she missed out on this moment.

I'm so overcome with emotions that my vision blurs so badly I can't even take in the dress she's wearing.

When she stops in front of me and comes into focus, I feel like I might fall over.

I'm so undone for this woman.

With a watery smile, she passes her bouquet to a heavily pregnant Bertie.

We say our vows, and at the end, I lean in to whisper in her ear. "I broke my own rules for you, baby, and fell hard. I never want to come back up."

And I mean it too.

Once upon a time, I thought Rosie was a temporary stop on the journey toward my future. In reality, she was the end game all along. If it weren't for Sammy, I might not have ever gotten my head out from my ass. I could've missed out on the love of my life. Sleeping with my professor may have been a reckless, stupid choice, but it's one mess I've made in my life that I can't regret.

Becoming a father is the best thing that could've happened to me. Because of Sammy, I cleaned up my act. He gave me back the things that matter in life, like family, but most importantly, Rosie. Sammy's the reason I have the love of my life.

We exchange our rings—the same ones as before; over the last several months, they've certainly become strong symbols of our love—then I'm told to kiss the bride.

This kiss is so different from the one we exchanged in the courthouse.

That one was intense, but full of hate and a strange intensity neither of us understood.

This one is pure passion and love melding together.

Cheers ring out, and we break apart.

Rosie smiles up at me with hearts in her eyes, and goddamn, I hope she keeps smiling at me like that for the rest of her life.

"What?" she asks, no doubt because I keep smiling at her like a complete and utter goof.

"I get to spend the rest of my life you. This ... today ... it's only the beginning of all the things we're going to do together."

"Don't you dare make me cry." She gives a laugh that's edged in a sob.

I take her hand, facing our gathered friends, family, and all kinds of people I've never met but her mom deemed worthy of inviting.

Behind us, the officiant says, "I present to you Mr. and Mrs. Daire Hendricks."

Heart leaping at those words, I dip Rosie, pulling a squeak from her, and kiss her again.

Before we can start down the aisle, I grab Sammy from Roman's arms. He's a part of us too, the biggest part. He looks adorable in his baby tux and black Converse sneakers. His blond hair is slicked over more to one side, making him look like a gentleman.

With him tucked in to my chest, I lead Rosie to the private room we sectioned off, where we can relax while our guests move to the reception venue.

"I can't believe we just got married." She spins around, her dress billowing around her.

Chuckling, I set Sammy down. He's walking now and toddles right over to her.

"Mama, pretty! Up!" He waves his arms dramatically. "Up, up, up."

She scoops him into her arms and plasters his face with kisses while he giggles, tossing his head back. "I think *up* has replaced *no* as his favorite word."

"You might be right."

I lean against the wall, loosening my tie. I'll have to fix it before we leave here, but I might as well have a reprieve while I can.

Sammy presses his cheek against Rosie's, pulling a smile from her. She doesn't seem one bit concerned that he might mess up her makeup.

"Well," she begins, eyeing me, "we've survived college and our first nine months of parenthood. Now you've made an honest woman out of me." She wiggles the fingers of her left hand at me and winks. "What do we do now?"

I take her in, smiling at the possibilities our future holds, then pull her close to me, pressing Sammy between us. He's the beating heart of our little family.

"Anything we want."

bonus scene

Rosie's POV

5 years later

Tired doesn't even begin to cover how I feel.

More like completely and utterly exhausted. Somehow in a good way. It's safe to say I'm the happiest I've ever been.

I gather the tiny bundle closer in my arms, sniffing at her soft brown hair. There's not a lot of it, but it's there. Daire brushes a kiss to my forehead, rubbing my shoulder.

"She's perfect."

She is. She really is.

BONUS SCENE

It feels like we've been waiting a long time for her.

We both knew we wanted to more kids, but we also wanted to wait for a while.

We started to get the feeling a year ago that it was time to start trying for a baby. It was further confirmed when Sammy asked if we were *ever* going to give him a sibling. All his friends have one and he wanted one too.

"Sammy's going to love her." I rub my finger against her plump cheek. My nails are painted a light pink for my little girl.

He rubs at my scalp, the feel of it so relaxing after the day I've had that I find my eyes wanting to drift shut. "We have to decide on a name. It's the first thing he's going to ask us."

"I know." The words leave me as a sigh.

If there's one thing we've disagreed over since I got pregnant it's names. I have a whole list of names crossed out in my notes app because Daire vetoed every single one. To be fair, his list was demolished as well.

"Why is this so difficult?" I grumble, staring at her cute face.

I thought for sure once I birthed her that I'd take one look at her and *know* her name like it would instinctually speak to me.

I couldn't have been more wrong.

If anything, I'm more confused now than before.

"Naming a human is hard. She's stuck with what we

BONUS SCENE

choose for the rest of her life." Daire frowns like the thought of his own words has him worried.

I look up at my husband, still just as stupidly in love with him as ever if not more so. "Unless we pick something horrible, and she hates it enough to change her whole name."

He stares me down, unblinking. "Unlikely. What about Annie?"

"Annie Hendricks? No. It sounds weird."

He wets his lips, eyes rolled upward in what I assume is a search for a name we haven't already nixed. "Harper?"

"Double alliteration? I don't think so."

"Rosie." He buries his face into the crook of my neck. "We're hopeless at this."

We really are.

"Bella?" I toss out.

"She's not a vampire wannabe *or* a dog."

This really is an impossible task.

"Next time, we're sticking names in a hat and picking at random."

Daire's grin is nearly blinding. I have to squint my eyes against it. "Next time, huh? Already planning on another."

"It's a figure of speech," I huff.

Though, we both do want at least one more. Being a parent is incredible. I love it more than I ever thought I would.

BONUS SCENE

Hours later, Daire is reclined in the chair beside me with our baby girl on his bare chest in nothing but her diaper.

I can't help but keep sending them heart eyes.

I'm obsessed with both of them.

Since he's got her, I know I should try to get some sleep, even if it's only a short time, but I don't want to miss any of this.

"I'm so happy," I mouth to him, not wanting to disturb our sleeping angel.

He smiles back, eyes crinkling at the corners. He splays his left hand against her back and I don't know what it says about me that the image has me feeling like I want to jump on him like a spider monkey. I thought for sure after I pushed a child out of my vagina that would be the *last* thing on my mind, but fatherhood is Daire's best look. He proves it every day with Sammy and now with … whatever her name is going to be.

"Ava," I blurt out. "What about Ava?"

Daire tucks his chin in, looking down at the baby on his chest. "Ava," he repeats. "I like it."

I smile just hearing him say it. "Ava feels right. Doesn't it?"

He nods in agreement. "Ava Hendricks. I love it."

"But no middle name," I say, pointing at him. "That'll make things too complicated."

He chuckles, nodding in agreement.

BONUS SCENE

"My Ava," he croons, nuzzling his nose into the top of her head.

Ava makes a small little sound that I take to mean approval of her name.

"I can't wait for Sammy to meet her."

Daire looks over at me, lips quirked. "He's going to try to steal her from us."

"He'll be the best big brother."

I'm stupidly excited to see Sammy with Ava. Tomorrow can't come soon enough.

After Daire's finished with skin-to-skin and I've breastfed the baby, exhaustion finally overtakes me.

❋ ❋ ❋

I've somewhat managed to make myself look presentable. I brushed my unruly hair and applied some mascara to my lashes. It's not my usual but I can't bring myself to do much more. I slept more last night than I expected, but I still had to feed Ava a few times — not to mention the nurses in and out through the night.

Daire looks from his phone over at me where I finish snapping Ava's onesie into place. 'Lil Sis is spelled out in cursive along the front.

"Your mom said they're getting in the elevator."

We exchange a smile, more than ready for Sammy to meet his sister.

A few minutes later he gets another text from my mother and goes to get them.

Despite my mom and sister dying to see the baby we

BONUS SCENE

told them that we want Sammy to come in first by himself.

Ava snoozes peacefully, hands curled into little fists on the sides of her face.

"Your big brother is going to love you so much." I rub her tiny nose, still marveling over the perfection of her.

I made that. In my body. With Daire's sperm.

Talk about cool.

The door creaks open and I'm already smiling before Sammy comes barreling around the corner. "Mom!" He cries, running up to my side with a small bouquet of wildflowers in one hand and a little pink bear in the other. "I got you these." He thrusts the flowers at me. "For a good job. And this is for sissy." He puts the bear in the empty bassinet.

"Thank you, sweetie." I take the flowers from him, giving them a sniff before I lay them beside me. "Do you want to meet your sister?" I pat the small space beside me for him to hop up if he wants.

He doesn't hesitate, eyes wide as he gets his first look at her face.

Daire watches everything with a shimmer in his eyes. Him holding back tears makes *me* want to cry.

Sammy reaches out to touch her cheek. "She's so pretty." He leans in close to her and whispers in her ear. "I'm going to look out for you."

BONUS SCENE

My emotions are all over the place, threatening to take me out like a giant wave.

Sammy straightens up, looking over at his dad. "Did you finally pick a name?"

Daire closes the short distance, ruffling Sammy's hair affectionally. "We did. Any final guesses?"

Sammy pushes his glasses back up his nose — a recent addition after he failed his eye test at school. "Samantha?"

Daire throws his head back with laughter. "Sam and Sam? Now that would've been good. Why didn't we think about that, Rosie?"

"A failure on our part, truly."

"Okay." Sammy taps his lips. "Not Samantha. I don't know. Just tell me."

I smile at him, so overcome by love for my little family. "Ava."

"Ava," he repeats, looking at her. "She looks like an Ava."

"Do you want to hold her?"

The immediate, "Yes!" tumbles out of his mouth almost as quick as his body does off the bed. He runs to the sink without being told and washes his hands thoroughly. He settles in the recliner chair, arms open and ready.

Daire takes Ava from me and gently places her in Sammy's arms. At six, he's been old enough to want to learn before her arrival about different things, including

BONUS SCENE

the proper way to hold her. He makes sure to support her head and body.

Sammy looks down at her with so much love that my own heart swells.

Happy.

I'm so blissfully happy.

Daire takes about a billion pictures of Sammy with Ava. I fear for both of our phone storage over the upcoming years.

Eventually, Daire fetches my mom and sister and my dad too since he tagged along.

My dad kisses the top of my head while my mom and Gracie coo over the baby.

"I'm proud of you," he whispers for only my ears.

"You are?"

He nods.

Our relationship has improved a lot over the years, but the sad thing is his initial reaction to my marriage to Daire did irreparable damage. We'll never have the same relationship we once did, but I'm okay with where we are now.

Everyone takes turns holding Ava and then they head out for the evening. Daire's dad is coming to visit next week to meet his new granddaughter.

It's just Daire, Ava, and me once more.

Daire climbs into the bed beside me, his big body nearly too much but we make it work, the two of us staring at Ava in my lap while she sleeps.

He presses a soft kiss to my lips and I melt into him.

I didn't think it was possible for me to fall more in love with my husband than I already was, but the past nine months and today have shown me that love doesn't just reach a point and stop. When they're the right person for you there are so many things that can make that love grow in new ways. The way he's looked after me since the test turned positive, the gentle way he's touched my belly every day, and soaked in every moment has only made me appreciate him more.

His lips graze over the shell of my ear. "Thank you."

I turn my gaze from Ava to him. "For what?"

"For agreeing to marry a guy who didn't deserve it just to help him get custody. For giving me a second chance. For loving me. For ... everything."

I lay my head on his shoulder. "I love you."

"I love you, too."

Ava makes a small sound in her sleep, arms fighting against the swaddle. When I look at Daire, he's wearing a smile that matches mine.

Life with him is more than I could've ever hoped for.

It might've been unconventional—how we got to where we are—but I've never regretted a bit of it for even a single second and I'd do it all over again to end up right where we are.

HONEST BOYS DON'T PLAY

Bertie and Luke's book coming 2025.

acknowledgments

Thank you, dear reader, for picking up not just this book, but any book of mine. The Boys series has been a blast to write, and whether this is your first venture into the series or your 6th, thank you for being here. I like to say this series is like home, and I love being able to return to it from time to time.

Emily Wittig, thank you for not only being an incredible cover designer, but for being my best friend. We've grown up together in this industry and I can't believe all the things we've both accomplished. You're a light, one I'm lucky to have in my life. Thanks for listening to my ten-minute-long voice messages and leaving ones just as long in return. Onto the next book!

Valentine, thank you so much for dealing with my

scatter-brained self. I'm forever thankful that you picked up my books and we were able to connect and I can have you as my PR. Also, thank you for always letting me talk about my love for Krista and Becca Ritchie. It's much appreciated. Ha!

To the entire team at Valentine PR, thank you for the hard work you put into every release. It never goes unnoticed. You guys are incredible, and it wouldn't be possible without you.

Melanie, I've lost count of how many books you've done developmental edits on for me at this point, but your input and feedback is an invaluable resource. I appreciate you so much and this book is 10x better because of you.

Beth, thank you a million times over for working with me. I honestly don't know what I would do without you now that I've found you. Thank you for helping me make my books even better and teaching me even more about writing. I love that I'm always learning and growing with every book.

www.ingramcontent.com/pod-product-compliance
Lightning Source LLC
LaVergne TN
LVHW031608060526
838201LV00065B/4770